Dark Secrets 2

ALSO BY
ELIZABETH CHANDLER

Kissed by an Angel

Dark Secrets 1

Dark Secrets 2

No Time to Die * The Deep End of Fear

ELIZABETH CHANDLER

SIMON AND SCHUSTER

A **simon pulse** book

First published in Great Britain in 2010 by
Simon & Schuster UK Ltd,
1st Floor, 222 Gray's Inn Road, London WC1X 8HB
A CBS COMPANY

Published in the USA in 2010 by Simon Pulse,
an imprint of Simon & Schuster Children's Division, New York.

No Time to Die copyright © Mary Claire Helldorfer, 2001
The Deep End of Fear copyright © Mary Claire Helldorfer, 2003
These titles were originally published individually by Simon Pulse.

A CIP catalogue record for this book
is available from the British Library

ISBN 978-1-84738-912-1

10 9 8 7 6 5 4 3 2 1

This book is a work of fiction. Names, characters, places and incidents are either
a product of the author's imagination or are used fictitiously. Any resemblance to
actual people living or dead, events or locales is entirely coincidental.

Printed by CPI Cox & Wyman, Reading, Berkshire RG1 8EX

No Time to Die

With thanks to Ray Stoddard
and the Mercy High School Footlighters

One

Jenny? Jenny, are you there? Please pick up the phone, Jen. I have to talk to you. Did you get my e-mail? I don't know what to do. I think I'd better leave Wisteria.

Jenny, where are you? You promised you'd visit me. Why haven't you come? I wish you'd pick up the phone.

Okay, listen, I have to get back to rehearsal. Call me. Call me soon as you can.

I RETRIEVED MY sister's message about eleven o'clock that night when I arrived home at our family's New York apartment. I called her immediately, if somewhat reluctantly. Liza was a year ahead of me, but in many ways I was the big sister, always getting her out of her messes—and she got in quite a few. Thanks to her talent for melodrama, my sister could turn a small misunderstanding in a school cafeteria into tragic opera.

Though I figured this was one more overblown event, I stayed up till two a.m., calling her cell phone repeatedly. Early the next morning I tried again to reach her. Growing uneasy, I decided to tell Mom about the phone message. Before I could, however, the Wisteria police called. Liza had been found murdered.

Eleven months later Sid drove me up and down the tiny streets of Wisteria, Maryland. "I don't like it. I don't like it at all," he said.

"I think it's a pretty town," I replied, pretending not to understand him. "They sure have enough flowers."

"You know what I'm saying, Jenny."

Sid was my father's valet and driver. Years of shuttling Dad back and forth between our apartment and the theater, driving Liza to dance and voice lessons and me to gymnastics, had made him part of the family.

"Your parents shouldn't have let you come here, that's what I'm saying."

"Chase College has a good summer program in high school drama," I pointed out.

"You hate drama."

"A person can change, Sid," I replied—not that I had.

"You change? You're the steadiest, most normal person in your family."

I laughed. "Given my family, that's not saying much."

My father, Lee Montgomery, the third generation of an English theater family, does everything with a flair for the dramatic. He reads grocery lists and newspaper ads like Shakespearean verse. When he lifts a glass from our dishwasher to see if it's clean, he looks like Hamlet contemplating Yorick's skull. My mother, the former Tory Summers, a child and teen star who spent six miserable years in California, happily left that career and married the next one, meaning my father. But she is still an effusive theater type—warm and expressive and not bound by things like facts or reason. In many ways Liza was like Mom, a butterfly person.

I have my mother's red hair and my father's physical agility, but I must have inherited some kind of mutated theater gene: I get terrible stage fright.

"I don't think it's safe here," Sid went on with his argument.

"The murder rate is probably one tenth of one percent of New York's," I observed. "Besides, Sid, Liza's killer has moved north. New Jersey was his last hit. I bet he's waiting for you right now at the Brooklyn Bridge."

Sid grunted. I was pretty sure I didn't fool him with my easy way of talking about Liza's murderer. For a while it had helped that her death was the work of a serial killer, for the whole idea was so unreal, the death so impersonal, I could keep the event at a distance—for a while.

Sid pulled over at the corner of Shipwrights Street and Scarborough Road, as I had asked him to, a block from the college campus. Before embarking on this trip I had checked out a map of Maryland's Eastern Shore. Wisteria sat on a piece of land close to the Chesapeake Bay, bordered on one side by the Sycamore River and on the other two by large creeks, the Oyster and the Wist. I had plotted our approach to the colonial town, choosing a route that swung around the far end of Oyster Creek, so we wouldn't have to cross the bridge. Liza had been murdered beneath it.

Sid turned off the engine and looked at me through the rearview mirror. "I've driven you too many years not to get suspicious when you want to be left off somewhere other than where you say you're going."

I smiled at him and got out. Sid met me at the back of the long black sedan and pulled out my luggage. It was going to be a haul to Drama House.

"So why aren't I taking you to the door?"

"I told you. I'm traveling incognito."

He rolled his eyes. "Like *I'm* famous and they'll know who you are when they see me dropping you off. What's the real reason, Jenny?"

"I just told you—I don't want to draw attention to myself."

In fact, my parents had agreed to let me attend under a

different last name. My mother, after recovering from the shock that I wanted to do theater rather than gymnastics, had noted that the name change would reduce the pressure. My father thought that traveling incognito bore the fine touch of a Shakespearean romance.

They were less certain about my going to the town of Wisteria, to the same camp Liza had. But my father was doing a show in London, and I told them that, at seventeen, I was too old to hang out and do nothing at a hotel. Since I had never been to Wisteria, it would have fewer memories to haunt me than our New York apartment and the bedroom I had shared with Liza.

I put on my backpack and gave Sid a hug. "Have a great vacation! See you in August."

Tugging on the handle of my large, wheeled suitcase, I strode across the street in the direction of Chase campus, trying hard not to look at Sid as he got in the car and drove away. Saying good-bye to my parents at the airport had been difficult this time; leaving Sid wasn't a whole lot easier. I had learned that temporary good-byes can turn out to be forever.

I dragged my suitcase over the bumpy brick sidewalk. Liza had been right about the humidity here. At the end of the block I fished an elastic band from my backpack and pulled my curly hair into a loose ponytail.

Straight ahead of me lay the main quadrangle of Chase College, redbrick buildings with steep slate roofs and multi-paned windows. A brick wall with a lanterned gate bordered Chase Street. I passed through the gate and followed a tree-lined path to a second quad, which had been built behind the first. Its buildings were also colonial in style, though some appeared newer. I immediately recognized the Raymond M. Stoddard Performing Arts Building.

Liza had described it accurately as a theater that looked like an old town hall, with high, round-topped windows, a slate roof, and a tall clock tower rising from one corner. The length of the building ran along the quad, with the entrance to the the-ater at one end, facing a parking lot and college athletic fields.

I had arrived early for our four o'clock check-in at the dorms. Leaving my suitcase on the sidewalk, I climbed the steps to the theater. If Liza had been with me, she would have insisted that we go in. Something happened to Liza when she crossed the threshold of a theater—it was the place she felt most alive.

Last July was the first time my sister and I had ever been separated. After middle school she had attended the School for the Arts and I a Catholic high school, but we had still shared a bedroom, we had still shared the details of our lives. Then Liza surprised us all by choosing a summer theater camp in Maryland over a more prestigious program in the New York area, which would have been better suited to her talent and experience. She was that desperate to get away from home.

Once she got to Wisteria, however, she missed me. She e-mailed and texted constantly, and begged me to come meet her new friends, especially Michael. All she could talk about was Michael and how they were in love, and how this was love like no one else had ever known. I kept putting off my visit. I had lived so long in her shadow, I needed the time to be someone other than Liza Montgomery's sister. Then suddenly I was given all the time in the world.

For the last eleven months I had struggled to concentrate in school and gymnastics and worked hard to convince my parents that everything was fine, but my mind and heart were somewhere else. I became easily distracted. I kept losing things, which was ironic, for I was the one who had always found things for Liza.

Without Liza, life had become very quiet, and yet I knew no peace. I could not explain it to my parents—to anyone— but I felt as if Liza's spirit had remained in Wisteria, as if she were waiting for me to keep my promise to come.

I reached for the brass handle on the theater door and found the entrance unlocked. Feeling as if I were expected, I went in.

Two

INSIDE THE LOBBY the windows were shuttered and only the exit signs lit. Having spent my childhood playing in the dusky wings and lobbies of half-darkened theaters, I felt right at home. I took off my backpack and walked toward the doors that led into the theater itself. They were unlocked and I slipped in quietly.

A single light was burning at the back of the stage. But even if the place had been pitch black, I would have known by its smell—a mix of mustiness, dust, and paint—that I was in an old theater, the kind with worn gilt edges and heavy velvet curtains that hung a little longer each year. I walked a third of the way down the center aisle, several rows beyond the rim of the balcony, and sat down. The seat was low-slung and lumpy.

"I'm here, Liza. I've finally come."

A sense of my sister, stronger than it had been since the day she left home, swept over me. I remembered her voice, its resonance and range when she was onstage, its merriment when she would lean close to me during a performance, whispering her critique of an actor's delivery: "I could drive a truck through that pause!"

I laughed and swallowed hard. I didn't see how I could ever stop missing Liza. Then I quickly turned around, thinking I'd heard something.

Rustling. Nothing but mice, I thought; this old building probably housed a nation of them. If someone had come through the doors, I would have felt the draft.

But I continued to listen, every sense alert. I became aware of another sound, soft as my own breathing, a murmuring of voices. They came from all sides of me—girls' voices, I thought, as the sound grew louder. No—one voice, overlapping itself, an eerie weave of phrases and tones, but only one voice. Liza's.

I held still, not daring to breathe. The sound stopped. The quiet that followed was so intense my ears throbbed, and I wasn't sure if I had heard my dead sister's voice or simply imagined it. I stood up slowly and looked around, but could see nothing but the exit signs, the gilt edge of the balcony, and the dimly lit stage.

"Liza?"

There had always been a special connection between my sister and me. We didn't look alike, but when we were little, we tried hard to convince people we were twins. We were both left-handed and both good in languages. According to my parents, as toddlers we had our own language, the way twins sometimes do. Even when we were older, I always seemed to know what Liza was thinking. Could something like that survive death?

No, I just wanted it to; I refused to let go.

I continued down the aisle and climbed the side steps up to the proscenium stage. Its apron, the flooring that bows out beyond the curtain line, was deep. If Liza had been with me, she would have dashed onto it and begun an impromptu performance. I walked to the place that Liza claimed was the most magical in the world—front and center stage—then faced the rows of empty seats.

I'm here, Liza, I thought for a second time.

After she died, I had tried to break the habit of mentally talking to her, of thinking what I'd tell her when she got home from school. It was impossible.

I've come as I promised, Liza.

I rubbed my arms, for the air around me had suddenly grown cold. Its heaviness made me feel strange, almost weightless. My head grew light. I felt as if I could float up and out of myself. The sensation was oddly pleasant at first. Then my bones and muscles felt as if they were dissolving. I was losing myself—I could no longer sense my body. I began to panic.

The lights came up around me, cool-colored, as if the stage lights had been covered with blue gels. Words sprang into my head and the lines seemed familiar, like something I had said many times before: *O time, thou must untangle this knot, not I. It is too hard a knot for me t'untie.*

In the beat that followed I realized I had spoken the lines aloud.

"Wrong play."

I jumped at the deep male voice.

"We did that one last year."

I spun around.

"Sorry, I didn't mean to scare you."

The blue light faded into ordinary house and overhead stage lighting. A tall, lean guy with sandy-colored hair, my age or a little older, set down a carton. He must have turned on the lights when entering from behind the stage. He strode toward me, smiling, his hand extended. "Hi. I'm Brian Jones."

"I'm Jenny." I struggled to focus on the scene around me. "Jenny Baird."

Brian studied me for a long moment, and I wondered if I had sounded unsure when saying my new last name. Then he smiled again. He had one of those slow-breaking, tantalizing smiles. "Jenny Baird with the long red hair. Nice to meet you. Are you here for camp?"

"Yes. You too?"

"I'm always here. This summer I'm stage manager." He pulled a penknife from his pocket, flicked it open, and walked back to the carton. Kneeling, he inserted the knife in the lid and ripped it open. "Want a script? Are you warming up for tomorrow?"

"Oh, no. I don't act. I'm here to do crew work."

He gave me another long and curious look, then pulled out a handful of paperback books, identical copies of *A Midsummer Night's Dream*. "I guess you don't know about Walker," he said, setting the books down in sets of five. "He's our director and insists that everyone acts."

"He can insist, but it won't do him any good," I replied. "I have stage fright. I can act if I'm in a classroom or hanging out with friends, but put me on a stage with lights shining in my face and an audience staring up at me, and something happens."

"Like what?" Brian asked, sounding amused.

"My voice gets squeaky, my palms sweat. I feel as if I'm going to throw up. Of course," I added, "none of my elementary school teachers left me on stage long enough to find out if I would."

He laughed.

"It's humiliating," I told him.

"I suppose it would be," he said, his voice gentler. "Maybe we can help you get over it."

I walked toward him. "Maybe you can explain to the director that I can't."

He gazed up at me, smiling. His deep brown eyes could shift easily between seriousness and amusement. "I'll give it a shot. But I should warn you, Walker can be stubborn about his policies and very tough on his students. He prides himself on it."

"It sounds as if you know him well." Had Brian known Liza, too? I wondered.

"I'm going to be a sophomore here at Chase," Brian replied, "and during my high school years I was a student at the camp, an actor. Did you see our production last year?"

"No. What play did you do?"

"The one you just quoted from," he reminded me.

For a moment I felt caught. *Twelfth Night.*

"Those were Viola's lines," he added.

Liza's role. Which was how I knew the lines—I'd helped her prepare for auditions.

Still, the way Brian studied me made me uncomfortable. Did he know who I was? Don't be stupid, I told myself. Liza had been lanky and dark-haired, like my father, while my mother and I looked as if we had descended from leprechauns. Liza's funeral had been private, with only our closest friends and family invited. My mother had always protected me from the media.

"It's a great play," I said. "My school put it on this year," I added, to explain how I knew the lines.

Brian fell silent as he counted the books. "So where will you be staying?" he asked, rising to his feet. "Did they mail you your room assignment?"

"Yes. Drama House."

"Lucky you!"

"I don't like the sound of that."

He laughed. "There are four houses being used for the camp," he explained. "Drama House, a sorority, and two frats. I'm the R.A., the resident assistant, for one frat. Two other kids who go to Chase will be the R.A.s for the other frat and the sorority house. But you and the girls at Drama House will have old Army Boots herself. I think last year's campers had more descriptive names for her."

Liza had, but Liza was never fond of anyone who expected her to obey rules. "Is she that awful?" I asked.

He shrugged. "*I* don't think so. But of course, she's my mother."

I laughed, then put my hand over my mouth, afraid to have hurt his feelings.

He reached out and pulled my hand away, grinning. "Don't hide your smile, Jenny. It's a beautiful one."

I felt my cheeks growing warm. Again I became aware of

his eyes, deep brown, with soft, dusty lashes.

"If you wait while I check out a few more supplies, I'll walk you to Drama House."

"Okay."

Brian headed backstage. I walked to the edge of the apron and sat down, swinging my feet against the stage, gazing into the darkness, wondering. Brian had heard me say Liza's lines, but he hadn't mentioned the voices that I'd heard sitting in the audience. I thought of asking him about them but didn't want to sound crazy.

But it's not crazy, I told myself. It shouldn't have surprised me that being in a place where I couldn't help but think of Liza, I'd remember her lines. It was only natural that, missing her so, I would imagine her voice.

Then something caught my eye, high in the balcony, far to the right, a flicker of movement. I strained to see more, but it was too dark. I stood up quickly. A sliver of light appeared—a door at the side of the balcony opened and a dark figure passed through it. Someone had been sitting up there.

For how long? I wondered. Since the rustling I had heard when I first came in?

"Is something wrong?" Brian asked, reemerging from the wings.

"No. No, I just remembered I left my luggage at the front door."

"It'll be okay. I'll show you the back door—that's the one everybody uses—then you can go around and get it."

He led me backstage, where he turned out all but the light that had been burning before, then we headed down a flight of steps. The exit was at the bottom.

"This door is usually unlocked," Brian said. "People from the city always think it's strange the way we leave things open, but you couldn't be in a safer town."

Aside from an occasional serial killing, I thought.

We emerged into an outside stairwell that was about five steps below ground level. Across the road from the theater, facing the back of the college quadrangle, was a row of large Victorian houses. A line of cars had pulled up in front of them, baggage was deposited on sidewalks, and kids were gathering on the lawns and porches. Someone waved and called to Brian.

"Catch you later, Jenny," he said, and started toward the houses.

I headed toward the front of Stoddard to fetch my luggage. As I rounded the corner I came face to face with someone. We both pulled up short. The guy was my age, tall with black hair, wearing a black T-shirt and black jeans. He glanced at me, then looked away quickly, but I kept staring. He had the most star-tlingly blue eyes.

"Sorry," he said brusquely, then walked a wide route past me.

I turned and watched him stride toward the houses across the street.

I knew that every theater type has a completely black outfit in his closet, maybe two, for black is dramatic and tough and cool. But it's also the color to wear if you don't want to be seen in the dark, and this guy didn't want to be seen, not by me. I had sensed it in the way he'd glanced away. He'd acted guilty, as if I had caught him at something, like slinking out of the balcony, I thought.

Had he heard Liza's voice? Had he been responsible for it? A tape of her voice, manipulated by sound equipment and played over the theater's system could have produced what I heard.

There was just one problem with this explanation—it begged another. Why would anyone want to do that?

Three

BY THE TIME I had picked up my suitcase, dragged it around the building, and crossed the street, the guy in black had disappeared among the other kids gathering at the four houses. Drama House, which had a sign on it, was the best kept of the three-story homes. Covered in pale yellow clapboard with white trim, it had a steep pyramid-shaped roof, gables protruding at different angles, and a turret at one corner.

A guy about my height and three or four times my width blocked the sidewalk up to Drama House, two stuffed backpacks and a battered suitcase resting at his feet like tired dogs. He gazed toward the porch, where a flock of girls chattered and laughed. "She's beautiful," he said.

I peeked around him, hoping he'd notice I wanted to get past, but he was lost in wonder. "Which one?" I finally asked.

He blinked, surprised. "What?"

"Which girl?"

He shoved his hands in his pockets and looked embarrassed, "I—I was talking about the house. It's a Queen Anne, the style built at the end of the 1800s. Look at the way they used the different shapes—triangular, rectangular, round, conical. Look at the texture in the roof and front gable."

He had a strong Bronx accent—the kind I associated with beer vendors at Yankee Stadium, not an admirer of nineteenth-century architecture. I stifled a giggle.

"If I was painting it, I'd use colors with more contrast," he went on. "Red, gold, green. Lime, maybe. Yes, definitely . . . lime." He swallowed the last word self-consciously. "I'm supposed to be over there," he muttered, slinging on his backpacks, then reaching for his suitcase. He started toward a peeling gray house that had a stuffed plaid sofa and purple coffee table on its front lawn. Obviously, a fraternity.

"Now, *that* house," I called after him, "could use a paint job."

He turned back and smiled for just a moment. Despite his thick dark hair, bristly eyebrows, and nearly black eyes, his round face looked almost cherubic when he smiled.

As he hurried on to the frat, I continued down the sidewalk to Drama House and up the steps of its wraparound porch. Four girls were gathered there in a tight group, talking loudly enough for three others to hear. I joined the quiet girls.

"So did you get yourself expelled?" asked a girl whose head was wrapped in elegant African braids. Her cheekbones were high, her dark skin as smooth as satin.

"No, Shawna, I did not," another girl replied, sighing wearily.

"How come?" Shawna asked. "Did they keep giving you second chances?"

"Something like that."

Shawna laughed. "Well, how many times did you try, Keri?"

"Not as many as I'd planned. I found out who went to the school where my parents threatened to send me. It would be entertaining for a while, but it'd get old."

As she spoke, Keri combed long nails through her hair, which was cut short and dyed, a high contrast job in black and white. Dark pencil lined her pale eyes—sleepy, half-closed eyes. I knew that look: Liza had used it occasionally to let others know they had better do something if they wanted to hold her interest.

"Hey, Keri, Paul's back," said another girl.

"Is he?" The bored expression disappeared.

"Still hot for Paul," the tall, thin girl observed.

Shawna shook her head. "I just don't understand you."

"Keri doesn't want to be understood," said the fourth girl of the group. She had long black hair and velvet-lashed, almond eyes.

"I mean, he's good-looking," Shawna began, "but—"

"Oh, look who's headed this way," Keri said coolly.

"Boots," muttered the thin girl.

All of us quiet ones turned to see whom the others were eyeing. I figured it was Brian's mother, a.k.a. Army Boots.

From a distance she appeared theatrical, with a wide scarf wrapped around her thick, bleached hair and a big gold chain around her waist, but as she got close, she looked more like a P.E. teacher and mother—with a strong jaw, a determined mouth, but lots of little worry lines around her eyes.

"Ladies," she greeted us, joining us on the porch. "How are you?"

"Fine, okay, good," we mumbled.

"I hope you can speak more clearly than that on stage," she said, then smiled. "I'm Dr. Margaret Rynne. You may call me Maggie."

I thought Brian had said his last name was Jones; perhaps she used her maiden name or had remarried.

"I'm the assistant director, and for the eight of you who have been assigned to Drama House"—she paused, counting to make sure we were eight—"your R.A., or housemother. We'll start promptly. Here are copies of the floor plan. Please find your name and locate your room."

I studied the diagram. Maggie's room, two bedrooms, a multi-bath, and the common room were on the first floor. Four bedrooms and another multi-bath were on the second, and two bedrooms and a bath were nestled under the roof. We were supposed to eat in the cafeteria in the Student Union, but there was a kitchen in the house's basement.

"On each door you'll find a rope necklace with your key attached," Maggie said. "Please remember to—"

"Who wants to switch rooms?" Shawna interrupted.

"No room switching," Maggie replied quickly. "Please be attentive to—"

"But I have to, Maggie," she insisted, fingering a braid. "I'll never be able to sleep in that room."

"You can sleep with me," Keri said. "I'm in the attic."

I rechecked the floor plan. So was I.

"Each girl will sleep in her own bed," Maggie said. "I would like to remind you all that this is theater camp, not a seven-week slumber party. When the lights go out at eleven, everyone is to be in bed. Our rehearsal schedule is a rigorous one and you must be in top form."

"But I can't be in top form if I have to sleep in that room," Shawna persisted. "My sister goes to college here, and she says the back room is haunted."

"Haunted how?" asked the thin girl, twisting a strand of her light-colored hair.

"There are strange sounds at night," Shawna said, "and cold drafts, and after the bed is made, it gets rumpled again, as if someone's been sleeping in it."

I glanced at Maggie, who shook her head quietly. The other girls gazed at Shawna wide-eyed.

"It's Liza Montgomery," Shawna continued.

Now I stared at her.

"That was her room last year, you know."

"You mean the girl who was murdered?" asked a newcomer. "The one axed by the serial killer?"

"Bludgeoned," Keri corrected with a dispassionate flick of her heavily lined eyes.

Inside I cringed.

"Four weeks into our camp," said the girl with the dark silky hair, "Liza went out alone in the middle of the night."

My stomach tightened. I should have anticipated this, my sister being turned into a piece of campus lore.

"She was found under the bridge, chased under there," the girl added.

In fact, the police didn't know why Liza was beneath the bridge—whether she was chased, lured, or simply happened to be walking there.

"She got it in the back of the head—with a hammer. There was blood like all over the place."

"Thank you for that detail, Lynne," Maggie said.

"Her watch was smashed," Lynne went on.

I struggled to act like the other girls, interested in a story that was making me sick.

"That's how the police knew it was the serial killer. He murders people under bridges and smashes their wristwatches, so you know what time he did it."

"What time did he do it?" asked a new girl.

"Midnight," said Lynne.

Twelve-thirty, I corrected silently, *twelve-thirty while I was still trying to reach her.*

"Well, I think that's enough for today's storytime," Maggie said, then turned to the four of us who were new. "Ladies, there was a horrible tragedy here last summer. It shook up all of us. But this is a very safe campus and a safe town, and if you follow the camp's curfew rules, there is no reason to be concerned. Keri, Shawna, Lynne, and Denise"—she pointed them out—"were here last year. And camp is camp, no matter how grown-up you get. Those of you who are new, don't be conned by the tales and pranks of the veterans."

"My sister wasn't making up tales," Shawna insisted. "The room is haunted."

"I'll take it."

The other girls and Maggie turned around. I thought Maggie was going to remind me that she had prohibited the switching of rooms, but perhaps she reasoned that Shawna's room was next to her own and seven weeks was a long time to live next to someone convinced she was sharing her bed with a ghost.

"Fine," she agreed. "And you are?"

"Jenny Baird. I was assigned to the third floor."

She made a neat correction on her own copy of the floor plan, then glanced at her watch. "We have a camp meeting and cookout at the college pavilion scheduled for five o'clock. I would like you all to deposit your luggage in your rooms and be ready to go in five minutes. Wear your key and lock your door when you leave."

There was general confusion as the eight of us pulled our luggage out of the heap and rushed toward the front door. "Don't dawdle in the bathroom," Maggie called after us.

"She means it," Shawna whispered. "She'll come in and pull you off the toilet."

One of the new girls looked back at Shawna, horrified.

"Just kidding," Shawna said, laughing in a loud, bright way that made *me* laugh.

The front door opened into a large, square foyer with varnished wood trim and a worn tile floor. The stairs rose against the back wall of the foyer, turned and climbed, then turned and climbed again. A hall ran from the foot of the stairway straight to the back of the house. The common room, where we could all hang out, was to the right of the foyer. Proceeding down the hall, there was a room on either side, Maggie's and Lynne's, then continuing on, my bedroom on one side and the multibath on the other.

I knew from Liza's e-mails that she had liked this room, and when I opened the door I remembered why. Its back wall had a deep double window with a built-in bench. I pictured Liza practicing every possible pose a heroine could adopt in the romantic window seat, but there was no time for me to "dawdle" and try it out.

I met up with Lynne in the bathroom, then we headed out to the front porch. When everyone had reported back, Maggie led us down Goose Lane, which ran past the backyard of the fraternity next door toward Oyster Creek.

"How do you like your room?" Keri asked as she strolled beside me, her short black-and-white hair ruffling in the breeze.

"It's nice."

"Yes," she said, lowering her voice, "if you like being next to Boots."

I shrugged. I hadn't come here to see how many rules I could break.

"Hey, guy alert," Denise called from behind us.

Everyone turned around but Maggie, who marched on like a mother goose assuming her goslings were right behind. Our group of eight slowed down, or perhaps the guys picked up their pace. However it happened, the two groups soon merged and we did what guys and girls always do, say things too loudly, make comments that seem terribly clever until they come out really dumb, while checking each other out. I saw the heavy-set guy from the Bronx hanging toward the back. Far ahead Maggie stopped and gazed back at us, counting her flock, I guessed.

"So where's Paul? I thought Paul was supposed to be here," Shawna said with a sly look at Keri.

"He's here. Somewhere," a guy replied. "Mike and Brian are looking for him."

Mike? Liza's Michael? I wondered. Would a guy in love with a girl return to the place where she was murdered? No way . . . and yet I had come here and I loved Liza.

"Paul's probably back torching Drama House," another guy teased. "Hope you girls didn't leave anything important there."

"I still think it was unfair for everyone to blame last year's fire on Paul," Shawna replied. "There was no evidence."

"Oh, come on. He did it," Lynne said, "probably with the help of Liza."

"Probably to get Liza," a guy observed.

"No way," argued another. "Paul wouldn't have hurt her. He was totally obsessed with her."

I saw Keri bite her lip.

"That's what obsessed people do when they don't get what they want," the boy continued. "They get the person's attention one way or another."

I didn't like this conversation.

"I thought Paul was weird before Liza was murdered," Denise said, rubbing her long, thin arms, "but he was even weirder afterward, wanting all the details."

"Most people do want the details," Keri said crisply. "He's just more honest than the rest of you."

"Anyway, it's not strange for *him*," observed another guy. "You ever seen the video games Paul plays? The more violent they are the better he likes them."

"Movies, too," someone else added. "I bet he watched slasher movies in his playpen."

Sounds like a terrific guy, I thought.

"Paul's great-looking—in a dangerous kind of way," Lynne said, picking up her dark hair and waving it around to cool herself. "But once he gets hooked on someone or something, he's scary."

"At least scary is interesting," Keri remarked, "which is more than I can say for the rest of you guys."

The boys hooted. The girls laughed. The conversation turned to other people who had attended camp last year.

Had Liza been aware of Paul's feelings? I wondered as we walked on. Did my sister realize that someone like that could turn on you? Call it a huge ego or simple naïveté, but Liza always believed that everyone liked her—"they like me deep down," she'd insist when people acted otherwise.

Goose Lane ended at the college boathouse. Beyond the cinder-block building were racks of sculls—those long, thin boats for rowing races—and a pier with floating docks attached. Oyster Creek, wide as a river, flowed peacefully between us and a distant bank of trees. To the left of the docks was the pavilion, an open wooden structure with a shingled roof and deck. Built on pilings over the edge of the creek, it seemed to float on a tide of tall, grasslike vegetation.

Two other groups of eight had caught up with us. Maggie conferred with a guy and girl whom I guessed were R.A.s, and the rest of us climbed a ramp to the pavilion. Inside it was furnished with wood tables and benches. I headed for its sun-washed deck, which provided a view of the creek. Leaning on the railing, I finally allowed myself to look to the left, past a small green park to a bridge, the bridge where Liza had been killed. I studied it for several minutes, then turned away.

"Are you all right?"

I hadn't realized Shawna was standing next to me. "Me? Yeah."

"You're pale," she said. "Even your freckles are pale."

"Too bad they don't fade all together," I joked. "Really, I'm all right. I, uh, look like this when I haven't eaten for a while."

She believed the excuse. "They're putting out munchies. You stay here, Reds. I'll get you some."

"Thanks."

I turned back to the water. When Liza came to this place the first day, when she saw the creek sparkling in the late-afternoon sun and heard the breeze rustling in the long grass, did she have any idea that her life would end here?

No. Impossible.

She had had so much ahead of her—a scholarship to study acting in London, a film role scheduled for spring. She had had beauty, brains, and incredible talent, and the world was about to get its first real glimpse of her. It was no time to die.

Besides, even if Liza had been a more ordinary girl, no teen believes death is waiting for her. Certainly, standing by the creek that sunny afternoon, I didn't.

Four

OUR DIRECTOR ARRIVED by motorcycle. The guys thought it was cool. I think a middle-aged man with a big paunch straddling a motorcycle looks like a jack-in-the-box before it springs—all rolled up in himself. In any case, it was a dramatic entrance, especially since he rode the cycle across the park grass and partway up a pavilion ramp, stopped only by Maggie running down it, waving her arms frantically, screaming that the machine was too heavy.

Walker backed up his vehicle and climbed off. He was greeted like a hero, the guys swarming down the walkway to see the cycle, the girls lining up on the deck of the pavilion, like ladies watching from the top of a castle wall. When Walker removed his helmet, I saw that he was bald. A few reddish strands of hair had been recruited from a low part and combed over his dome; the remaining hair grew long enough to curl over his shirt collar.

"This is a merry troupe," he said, striding up the ramp.

Inside the pavilion we sat in a circle with Walker at the center. He asked us to introduce ourselves, say where we lived, and tell something about our interests.

My parents had known Walker Burke years ago in New York, but I couldn't remember meeting him, and if I had, I would have been too young for him to recognize me now. The autobiography submitted with my application was mostly true. Realizing that whoppers would make it too easy to slip up, I had changed only what was necessary to conceal my identity, like making myself the child of a magazine editor and his wife. I had showed the bio to the two people who had agreed to recommend me under the name of Jenny Baird so there would be no inconsistencies. When called on, I was brief.

Other kids went on and on. It took at least forty minutes to get all the way around the circle of introductions. At last the final person spoke, the heavyset guy who had admired the architecture of Drama House.

"Tomas Alvarez," he said, using the Spanish pronunciation of his first name.

"My set designer," Walker replied.

"I am?"

Applicants had been invited to submit a design for the set

of the play; apparently his had been chosen. Tomas's face lit up like a Halloween pumpkin's.

"It needs revision, of course," Walker said, then rose to his feet. He wiped his neck, cricked it left and right, and rolled his shoulders. He seemed to be winding up for a speech.

"Now, people," he said, "let me tell you what I expect from you. The absolute best. A hundred percent and more. Nothing less than your heart, soul, and mind."

He began to pace.

"From eight-thirty a.m. to four-thirty p.m. you will be mine. I will work you hard, so hard that at dinnertime your faces will drop onto your plates. And after dinner I will expect more of you."

He took a pair of glasses from his pocket, a nice prop with which to gesture.

"That means I expect each of you to keep yourselves in top physical shape. I expect you to eat right, to sleep eight hours a night, and to avoid risky behavior. You are old enough to know what I mean by risky behavior."

We glanced at one another.

"You will have studying to do, lines to memorize, films to watch. Your life here will be utterly devoted to drama. You will eat, breathe, and sleep drama. You will feel as if the theater owns you. If you had something less than this in mind, you should transfer to one of those cushy New York moneymakers."

I wondered how many people were considering it.

"Other directors coddle their young actors. They treat their tender egos with kid gloves and teach them to think better of themselves than they should. What I am going to teach you is to act. Come hell or high water, you'll learn."

Welcome to drama boot camp, I thought.

"In the long run," Walker said, "you'll find the skills I teach you more useful than a New York attitude."

Clearly, he didn't like the Big Apple.

Walker then asked Maggie to go over the rules—procedures at mealtime, curfew, and special instructions for campers who opted to stay through the weekend. Brian arrived while she was talking. Curious about Mike, I glanced around, but the faces were too unfamiliar for me to notice if someone new had arrived. Brian was introduced to us as the stage manager and gave us the schedule for the coming week: auditions tomorrow, a read-through on Wednesday morning, and blocking beginning that afternoon.

"Everyone will audition and everyone will do crew work," Walker told us. "There are thirty-two of you. I'm casting twice the number of fairies, which gives us twenty-six roles. But everyone, including my six techs, will be involved at least in understudy work. Got it? Any questions?"

Tomas raised his hand and waited for Walker to acknowledge him. "About trying out," the boy said, "I'd rather not."

Walker gazed at him for a long moment. "Tomas, do you have a hearing problem?"

"No, sir."

"Do you have attention deficit disorder?"

"Uh, no."

"Do you have any excuse at all for not hearing what I just said?"

"No, sir."

"Are you fat?"

Kids snickered.

"Yes," Tomas said quietly.

"Obviously, but that's no excuse for not trying out."

It's no excuse for embarrassing him, either, I thought, though I had hung around enough shows to know there were directors who made an art form of bullying others. Not wanting to offer up myself as the next public victim, I decided to talk to Walker later about my problem with stage fright. I hoped Brian would keep his promise and ease the way for me.

Maggie ended the meeting, telling us to get to know one another and reminding us to stay in the area between the bridge and the school docks. The grills had arrived by truck, and burgers would be ready in about forty minutes.

I followed a group of kids down the pavilion ramp and into

the small park, where there were swings and a gazebo.

"Hey, Jenny," Brian called, "wait a sec." He caught up and started walking with me. "I haven't had a chance to talk to Walker about your stage fright, but I didn't want you to worry. I'll do it before tomorrow, okay?"

"Thanks. He comes on strong."

Brian laughed. "Don't be snowed by him. Walker puts on a great act, but really, he's just a frustrated director who didn't make it in New York. Thanks to my mother—she knew him when she was a grad student at NYU—he can still live out his dream, creating magic moments of theater in the midst of cornfields. If there are empty seats at a show, we fill them with scarecrows."

"That's too bad," I said.

Brian cocked his head.

"I mean, I don't like him very much, but I feel bad for anyone who isn't where he wants to be."

"Oh, don't worry about Walker. Here he is king of drama, just as he always thought he should be."

I didn't respond.

"Maybe I'm being too harsh," Brian added quickly. "Try to understand. I've spent most of my life hanging around the theater, and sometimes I get a little cynical about the people who do it."

I smiled at him. I knew how that was.

"I wish I could hang out with you, Jenny," he said, returning my smile, "but I'm staff and right now I'm head burger flipper."

He turned back toward the grills, which had been set up along the walkway between the pavilion and the park. I continued past the gazebo, where some of the campers had gathered, crossed the grass toward the creek, then followed a path along its bank. Plumed grasses six feet tall, like those that grew around the pavilion, gave way to a timber bulwark that lined the creek almost as far as the bridge.

After Liza died, my mother thought we should come to Wisteria and toss flowers in the water beneath the bridge, but my father said he couldn't bear it. So we huddled together in our New York apartment while Sid and a family friend accompanied Liza's body home. Now I had to see for myself the place where she had died.

I guess one expects the location of a life-changing event to be remarkable in some way, but as I approached the bridge, I saw that it was quite ordinary, supported by round pilings, its undergirding painted a grayish blue, its old concrete stained with iron rust and crumbling at the edges. Stepping into the bridge's shadow I studied the mud and stones by the water's edge, where they had found Liza, then quickly pulled back.

The guy in the black clothes was there. I leaned forward

again, just far enough to see him. He was sitting on the bank beneath the bridge, staring out at the water, his wrists resting on his knees, his hands loose and still.

He suddenly turned in my direction. His eyes had changed mood, their brilliant blue darkened like the water in the bridge's twilight.

I waited for him to speak, then finally said, "I saw you inside the theater."

He didn't reply.

"You were in the balcony."

Still he was silent.

"You acted as if you didn't want to be seen."

The way he listened and focused on me, as if picking up something I wasn't aware of, made me uncomfortable.

"What were you doing?" I persisted.

"Tell me your name," he said softly.

"Jenny. Jenny Baird. You didn't answer my question. What were you doing?"

He stood up. He was a big guy, over six feet, with broad shoulders. When he walked toward me, I instinctively took a step back. He noticed and stopped.

"I'm Mike Wilcox."

My heart gave a little jerk. Liza's guy.

"Where are you from, Jenny Baird?"

"New York."

"City or state?"

"The city."

"You don't talk like it," he observed.

It was true. Mom and Dad's trained voices and their constant coaching of Liza and me had ironed out any trace of a New York accent.

"We traveled a lot," I told him. "My father kept getting different jobs. But Manhattan is home now."

"At camp last year we had a girl from Manhattan who had a schooled voice like yours. Her name was Liza Montgomery. Did you know her?"

I met his eyes steadily. "No. But I've heard about her. She's a hot topic among campers."

"I bet," he replied with a grimace. "In answer to your question: I was thinking about Liza."

"Were you close to her?"

"No. Just friends."

"But I thought—" I broke off.

He observed my face shrewdly. "You thought what?"

"I heard you and Liza Montgomery were in love."

Check the actor's hands, my father always told us. Mike's face was composed, but his hands tense, his fingers curled. "You're confusing me with Paul."

"No, Paul was obsessed with her—that's what they said. You were in love." *That's what Liza said,* I added silently.

"I think I should know better than they," he replied shortly.

"Today in the theater, did you hear"—I hesitated, remembering at the last minute that I wasn't supposed to know what Liza's voice sounded like—"voices?"

"I heard you reciting the lines from *Twelfth Night.*"

"Anything else?"

He gazed at me thoughtfully. "Well, Brian came in then."

"Before that—how long had you been there?"

"I arrived just before you began to speak."

Maybe, I thought, *but I had heard a rustling noise well before that.*

"Why?" he asked.

"Just curious."

We stared at each other, both of us defiant, each aware that the other person wasn't being candid.

"Well, I'm headed back to the party."

"Enjoy it," he said. "I'm going to stay here a little longer."

"To think about Liza?"

He nodded. "She was a very talented girl. And a friend," he added.

Liar, I thought, and strode away.

Five

WE ARRIVED BACK at Drama House about eight-thirty that evening. Some of the girls got sodas from a vending machine and holed up in the common room to talk, but I was tired of being someone other than myself, always thinking about how to respond as Jenny Baird, and was glad to escape to my room.

While I unpacked, I thought about the things that the kids from last year had said about Liza. I didn't like the idea that a creepy guy was obsessed with her. And it bothered me that the guy she had fallen in love with now claimed they were no more than friends. Maybe I remembered Liza's e-mails incorrectly, I thought, then turned on my laptop and opened a file named Liza. Sitting sideways in the window seat, I pulled my feet up, and began to read.

Jen—Hi!

*I finally made it here and it's great. I had no idea so
many cute guys hung around a nothing-happening place.
Lucky for me, there aren't many cute girls. But our curfew
is unbelievable. 10 p.m.!!! And lights out at 11!!! I'm just
waking up then. I've got an awesome room on the first
floor with a window seat (a real window seat! Where's
Jane Austen?) and another big window to climb out of.
I'll be in at 10:00 and out at 10:05. Miss you.*

Miss you a lot. Love, L

*P.S. Would you look for my silver barrette and mail it to
me? It should be in my top drawer, or my jewelry box, or
on the bathroom shelf, maybe the kitchen, check Sid's car.
Thanx.*

I continued reading through the batch of notes—her description of Stoddard Theater, her account of the funny things that had happened during auditions, and her reaction to Walker.

*He's always criticizing me, Jen, me more than anybody
else. I make him mad because I don't cringe like the others at his stupid remarks. I just stare at him. One of these
days I'm going to give it back. He's a nobody acting like*

he's directing Broadway. Somebody's got to put Walker in
his place. Looks like it'll have to be me.

There were frequent references to "Boots." Of course, given Liza's difficulty in following rules, she and Maggie had had a few run-ins. Liza thought Brian was nice. I found only two mentions of Paul. She was aware of his interest in her, but seemed to consider him just another of her fans. Maybe she had seen too many psychos in New York to be alarmed, I thought.

  She didn't get along with Keri.

Talk about a snob! She finds the whole world boring,
which, if you ask me, is the ultimate in snobbery. Her
parents have given her so much that the only thing left to
want is something she can't have—like Paul. In front of
everybody she announced that she couldn't stand my jas-
mine perfume. Fine, I told her, stay away from me so you
don't have to smell it—make us both happy!

I remembered correctly the romantic way Liza had described her relationship with Mike—Michael as she called him.

"It's Mike," he keeps saying, but I like the sound of
Michael better—Mikes are guys who work at Kmart.

*He is so gorgeous—dark hair, blue eyes to die for, tall but
not one of those skinny Hamlet types—a real guy. We're
like so in love, but we both fake a little. I don't discourage
the other guys who are interested in me because it's
always good to keep each other wondering. But really,
Jen, this is true love!!! You've got to come down and meet
my incredible guy. Please come soon.*

The descriptions of Michael and Liza's shared moments filled
the rest of her e-mails. I remembered thinking when I first read
them that Liza had finally figured out what counted, for the
things she was talking about so romantically were small acts of
kindness, little bits of gentleness, not wild kisses. Usually, Liza
went for cool, star types like herself, and after she and the guy
grew tired of showering each other with flattery, the fighting
got ugly. Maybe Liza had finally fallen for a guy who was terrific
on the inside, too.

And maybe I should have been gentler, I thought, *not trying to
force Mike to admit his feelings for my sister.*

I read all the way through the correspondence and came to
the last e-mail, the one that had been sent after lunch the day
Liza died.

Jenny,

Don't tell Mom and Dad, but I'm thinking about coming home. I know they won't want me to pull out of the production, but I think I have to. I've hurt someone very badly, and I don't know how to make it up. I had no idea—I didn't mean it—it's terrible. I need to talk to you.

1:20—rehearsal's started. Talk later. L

Whom Liza had hurt, I never found out. I showed the note to the police, but they dismissed it as normal high-school stuff. The pattern of the serial murderer had been established, and his victims appeared to be random. They weren't looking for suspects who knew Liza and would have had some kind of personal motive.

I wondered again what had happened that day. Had Liza suddenly realized she was hurting Paul? Had something occurred between her and Mike? Maybe that's why he denied their relationship now. Or, had she let Walker have it between the eyes? My sister had a better command of language than she had realized and could sometimes be cruel in what she said.

It wasn't until I got her phone message that night that I checked my e-mail. If I had checked earlier, I might have reached her before she slipped out the window. If I had gone to Wisteria when Liza invited me, I might have helped her get out of whatever mess she was in. I could have been with her and kept her from venturing out the same night as the murderer.

After shutting down my laptop, I turned out the lamp by my bed and climbed back in the window seat. I listened to the sounds of the summer night and the mix of music and laughter that floated down from open windows. A moth flicked its wings against my screen. Though I wasn't tired, my eyelids felt as fluttery as a moth. There was a cool breeze and my head grew light, so light it could have floated off my shoulders. Closing my eyes, I leaned against the soft wire screen. My mind slipped into a strange, textureless darkness. Its edges glimmered with pale blue light.

Then my body jerked and I was alert, aware of the sound of my own breathing, quick and hoarse. I felt as if I had been running fast. I held my side, massaging it. I opened my mouth, trying to catch my breath silently, afraid to make the slightest noise.

It was swampy where I was—I could smell the creek and feel the ground ooze beneath my feet. A rooflike structure supported by pilings stretched over the dark area. I listened to the lap of water against the pilings, then footsteps sounded above. Fear flashed through me like light off a knife blade.

I made my way forward into the shallow water—slowly, so as not to make a ripple of sound. I heard the light thump of feet on wet ground, then mud sucking back from shoes. My pursuer was close—whether male or female, I couldn't tell—the night was cloudy and the person's face and body covered. I hid behind one of the pilings.

I heard the person walking slowly, prowling and listening, prowling and listening. I guessed that only ten feet remained between us. If I moved, the person would know immediately where I was. But if I waited any longer, I might get trapped.

I bolted. The pursuer was after me fast as a cat. I tripped and fell facedown, splashing into the muddy ebb of the creek. I scrambled to my feet and rushed forward again.

The tumble had jolted me, and I realized that my knees, though sore from falling, were dry. I had fallen out of the window seat and rushed toward a door, my bedroom door in Drama House. There was no muddy creek here. I was safe.

Still, I shook so badly I knocked into my bedside lamp trying to turn it on. I crept into bed and pulled the sheets up to my chin, shivering despite the July heat. I reached for the lamp a second time. The darkness retreated from the glow of the dim bulb, but I didn't dare look in the corners of the room, lest the shadows turn blue—blue like the lighting in the theater this afternoon, blue like the edges of the nightmare vision I'd just had.

It was only a dream, I told myself, a natural one to have after seeing the place where Liza had died. But the blue light . . . *Please, not again,* I thought.

When I was a child I had horrible nightmares, dreams as strange as they were frightening, about people and things I couldn't remember seeing in real life. All of the dreams had a strange blue cast. Waking up from them terrified, I would tell Liza, and she would put her arms around me, holding me tight. Sometimes she would tell me she had had the same dream. As I grew older I didn't believe her; still it had helped me not to feel alone. "Sweet dreams," Liza would always say, soothing me, tucking me back in bed, "sweet dreams only for you and me." Eventually the nightmares stopped.

Now I scrunched down under the sheet, sweating and shivering, missing Liza more than ever, and wondering why the dreams had come back.

Six

WE GATHERED IN the seats of Stoddard Theater at eight-thirty the next morning. Walker came up the back steps, strode across the stage, then stopped, scanning us slowly, like a shopper carefully eyeing apples before reaching into the pile. Our nervous chatter died.

"Oh, don't be bashful," he said.

Maggie called roll. Next to Mike, two rows in front of me, sat a guy who answered to Paul McCrae, but all I could see of him was brown hair hanging thick and wavy down the back of his neck. Maggie handed out adhesive name tags, which we were to stick below our left shoulder. Anyone who put it on his or her right was corrected. Brian gave out the books.

"Put your names in them immediately," Maggie instructed. "Katie, no more free replacements of lost scripts."

"She doesn't forget anything," the girl named Katie hissed to Shawna.

Walker continued to study us. "Okay, people," he said, putting on his half-moon glasses. "I am assuming you are all intimately familiar with *A Midsummer Night's Dream* and are fully prepared and eager to impress me with your auditions. Let's begin."

"Excuse me, Walker."

His eyes rolled up over his glasses. "Maggie."

"I think we should review the plot."

His smile was a tiny bow. "You have my permission to think whatever you like. Meanwhile, I'm starting the auditions."

"And is that because you prefer to review the story halfway through, once it becomes obvious that everyone is confused—as we did last year, and the year before that, and the year before that?"

"I told you she doesn't forget," Katie whispered.

Walker sighed, then eyed us. "I believe in learning from my mistakes," he said, "but I keep making Maggie assistant director."

There were muffled laughs. I glanced at Maggie, but she didn't seem to care, perhaps because she knew what he would do next—exactly what she had suggested.

"As you all no doubt already know," Walker boomed, "there are four lovers in this play. The two guys, Lysander and Demetrius, are both in love with Hermia. Hermia is in love with Lysander, but Hermia's father has chosen Demetrius to be her husband. Meanwhile, we have poor Helena, Hermia's friend, who is hopelessly in love with Demetrius. Got it?"

We nodded.

"Like all good star-crossed lovers, Hermia and Lysander plan to run away. Helena thinks she can score some points with Demetrius by telling him of Hermia and Lysander's departure. So, what do we have? Hermia and Lysander running off to the forest, Demetrius running after Hermia, and Helena after Demetrius. We have four lovers wandering around the Athenian woods on Midsummer Night."

Walker strode back and forth across the stage as he spoke, gesturing with the script. He held our attention as if he were Shakespeare himself.

"Enter the fairies: Oberon the fairy king and Titania, the queen. They're married and they're quarreling. Oberon has a jealous, vengeful streak in him. He also has a very mischievous fairy working for him, Puck, and, with Puck's help, he plans to spread a magic flower ointment on his wife's eyes while she is sleeping. The first person, beast, or thing Titania sees when she awakens, she'll fall madly in love with."

A couple kids giggled, as if just now figuring out what would happen, which told me they hadn't read the play, at least not too well. Maggie knew what she was doing.

"Now, there are some interesting candidates for Titania to fall in love with that night," Walker continued. "A group whom we refer to as 'the rustics,' six bumbling guys, are rehearsing a play in the woods to present to the Duke of Athens at his wedding. The Duke's wedding frames the entire play. Puck has some fun and transforms one of the rustics so that he has an ass's head instead of a human one, and it is he whom Titania sees first when she awakens.

"As for the lovers, Oberon gives Puck instructions to use the flower ointment to work out their problem, that is, to make Demetrius fall in love with Helena, so the four are neatly paired up. Unfortunately, Puck gets the guys confused, and we end up with a wonderful reversal, with Demetrius and Lysander now in love with Helena and chasing her, while Hermia is left out in the cold. Got it?"

We all nodded again and Walker hopped down from the stage steps, surprisingly light on his feet.

"Now, Maggie, may we begin?"

"I'm waiting," she said with a smile.

Walker started by assigning the parts of the lovers, trying different combinations for the two guys and two girls. Watching Mike read, I was amazed at his skill. I had imagined that he had just enough talent, or more accurately, the good looks to earn a small high school part. I was wrong—or perhaps the part of a lover came quite naturally to him. I glanced around: I wasn't the only girl who had trouble taking her eyes off him.

"Jenny Baird."

I didn't respond; it wasn't the name for which I was used to snapping to.

"Miss Baird." Walker's voice could roll low like thunder. Shawna nudged me.

"Walker," Brian said in a quiet voice, "I spoke to you about Jenny, remember?"

Walker turned to Brian very slowly, demonstrating for all of us how an actor can make an audience wait for a line. "I remember. Get up there, Miss Baird."

I walked to the stage steps carrying my book.

"I can try out," I told Walker, "but I get terrible stage fright when it comes time for performance."

"Act Two, Scene Two, after Puck has exited," Walker replied, as if he hadn't heard a word I'd said.

Brian stared at him and shook his head.

"Helena," Walker said to me when I was on stage, "you've just come upon Lysander, who is sleeping. What you don't know is that Puck has put the magic ointment on his eyelids, and the first person Lysander sees—you, not his beloved Hermia—he will now be madly in love with. Not knowing what has happened, you think he's making fun of you. Pick it up on *'But who is here?'*"

We positioned ourselves, Mike on the stage floor and me bending over him. I began:

> "But who is here? Lysander! on the ground?
> Dead or asleep? I see no blood, no wound.
> Lysander, if you live, good sir, awake."

Mike opened his eyes, then pulled himself up quickly, responding fervently: "'And run through fire I will for thy sweet sake.'"

I blinked and drew back. The incredible blue of his eyes and the intensity with which he zeroed in on me made my heart jolt, made me feel as if I were on an elevator that had suddenly dropped from beneath me. All I could do was stare at him, surprised. Of course, the character of Helena would have reacted the same way. I wasn't acting, but I looked like I was.

"'Transparent Helena,'" Mike began softly, kneeling now, his eyes, his whole person focused on me, the way a lover's would be. My heart did strange flip-floppy things. I struggled to make sense of the instinctive way I responded to Mike; in the play, Helena struggled to make sense of Lysander.

I dutifully told Lysander why he should be happy with his Hermia.

"'Content with Hermia?'" Mike responded. "'No, I do repent the tedious minutes I have with her spent.'" He reached out and touched my face. I tingled at the brush of his fingers and could feel my cheeks getting pink. Of course, Helena's cheeks would have reddened as she got increasingly angry at Lysander.

"'Not Hermia, but Helena I love,'" Mike said. "'Who will not change a raven for a dove?'"

But *I* was the raven and Liza his dove, I wanted to say. I stood up quickly, feeling mixed up, caught between the play world and the real one. He gazed at me as if his eyes would hold and cherish what his hands could not. I reminded myself that this was acting.

At last he got to the end of his lines, and I pulled myself together. I was mad—mad at him for using his eyes and voice that way, madder at myself for being caught in their spell. Hadn't I seen a million actors deliver lines like that? Hadn't I fallen for not one, but two guys who were pretending to like me because they wanted to know Liza?

Just as anger was boiling up in me, it was bursting from poor Helena: "'Wherefore was I to this keen mockery born?'" I exclaimed—ironically, totally in character.

Finishing my speech, I exited quickly, exactly as Helena should have. In fact, I wanted to run back to my seat, but I figured that Walker, upon observing my flight, would make me stay and read some more. I stopped onstage about twenty feet from Mike, waiting to be dismissed by Walker.

He looked from Mike to me, then turned to Brian. "Your new best friend doesn't seem all that shy," he observed. "I believe she has some talent."

"I never said she didn't," Brian replied coolly.

"You two are done," Walker said to us. "For now."

Mike headed for the steps stage left, I went stage right.

Lynne was called on to read as Hermia. She was so strong in the role she made the guy who played opposite her look good. Shawna tried out as Helena and Queen Titania, then Keri read for the queen's role opposite Paul as Oberon.

"No accents, Keri," Walker told her halfway through. "Save that lovely Jersey British for New York, where they can't tell the difference."

Paul was destined to be Oberon, I thought. His face was handsome, a model's face, and yet there was something wasted about it. His green eyes had circles under them—right for a jealous and somewhat vengeful king of the fairies. His body was hard—wiry, like a rock star's, his hands strong and expressive, but too thin, a thinness that could suggest cruelty.

By lunch everyone had read but Tomas, the heavyset guy who had said he'd "rather not." I thought Walker was showing some heart, or perhaps knew better than to torture the guy who had provided the winning set design for the play. I was wrong.

"All right, Tomas," Walker said as soon as we had gathered again, "this is your big chance."

Tomas was jolted out of what appeared to be the beginning of an afternoon nap.

"Get up there. You're Oberon."

There was a snicker from the vets. If Tomas played any role, it would have to be one of the rustics; there was no way he was going to prance around the stage as if there were magic in his feet.

"Paul, you're Puck," Walker said.

The contrast between the two guys was striking, and I wondered if Walker was pairing them up for his own amusement.

"Kimberly, you're Hermia." A blond girl giggled and made her way to the stage.

"Mike, Demetrius again. Act Three, Scene Two," Walker said, when the cast had assembled. "Puck is reporting back to Oberon about how he fared with the magic ointment. Demetrius and Hermia enter, and it is discovered by Oberon and Puck that Puck got the wrong guy when he tried to fix things for the lovers. Got it? Take it from the top, Oberon. Oberon?"

Tomas was paging frantically through the book; the more quickly he tried to find the scene, the harder it became. Kimberly giggled annoyingly. Paul finally snatched the script and found the page. When he shoved the book back in Tomas's face, Mike walked over to the embarrassed boy, leaned close, and ran his finger down the page. "You start here," I heard him say quietly. "Then Hermia and I enter—see?—and you don't say anything more until I lie down to sleep. Okay?"

Tomas nodded. Without waiting for Mike to get back in position, he began what had to be the most painful reading I'd ever witnessed. "'I wo-wonder if Titan be—'"

"Titania!" Walker called out. "She's a fairy, not a football team."

Kids laughed.

"'—if Titania be awak'd.'"

He didn't know how to pronounce the *k'd* and stumbled over it as if it were a piece of broken concrete. Kimberly, waiting for her entrance, rolled her eyes and made faces at her friends in the audience.

Fortunately, a long speech by Puck followed. Unfortunately, while Paul read, Tomas practiced his next few lines so intently, his lips moved and little whispery sounds came out. Paul paused halfway through his piece.

"Which one of us is talking here?" he asked, provoking more laughter.

Tomas continued to work on his lines, though silently now, with such focus that he missed his cue.

"Oberon!" Walker hollered.

Tomas looked up and promptly lost his place. When he found it again, his voice shook badly. He got through the last line before Mike and Kimberly's entrance, but he didn't look as if he were going to make it through the entire scene. As the dialogue ran back and forth between Mike and Kimberly, Tomas's face grew redder. He looked as if he was going to cry. Given his size and his bristly eyebrows, I knew it would be a terrible sight. He began blinking his eyes. He was never going to live this down.

"Excuse me." I stood up. "Excuse me."

Mike, who had just finished a line, turned with surprise, as did everyone else.

"I'd like to play Puck if you don't mind."

It was a strange request for a person with stage fright. Brian looked baffled. Maggie frowned at the interruption. But Walker studied me with a shrewd look on his face; he knew I was trying to distract people while Tomas regained his composure.

"Would you now, Miss Baird," Walker said. "That old menacing stage fright seems to be waning, does it?"

I glanced at Tomas out of the corner of my eye. "Seems to be."

"All right. Paul, sit down."

Paul stared at Walker a moment, caught off guard by the

abrupt change, then slowly left the stage, pressing his lips together, giving me a smile that was meant to chill. I ignored him, glad he was walking slowly and giving Tomas time to pull himself together. Giving me time as well—I quickly bent over and stretched before climbing the steps to the stage. Onstage I worked my back, my wrists, and my ankles, knowing I looked silly to everyone in the audience and buying Tomas even more time.

"We'll start from the top," Walker said.

Of course, I thought, let's drag him through it all again. But Tomas's eyes were clear now. If I could give the scene some lightness, play with him a little, I might get him through it and he'd have a chance of surviving camp. He looked at me curiously when I placed my script next to his feet and told him not to move an inch. I withdrew to the wings and removed my sandals. Walker sat back in his seat, arms folded over his chest, waiting.

Tomas delivered his first three lines with one less stutter. I listened, measuring with my eyes the distance between him and me. When the cue came, I raced forward and sprang, executing a handspring and round-off, landing five inches from his face. He laughed.

"'Here comes my messenger,'" he read, still laughing some. It worked well for his character. "'How now, mad spirit?'"

I had done gymnastic routines to music, but never to Shakespeare's iambic pentameter. The report to Oberon ran twenty-nine lines. I performed only easy stunts and thoroughly mashed my script, but I kept everyone entertained—most important, Tomas. I made sure to finish up close to him so I could give him a nudge if he missed his cue, but he was ready for me. We ran through a bit of dialogue, and Mike and Kimberly entered to read their parts. Then it was our turn again with lines Tomas hadn't yet read, but he did okay, I guessed because he felt more relaxed.

When we finished, some of the kids broke into applause. Walker didn't say a word, just went on to the next group. I had probably ticked him off. I wondered what Mike was thinking. I was careful not to look at him; hoping for his approval seemed too much like competing with Liza.

The audition went on with Walker trying different combinations of actors. He dismissed us at four o'clock, a half hour early, instructing us to read the play once again for tomorrow. The cast would be posted in the morning.

Brian showed the group the way down to the back exit and we filed out quietly. As I reached the grass outside, someone yanked on me from behind, pulling my arm so hard it hurt, forcing me to turn around.

"That role was mine," Paul said.

I could have insisted that I didn't want to play Puck, but he wouldn't have believed me, and if I explained why I had interrupted the scene, I'd embarrass Tomas.

"My name is Jenny," I told him. "If you want me, call my name, okay?"

"There's only one girl I ever wanted."

I could guess who.

"Since you're new around here, Jenny, I'm going to give you some advice." He gazed at my mouth, the only feature of mine that was like Liza's. "Watch your step. Don't play too many games with people. Don't cross Walker. Last summer there was a talented actress who did, and she ended up dead."

For a moment I could say nothing. "If you mean Liza Montgomery, I believe she was the victim of a serial killer."

"That's what people say," Paul replied, walking past me. "That's what people say."

Seven

KERI AND MIKE hurried after Paul and a stream of campers followed. Realizing that I had better straighten things out with Brian and that this would be a good time to catch him alone, I ducked back inside Stoddard. I found him walking down the ground floor hall, deep in thought, jangling a ring of keys.

"Can I talk to you?"

Brian turned around. "Sure. What's up, Jenny?"

"I want to apologize. I shouldn't have gotten you involved with my stage fright stuff."

"No problem," he assured me.

"And I want to explain about playing Puck."

Brian grinned. "I have to admit you had me very confused for a moment, then I figured you were rescuing the fat guy."

"Tomas," I said, wanting Brian to use his name.

"*Tomas*. Really, there's no need to apologize. It was worth it to see someone stand up to Walker. Most people don't."

"Why does Walker act the way he does?" I asked. "One moment he's nice, the next moment, obnoxious and insulting."

"It's how he keeps control," Brian replied. "Walker would say it's how he gets the best from us. Since we never know what's coming next, we stay on our toes."

"Why do *you* put up with him?"

"Good question." Brian leaned against the stairway railing and smiled that slow-breaking smile of his. "Basically, for the money and experience. I can't go to L.A. broke. I can't go there with nothing on my résumé."

"You mean to do film?"

He nodded. "Of course, it annoys Walker that I'd choose film over stage. It shouldn't matter to him, since he's always telling me I can't act. But Walker has this loyalty thing. The way he sees it, everyone is either for him or against him, there's no in-between. He takes everything personally."

I could imagine how personally he took Liza's response to him. "That's a narrow way of looking at the world."

"It's a very egotistical way," Brian replied. "And stupid. I mean, in the end, everybody is out there for himself. Sometimes it makes a person seem for you. Sometimes it makes a person seem against you."

"*That's* a very cynical view!"

"Probably." He smiled at me, then continued down the hall.

I'd had enough of theater types, and when I exited the building, I turned away from Drama House, heading left on Ink Street, the road that separated the quad from the houses, then taking another left on Scarborough, walking toward the main street of town. I remembered from Liza's e-mails that there was a café called Tea Leaves with terrific pastries and cappuccino.

Wisteria had to be the most peaceful town I'd ever strolled through. You could almost hear the flowering vines climbing their trellises. Every house had a sitting porch, every shop a tinkling bell on its door. Pedestrians moved much more slowly than in New York, adding to the sense of a town not subject to time. At the end of the long street of sycamores, sun glittered off the river. I walked all the way down to the harbor, then retraced my steps back to Tea Leaves.

The café was like a great-aunt's kitchen, with painted wood furniture and a linoleum tile floor, everything scrubbed clean. I had just settled down at a table with a chocolate doughnut and a cappuccino when I saw Tomas across the room from me, sitting by the big window. He gave me a small, self-conscious wave. I smiled back at him but stayed where I was.

When I looked up again, he was gazing intently out the window. His hand was moving quickly, sketching on an open pad. For fifteen minutes he managed to ignore the decadent pastry on his plate, drawing like a person possessed. I finished my doughnut and carried my cappuccino over to his table, wondering what he was working on.

"Hi."

He looked up and flushed. "Hi."

"May I sit with you?"

"Oh, uh, sure," he stammered and tried to clear a space quickly, knocking his backpack on the floor. It landed with a heavy thud. "Oh, nooo!" His head disappeared beneath the table, there was a lot of rustling around, then he popped up again. "Sorry."

"Everything okay?"

"I hope so."

"What do you have in your pack?" I asked curiously.

"Stuff. Sketch pads. Pencils. Pens. Chalks. A camera—two of them—digital and film. Lenses. They're in padded cases, they're okay."

"That's an awful lot to carry around."

"I like to be ready," Tomas explained. "You never know what kinds of interesting things you're going to see."

"I guess not." I leaned closer, trying to see his sketchpad, but he was practiced at covering his work with his arms. "May I look at what you're sketching?"

He glanced down at his drawing, then passed it over.

It was a street scene showing the buildings across from the

café, an old movie theater, a Victorian-looking hotel, a restau-
rant, and a large brick home.

"Wow, you're really good!"

"When I sketch buildings," he agreed. "I've always been
better with things than people."

"May I look at the rest of the sketches?" I asked.

He nodded. "It's a new book. There's just a couple."

Two of them were of Drama House, one of a tree and patch
of brick walk, another of Stoddard Theater from the outside.
I admired the way Tomas used lighting to create drama and
emotion.

"You know how to give buildings and objects feeling," I
said. "I guess that's what makes you a good set designer."

"I love doing art," he replied happily. "People look at what
you produce, rather than at you."

I imagined that both acting and athletics were miserable
activities for him.

"Thanks for earlier this afternoon," he went on. "I know
why you interrupted the scene."

"It was fun," I said, taking a sip of cappuccino. "Walker is
lucky to have a real artist in his troupe. I hope he figures that
out."

Tomas flushed again and studied his pastry. I began to
talk about New York and gradually he relaxed with me. We

compared notes on schools and friends and art exhibits we had seen in the city. Finishing our snacks, we walked up and down Wisteria's streets, poking around in shops. Time slipped away and we had to rush back to the meal hall. When we carried our food trays to the table area, everyone else was already seated.

I looked around for a place to sit. Keri's black-and-blond hair made her easy to spot in a crowd. She raised her head, saw Tomas and me, then leaned close to Mike, whispering something. He glanced up, then looked away. Just then Shawna held up a fork with a napkin stuck on its end and waved it like a flag.

"Come on, Tomas," I said.

"You sure?"

"About what?" I asked, though I knew what he meant and wasn't sure.

"That I'm invited, too."

"Of course you are."

"It's all girls," he observed.

"Lucky you!"

Tomas got an earful at dinner. The girls were annoyed because Maggie had announced that those of us who lived in Drama House would read together in the common room that evening.

"She says she wants to build camaraderie," Shawna said.

"Yeah, right. She wants to make sure we do our homework," Denise observed.

Several girls had already made plans to sneak over to the frats—not that we were supposed to visit unchaperoned.

"You guys, we've got to speed-read," one of them said.

Back at Drama House we tried, but Maggie wouldn't let us. Every time we rushed, she told us to slow down, explaining why this or that line was particularly meaningful. We lost more time than we gained. Two and a half hours later, just thirty minutes before curfew, we finished.

Keri and a new girl went immediately to Lynne's room, which had a first floor window, an easier exit than the fire escape. Shawna waited for me outside Lynne's door.

"Want to go with us?" she asked.

"Not tonight, thanks."

I returned to my room, turned on the bedside lamp, and carried a sketchpad belonging to Tomas to the window seat. Sitting down, I pulled my legs up on the bench and opened the spiral-bound book. Tomas had said that most of the drawings were done in New York. On the first page I discovered the carousel in Central Park, which Liza and I had ridden about a million times. I continued to turn the pages, feeling a twinge of homesickness—a park bench and street lamp, a green-grocer's striped awning and boxes of fruit, St. Bartholomew's

Church. Then I found myself in Wisteria.

All three drawings were of the bridge over Oyster Creek. I studied one, tracing with my finger the dark lines of its pilings. I began to feel light-headed. The moonlit paper turned a cool silvery blue. The image of the bridge swam before my eyes like a watery reflection.

It was happening again, the same strange experience that I'd had last night and in the theater. Frightened, I tried to pull back, tried to pull out of it. My muscles jumped, my head jerked. I felt wide awake and relieved that I could focus again. But when I looked around, I wasn't in my room.

Oyster Creek Bridge stretched above me. I heard a car drive over it, its wheels whining on the metal grating, the pitch rising, then dropping away. Silence followed, a long, ominous silence.

"Liza," I whispered, "are you there? Liza, are you making this happen? Help me—I'm scared."

The image of the bridge dissolved. I could see nothing now, nothing but darkness with an aura of blue, but I could sense things moving around me. The air was teeming with words I couldn't discern—angry words and feelings worming in the blackness.

I felt something being fastened around my wrist. I didn't know who was doing it or why and tried to pull my hand away. My arms and legs wouldn't respond.

"Help me! Help me, please."

The words stayed locked inside me. I tried to move my lips, but I had no voice.

Then a pinpoint of light broke through the darkness. I moved toward the light, and it grew larger and radiant as the sun. But something stirred in the darkness behind me and I quickly turned back. I saw another light, a smaller, dimmer image, like the reflected light of the moon. Suddenly there was the sound of breaking glass. The moon shattered.

I blinked and looked around. I was back in my room at Drama House, and the moon was in one piece high in the sky, shining down on a mere sketch of the bridge.

I clutched the art pad till its spiral bit into my fingers. What was happening to me?

When I had the blue dreams as a child, I was always asleep, but these visions were invading my waking hours. If I was awake, they had to be daydreams, imaginings about the place where Liza had died. And yet they came unsummoned like nightmares—dreams I couldn't control.

Now, more than ever, I needed Liza here to comfort me. And yet, it was the memory of her that gave these visions their terrifying life.

Eight

FEAR OF SLIPPING into another nightmarish vision made it difficult for me to fall asleep that night, but once I did, I slept solidly and could not remember any dreams when I awoke Wednesday morning. I walked to the meal hall with Shawna and Lynne, who reported that last night's adventure had been pretty dull. The girls had simply stood at a window of one of the frats and talked for a while to the guys.

In the middle of her analysis of this year's selection of guys, Shawna suddenly stopped and pointed to a group of kids clustered around the back door of Stoddard. "They posted the cast. Come on!"

She and Lynne rushed down the path. Tomas, who had been standing at the back of the crowd of campers, hurried toward me, grinning.

"You did it, Jenny. You did it! Congratulations! I knew you would get the part."

"Part—what part?"

"Puck," he said.

"As understudy, you mean." Please let that be what he means, I thought.

"No, no, you're it," he announced happily. "Isn't that great?"

"Yeah, *real* great . . . if you like a fairy that looks nauseated, sweats profusely, and speaks in a squeaky voice. I have to talk to Walker."

"Jenny," Lynne called to me, "you're Puck."

"Way to go, Reds!" Shawna hollered.

"I'm Hermia," Lynne called. "Shawna is Peter Quince, the director of the rustics."

"Congrats!" I turned to Tomas. "Did you get a part?"

"Not even understudy," he said with relief. "I'm head of scenery and props. This is going to be great. Want to eat? I sure do."

"You go ahead. There's something I have to take care of. Tell Shawna and Lynne I'll catch up with you at the theater."

Tomas walked on happily and I retreated to the porch of Drama House. From there I watched the four houses empty out. When it looked as if everyone had seen the posting and gone on to breakfast, I headed back to Stoddard. At the door I stopped to check the list. Mike had gotten the role of the lover

Demetrius, Paul was Oberon, the jealous king of the fairies, and Keri, his queen, Titania. I—under my new "stage name," Jenny Baird—was listed next to *Puck*. Liza would have been astonished.

When I entered the building I heard voices coming from a distance down the hall. One of them, Walker's, bristled with irritation.

"You've always got an excuse."

"I asked for a ladder," came the quiet reply. "Asked for it last Friday. When I get it, I'll do the job."

"I want it done *now*, Arthur."

I followed the voices past a series of doors marked WOMEN'S DRESSING ROOM, WARDROBE, AND PROPS, and reached the corner of the building, where the hall made a right-angle turn. Rounding the bend, I came upon Walker standing in an office doorway, his hands on his hips, a scowl on his face. He was talking to a man whose streaky hair was either blond turning gray or gray turning yellowy white. His veined hands had a slight tremor. Suddenly aware of me, he glanced back nervously.

"You don't need a ladder to get to the catwalk," Walker continued. "I told you before, there are rungs on the wall."

I tried to imagine this fragile man climbing the rungs to a narrow walkway hanging thirty feet above the stage. I had seen custodians like him before: tired, emotionally worn men just trying to get to the end of each day.

"Tell your boss I want to speak with him," Walker went on. "I'm tired of the crap they're sending me for custodians. You're worse than the last guy."

The custodian took a step back. "Yes, sir, I'll tell 'im. And maybe he'll climb up those rungs," he added. "You and him together."

I fought a smile. Arthur was tougher than he looked. He walked away, his pale blue eyes glancing at me as he passed.

"Miss Baird," Walker said, "we don't meet till eight-thirty."

"I wanted to talk to you about the casting. I can't play Puck—you know I can't and you know why."

He cocked his head. "I'm afraid I don't. You do gymnastics."

"Yes, but—"

"Don't you ever compete?"

I shifted my weight from foot to foot. "Well, yes, I'm on the school team, but—"

"Performance is performance," he said. "If you can do one, you can do the other." He turned to go back in his office. "Now, if you don't mind, I—"

"I do mind," I said, following him in. "I need you to listen."

He sat in his chair and checked notes on his desk. He didn't look too interested in listening.

"We are talking about two different things," I explained. "When I compete in gymnastics, the performance is on a gym floor, not up on a stage. I don't see a sea of strange faces looking up at me. I'm not in a spotlight—the gym is fully lit. And any butterflies I get are over as soon as I start, because I can shut everyone out."

Now he was attentive.

"I don't have to interact with other actors. I'm not supposed to respond to the audience. I seal them out and concentrate on my routine."

"Concentration is essential in theater as well," Walker said. "You already have tremendous energy and instinctive stage presence. I am going to teach you to transfer your ability from gymnasium to theater. You'll be doing your gymnastics as Puck, giving Puck quickness and strength, making him lighter than air. Oh, yes, you'll do well."

"Maybe in rehearsal," I argued. "But I told you—"

"You mystify me, Miss Baird," he interrupted. "I checked your application last night. Unlike my friend Tomas, you listed no specific skills in set design, costume, makeup, lighting, or sound. What on earth did you plan to do here?"

I felt caught. "I, uh, I guess I thought I could overcome my stage fright, but when I saw how good everyone was, I figured this wasn't the place to do it. I don't want to sink the production."

"But you're not going to. You're going to pull this off."

"You're taking a big risk," I warned him.

"I've always been a director who takes risks. That's why I didn't make it in New York, where bottom-line mentality rules."

It was the usual artistic gripe, but I was surprised by the bitterness in his voice.

"You will discover, Jenny, that my shows, cast with a bunch of kids and produced in the boonies, are better theater, more imaginative and compelling fare than Broadway shows in which people pay to see Lee Montgomery play himself over and over again."

"Really."

"You're not a fan of his, I hope."

I wondered if my face had given me away. "I've seen him perform," I replied, "in *Hamlet.*"

"Ah, yes, he played that role a good fifteen years longer than he should have. I began to think it was a play about a man in midlife crisis."

Tell that to the people who flocked to see him, I thought, but I couldn't defend my father aloud.

"So, Puck, we understand each other," Walker said, his eyes dropping down again to the notes in front of him.

Hardly, I mused, and left.

We spent Wednesday morning reading the play aloud as a cast. A few kids sulked about not getting the parts they wanted, but most were pretty excited. Brian worked with Tomas and two other tech directors—heads of lighting and sound—putting down colored tape on the stage, mapping the set we would soon be building. In the afternoon we began blocking the play.

My part was blocked sketchily. It was decided that I'd be given certain parameters—where I had to be, by when—and that over the next few days Maggie and I would work on the gymnastic details. She had also volunteered to help with my stage fright, teaching me relaxation exercises and pacing me through extra rehearsals in which she'd expose me to increments of stage lighting in a gradually darkened theater.

Rehearsal ran late that day and was followed quickly by dinner, then a showing of *The Tempest*. Each Wednesday evening was Movie Night during which we'd watch and discuss a film of a Shakespearean production. After the movie I hung out with Shawna and two other new girls in her cozy room beneath the eaves. Everything was fine until ten o'clock, when I returned to my room.

For the first time since early in the day I was alone and had the opportunity to think about the strange visions I'd had the last two nights. I found myself glancing around anxiously and turning on lights, not just the bedside one, but the overhead and the desk lamp as well. I didn't want any blue shadows tonight.

I pulled down the shades, then drew the curtains over them. It made the room stuffy, but I felt less vulnerable with the windows covered, as if I could seal the opening through which thoughts of Liza entered my mind. It was eerie the way the visions occurred when I sat in the window where she would have sat and stood on the stage where she would have stood.

I walked restlessly about my room, then tried to read. At ten-twenty I knocked on Maggie's door.

"Jenny. Hello," Maggie said, quickly checking me over the way my own mother would have, making sure there was no physical emergency. "Is anything wrong?"

"No, but I'm feeling kind of jumpy. May I go out for a walk? I know it's past curfew, but I'll stay close."

"Come in a moment," Maggie said, stepping aside.

I was reluctant.

"Come on."

I entered the room. It was extremely neat, her bedspread turned down just so, the curtains pulled back the exact same width at each window, all the pencils on her desk sharpened and lined up. But Maggie's pink robe was a bit ratty, the way my mother's always was, making me feel more comfortable with her. She gestured to a desk chair, then seated herself on the bed a few feet away.

"Are you worried about your role in the play?" she asked.

What could I say? No, I'm worried about my dead sister haunting me. "Sort of."

"We'll get you over the stage fright, Jenny, truly we will. Tell me, do you remember how it started?"

"How?" I repeated.

"Or maybe when," she suggested.

"I don't know—I just always had it, at least as far back as kindergarten. I was supposed to recite a nursery rhyme for graduation, 'Little Bo Peep.' We have a video of me standing silently on stage, my mortarboard crooked, the tassel hanging in my face, my eyes like those of a deer caught in headlights."

She laughed. "Oh, my!"

"Why do you ask?"

"I was looking for a clue as to why stage fright happens to you. Psychologists say that performance anxiety is often rooted in unhappy childhood experiences, such as rejection by one's parents, or perhaps physical or verbal abuse by those who are close to the child."

"I wasn't rejected or abused," I said quickly. "Nothing terrible has ever happened to me." Till last summer, I added silently.

She smoothed the bedcover with her hand. "Sometimes memories of traumatic events can be repressed, so that the individual doesn't consciously remember those events, and therefore doesn't know why she is reacting to a situation that is similar in some way."

"I don't think that's it," I said politely.

"Let me give you an example," Maggie continued. "A child is wearing a certain kind of suntan lotion. That day she watches someone drown at the beach. Years later she happens to buy the same brand of lotion. She puts it on and finds herself paralyzed with fear. She doesn't know why, but she can't go on with whatever she planned to do at that moment. The smell has triggered the feelings of the traumatic event she has long since repressed. Only by remembering the event, understanding what has triggered such an extreme response, can she overcome it."

I shifted in my chair, uncomfortable with the psychological talk. "Repressed memory isn't my problem," I told her. "But I will try the relaxation exercises you mentioned."

"And the incremental exposure."

"That, too."

She smiled agreeably. "Still need a walk?"

"Yeah."

"Stay on this block within the area of the four houses we're occupying. It's perfectly safe, but I'm an old worrywart. Check in with me in twenty minutes, all right?"

I nodded. "Thanks."

For the first few minutes I sat on the front steps of Drama House and gazed at the night sky. Across the road the tall tower on Stoddard cut a dark pattern out of the glittering sky, its clock glowing like a second moon.

I walked up and down the block, then circled Drama House, curious to see my room from the outside. Just as I reached the back of the house, I heard a noise from the fraternity next door, a grunt, then a thud, like a fall that had been muffled by grass. A guy swore softly. I peered around the lumpy trunk of an old cherry tree at the same time that Mike, standing by a window of the frat, turned to look over his shoulder. He grimaced when he saw me.

Maybe he thought I'd mind my own business and walk on, for a moment later he checked to see if I was still there and grimaced again. I wasn't moving; I wanted to know what was going on.

He threw a stone against a second-floor window and someone raised the shade. "I need your help," Mike called quietly.

He waited—I guessed for his helper to come downstairs— and looked back over his shoulder a third time.

"Still here," I said.

The light in the first-floor room went on. The shade rolled up—it was the guys' bathroom. *Maybe I shouldn't be looking*, I thought, but of course I did. A stubborn window screen was yanked up.

"Ready?" I heard Mike ask the guy inside, then he leaned over, grunting and pulling. I stepped to the right of the tree to get a better view and saw a heap of a person on the ground, then a head come up above a set of shoulders as Mike heaved him onto the windowsill.

"Got a good hold?" Mike asked. "On the count of three. One, two—"

In the bathroom light I saw Paul's head, then torso go over the window frame.

"Glad he's not any heavier," the guy inside said, tugging on the screen.

"Splash some cold water on his face," Mike instructed, "and let him stay in the bathroom for a while."

The shade was yanked down from the inside, and Mike turned away from the window. He seemed to be debating what to do, then strolled over to me.

"Out for a walk?" he asked.

"Yes."

"I guess you know it's past curfew."

"I have permission," I said. "What about you?"

He grinned. "I don't."

"What happened to Paul?"

"Oh, nothing too bad."

"Nothing too bad like what?" I asked.

Mike gestured toward the tree. "Want to sit down?"

Under a tree, alone with him in the moonlight? I wasn't sure.

"You climb trees, don't you?" he persisted. "You must if you're a gymnast."

The first strong limb was about four feet off the ground. I hoisted myself onto it—Mike was going to help me but thought better of it. Then I climbed up to a limb that grew in the opposite direction, about seven feet high. Mike made himself comfortable on the long lower limb. I wondered if he and Liza used to sit there together.

"Paul hangs around town and gets himself in trouble with the locals," Mike said. "I should have let him get his head split open by the giant he took on tonight. It's the only way he'll get any sense knocked into it."

"You rescued him?"

"Are you kidding? I'm not an idiot. I grabbed him and ran like a good coward."

I smiled.

"Listen," Mike said, "you've got to keep this quiet, okay?"

"Give me a reason why."

"We need Paul for the production. But more important, Paul needs us," he added, his blue eyes intense, persuasive. "Theater is the only thing that has kept Paul in school. It's what has kept him from getting into the really bad stuff. We can't get him bounced out of here."

"He makes me very uncomfortable."

"He aims to," Mike replied. "It's just an act."

"Brian said the same thing about Walker."

Mike smiled. "Don't be fooled by Walker. At heart, he's a good guy."

I must have made a face, for Mike laughed up at me. "Yeah, I can see he's got a fan in you. But really, I don't know what I'd do without him. He found grant money for me so I could attend last year and this. He has taught me more than the books I've read or any of my other teachers. I'm really grateful to him."

"I'm glad he has helped you," I said, "but I still think he's an egotistical tyrant with a nasty streak in him."

"A lot of creative people are that way."

I prickled. I'd heard that justification one too many times. "Creativity is no excuse for obnoxious behavior."

"Are you worried about performing?" Mike asked quietly.

"That's *not* my reason for disliking him."

"I didn't think it was. I just wanted to tell you that there is nothing to be afraid of. The audience is rooting for you, Jenny. They see you on stage and want you to do well. Everyone out there wants to love you."

Speaking of ego, I thought to myself, *what an assumption!*

"Trust me," Mike said, his face animated, "it's a blast."

"For you, maybe."

"There's nothing like it. I've been putting on shows since I was five."

"Are you part of a theater group?"

He grinned. "No, the kid of a minister. I spent a lot of growing-up years hanging around the church next to our house in Trenton. It had a stage—the altar; a balcony—the choir loft; sort of an orchestra—the organ; even costumes—my father often wondered why his vestments were wrinkled on Sundays. I put on a lot of performances for my friends, all of them unauthorized."

I laughed out loud. Mike laughed with me, gazing up at my face. His smile, the brightness in his eyes made my heart feel incredibly light. Then I remembered Liza and looked away. I could imagine her slipping out to meet him here in the moonlight.

"Anyway, my parents aren't thrilled about my dream of being an actor. My oldest brother is doing mission work in Appalachia. The second one is studying at Union Theological. And then there's me. Since I don't seem to have a religious calling, they would like me to pursue something practical, you know, something that guarantees a good salary."

"But you have to follow your heart," I said.

"Yes . . . Yes, you do."

He waited for me to meet his eyes, but I didn't. I couldn't.

"You know, some of the guys have been talking about you, Jenny."

"They have? Saying what?"

"They're disappointed that you paired off so quickly with Tomas."

"Why should it matter to them that we're friends?"

He looked at me curiously. "You really don't know, do you?" he said. "'Her hair gives dawn its fire, her eyes give dusk its soul.'"

He knew how to use his voice to melt a girl's heart, to make a girl want to believe. I steeled myself against the seductive words. "Excuse me?"

"It's a line of poetry describing a beautiful girl, one who doesn't seem to know it."

I dug my fingernails into the bark of the tree. "Well, there's your answer, the reason I like Tomas. He's real. He's not an actor."

"What's wrong with actors?"

"They quote poetry. A girl has to be crazy to believe one," I told him. "It's far too easy for an actor to give you a good line."

"You're quick to judge."

"No," I argued. "I've had experience with theater types. After a while they can't tell real from unreal. They believe their own creation of themselves and can't understand why everyone else isn't convinced they're wonderful."

He jumped down from the limb, then stared up at me, his eyes sparking with anger. "It's efficient, I guess, judging an individual by a group. You don't waste any time trying to know somebody."

But I don't want to know you! I thought as I watched Mike walk away. *I can't risk knowing you.*

Experience had taught me not to get close to guys who fell in love with Liza. I had been burned twice and knew I couldn't compete. It didn't matter that I could no longer give a guy access to my sister; if Mike knew who I was, I'd be access to his romantic memories of her. He'd start looking for traits and signs of her in me. And I wasn't setting myself up for that kind of heartache.

Nine

"How are you doing, Jenny?" Maggie asked me Thursday morning.

"Good. Ready to go."

"Glad to hear it," she said. "We're going to work at the gym later today to block your movements. Walker thought it would be good if Tomas went with us. Knowing the set and being as visual as he is, he might see some possibilities we don't."

"Sounds like fun."

"Also, I'm photocopying a set of relaxation exercises and organizing CDs for you to listen to."

"Sorry to be so much trouble," I said.

"Nonsense," Maggie replied, putting an arm around me, giving me a hug. "I love a good challenge."

"Maggie," Walker called. "I need you to get maintenance. Arthur still hasn't replaced those lights."

She winked and moved on. From across the stage, Brian smiled at me.

"I know who the camp pet is," a girl said.

I turned my head to see who had spoken, then wished I hadn't. Keri was standing next to Paul and Mike, hoping for a reaction. I ignored her and called to Shawna, who had just come in.

"Jenny didn't hear you," Paul said.

"Oh, I think she did," Keri replied. "Hey, Shawna. Don't you think Jenny is the camp pet?"

"She's the camp redhead, that's for sure," Shawna answered.

"Obviously, I'm not *Walker's* pet," I pointed out.

Keri flicked her long, dark-lined eyelids. Perhaps conflict kept her from being totally bored. "Walker gave you a hard time at first," she said, "something he does with all his favorites. Usually, he doesn't share favorites with Maggie. She likes girls who aren't sure of themselves, girls she can mother. But then, there is that little problem of yours."

"Ease up, Keri," Shawna said.

"So she's adopted you," Keri continued, "made you her project for camp. And Brian is close to sending kisses from across the stage."

I glanced at Mike, who stood silently, his face providing no hint of what he was thinking. I knew my cheeks were red.

Paul laughed. Standing close behind Keri, as if he would hug her from behind, he leaned his head over her shoulder and pressed his face against hers. I saw Keri's shoulders relax, her body rest back against him. But the glimmer in Paul's green eyes told me he didn't feel any real affection for her; he was just yanking her chain.

"I don't like Jenny," he said, his mouth against Keri's cheek. "She's not my pet."

Keri turned her face toward his, letting her mouth brush his mouth.

Paul's hands cupped her shoulders and he pushed her away. "You try too hard."

Keri spun around to look at him.

"The girls who are worth it don't try," Paul told her. "They are helpless to stop a guy from wanting them."

Keri's eyes flashed. "Liza was never helpless," she spat. "Only you were."

They walked off in opposite directions. Shawna, Mike, and I stood silently for a moment.

"Walker sure is good at casting people," Shawna observed. "It won't be hard for anyone to believe they're a quarreling couple."

"I don't know why he can't let go of Liza," Mike said.

As much as I didn't like Paul, I knew how Liza could haunt a person's thoughts.

"It's not easy when you love someone," I said. "A year is not enough time to get over anything."

Mike's eyes met mine.

"Unless you're *acting*, of course."

"Of course," he replied stiffly.

"Did I just miss something?" Shawna asked as Mike strode away.

"Like what?"

"Well, you can begin by explaining to me why you just defended Paul, who's being ignorant and creepy. You know, he has pictures of Liza hanging in his room, hanging all around it, that's what Andrew told me."

I wriggled my shoulders at the thought of it—a museum for the dead.

"Paul needs to get on with his life. It's not like he and Liza were the love story of the century. The guy Liza was hot for was Mike."

"So I heard."

"Not that she was alone in that," Shawna added. "How 'bout you, girlfriend?"

"How 'bout me what?"

"What do you think of Mike?"

I shrugged. "He's okay."

Shawna grinned. "This place is just full of actors."

The acting began in earnest shortly after that. Walker required that we all be attentive to the blocking that was going on whether we were in the scene or not. It was slow work as we highlighted our lines and noted Walker's directions in our books—the cues on which we were to enter, or rise, or cross over, that kind of thing.

We dragged through Act 2 with the fairies. Having doubled them in number, Walker had created more parts and a lot of confusion. But the pace picked up when Oberon and Titania—Paul and Keri—began to quarrel. I watched them from the wings, waiting for my cue. Walker folded his arms over his chest, looking very satisfied when Titania finally exited with her fairies.

I waited in the wings.

"'Well go thy way,'" the angry Oberon said to Titania's back. "'Thou shalt not from this grove till I torment thee for this injury.'"

I began to move.

"Wait! What are you doing, Puck?" Walker barked.

I stood still. "Entering?"

"Has Oberon summoned you yet?" Walker asked. "Has he? He's king. You don't emerge till he tells you to."

I backed up.

"I want you in at the end of 'My gentle Puck,'" Walker added in a milder voice, "and I want you to move close to him. You're conspirators. That line again," Walker said to Paul.

"'Well go thy way. Thou shalt not from this grove till I—'"

The lights flickered.

"'—torment thee.'"

The lights blinked off. We were swallowed by darkness. Someone screamed, then muffled it.

"What the . . . ?" growled Walker. "Arthur!"

Our only light was the glow of the emergency exit signs and the strings of tiny floor lights that marked the way to them.

"Everyone stay where you are," Maggie said. "We don't want an accident."

"Brian, find Arthur!" Walker ordered.

"Does anyone have a flashlight?" Brian asked. "Even a small one on a key chain would help."

Two girls seated in the audience volunteered theirs.

"Pass the flashlights toward the center aisle," Maggie instructed.

There was whispering and nervous laughter as Brian retrieved the flashlights, then crossed the stage to the steps that led to the ground floor hall. Suddenly the whispering stopped.

"What's that?" someone asked, her voice thin with apprehension. "What do I smell?"

"Perfume," a guy answered.

I sniffed and my skin prickled. I knew the scent.

"Smells like jasmine," said another girl.

Liza's perfume. I remembered the weeks after she'd died, packing her sweaters in a Goodwill bag, smelling the jasmine. I had felt as if she would walk into our bedroom at any moment. It was a scent that haunted.

The lights suddenly came back on.

"Nobody move," Maggie commanded. "I'm doing a head count."

The vets exchanged glances—perhaps they recognized my sister's trademark scent.

"Look at Paul," someone whispered.

His eyes were shut, his lips closed and smiling. He was inhaling deeply, as if he loved breathing in Liza's scent, as if he couldn't get enough.

I felt sick to my stomach. Turning away from him, I discovered Mike watching me.

Walker paced up and down the stage, obviously irritated.

"What was the problem?" he asked when Brian emerged from behind the stage.

"I don't know. The power came back on before I reached the electrical room."

"Did you see Arthur?"

"No, but I came right back."

"All of us are accounted for," Maggie reported to Walker.

Placing his hands on his hips, Walker eyed Paul and me, then Keri in the wings with her fairies, then the kids in the rows of seats below.

"It was a nice bit of theater," he said. "We might even incorporate it in our production, releasing a certain scent through the air duct system when Puck does his magic or Titania sweeps through. That said, I don't wish to be entertained by further improvisation. Got it?"

Kids nodded and looked suspiciously at one another.

I wanted to believe it was a piece of theater, but I couldn't shake the eerie feeling I'd had the day I arrived here, the strong sense of Liza's presence. I had thought I came out of my own need for closure; now I wondered if Liza had summoned me.

What do you want, Liza?

To find things for her, it was always to find things. Had someone at the camp heard something, seen something? If I probed, would I find clues that could solve her murder?

"Miss Baird," Walker was saying, "please join us on this planet."

No way, Liza, I answered my sister silently, *don't ask me to do it.*

I'd hunt for barrettes, socks, homework, and phone numbers, but not for serial killers.

Ten

THE BEST MOMENTS of Thursday and Friday were spent in the gym with Maggie and Tomas, the three of us working on how to make Puck "lighter than air." Tomas, seeing what I could do, was full of ideas on how to rework the set to accommodate vaults and tumbles. Maggie acted different than she did at the theater. She still worried, and still was unrelenting about getting things right, but sometimes, when we'd clown around, she'd laugh. We even "played hooky" for an hour, going to a nearby store to buy leotards for me. When Maggie heard that Tomas and I would be staying through the weekend, she invited us for dinner at her home Saturday night.

I learned from Shawna that Mike, Paul, and Keri were also staying over the weekend. I avoided the three of them as much as possible Friday and saw them only from a distance walking down High Street on Saturday. I also avoided the window seat and the bridge and kept the lights on in my room. I slept badly Thursday and Friday night, wanting to close my eyes, but fighting sleep each time I'd feel myself slipping away. Still, I got a few hours each night with no haunting images. By the time Tomas and I were walking to Maggie's house Saturday night, I had convinced myself that the strange events of the first week were simply my initial reaction to facing the place where Liza had died. My second week here would certainly be easier.

Maggie lived in a pretty wooden house on Cannon Street, one block over from High. Its front porch was welcoming with wicker chairs and pots of pink and white flowers. Brian answered the door smiling. "Any trouble with my directions?"

"No," I said, "the only trouble was keeping Tomas moving. He has to stop and look at everything." I turned to my friend. "Next time we go somewhere, I'm leading you blindfolded."

"Okay," he replied, half-listening, more interested now in peering beyond Brian to see what was in the living room.

It was a homey room, though a little too flowery for me, with prints of cabbage-size roses on the slipcovers and curtains. Brian led us through a small dining room and into a square kitchen, where Maggie was stuffing potato skins.

"What can we do to help?" I asked.

"Just enjoy yourselves," she replied. "I've got everything under control here."

Brian placed a tall kitchen stool next to Maggie for Tomas to sit on.

I thought he'd get one for me too, but when Maggie started talking with Tomas about the dinner she was preparing, I felt a tug on my arm. Brian winked, then pulled me toward the door. I followed him to the living room, though I felt a little rude leaving Tomas and Maggie in the kitchen. I glanced back over my shoulder.

"I never get a chance to hang out with you," Brian said. "Tomas always does."

"Yes, but I'm your mom's guest, too."

"She understands my situation. I think that may be why she invited you tonight. I'm only two years older than you, but you're a student and I'm staff, so I'm not supposed to ask you for a date."

"Otherwise you would?"

He laughed in response. "Sometimes I can't believe you, Jenny! You're as naive as Tomas. You make quite a pair."

"Guess we do."

His brown eyes swept over my face, the dusty lashes making his long gaze soft. His lips parted for a moment as if he was going to say something more, but he simply smiled. I glanced around the room for something to talk about.

"Is that you?" I asked, pointing to a photograph. "Or did Superman get a lot shorter?"

"That's me, Halloween, our first year in Wisteria."

I walked over and picked up the framed picture. "You were awfully cute!"

"Do you have to use the past tense?" he asked.

I laughed. "How old were you?"

"Six, I think." He crossed the room, stood beside me for a moment studying the photo, then sat on the love seat next to the table of pictures, leaving space for me.

I remained standing and picked up another photo. "Your mom. How pretty!"

"That's her college picture. You can sit down and look at them, Jenny."

I did, and he pulled his arm up, resting it along the back of the love seat, conveniently close to my shoulders. I wondered what to do when I ran out of pictures. I wasn't ready to get romantic with him, but I didn't want him to think I *never* would.

"Who's this?" I asked, pointing to another photo. Maggie and Brian were sitting on a picnic blanket with a child who looked two or three years younger than Brian. There were several pictures of the child, a beautiful little girl with brown hair and blue eyes. I picked up the closest one.

"That's my sister, Melanie."

"Where is she now?" I asked, then wished I hadn't. As I

gazed at her face, a strange feeling came over me. I knew she was dead.

"She died about six months after that picture was taken."

"I'm sorry. I shouldn't have asked."

"Don't worry about it," Brian said. "It was a long time ago. I was only five at the time."

I kept looking at the picture. With her dark hair and puffy party dress, Melanie reminded me of a young Liza.

"What is it?" Brian asked gently. "You look so—so sad."

"It is sad," I replied, tempted to tell him what we shared. I thought about the way Maggie watched us campers like a worried mother hen. Since Liza's death, I had caught my own mother watching me that way

I placed the picture back on the table, and Brian reached over and picked up another. "This is my favorite photo of Melanie," he said, laying it in my lap. "This is how I remember her."

I held the picture gently. His sister was wearing little green overalls with a bunny on the front. She had a wonderful, merry smile and eyes full of mischief, as if she were keeping a delicious secret.

The image grew blurry and I felt tears in my eyes, helpless tears for Brian's family and mine. I blinked them back, but the image still wavered before me, its edges softening and shifting, another image rising up through it, like an object at the bottom of a pond that suddenly clears. The little girl was in a long, narrow box and she was scared. A soft black blanket dropped down over her. I felt horribly afraid. Then Liza stood next to me. I couldn't see her, but I knew it was she. "Don't be scared, Jenny," she said. "I'll help you."

"Jen," Brian said, "Jenny!" He pulled me close to him. "I didn't bring you over here to make you sad."

My eyes cleared; the little girl was smiling up at me again. "How did Melanie die?"

"In a fire. She became frightened and hid in a closet."

My throat tightened. "In a closet?"

"The baby-sitter couldn't find her. She died from smoke inhalation."

I swallowed hard. What in the sunny picture before me had allowed me to see her in a long box—a closet—with a blanket of black smoke descending upon her?

"Have you ever been in a fire?" Brian asked.

"No. No, it must be very frightening."

"You feel so powerless," he said.

Powerless was how I felt now, unable to stop the images that invaded my mind. I had been careful the last two days, but as soon as I let down my guard, Liza crept back into my head.

Was there something real about these images, I wondered, something true about them?

Liza and I used to watch Mom's old films and laugh ourselves silly at one called *Teen Psychic*. There were a lot of close-ups of Mom's green eyes widening with terror as she gazed at photos of murder sites and touched things that belonged to dead people. In a singsongy voice she would describe the visions she was seeing, images that would help solve mysteries. I wished I could laugh about it now, but I was scared and desperate to believe there was nothing psychic about me and my visions.

I glanced up at Brian.

"Good move, guy," he said to himself. "A girl comes over, you get time alone, and you depress the heck out of her."

I forced a smile. "I like knowing about your family—family is what makes a person who he is. And I like seeing your house," I said, seizing the excuse to get up and walk around again. "Houses are full of clues about people."

"You know a lot more about me than I know about you," Brian pointed out.

"Well, I don't have much to tell. My family's boring."

Another picture of Melanie sat on a desk, and another on a bookcase.

It would be easy to guess that the child was dead, I reasoned, since there were no pictures of her growing older. And knowing she had died, it would be natural to imagine her in a long box—a casket, not a closet—with a symbolic black blanket drawn over her. These images had been triggered simply by my empathy with Brian as someone who lost a sister. And that, of course, was why I had thought of Liza. Liza was not sending me messages from the dead, and I was not "Teen Psychic."

I pulled a worn book off the shelf, *Handbook to Acting*, and started paging through it as if I were interested.

"How do you think it's going between you and Walker?" Brian asked.

"A lot better than I thought it would."

"He likes your feistiness," Brian said. "And it doesn't hurt that you're new to theater. I know you won't believe it, but Walker is easily threatened by people with talent and experience."

"You're right, I don't believe it."

Brian laughed and swung his feet up on the love seat, sitting sideways, watching me as I closed the book and chose another.

"To understand Walker," he said, "you've got to understand his history. When he bombed in New York, he really bombed. The last show he directed, his big chance, the one he thought would bring him fame and fortune, starred Lee Montgomery."

I turned toward Brian—a little too quickly, I realized. I knew my father had worked with Walker, but I had been too young to remember anything about the situation. "It didn't do well?" I asked aloud.

"Montgomery pulled out. He saw the ship going down and jumped fast. The show sank immediately, closing three days after he left the cast."

I turned back to the bookcase so Brian couldn't see my face. "Are you sure? Did Walker tell you this himself?"

"Walker would never tell me anything he'd consider so humiliating. My mother did, last summer, when Liza Montgomery came here. I had seen Walker go after actresses he thought were prima donnas but never with such passion as he did with Liza. Of course, Liza could defend herself. She dished it back, right in front of the other kids, and wasn't shy about reminding him that he had failed in New York, that he was just some drama teacher in the middle of nowhere."

I winced inwardly. I knew how sharp Liza's tongue could be.

"I don't think she realized what a tender point it was with him. Anyway, my mother, who knew Walker from her grad school days in New York, explained the situation to me. Don't repeat it, Jenny, I wasn't supposed to."

"I won't."

There was a clinking of silverware in the next room.

"Sounds like it's almost time to eat," Brian observed.

I returned my book to its place, and he rose from the sofa. Just before I reached the dining room door, he pulled me back. "Jenny, I realize I'm blowing my chance with you," he said softly.

"I promise we'll talk about all happy things during dinner and after."

We did, and there was a lot of laughter as we discussed high school life from math class to prom dates, even Maggie chiming in with a funny account of her first date. But I felt like a person split in two, one part of me chattering away and putting on a good show, the other plagued by a growing uneasiness. What had happened between Walker and my father? What exactly had happened when Liza was here? How deep did the bitterness run?

When the evening was over, Brian insisted on escorting us back to campus, even though he was off for the weekend while other Chase students covered the dorms. It took a while for Tomas to figure out that Brian was waiting for him to go inside and leave us alone. As soon as he disappeared, Brian walked me over to the porch steps of Drama House and pulled me down next to him.

"I'm not supposed to date you, Jenny."

"That's what you said before."

He leaned forward, his elbows on his knees. "I didn't think this was going to be a problem. I mean, I'm pretty good at not letting someone become important to me. I have to be if I want to make it to L.A."

"I understand."

He laughed. "How nice of you to understand, since you're the one making it a struggle for me! It would be so easy to make you important."

"Then be careful," I told him.

"I don't think I want to be." He took my face in his hands.

"You know how important the rules are to your mother," I reminded him.

"I heard it's a rule that you have to kiss a girl when you walk her home beneath a full moon."

"The moon isn't full."

He smiled and glanced toward the tower on top of Stoddard. Its clock gleamed in the dark. "This is drama camp. The clock is shining. We'll make it a moon."

He kissed me on the lips. "Good night," he said softly, then rose and walked away whistling.

I leaned against the stair railing. Brian's kiss was nice—as nice as a handshake, I thought. How could I feel romantic when there was so much else going on in my life? I debated whether I should confide in Brian, so he would understand why I couldn't get interested. *Not quite yet,* I decided.

He was right, the tower clock did look like a full moon. I stood up quickly. The image I had seen Tuesday night, the shattering circle of light, flashed through my mind. Perhaps the image wasn't a moon, but a clock—a watch, for I had felt something being fastened around my wrist. I grasped my wrist as I had done then and thought of Liza's watch being smashed by the murderer.

But it was my left wrist that I grasped tonight, and the left wrist in my vision. As left-handers, Liza and I wore our watches on our right. I sat back down on the steps.

Was this detail a meaningless mistake in the way my mind re-created the events beneath the bridge, or was it true? I tried to remember what the police report said, but I had worked so hard at blocking out the facts, I couldn't recall.

Liza didn't always wear a watch. Maybe the serial killer supplied a watch if his victim wasn't wearing one and fastened it to the wrist on which a person usually wore her watch. Maybe the watch would be a clue to the killer's identity. Was this what Liza wanted me to discover?

Of course, anyone could have fastened a watch on her, then smashed it. What if someone had done so to make it look like a crime by the serial killer? I shuddered at the idea and dismissed it, for that kind of murder suggested a more personal motive. And no one could have hated my sister enough to kill her.

Eleven

SUNDAY MORNING I went to church. I sat in the back and prayed my visions would go away. I knew it was a dangerous thing to do—God has a habit of answering prayers in ways different from what we have in mind.

When I returned to Drama House, I found a note from Tomas asking if I wanted to hang out in town. I changed into a sleeveless top and shorts, slipped some money and tissues in my pockets, then went next door. Tomas emerged carrying his stuffed backpack, like a snail hauling his shell.

"Would you like to put anything in here?" he asked as he adjusted the pack on his shoulders.

"Yeah, and never see it again," I teased.

We spent an hour visiting shops on side streets, then bought two iced cappuccinos and strolled down to the river. The town harbor had a public dock, a rectangular platform extending over the water and lined with benches. It was a perfect place to sit and sip.

Tomas pulled out his spiral pad and began to sketch. I lay my head back on the bench and sprawled in what my mother would call "an unladylike manner," happily soaking up the late-morning sun.

"Ahoy!" I heard Tomas call out.

I grinned to myself and kept my head back.

"Ahoy!" he called again.

"Are there pirates on the horizon, Tomas?"

"No, just Mike."

I sat up.

Mike waved. He was in a small boat, maybe fifteen feet long with an outboard, painted in the maroon and gold colors of Chase College. He guided the skiff toward the dock, nosing it in, then lassoing the piling next to us.

"What's up?" he asked.

"Just hanging out," Tomas said. "How about you?"

"The same, only on water. Hi, Jenny."

"Hi." I wished his eyes weren't so much like the water and sky. The anger I had seen in them the other night had disappeared, leaving them a friendly, easy blue. Like the river, they made me feel buoyant.

He turned back to Tomas. "What are you working on?"

"Just sketches—boats, docks, houses, trees, whatever I see."

"Want to see some things from the water?" Mike invited.

"Well—" I began.

"Yes," Tomas replied quickly.

But Mike had heard me hesitate. The light in his eyes dimmed. "Maybe another time," he said. "Your sketches could be ruined if they got wet."

"They won't," Tomas assured him. "My backpack is waterproof. I'll tear out a couple sheets and use my clipboard." He rummaged through his pack, pulling out an assortment of things, then putting them back in.

"What all do you have in there?" Mike asked curiously.

"Everything but a refrigerator," I told him. "I'd like to come, too, Mike."

He smiled and I felt that buoyancy again.

Tomas strung two cameras around his neck, then grasped a clipboard and pencils in one hand and his cappuccino in the other. "Ready."

"Why don't I hold your art supplies and drink while you get in?" I suggested.

Mike, looking as if he was trying not to laugh, guided the two of us down the four-foot drop into the boat. We settled onto its plank seats, Tomas in the middle, me at the bow.

"I'm glad I didn't sign out a canoe," Mike observed as we rocked back and forth.

"Next time," I replied.

"Next time I'll let you go by yourselves," he answered, smiling, then tossed us two life jackets. "When I'm chauffeur, I make people wear these."

"How about you?" I asked, when Mike didn't put one on.

"I can swim."

"So when the boat turns over and bonks you on the head and you're unconscious, you expect me and Tomas to save you?"

"Good point," he said. "After all, I am with two such graceful boaters." He put on the orange vest, grinning at me. Then he untied the rope and pushed off from the dock.

"Can anyone sign out a boat?" Tomas asked as Mike started the motor.

"You're supposed to have experience on the water and be connected to the college somehow," Mike replied. "My grandfather was from the Eastern Shore and used to take me crabbing. He lived down in Oxford, which is where the manager of the college boathouse grew up."

We puttered out of the tiny harbor. With each boat length we put between us and the shore I felt more at ease, free from the things that had been haunting me recently. The sun was warm on my skin and the breeze cool, ribboning my hair across my eyes. I drew an elastic from my shorts pocket, leaned forward to catch my blowing hair, then pulled it through the elastic in a loopy ponytail. When I looked up, Mike was watching me.

"She's beautiful!" Tomas breathed.

Mike glanced at him, startled.

"Yes, that yacht sure is pretty," I said, nodding toward the moored sailboat that we were passing.

Mike laughed and Tomas photographed the boat.

"Cool perspective! Jen, can you believe it? There are so many cool perspectives out here."

In the next forty minutes Tomas found heaven: a house with double-decker porches overlooking the river, an old bridge across Wist Creek, an abandoned mill. "I'm going to have enough stuff to draw for the next year and a half," he said, clicking away on his camera. We motored a distance up Wist Creek then turned around and headed back to the river.

"I'd like to stay out awhile longer," Mike said. "You can stay on or I can drop you back at the town dock."

"Stay on," Tomas replied immediately. "I mean, if Jen wants to."

"Sure."

We sailed past the town harbor again, then two marinas.

"That's the commercial harbor over there," Mike said, pointing toward shore. "They have all kinds of interesting boats, Tomas. See those long ones with low sides and little houses on one end? They're like my grandfather's. They're used for crabbing."

"Can we stay here a few minutes?" Tomas asked.

"I can drop anchor."

"Great! Then I can sketch."

"Is that okay with you, Jenny? You're not nodding off on us, are you?"

I was.

"I'd hate to see you fall asleep and fall overboard," Mike said, smiling. "It would be useless this time of day. The crabs don't bite when the sun's high."

"Lucky for you, I don't, either."

Mike smirked, shut off the motor, and dropped anchor. "Lift up your seat, Jenny, and slide the board beneath Tomas's, then you can hunker down safely,"

I did and Mike tossed me two extra life vests, which I placed in the bow to cushion my back. He did the same thing on his side, then pulled his sunglasses and script from a boat bag.

With the motor off it was quiet enough to hear the light scratch of Tomas's pencil, the occasional turn of a page by Mike. I nestled down happily. The gentle rocking of the boat made me feel safe as a child in a cradle. I fell into a warm, luxurious sleep.

I don't know how long I napped, but I had slept so heavily that I couldn't open my eyes at first. I just lay there, too content to stir, and listened to their voices.

"Do you think we should wake her?" asked Tomas. "I sort of hate to. She told me she hasn't been getting much sleep."

"I'm afraid she's going to get burned," Mike replied.

"We could cover her with our shirts and let her rest a little more," Tomas suggested.

"That's an idea."

There was some movement and a bit of boat rocking, then I felt a soft cloth being laid over my legs and another one over my arms.

"Her ankles are sticking out," Tomas reported.

"I'm more worried about her face," Mike replied. "I think I have sunblock. Yeah, here it is. Put some on her face."

"On her face?"

"And her ankles."

"I can't do that."

"Why not?" Mike asked.

"I just can't."

"Tomas, it's no different from helping people put on their stage makeup."

"Then you do it."

"You're closer to her," Mike pointed out.

"So switch seats."

"Why? It's no big deal," Mike said.

"You have experience," Tomas insisted. "Switch seats."

There was more movement. "Jeez! Careful."

I'd probably get us capsized, but there was no way I was going to open my eyes, not yet. This was too interesting.

"Okay," I heard Mike mutter, close to me now. "Okay."

He dabbed a bit of lotion on my left cheek, waited a moment, then rubbed it in. He added some more, then rounded a glob over my chin. He spread the lotion across my forehead and down my nose, the way my mother used to, but more slowly. He must have remembered my right cheek and added some there, working it in gently and even more slowly than before. His hand stopped, resting on my cheek. A tip of a finger touched my mouth, lightly tracing the shape of my lips.

This was how he put on stage makeup? I opened my eyes.

"Oh, hello," he said.

"Hi."

I thought he'd draw back, but he simply pushed up his sunglasses. His face was ten inches from mine and in its own shadow, his eyes bright with reflections off the water. I couldn't stop looking at him.

"I guess you're wondering what I'm doing," he said.

"Um . . ." I tried not to look in his eyes and ended up staring at his mouth. "Sort of."

What a mouth! I thought. If *he* had fallen asleep, I would have been tempted to touch it.

Why wasn't he wearing his shirt? *Because you are, stupid,* I reminded myself.

I tried not to stare at his muscular shoulders and found myself gazing at the bare expanse of chest between the flaps of his life jacket. I quickly lifted my eyes to focus on his ear. Cripe, even his ear was good-looking! I didn't need this—I didn't need to notice these things about Liza's old boyfriend.

"I have some fairy ointment here," he said.

"You do?"

"Magic stuff, just like Puck's. I spread it on your eyelids."

"You did?"

"As you know, you must fall in love with the first person you see upon opening your eyes."

I stared at him, speechless.

"Oops!" He pulled back. "Wrong stuff. This is sunblock."

I sat up and managed to laugh.

"We were worried about you," Tomas said.

"Redheads shouldn't go out without their sunscreen," Mike added, then handed the tube to me. "You need it from the neck down."

"Thanks."

He changed places with Tomas, and I began spreading the stuff on my neck and arms. "How are the sketches going?" I asked. "I'd like to see them."

The truth was I'd liked to have seen anything that would distract me from Mike. Brian had held my face in his hands; he'd even kissed me. Why didn't I think *his* ears were cute?

"Tomas wants to stop by the Oyster Creek Bridge to take some photos," Mike said. "Is that okay with you, Jenny?"

Just what I needed, visiting Liza's bridge with Liza's guy—talk about a reality check!

"Why wouldn't it be?"

Tomas looked up, surprised by the snap in my voice.

"Because you have gotten so much sun," Mike answered patiently. "I thought you might be feeling it."

"I'm fine. Thanks for asking," I added lamely.

Surprisingly, I didn't feel much of anything when we anchored by the bridge or slipped beneath its shadow. We passed the pavilion, ringed by the tall, plumed grass, then turned in to the floating docks that belonged to the college and tied up silently.

"I'm going to stay down here and hose off the boat," Mike told us.

"Do you need some help?" Tomas asked.

"No, it's a one-person job."

"Well, then, thanks! It was cool," Tomas said. "I mean really, really cool."

"Glad you enjoyed it," Mike replied.

"It was nice. See you," I said quietly, anxious to escape up Goose Lane.

Did Mike have any idea how he affected me? I wasn't as good an actor as he, but I doubted he could see through my rocky performance. I probably just confused him, running hot and cold as I did. In the future I'd be more careful around him. As long as I kept my distance and he didn't learn my identity, I was safe—safe from being compared to Liza and getting my heart broken again.

Twelve

MONDAY MORNING TOMAS, several strong guys, and Arthur moved the gymnastic equipment I needed. The athletic department had given us permission to keep it at the theater for the next six weeks.

Tomas explained to the cast and crew the changes to the set that Walker had authorized. Walker sat back looking a bit smug, as if the rough time he'd given Tomas at the beginning of camp was responsible for bringing him out of his cocoon.

As before, there would be a waterfall—shredded Mylar lit with stage lights—cascading down the back stage wall. But now a stream would run from its base, and the bridge over the stream would have a balance beam as its downstage side. The vaulting horse, disguised as a stone wall, would be placed near the right wing, its springboard offstage. For one entrance I would appear to fly forward and upward, launched from behind the curtain, then use the "wall" and my arms to propel myself even higher into a one-and-a-half twist.

"How about adding a rope?" Walker asked. "Jenny, can you shinny up and down a rope?"

"Sure."

"Brian, I want you to check out a sports store and acquire what is needed for decent climbing rope. Arthur—"

Perhaps guessing where the rope would be hung, the custodian was slinking toward the exit.

"—we're going to hang the rope from the catwalk. Put it on your list."

"When the ladder comes," he replied, and continued on.

I had a feeling I'd be climbing the rungs to attach the rope, but I preferred that so I could make sure the rope was secure.

Walker wanted to see the blocking we had worked on for Act 2, Scene 1. I was wearing a leotard beneath my shirt and shorts and began to remove my outer clothes. Out of the corner of my eye I saw Paul watching me. Of course, guys do that at gym meets and swimming pools, but his gaze wasn't the usual curious or flirty one—more like that of a cat, still and silent, observing its prey.

Keri joined him onstage since she, too, was part of the scene. I turned my back on them.

"Show 'em your stuff, Jen," Tomas encouraged me.

I would. I wanted to do both of us proud.

The scene went better than I had hoped. Though we weren't yet expected to be off book, I had spent the rest of Sunday memorizing my lines for that scene. And, as chilling as Paul could be offstage, he did his work like a professional onstage. There was spontaneous applause at the end, which made Maggie smile. Walker frowned a bit and made a few changes that I noted in my script. I was careful not to look at Mike until I was in the audience and he onstage and in character.

Walker reviewed Friday's work on the end of Act 4, then began blocking Act 5. It came to a screeching halt at the play-within-the-play that is performed by the clownish rustics—Walker doing the screeching. Shawna was on top of things, but the other five actors couldn't get straight stage left and stage right, or anything else for that matter.

Walker erupted. "What the hell are you doing?" he shouted.

The kids on stage froze and glanced at one another.

"Don't any of you listen? Do I need to put up traffic signs? If I did, would you bother to read them?" He paced the stage. "Perhaps I should get an orange vest, white gloves, and a whistle," he suggested sarcastically. "Make a note, Brian—a vest, gloves, and whistle."

Brian glanced up and said nothing.

"Did you make a note?"

"A mental one," Brian replied calmly.

"Dumbbells!" Walker exclaimed, turning on his actors again. "You're supposed to *play* ignorant people, not *be* them. When I speak, you listen. When I say something, you do it. Is that a difficult concept for you to grasp?"

The kids onstage had drawn together like a herd of sheep.

"Following directions—is this something new to you? You speak English, don't you? Next to *you*, Shakespeare's ignorant rustics are rocket scientists!"

Well, I thought, *with that kind of encouragement and confidence boosting, everyone should be nervous enough to make more mistakes.* Feeling bad for the kids, I made a suggestion. My father always talked about understanding the whole pattern of a play's blocking, seeing it as a large piece of choreography. I pointed out the pattern Walker was creating so that the individual directions would become clearer to the actors. I could tell from their faces that they understood.

"I get it," Denise said.

"Yeah, that makes sense," added a guy named Tim.

Shawna gave me the thumbs-up sign.

Walker sent me a cool, thankless stare. To the rustics he said, "We'll work on this after lunch."

We all figured we'd been dismissed early and started gathering our things. Then Walker turned to me. "There are fifteen minutes remaining. Puck, fairy group, Oberon, Titania. Act Two, Scene One. Let's go."

I wondered why we were doing the scene for the second time that morning.

"Brian and Doug," Walker added, addressing one of the tech directors, "I want it run with lights."

I saw Brian's eyes narrow and I realized then what was going on.

"I think that's a bad idea, Walker," Maggie said.

"And I think you're not the director," he replied, then descended the stage steps. "I want house lights all the way down, stage lights up. Doug, who do you have working with you?"

"Samantha."

Walker nodded. "Good. Do it."

I walked up on the stage knowing it was useless for me to argue. Walker was in a bad mood, my suggestion had come unsolicited, and worse, it was a good one. Now he planned to put me in my place and erase the applause from earlier that morning.

I took off my shorts, but left on my T-shirt; it made me feel less vulnerable.

"Walker, we have already discussed the best program for Jenny," Maggie reminded him. "You agreed that incremental exposure was the remedy. There is no point in doing this."

Oh, there's a point, all right, I thought.

"Places," Walker said, ignoring Maggie. "Lights."

I stood in the right wing, watching as the lighting shifted, then measured my steps back from the springboard.

"Enter Fairies and Puck," Walker directed.

I raced forward and sprang. Flying through the air, propelling myself off the horse, tucking for my rotation—I was focused totally on the gymnastics. Then my feet touched ground and I was in a flood of light, aware of a sea of dark faces below me. Fear clutched my heart. I fought it—it was stupid, irrational, senseless—but it was as strong as ever.

"'How now, spirits, whither wander you?'" I asked the fairies, my voice thin as thread.

Katie and another girl, who split that particular fairy part, began their speech of fifteen lines:

> "Over hill, over dale,
> Thorough bush, thorough brier,
> Over park, over pale,
> Thorough flood, thorough fire. . . ."

I tried to concentrate on what they were saying, but my stomach felt queasy. My hands grew moist.

> "We do wander everywhere,
> Swifter than the moon's sphere;
> And we serve the Fairy Queen,
> To dew her orbs upon the green."

My heart beat fast. I took deep breaths, trying to slow it down.

> "The cowslips tall her pensioners be,
> In their gold coats spots you see:
> Those be rubies, fairy favors,
> In those freckles live their savors."

My knees shook. I was drenched with sweat. I needed chalk to grip the beam.

"'Farewell, thou lob of spirits,'" the fairies concluded. "'We'll be gone. Our Queen and all her elves come here anon.'"

The next set of lines was mine.

"'The King doth keep his revels here tonight,'" I said, pulling myself up on the beam as if I'd never mounted one before. "'Take heed the Queen come not within his sight.'"

I rose slowly from a crouch, my heart pounding.

"'For Oberon is passing fell and wrath because that she as her attendant hath—'"

It was unnerving the way the others watched me, as if waiting for me to slip.

"'—A lovely boy, stolen from an Indian king.'"

I struggled to keep my focus.

"'She never had so sweet a changeling. And jealous Oberon—'"

A wave of sickness washed over me.

"'And jealous Oberon—'"

I clutched my stomach. My mind went blank. I couldn't even think to call "line," as actors do when they forget one. I began to teeter. I caught my balance then heard a collective catching of breath.

"For heaven's sake, Walker!" Maggie chided.

"All right. House lights."

I dismounted the beam, then grasped it like a stair rail, trying to steady myself. The lights came on. Walker climbed up the steps and stood in the middle of the stage, pivoting slowly, looking us over.

"Take lunch," he said, then strode toward the back stairs. No one moved until the sound of his footsteps disappeared.

I returned to the seats to gather my things, but Shawna already had them for me. Brian spoke to his mother, and everyone else filed out quietly. I left with Shawna on one side and Tomas on the other, avoiding everyone's eyes. When we got outside, I found that Mike had positioned himself at the top of the concrete steps.

"Jenny? Jenny, look at me."

I glanced up, miserable and ashamed, knowing I could never explain my fear to someone who, like Liza, thought being onstage was "a blast."

"It takes a certain kind of person," I told him, "to believe that everyone wants to love you. And I'm not her."

Dear Uncle Louie,

I'm here at drama camp. (Thanks again for your recom-
mendation.) I have a question, one I'd rather ask you
than my father. Our director, Walker Burke, knew Dad
years ago in New York. Here at camp Walker is quick
to criticize New York theater and put down Dad. (Of
course, he doesn't know I'm a Montgomery.) Someone
here told me that Dad was in Walker's last show—that
Dad pulled out of it and the show failed. Could you tell
me what happened? I'm not going to say anything to
Walker—I just want to know what stands between them.
Thanks.

    Jen

I sent the e-mail to my godfather, then took a long shower. I was
grateful to Maggie for allowing me to spend lunch alone at Drama
House, and I returned to the theater feeling much better. Things
seemed back to normal, except that Brian was watching me a lot.

"I'm fine," I whispered to him. "Don't stare. People will notice
and I don't need any more attention than I've already gotten."

Walker had decided to spend the afternoon getting the rustics straight. Tomas was told to divide the crew work among

the rest of us and proved that he was more savvy about people than he let on. He gave Keri, Paul, and two others flats to paint inside, where they could be supervised, and sent Lynne and three responsible types outside with the spray paint. Two neat, quiet girls were assigned leaf stencils. Maybe he thought Mike and I were friends after yesterday: he asked us to paint the canvas that would cover the vaulting horse.

We worked on the ground floor, underneath the theater, across the hall from the dressing rooms and wardrobe. Saw-horses, drafting tables, and workbenches were spread throughout the cavernous room. There were pegboard walls of tools, shelves of paint supplies, and large rolls of canvas and paper, along with flats and screens that looked as if they had been painted over a hundred times.

After getting the other kids started, Tomas explained the job he was giving Mike and me. He unrolled a piece of prepared canvas, ten feet by five, on which he had chalked outlines of stones to create a wall. He showed us the finished version of pieces that would cover the ends of the horse and how to use varying shades of gray and brown paint to make the stones look three-dimensional.

Mike and I poured our paint and set to work. We talked little and about nothing important, but both the small talk and the silences were comfortable between us, as they were on the boat. I enjoyed the rhythm of our work, dipping and brushing, dipping and brushing. Mike began to sing to himself, snatches of songs. I giggled when a rock song wavered into a religious hymn, then shifted back into hard rock.

The music stopped. "Is something funny?"

"No," I said, but couldn't keep from smiling.

"You're laughing at my voice."

"No, just at you," I told him. "Uh, that didn't come out right."

"No, it didn't," he agreed.

I glanced up and saw his eyes sparkling.

"It's just funny the way you sing, mixing up all your songs. My friend in kindergarten used to sing like that when he finger-painted."

"So am I your friend?"

The question caught me off guard. "Sure."

He must have heard the uncertainty in my voice. "Maybe you'd like to think about it some more."

I didn't want to think about him any more than I already was. I focused on my brush strokes. Mike was silent for a while, then started singing again. Tomas stopped by to see how we were doing.

"Looks great!" he said. "When you're finished, take it to the drying room next door. You'll see clothesline there. Hang it up securely."

About three-thirty Mike and I carried our canvas to the next room. We lined it up along a rope, each of us attaching an end with a clothespin. Standing on opposite sides of our painted wall, we continued to work our way toward the middle of the ten-foot piece, clipping it every six inches. I made slower progress, having to climb up on a stool each time to reach the high clothesline. Mike waited for me at the center.

"Do you know how many freckles you got yesterday?" he asked when I had attached the last clothespin.

"One point six million."

He laughed.

Aware of being eye level with him, feeling self-conscious, I surveyed the painted rocks, which were on my side of the canvas. "We did a good job."

"Sometimes you look at me, Jenny, and sometimes you don't. Why?"

"You expect girls to look at you all the time?"

He smiled a lopsided smile. "No. But it's as if sometimes you're afraid to meet my eyes."

"I'm not," I assured him, and stared at his neck. It was strong with a little hollow at the base of his throat.

"Higher," he said.

I gazed at his mouth.

"Higher."

But when I found the courage to look up, he was looking down, gazing at my lips, his lashes long and dark, almost hiding the shimmer of his eyes. His face moved slowly closer to mine. He tilted his head. If I wanted to bail out, it had to be now. I held still. Feeling the nearness of him, I waited breathlessly. His lips touched mine.

How could a touch so soft, so barely there, be so wonderful? He wasn't even holding me. It was just his mouth against mine, light as a whisper.

"Hey, you guys. What have you been working on?"

We both pulled back. Shawna entered the room.

"Walker's going to keep my group till five," she said, "but we're taking fifteen. Let's see what you've done."

"A wall," Mike said quietly.

"This side," I mumbled, stepping down from the stool. I fought the urge to touch my hand to my lips. Had his kiss felt as incredible to Liza? What had made it that magic?

Shawna ducked under the rope.

How had my kiss felt to him?

Shawna studied the canvas, then me. "You sure did get a lot of sun this weekend, Jenny," she said, smiling. "You white people ought to be more careful."

Mike flashed a sly smile over the top of the clothesline.

Shawna caught it.

"What?" she asked. "Did I miss something?"

"I didn't say anything," Mike replied.

Shawna got a knowing look on her face. "Come on, girl," she said to me. "Take a break. I need some air."

I knew I was going to be interrogated but decided I could handle that better than one more moment alone with Mike. I did not want to fall for him—fall farther than I already had.

Shawna and I took the back exit of the building, climbed to the top of the outside stairwell, and sprawled on the grass.

"Okay, Reds, what's going on between you two?"

"You two who?" I asked.

"Don't play dumb. You and Mike."

"Nothing."

"Un-hunh."

"Really, nothing!"

"That's the fastest fading sunburn I've ever seen," she remarked.

I plucked at the grass.

"Did he kiss you?" she persisted, "Is that what you were doing when I barged in?"

"Why would you even think something like that?" I replied.

"Oh, I don't know," she said, smiling. "Maybe it's those glances you keep stealing at each other during rehearsal, or maybe the way Mike murmured, 'A wall,' as if he was still feeling your kiss on his lips." She eyed me. "Whoa! There it is again, that mysterious recurring sunburn."

I bit my lip.

"Why are you fighting this?" she asked.

Because he was Liza's boyfriend and had lied about it. Because I knew I couldn't compete. Because it was scary, the spell he cast on me, the way I felt when he was near.

"He lives in Trenton," I told Shawna. "I live in New York."

"So what's that—an hour and a half by car, less by train? Ever heard of Greyhound? Amtrak? E-mail? Texting? I think you're making excuses."

I didn't deny it.

"But I'll play along," she said. "This afternoon, at least," she added with a grin, then mercifully changed the subject.

When she returned to rehearsal I went downstairs to see what Tomas wanted me to do next. Mike must have cleaned up our paints. He and Paul were in the corner of the room, Mike measuring a board, Paul standing a foot away, running his finger up and down the length of a saw. Keri sat nearby, chipping at her fingernails, looking bored.

Brian had come downstairs and was talking with Tomas. I watched them a moment, feeling proud of Tomas, the way he was managing everything and earning people's respect.

"Hey, Jen," Tomas called, "would you bring over a hammer? There's one in the toolbox right behind you."

I nodded and knelt down to unfasten the latches of the metal box. Lifting the lid, seeing that the hammer's handle was buried beneath other tools, I reached for its head, trying to extract it. I pulled back in surprise. The steel felt ice cold. Reaching down to grasp it again, I saw the metal glimmering blue. I touched it and cold traveled up my arm, as if my veins had been injected with ice. My shoulders and neck grew numb, my head light, so light I had to close my eyes.

Then I jerked and was free of the floating feeling, but I wasn't at Stoddard anymore. I stood breathless, as if I'd been running fast. Clutching my side, I opened my mouth trying to breathe silently, afraid to make the slightest noise. I could see little in the darkness that surrounded me, but I smelled the creek and heard its black water lapping against the pilings. I knew I was in terrible danger.

Soft footsteps hurried across the structure above me. I looked up and listened, trying to judge the direction the person was heading. *My direction*, I thought, panicking, no matter what, it would be my direction.

Step by step I moved forward in the darkness, hating the feel of the swampy ooze but knowing I had to keep on. About twenty feet behind me I heard the muffled thud of feet landing on wet ground.

I hid behind a piling and listened to my pursuer walking in the mud, moving steadily closer. My heart pounded so loudly I thought the person had to hear it. If he or she discovered me now, I'd be trapped.

I bolted, splashing through the shallow water. The person was after me in a flash. I tripped and fell facedown. Tasting mud, gasping for breath, I scrambled to my feet. A distance ahead I saw a wall of grass, tall as corn, and beyond that, a lighter, open area. Bright lights shone from the tops of poles. If I could make it as far as the lights, maybe someone would see me, maybe someone would help me.

Then I felt a powerful blow from behind. Pain exploded at the base of my skull. Every nerve in my body buzzed with it—every second of agony so excruciating, I could not stay conscious. I fell headfirst into darkness.

Thirteen

When I opened my eyes I was in Brian's arms. He knelt on the floor next to the toolbox, holding me, searching my face, his own face lined with worry.

"Jenny, Jenny, are you all right?"

I nodded, unable to speak. The crushing pain at the back of my skull had disappeared, but the memory of it was so intense it dulled my senses and made the present seem less real. Tomas and others working on scenery had gathered around me. Paul watched me with keen eyes. Keri stood next to him, looking as if she'd finally seen something of interest. I knew Mike was next to Keri, but I didn't allow myself to look at him, afraid he'd see how much I wished he was the one holding me.

"What happened?" Brian asked gently.

"I don't know."

"Why did you faint?"

I shook my head, unable to think of an answer that would make sense to him and the others.

"Did you get lunch, Jen?" Tomas asked. "When you went back to Drama House, did you get something to eat?"

"No. I'm sure that's it," I said, seizing upon the excuse.

Brian brushed my hair back from my cheek, his dark eyes doubtful.

"I'm okay," I told him, sitting up, pulling away from him.

He let go reluctantly. Tomas, who had been searching his pockets, leaned over and handed me a candy bar.

"Perfect," I said. "Thanks."

"Why don't I walk you back to Drama House?" Brian suggested.

"No, I'm fine and want to keep working. There's the hammer, Tomas."

He picked it up, then glanced at his watch. "Everybody, let's start cleaning up. It's going to take us a while."

I stood and followed some of the others to the corner of the room where they had been cutting out leaves. Brian, shaking his head at my stubbornness, returned to rehearsal.

For five minutes I picked up scraps of paper, then, when I thought no one was paying attention to me, I walked back to the toolbox. I sorted through it and grasped a hammer, first by the handle, then by its steel head, wrapping my fingers tightly around it. Nothing, I felt nothing, just a tool that was cool to the touch like the others in the box. It didn't turn icy cold, didn't make my head grow light; nothing glimmered blue.

I walked to the bench where Tomas had been working and laid my hand on the first hammer. Just cool, I told myself, but then the cold began to seep through the tips of my fingers. It flowed through my veins and up my arm. The bench's fluorescent fixture buzzed blue. My head grew light. I quickly thrust out my other hand, grasping the edge of the workbench to steady myself.

"You doing okay?"

I let go of the hammer. "Fine."

"Sorry," Mike said, "but I don't believe you."

"I've never been better."

"Better at what? Acting?" He waited, as if he thought I would change my answer. "So I guess there's nothing I can do to help," he concluded.

"No, but thanks."

He took a step closer, leaned down, and whispered, "Just so you know, you're supposed to swoon when I kiss you, not a half hour afterward."

"That's not why I fainted."

"Darn! And I was so sure."

"Our kiss—that was just an accident," I told him.

"An accident? You mean you were aiming for someone else's lips and ran into mine instead?"

"I—I mean the kiss didn't mean anything."

"I see."

"Sometimes things just happen," I said. "They happen and don't mean anything at all."

"Really."

Paul called out to Mike then, asking for help in lifting a flat.

"Well, hope you're feeling better," Mike said, and went to help his friend.

I took a deep breath and glanced down at the hammer. I couldn't bring myself to touch it again. My blue visions were becoming like the frightening blue dreams I'd had as a child—bizarre and yet very, very real.

The *real* "Teen Psychic," I thought. What if I were? What if the images that had seemed so strange to me as a child had been retrieved from other people's minds? Maybe Liza wasn't simply comforting me after those dreams; maybe I really did share her mind and the minds and lives of others.

If so, I must have learned how to suppress the ability. But the visions I had now felt too powerful for me to control, triggered by things that formed a physical link to Liza: the window seat where she had sat, the place on stage where she had liked to stand, pictures of her murder site, and now, the hammer. I couldn't prove it, but I knew beyond a shadow of a psychic's doubt, this hammer was the weapon that had killed my sister.

Chase Library kept short hours during the summer, so I went there directly from the theater, needing a college computer to access newspaper archives. In every account I read, the facts were the same. The murder weapon was determined to be something heavy, a metal tool with a small blunt surface. The police believed it was a hammer, but the weapon had never been found. None of the news articles noted whether it was Liza's left or right wrist that bore the smashed watch.

At first I was comforted by my vision of the watch on the wrong wrist, reasoning from that small detail that the murderer hadn't known Liza. But the truth was that anyone in a hurry to escape the crime scene could have easily overlooked such a small matter.

I knew what I needed to do—carry the hammer to the bridge tonight and see what images came to me—but I was afraid. I didn't want to feel the crushing blow. Knowing what it was, realizing that I was reliving my sister's death, I felt sickened by it long after the physical pain receded.

As I gathered my things at the library, I realized that I had left my script at the theater. It was five-thirty when I reached

Stoddard, but the back door was unlocked as usual, as was the room where we had been working. I retrieved my book from a bench.

Emerging from the room, I thought I heard voices at the end of the hall, but they had a strange, echoing sound, as if the people and I were separated by a very long passage. Curious, I followed the hall, rounding the corner, passing Walker's office, then Maggie's. No one was in sight. The next three doors, all offices belonging to professors, were closed. Then I saw the last door in the hall ajar and strode toward it.

I thought I was peering into a dark closet, but when I heard the voices again, I opened the door wider and saw the outline of a metal stairway. It rose inside the small, square space, four or five steps up one wall, then met the corner and turned, rising several steps along the next wall, continuing to spire up into the darkness, a murky darkness, as if there was light at the top. The steps to the tower!

I was tempted to climb them. The platform above the clock must have been high enough to command a view of both the river and creek. But the voices above me were becoming louder and more distinct. A guy and a girl—Paul and Keri, I realized—were coming down. I didn't want to meet up with them, not when I was alone. I exited quickly and hurried along the hallway. Then curiosity won out. Were they simply enjoying a romantic moment in the tower, or were they up to something? I ducked inside the room from which I had fetched my book, extinguished the lights, and hid behind the open door.

"You're losing your edge," I heard Keri say, as she and Paul walked down the hall.

Paul laughed. "I'm not here to entertain you."

"But you do entertain me," she insisted. "That little mean thing that crawls around inside your brain fascinates me."

I pressed my head against the door, watching them through the vertical crack between the hinges.

"Did you ever think that it might be crawling around in *your* brain?" Paul asked. "You don't know who I am, Keri. You keep inventing me, trying to make me into the guy you want me to be."

"That's good," she answered sharply, "real good coming from a guy who turned a girl into a fantasy, who made her so perfect in his mind he can't give her up, not even when she's a corpse."

Paul turned away so I couldn't see his face.

"Do you know why Liza went out that night?" Keri asked.

"Why don't you tell me?" he replied. "I know you want to."

"She got a note from Mike asking her to meet him by the creek."

I felt as if someone had just punched me in the stomach.

"If you're trying to turn me against Mike—" Paul began.

"I saw the note," Keri went on. "Liza couldn't wait to show me what he had written. It was poetic. He was counting the minutes till he could meet her by the water."

"Maybe you should have shared that information with the police," Paul suggested coolly.

"I've told you before, I don't go running to teachers or police. It's us against them. I'm loyal—unless, of course, someone gives me a reason not to be."

Paul faced her.

"But I find it interesting," she went on, "that a note Liza would have saved for framing wasn't found on her body or in her room. Someone must have destroyed it before the police could get their hands on it. Was it you?" She stepped close to him. "Was it?"

"Do you want it to be?" he asked, placing his hands around Keri's neck and running his fingers lightly over her skin.

For a moment she didn't say anything. She closed her eyes as if she hoped the tease would become something more, then she pushed him away.

"I just want it over," she said, her voice low and angry. "Liza's dead. Why can't you bury her?"

She turned and stalked away. I heard the outside door swing open and closed. Paul left a moment later.

I emerged from the room, still reeling from my discovery. I

had made up my mind: after curfew tonight I'd go down to the bridge. I'd find out what happened when Mike asked my sister to meet him.

At eleven-thirty I climbed out the same window Liza had and followed the lane down to Oyster Creek. I didn't have the hammer with me. After Keri and Paul had left the theater, I searched the scenery and drying rooms, and even the stage, in case someone carried the tool upstairs, but I couldn't find it. I tried the tower, too, but the door had been locked.

Now, having escaped Drama House, I rushed down Goose Lane, then turned left on Scull, which ran parallel to the water. I didn't stop walking till I reached the bridge, afraid I'd lose my nerve. As I had hoped, the waterfront was deserted. I sat down quickly on the bank of the creek, pulling my knees up to my chest, pressing my face against them.

"I'm here, Liza," I whispered.

Nothing happened. My mind felt rigid like my body, locked into a protective position. I took a deep breath, rose, and walked five feet down to the edge of the water. I lay on my back beside the water and ever so slowly let go, as I had learned to do in my relaxation exercises, allowing my shoulders, my elbows, the calves of my legs to sink down into the mud and stones. I cringed when I felt the trickle of creek at the back of my skull—it felt like blood—but I continued to work through Maggie's exercises till my body and mind relaxed.

The bridge above me was lost in darkness. I turned my head to the side and gazed at the creek, at the concrete pilings and the wavering reflections of the bridge's street lamps. The water shimmered blue. I closed my eyes and still I saw blue. I grew light-headed, so light I felt as if I were floating above myself. Suspended in the air, I looked down on a dark body and a glowing watch face. Someone in black bent over the body, drew back, then smashed the watch.

I sat up quickly and grabbed my wrist, but there was no pain, not like there had been in the hammer vision. I felt confused and frustrated. Why couldn't I see who was shattering the watch? In the chase visions my pursuer was cloaked in black and had struck from behind, so I couldn't see the face. But why couldn't I now, when the person was bent over Liza?

I had thought I was inside Liza's mind reliving the events—I knew I had felt the murderer's blow as she would have felt it. Then it occurred to me: when the watch was strapped to my sister's wrist she was already dead. People who have near-death experiences talk about the spirit leaving the body, hovering above it. That was why I hovered in this part of my vision, looking down on the body and the watch face just as Liza's spirit had.

I stood up, my skin feeling clammy and chill despite the

warm night. Slowly I walked toward the gazebo, running my hands through my matted hair, brushing the gritty mud from my arms.

At the gazebo I sat on the steps to think. I wondered if this was the place by the creek where Mike had met Liza. Here or the pavilion, I thought. In the pale moonlight, the pavilion, sitting high on its pilings and surrounded by tall grass, seemed its own little romantic island.

I blinked. Tall grass, grass high as corn. I had assumed the pilings of my visions were the supports beneath the bridge, but there were pilings beneath the pavilion, too, and the creek washed through the grass and under the wooden structure just as it did under the bridge. I jumped up and ran toward the pavilion, stopping at the grass jungle encircling it. It grew thick as bamboo. I thrust my arms into it, parted the long stalks, and stepped in, then continued to push aside swordlike leaves, gradually working my way through the dense vegetation. It stopped abruptly at the edge of the pavilion floor, where sunlight would end.

The moonlight ended there, too. Step by step I moved into the darkness beneath the pavilion. The ground turned soggy under my feet. I could hear the light lap of water against the pilings and small rustlings in the surrounding grass. As I moved farther beneath the structure, the water began to pool around my ankles. Mosquitoes whined in my ears. I thought I heard something and paused for a moment to listen, resting against a piling. My head buzzed and grew light. The darkness around me glinted blue.

Behind me, twenty feet back, there was a soft thud, a sound light as a cat landing on leaves, then quiet footsteps. The person had found me.

My heart pounded in my chest. I could hardly breathe, my throat raw, my side aching from running. I slipped behind a piling hoping to see something—if not the face, the size or gait of the person—some clue as to who it was, but I couldn't. I heard the person coming closer and closer. I debated what to do.

Instinct took over. I bolted, then felt the sudden movement, the rush from behind. I wanted to pull out of the vision. I wanted it to stop now. But I had to turn around, had to reach for the face of my pursuer, to feel the shape I couldn't see.

I tried to and tripped, falling facedown in the water. Scrambling to my feet, I was too terrified to stop now. I raced forward. A hand grasped me and clamped down hard on my shoulder, fingers biting into me. I screamed and screamed. Another hand clapped over my mouth. The person pulled me back against him so violently the breath was knocked out of me. The blue light faded. The person laughed close to my ear, his moist lips touching my cheek. Paul.

"Going somewhere?"

I struggled against him, but he held me all the tighter. "Let me go!" I shouted. "Let me go!"

"Not yet."

I kicked backward, striking him in the shin.

"Don't make me get rough," he said.

"Let go, Paul. *Now!*"

"Not till you tell me what you were doing."

I continued to struggle.

"Tell me!" Paul jerked me around, lifting my whole body, making it clear who was in control.

"I was taking a walk."

"In a swamp?" he replied. "I don't think so."

I stopped struggling, deciding to save my energy for the instant he relaxed.

"I was walking through the park," Paul said, "and saw you duck under here. What a surprise"—his voice mocked me— "our best little camper, sneaking around after curfew! It's not like you, Jenny, being out late like this—it's not like the dear little Jenny we all know and love."

I didn't respond.

"Come on, talk! Are you making a pickup? Did someone leave something down here for you?"

"Nothing much," I said. "And I couldn't find it anyway."

He looked around, loosening his grip. I seized the chance

to pull away from him, racing forward, then glimpsing lights through the grass, lights on poles as they were in an earlier vision—dock lights. I crashed through the grass and into a clear area, running toward the college boathouse. From a distance behind me I heard his laughter. Paul wasn't bothering with the chase. Still, I didn't stop until I reached the racks of sculls. Crouching in the shadows, I gazed back toward the pavilion.

Paul emerged from the grass surrounding it and walked toward the street. I didn't know whether he was leaving me alone or setting a trap. He knew the route I'd take back. But if he had wanted to hurt me, he would have done things differently, I reasoned; he would have kept himself hidden so I couldn't accuse him later. And if he had wanted to kill me, he would have done it under the pavilion. I could have lain there for days before anyone found me.

It was an ideal place to murder and dump a body. And I was sure from my visions that my sister had been struck down beneath the pavilion. But that wasn't where the serial murderer liked to do his killing. If the police had discovered her body beneath the pavilion, they would have searched for a different killer, someone from the town or campus. And if they had known about the hammer I found in the theater, they would have focused on the people connected to the camp. I could no longer deny the probability that Liza's killer had known her.

If that person wanted the police to think the serial killer was responsible, then Liza's body had to be transported to the bridge without leaving a trail. Given that her death was bloody, the job seemed more than one person could handle. If so, there could be two people in Wisteria who knew the truth about Liza's death.

I intended to find them.

Fourteen

"So what do you think, Jen?" Tomas asked me the next morning as we waited for rehearsal to begin. "You don't like it," he guessed, fingering a bolt of filmy blue fabric.

"Tell me again. I wasn't quite listening."

He patiently explained a second time how he was going to create a sky for the set by stretching his semi-transparent fabric between the thirty-foot-high catwalk that ran across the front of the stage and the eighteen-foot ridge and waterfall that formed the set's back wall.

I struggled to follow what he was saying, uneasily aware of Mike and Paul standing nearby, as if they were waiting to speak to me. I wondered if Paul had told Mike about last night's incident. It annoyed me that I had let Paul see how afraid I was, though I would have been an idiot not to have feared him in that situation.

"So what do you think?" Tomas asked again.

I glanced down at the fabric. "It's beautiful. When the lights shine through, it will shimmer like a summer sky."

Tomas beamed.

"Just one question. Who's attaching it to the catwalk—besides me?"

"Arthur's getting an extension ladder," he said. "Someone will volunteer. I don't think I'd better—you saw me on the boat."

Mike stepped forward. "I'll help."

"Terrific," Tomas replied. "I'll see if I can find one more person."

He headed off quickly, perhaps wanting to sidestep an offer from Paul.

Gazing upward, Paul surveyed the length of the high, metal walkway. His face warped into a smile, as if something amusing had occurred to him. Then he turned to me. "Need some coffee this morning, Jenny?"

"No."

"You look tired," Mike observed.

Paul grinned. "That's the price of climbing out your window after eleven p.m. Yes," he added, noting Mike's surprise, "our own little Jenny."

"Why did you go out that late?" Mike's tone was disapproving.

"Someone sent me a note," I replied, "asking me to meet him by the river."

The light in Mike's eyes darkened. The muscles in his jaw tensed, hardening his face. I gave up the scrap of hope to which I had been clinging—he knew what I was referring to. He had sent the note to Liza.

"You ought to be more careful," he said.

"Yeah, you never know who you're going to meet out there," Paul added.

From across the stage Maggie called out, "Jenny. May I see you a moment?"

"She's on to you, girl," Paul whispered.

I ignored him and crossed the stage.

"How are you doing today?" Maggie asked, resting a hand on my shoulder.

"Good. Ready to go."

"Then what do you think of rehearsing with the stage lights up twenty-five percent and the house lights down about the same? Think you can handle it?"

"I'd like to try."

"I want everyone who is not in your scene to be sitting in the audience. Is that pushing you too hard? We can cut the scene immediately if you start to feel ill."

"Let's cut the scene only if I give you a signal," I proposed.

"I might turn a little green, but I want to try to get through it."

Maggie smiled. "I knew from the start you'd be a great kid to work with. I'll tell Walker."

Walker wanted to run the same scene as yesterday since he thought it best to "get back on the horse you were riding when you fell off." The lights were adjusted and kids settled into their seats in the audience. Paul and Keri, as Oberon and Titania, stood in opposite wings, waiting for their entrances. Katie and her fellow fairy entered from stage left, I from stage right, vaulting, spinning, landing lightly on my feet. "'How now, spirits, whither wander you?'"

My voice came out strong—not with as much expression as I'd have liked, but I was in control. The fairies gave their speech about how they served Queen Titania and I began my account of Oberon and his feud with the queen—the speech that I had blown yesterday.

As I spoke my lines and worked on the balance beam, I became increasingly sensitive to the stage lights in my eyes. It was like watching a sunrise and suddenly having to look away from the brightness. I paused, took a deep breath, then continued on, "'And jealous Oberon . . . And jealous Oberon'. . . Line."

"'Would have the child,'" Brian said softly.

"'Would have the child, Knight of his train to trace the forest wild.'" I knew where I was again and carried on, a little shaky, but determined.

The fairies spoke the next ten lines, leading up to my favorite speech, in which Puck tells of all the mischievous tricks he likes to play. We had woven lots of gymnastics into those lines. My first stunt was a cartwheel on the balance beam.

"'Thou speakest aright,'" I began, "'I am that merry wanderer of the—'"

My right hand had just touched the beam. The stage lights flickered. A beat later my left hand touched. The lights went out. Total darkness. My left leg came around to find the beam but missed it. I slid off, banging my arm against the wood.

"Arthur!" Walker shouted.

"Jenny, are you okay?" It was Brian's voice.

"Fine. Fine." I was angry, not hurt. I should have been able to complete the wheel in darkness. It was a loss of concentration, my own fault.

"Be still. Everyone be still till we get the lights on," Maggie said.

"Arthur!" Walker hollered again. "Brian, get him."

Kids giggled.

"This is nothing to laugh about," Maggie said sternly. "These pranks are dangerous. Someone could get hurt."

The nervous laughter was stifled. Kids whispered. I heard Brian's footsteps crossing the stage.

"If I find out who is behind this . . ." Walker's voice resonated in the darkness, deep and threatening. The whispers ceased.

In that moment of silence something dropped. It sounded small but heavy, like a metal object. It rolled across the stage and stopped close to me. Kneeling, I groped with my hand along the edge of the gym mat and found it. A ring.

The lights blinked on and I inspected the piece of jewelry. It was large with a gaudy red stone, the kind of ring that would be used as a stage prop. I slipped it on my finger. Glancing up, I noticed that everyone was looking at me. Katie, Keri, and Paul . . . Shawna and Lynne . . . Denise and Mike—everyone who had attended last year's camp was staring at the ring with troubled expressions. I pulled it off.

"It's from *Twelfth Night,*" Shawna said. "Remember? It's the ring Viola received, the one that Liza wore. We couldn't find it after Liza died. We looked everywhere."

Brian walked toward me and held out his hand. Knowing that Liza had worn the ring, I gave it up reluctantly.

"Who brought this in here?" Brian demanded.

Kids looked at one another suspiciously. Walker wiped the sweat off his brow, and Maggie bit her lip. Mike's face was grim. No one answered Brian's question.

"I want it," Paul said at last "Give it to me."

"No," Walker said firmly, "it's theater property. Put it where it belongs, Brian."

Brian nodded, then headed for the backstage steps.

I rubbed my palm, thinking. I hadn't felt anything when I held the ring, and there had been no glimmer of blue during this incident. Nor had there been blue light when I smelled my sister's perfume or heard her voice. These incidents were different from my visions and the last two were witnessed by others besides me. I didn't know how to account for them. Was my sister haunting the theater? Or was there a living, breathing person behind these three events? If the latter, someone among us wanted to rattle nerves.

Perhaps someone suspected I was Jenny Montgomery and wanted to unmask me. Or maybe these pranks were aimed at torturing and unmasking another person, the murderer.

What would Liza's murderer do if it was discovered that I was her sister? Till now it hadn't occurred to me that my relationship to her might put me in danger. I would have to be more careful that no one found out.

Tuesday night I went to bed early. My room, where I had feared having more visions, was now my refuge. Not that I sat in the window anymore. I stretched out in bed and listened to another of Maggie's relaxation CDs, then read until I fell asleep.

The sound of a bell startled me, pulling me out of a dreamless slumber. It was a repeated, echoey sound, like a bell in a school building—a fire alarm! I had to get up, I had to leave, but my arms and legs felt too heavy to lift. I lay there listening to the bell.

"Jenny, come on! Jenny, please!"

Liza reached for my hand: I couldn't see her, but I knew it was she.

"Don't be afraid," she told me, grasping my fingers.

"But I am afraid!"

"I'll help you," she said, her hand tightening around mine.

"Jenny, Jenny, wake up!"

I was shaken hard. Shawna was tugging on my hand, and Maggie was bending over me, her face pale and glistening with sweat.

"It's a fire alarm," Maggie said, raising her voice above the shrill pulsing of the bell. Sirens sounded in the distance. "We have to get out."

Shawna dragged me to my feet.

"Where's the fire?"

"Don't know," said Shawna.

"May be a false alarm," said Maggie. "But go out the window. Go, girls!"

We climbed through in our bare feet and landed softly on the grass below. Maggie followed us and pushed us away from the house, toward the fraternity, where others were gathering. I saw her mouth moving silently: she kept counting heads.

"That's everyone from our place," Lynne assured her.

Guys had come out of the fraternity and kids from the other two houses were arriving, awakened by the sirens. As the first fire engine pulled up in front of the house, Brian joined his mother and us.

"In the kitchen again?" he asked, and I remembered that there had been a small fire at Drama House last year.

"I didn't smell any smoke," Maggie replied.

They headed toward the firefighters to talk to them. Our crowd was growing larger, not just with students but also curious neighbors who had heard the sirens. Keri stood next to Paul, her face flushed slightly. Paul's eyes roved the crowd. Mike stood apart, watching the firefighters who were circling the house. His eyes flicked over to me, studied me for a moment, then shifted away. Brian was at my elbow.

"Everyone okay here?" Brian asked, addressing me and the other girls who were clustered together, but his eyes lingered on me.

We all spoke at the same time, asking him what was going on.

"It's probably a false alarm," Brian told us. "Did you notice anything odd? Did you hear anyone moving around inside the house or creeping around the perimeter?"

I shook my head with the others, and Shawna burst out laughing.

"Didn't hear anything, Jenny?" she teased. "Talk about waking the dead! From now on I'm keeping a trumpet handy to blow in your ear."

"Did you have trouble waking up?" Brian asked.

"I heard the alarm bell, but it became part of a dream, a dream I couldn't shake off."

He frowned. "What do you mean?"

"I just couldn't wake up."

"Don't worry," Shawna told him. "If it happens again, I won't mess around. She'll be up."

Brian rejoined his mother. Tomas came over and Shawna filled him in on the situation. I sat on the grass next to them, thinking about my dream. I found it scary that a dream could take hold of my mind so powerfully, I could barely break free of it. Even when bells were ringing and someone was shaking me, I had struggled to find my way back to waking life. I felt as if Liza had grasped my mind the way she had clutched my hand in the dream, and she wouldn't let go—not until I found her murderer.

While the firefighters continued to search the building, making sure this was a false alarm, Maggie came over and called all of the students together.

"This is unbelievable," she said, her gray eyes dark with anger. "It is senseless, stupid, and, most of all, dangerous. False alarms make people reluctant to respond quickly the next time they hear an alarm. And when a real fire occurs, thirty seconds can make the difference between life and death.

"It is the policy of Chase College to expel any student found guilty of this kind of dorm prank and to press criminal charges. We know the alarm on the outside of Drama House was pulled. If we find out who did it, you know the consequences. I don't expect it to happen again."

She strode away and everyone exchanged glances.

"Has anyone seen Walker?" Denise asked after a moment of silence.

"No, he lets Maggie take care of this kind of stuff," Katie replied. "She's a natural at lecturing."

"Look, there's that strange custodian guy."

I saw Arthur standing at the edge of the yard, half hidden by a bush, his eyes darting nervously here and there.

"He gives me the creeps," said Lynne.

"Me too," agreed another girl. "You ever seen how his face twitches? It makes my own skin crawl."

"He's been nice to me," Tomas told them. "He's helped me a lot with setting up scenery."

"Why is he here? He doesn't live on campus, does he?" asked Shawna.

"I bet he pulled the alarm," said Denise. "I bet next time he'll set a fire."

"I bet he's a psychotic murderer," Katie added.

"Maybe he just heard the sirens like everyone else," I suggested.

"Hey, don't ruin our fun, girlfriend," Shawna chided me. "Every camp needs a murderous maniac."

"This camp already had one." As soon as I spoke, I regretted it.

Shawna raised an eyebrow at me, puzzled by the sharpness in my voice. "Okay," she replied with a shrug.

We were finally allowed back in the building. Brian and his mother continued to talk, while the other R.A.s shepherded their campers back to the dorms. As those of us from Drama House started toward the porch, Arthur cut across the lawn. We reached the steps at the same time, and some of the girls shied to the other side. Shawna and I turned to him.

"Don't trust anyone," Arthur said softly. "Not anyone."

Fifteen

WALKER MUST HAVE been told what happened before rehearsal the next morning, but he didn't bring it up. Katie was right: Maggie got stuck with the disciplinary stuff. Given that everyone was short on sleep, rehearsal went amazingly well. The play had been blocked in its entirety, and Walker was talking about our getting off book—getting our lines down—by next week.

During our midmorning break I went downstairs to return a relaxation CD to Maggie and get the next one in the series. Finding her office door closed, I raised my hand to knock, then heard someone speaking.

"You're blowing this way out of proportion," Brian said.

"I don't think so," Maggie replied coolly. "I think it's rather important that a mother be able to trust her son."

"But there was no point in telling you until—"

"It was too late?" she suggested.

"Don't put words in my mouth!"

"Brian, how can I trust that you're not—"

"You just have to," he told her. "I'm better at these things than you are. Let *me* handle the situation, Mom, okay? Okay?"

"She won't," a hushed voice interjected.

I jumped at its closeness. Arthur seemed to have materialized out of nowhere.

"Those two are always fighting," he said.

"Parents and kids do," I replied quietly.

"They make me jittery," he went on. "People like that, you don't know what they're going to do."

"What do you mean?"

"People like that just go off suddenly," he said. "I've seen it happen."

I wondered if Arthur knew of some real trouble between Maggie and Brian or if he was projecting on them his own uneasy state of mind.

"Arthur, last night, when we were returning to Drama House, why did you tell us not to trust anyone?"

He didn't answer, just chewed a square yellow fingernail. His clothes smelled smoky. Farther down the hall was the door to the tower. I reasoned that he had slipped in there to have a cigarette, then emerged and surprised me. He probably knew all the nooks and crannies of the theater. According to my mother, it isn't the CIA who knows the secrets of the world, but building custodians and hairdressers.

"Have you worked at Stoddard long?" I asked.

"Long enough," he replied.

"Did you work here last summer? Were you around for last year's camp?"

He shoved nervous hands in his pockets. "No. I move in winter. Winter always makes me feel like I should be somewhere else. I came here last winter."

So he couldn't have observed something suspicious when my sister was killed. But he might have noticed some recent activities that would be useful for me to know.

"When the electricity went off yesterday, were you around?"

"I'm always around," he replied guardedly.

"Oh, I know, I know you do your job. I was just wondering if you saw anyone doing something he or she shouldn't. Or perhaps you saw one of the campers alone in the building, not with the group of us."

"You came back alone on Monday," Arthur noted.

Oh, good. He'd seen *me* being suspicious, and I hadn't even been aware of him.

"Anyone else?"

"Paul and the weird girl."

"Arthur, do you have any idea who could be cutting the power?"

"No," he replied quickly. "I don't know nothing! I don't see nothing!"

"Okay, okay, no problem, I was just wondering."

He was too nervous and worried to provide information now, and the best thing for me to do was back off. But I had been around a lot of custodians in my life; I would slowly make him my friend.

"Where are we going?" I asked, two hours later.

"If it were up to me, California," Brian said, taking my lunch tray from me, setting it down at the base of a maple at the far end of the quadrangle. "But that's a long walk, so let's stop here."

The energy our troupe had shown earlier in the day had run out by lunchtime. Maggie didn't want kids returning to the dorms unsupervised, but she let us bring our lunches out on the quad and take a nap there, where she could keep an eye on us. Kids had scattered over the grass, some in the shade of tall, leafy trees, others basking in the sun.

Brian stretched out on the grass. I sat and rested my back against the maple's rough bark.

"The truth is, Jenny, there are two more long days till the weekend. Lots of stupid stuff is happening around here, and I have to deal with it. I need a reward—lunch with you."

"It must be tough for you and your mother. Being in charge of the dorms as well as working all day in the theater, you never get a break."

"I think it's getting to her more than me," he said.

"How so?"

Lying on his back, Brian gazed up at the tree, thinking before he answered. The movement of the branches, the shifting sun and shade, were reflected in his dark eyes. "She's overreacting to things. The pranks in the theater have got her really upset. This morning she accused me of them."

I decided not to tell him I'd heard part of their argument. "Why does she think you'd do something like that?"

"To mess things up. To get back at Walker."

"I didn't realize you disliked him that much."

"I don't. I know I'm a good actor, a good stage manager, too, and let what he says run off me. But I think his criticism of me over the years has gotten to my mother. She tries to act professional and doesn't let people see what upsets her, but she's pretty sensitive. She can get down about stuff, really down, and she imagines I feel the same as she does."

"Do you have any idea who could be behind these pranks?" I asked. I was not about to mention my first theory that Liza was haunting us. I knew Brian was too practical to consider it.

"Paul, but I don't have proof. Paul and someone else who can cut the electricity, maybe Arthur, someone not expected to be present when my mother counts heads."

"Does Paul have a case against Walker?"

"Not really. Walker has given him a lot of breaks." Brian rolled on his side and pulled himself up on his elbow. "I don't know if I should say this. I could be way off, but I think Paul does the pranks as a way of making Liza Montgomery live on."

I thought of how Paul sniffed at her perfume, as if he couldn't get enough of it. My stomach felt queasy and I set down my sandwich.

"Is something wrong?"

"No."

Brian sat up. "Jenny, I have to tell you something. It may sound crazy, but I have a feeling it won't."

I met his eyes warily. "All right."

"This morning, when I was talking with my mother, I remembered a conversation I had last summer with Liza Montgomery. I remembered that Liza had a sister named Jenny."

I looked away.

"According to Liza, Jenny knew a lot about theater, and she had talent, but she was afraid to get up on stage. She never did any acting."

"No," I said quietly, "she did gymnastics."

I heard his quick intake of breath. He rested his hand on mine. "Why did you come here?" he asked. "It has got to be miserable for you."

"I told her I'd come. I promised Liza I'd visit her. I just"—my voice caught in my throat—"arrived a little late."

He lifted his hand and touched my cheek gently. "I'm sorry. I'm really sorry about what happened."

I nodded, pressing my lips together, hoping he wouldn't hear the sob building in my throat. He leaned closer and brushed my hair back from my face.

"There is something else I want to know, but I'll ask when you're feeling better."

"Ask now," I said.

He waited a minute, until I was breathing more regularly. "Does anyone here know who you are?"

I shook my head.

"You're sure?"

"There would be no reason for them to know. I don't look like Liza or act like her, and most people, like you, wouldn't expect me to come here after what happened. I love Liza with all my heart, but, as you probably noticed, she was a person who spent a lot of time thinking and talking about herself. I'm sure she bragged about Dad, but truthfully, I'm surprised you ever heard she had a sister."

"It came up once, in a conversation about the pros and cons of being involved with theater when your parents are. That's something Liza and I shared. But, Jenny, don't you see, if I heard your name and finally made the connection, somebody else might."

"I suppose."

"Does Mike know?"

"I'm sure he doesn't." If Mike had figured it out, he wouldn't have lied to me about his relationship to Liza.

"It worries me," Brian continued. "Because if Mike knows, Paul knows—they're close. And Paul was totally obsessed with Liza, still is. If he finds out you're her sister, he might . . ." His voice trailed off.

"What?" I asked.

I thought he was going to answer, then he changed his mind. "I don't know. My imagination's working overtime."

"Brian, have you ever thought that Liza might have been killed by someone other than the serial murderer?"

"I guess everyone here looked at everyone else when we first heard about her death. But then we learned that the murder had the trademark of the serial killer who was working his way up the East Coast."

"Which doesn't mean anything," I replied. "Imitating the style of others is something theater people do very well."

"What do you mean?" he asked. "Do you suspect someone?"

"I'm mulling over the possibility."

Brian's face grew worried. "Jenny, I think you should leave."

"Not yet."

"Before anyone else figures out who you are."

"I can't. Not until the dreams stop."

"What dreams?" he asked.

I knew better than to say I was having psychic visions. "I keep dreaming of Liza. It's as if she is trying to tell me something."

His eyebrows drew together. His mouth got the same determined look as his mother's. "I'm trying to tell you something, with no *as if*. You need to get out of here."

I shook my head stubbornly.

"Listen to me, Jenny. Paul's room is like a shrine to your sister. Sometimes I'm not sure he knows she is dead. It's as if a switch suddenly flips inside his brain, and he can't tell real from unreal."

Brian detached a set of keys from his belt. "This is my master key," he said, pulling it off the ring. "It opens all the doors in the frat. This afternoon, when you're not rehearsing and everyone else is occupied, I'll send you on a fake errand. I want you to go to Paul's room and see for yourself. Second floor. His name's on the door."

I gazed at the brass key Brian dropped in my hand.

"No, it isn't ethical," he added as if he'd read my thoughts, "and I don't care. All I care about is you seeing what you're dealing with." He took my face in his hands. "Believe me, Jenny, I don't want you to go. New York is a long way from here. But I think you're taking big chances."

"I'm not ready to leave yet."

"This afternoon ought to make you ready." He let go and glanced around. "We'd better eat."

We gulped down our food and Maggie called everyone in. Brian returned my tray and his to the cafeteria, sending me ahead to the theater. I joined Tomas and Shawna at the back of a crowd filing into Stoddard. Too late I noticed that Mike was in front of them. I fussed with my backpack and pretended not to see him.

"Hello," Mike said cheerfully.

I hoped he was speaking to someone else.

"Hello, Jenny. Is anyone home?"

Shawna and Tomas laughed at his question.

I glanced up. "Hi."

"Did you have a nice lunch?" he asked.

Had he been watching? I wondered.

"We were going to join you," Shawna said, her eyes bright with teasing, "but Tomas said it looked like a tree-for-two, so we didn't."

Tomas gave a little shrug and smile, then followed Shawna into the building. Mike stayed behind and caught me with a light hand before I could enter. He stood close, his neck and shoulders blocking out the light, making me acutely aware of his size and strength. When I glanced up at his face, I saw his eyes following a trickle of sweat down my neck.

"For a moment during lunch," he said, "I was afraid you were going to have another accident."

My cheeks got hot. "Must have been a pretty boring lunch," I replied. "I hope your dinner is better."

Sixteen

SOON AFTER WE came back from our three o'clock break, Brian handed me a diagram of the play's revised set and sent me off to "make copies." I circled Stoddard then headed toward the fraternity.

The house's design was almost identical to that of Drama House, but the peeling gray paint on the outside and its dilapidated condition inside made it seem like a very different place. The foyer was painted dark purple, its only light a bare bulb dangling from the ceiling. The stairway's banister, also purple, had deep gashes in it, and several of its balusters were missing.

I set the folder Brian had given me on the steps, then continued upstairs and found the door to Paul's room. Only then did I hesitate. I was invading his privacy, and I wasn't sure the private part of Paul's life was something I wanted to know. But I had to do this, for Liza's sake and my own. I slipped the key in the hole.

As soon as I opened the door, I smelled the perfume, Liza's perfume. Then I saw the pictures. She was everywhere, on the bureau and desk, hanging inside the mirror frame, taped to all four walls, her face large as life in some of the photos. I felt as if I'd walked inside a house of mirrors with my sister. Her image and perfume overwhelmed me, and I reached for a desk chair to sit down.

Turning slowly in the chair, I studied the photos one by one. Many I had never seen before and must have been taken at camp. Since Paul didn't occupy this room during the college year, he had brought them back with him. Why did he surround himself with these pictures? Perhaps for the same reason that Brian believed he played the pranks: to keep Liza "alive." But was it obsessive love which made him try to keep her alive, or the need to deny that something terrible had occurred? My eyes scanned the surface of the battered desk, then stopped. I picked up two pens and scribbled with them on my palm, leaving bright green and pink marks. Guys didn't usually write with those colors, but Liza had loved to. I opened the desk drawer and spotted a pink address book. I checked the entries, but I already knew it was Liza's. Then I saw her turquoise hair clip. It was as if my sister were living here!

I pushed back from the desk and walked around the room. The bookshelves had photos of Liza, but nothing else belonging to her. I stopped at the bureau: Liza's necklace with the opal pendant, the little bit of stone fire she defiantly kept as her good luck charm. I held it gently, then closed my hand around it.

I wanted it back, and I wanted her hair clip, her address book, her pens, even the photos that had not been ours. I hated the thought of Paul's eyes roving over the image of her face, his narrow fingers touching her belongings, but I had to leave everything where I found it.

I set down the necklace and noticed the shimmer of an object half hidden by a computer game magazine with a lurid red cover. Lifting the magazine, I found my sister's bracelet, the wide silver bangle I had given her for her sixteenth birthday. I picked it up and slid it over my hand.

The moment the silver touched my wrist I felt its icy sting. Cold traveled up my arm and fear rippled through me, wrapping my heart in a chilling web. Paul's room slipped into shadow, then darkness, its edges glimmering blue. I could smell the creek.

Not again! I thought. *Please, don't make me go through it again!*

I yanked the bracelet over my knuckles and heard it land on the bureau. The blue glint disappeared and the darkness of my vision frayed until the sunlit room shone through again. But fear still made my heart beat fast; Liza's fear throbbed inside me.

I held my head with my hands, trying to sort out what was happening. Most of my sister's belongings, such as her pens and hair clip, did not affect me when I touched them. It was as if the emotion coursing through her the night she died had imprinted certain things she touched—the window she had climbed through to meet Mike, the bank beneath the bridge, a piling beneath the pavilion—enough so that when I touched them they could engender my visions. Liza's extreme fear and pain the moment she was murdered had charged the hammer even more. Feeling the same sensation when I touched the bracelet, I wondered if she had been wearing it when she died.

I looked quickly inside Paul's bureau and closet and probably should have searched further, but I had seen all I could endure for the moment. After placing the magazine so that it partially covered the bracelet—I didn't dare touch the bangle again—I checked that everything else was as I had found it, then left and locked the door. Heading toward the stairway, I noticed Mike's name on the door across the hall.

I didn't try to rationalize my snooping, but simply unlocked the door and let myself in. Mike was neater than Paul, though his concept of order appeared to be leaving everything out and stacking his belongings in thematic piles. Clothes, books, CDs, tennis balls, sunscreen and shaving lotion—all of it in organized piles—covered the tops of his desk, bureau, and chair.

Glancing down at a stack of books, I noticed a satiny edge of paper protruding from the pages of one. A photograph. Curious, I pulled it out.

It caught me completely by surprise. Liza and I, our arms around each other's shoulders, wearing T-shirts made in honor of our father, laughed into the camera's eye. It was a favorite photo of my sister's because, as she used to say, "We look just like us!"

Mike knew who I was. He had known from the start. But if he knew my identity, why had he lied to me about his and Liza's relationship? Did he fear I would pepper him with questions until he revealed something he didn't want me to know?

I slipped the photo back in the book. I had seen what Brian wanted me to see, and then some, but the more I knew, the less I understood.

Walker ended rehearsal early that day, reminding us that it was Movie Night. Kids left the theater quickly, and Walker followed Maggie down to the offices. Both had been edgy that afternoon; according to Shawna, they had argued fiercely while I was gone on my errand. Brian followed them downstairs, hoping, he said, to get them to cool it.

I had already returned the master key to him, choosing a time when there were too many people around for us to confer. I didn't want to discuss what I had discovered.

Tomas and I were about to leave the set when Arthur and another guy from maintenance arrived, carrying the extension ladder that Tomas had been calling about all day. The two men made a hasty exit, perhaps afraid of being asked to do something else. After several clumsy efforts Tomas and I managed to rest the ladder against the catwalk thirty feet up.

"Shall I give it a try?" I asked.

Tomas shook his head. "I'd rather have a couple people here holding it."

"Don't worry. I'm not going far."

Tomas held the ladder and I started up the aluminum rungs. On the sixth one I stopped. I didn't like the give of the ladder, the way it vibrated in my hands and the metallic noise it made.

"Everything okay?" Tomas asked, pulling his head back to look at me.

"You're going to have to find someone else for the job," I said, climbing back down.

"I've already got them lined up."

"Shall we store this on its side?" I asked.

"No." He gestured toward a table full of tools and the bolt of blue fabric. "I'd like to get the sky hung right away tomorrow."

"Walker might get irritable if he starts the day with a ladder in the middle of his stage."

"If he does, I'll say I'm sorry," Tomas replied.

"I see. Better to say you're sorry later, than ask for permission before?"

He smiled. "Sometimes, with some people, yes."

"Tomas, you continually surprise me."

We gathered our belongings and walked back to the dorms together, passing Mike, who was carrying a tennis racket and a can of balls. He said hello, more to Tomas than me, and continued on. After Tomas and I parted, I headed in the direction Mike had taken, figuring there were courts somewhere beyond the Stoddard parking area and athletic fields.

I found him playing alone, hitting a tennis ball against a wall in a practice court, driving it hard. *Thump! Thump!* A day's worth of heat radiated from the pavement, and the humidity wrung every last degree from the lowering sun. Mike's shirt was soaked through and his forearms shone with sweat, still he played on as if some demon were goading him. Sometimes he slammed the ball hard, too hard to get the rebound—that seemed to give him the most satisfaction.

He didn't notice when I sat on a bench outside the court's wire fence. I brushed the gnats away from my face and waited. At last he stopped to drink from a water bottle.

"May I talk to you?"

He spun around, surprised, then glanced about to see if anyone else was there. "All right," he said, but he stayed where he was, midcourt on the other side of the tall wire fence. "About what?"

"My sister."

He didn't move.

"My sister Liza."

He wiped his face on his shirt and walked toward me, but only as far as the fence, keeping it between us.

"When did you know who I was?" I asked.

"As soon as I saw you."

"Why didn't you say something?"

"Why didn't you?"

"I have reasons," I replied.

"So do I."

I kicked at the grass, frustrated. He turned the face of his racket horizontal and bounced the ball against the court.

"Why did Liza give you the picture of her and me?"

"I guess she told you I liked it," he said, continuing to dribble the ball. Then his hand swooped down and snatched it. "No, she couldn't have, or you would have realized that I recognized you. How do you know about the photo?"

"I saw it in your room this afternoon."

"In my room?" His eyes narrowed, turning the color of blue slate. "What were you doing there?"

"Snooping."

He looked at me, amazed. "I can't believe it," he said. "I can't believe you'd do something like that."

"At least I'm honest in admitting it. You lied to me about Liza."

He turned his back on me and drove the ball hard against the wall. "You lied the day you introduced yourself as Jenny Baird."

"If you knew who I was, why did you lie to me about her?" I persisted.

He faced me again, frowning.

"Why didn't you admit you were dating, in love, whatever?"

"Whatever," he echoed.

"You had to realize she'd tell me about the two of you. Sisters share almost everything."

"I don't know what Liza told you, but we were just friends."

I shook my head and turned to walk away.

"Jenny, listen. I may have . . . misled Liza," he said haltingly.

I glanced back.

"When we first got to camp we became friends almost

instantly. We spent a lot of time together and told each other stuff about our families. We had a lot in common—I mean, our dream of being actors and all. I realized too late that Liza was misinterpreting things, that she thought I was interested in her romantically when really I was—" He broke off.

I stepped toward the fence and finished his statement: "Interested in my father, interested in his connections. Maybe he could get you a scholarship, like Walker did," I said and started to laugh, though I didn't think the situation funny. "You know, I've been used by guys who wanted to date my sister. I've been used by theater groupies who wanted access to Dad, but I didn't think something like that would ever happen to Liza."

Mike said nothing.

"Do you have any idea how much it hurts to be used that way—how much it makes you feel like a nothing?"

"I tried to let her down easy. I tried to back out, but she wouldn't let go."

"Did you kiss her?" I blurted.

He looked at me curiously. "Does it make any difference to you?"

"No, of course not." Talking about lying, I thought, I had just told a big one.

Mike was silent for a moment. "Well, as you know, accidents happen."

I stared at him angrily. "Next time, kiss up to my father, not me and my sister."

He took a step back.

"Why did you send Liza the note asking her to meet you by the river?"

"I didn't."

"You know what note I mean," I went on.

"The one Keri claims she saw, asking Liza to meet me at the gazebo. If there was one, I didn't send it. And, besides, Liza was killed under the bridge."

"Under the pavilion," I corrected him.

His forehead creased. "They found her under the bridge."

"She was murdered under the pavilion."

"How do you know that?" he asked.

"I"—I was reluctant to tell him about the visions—"I sense it."

He moved closer. "Sense it how?"

I was tired of lying. "I have dreams about it, visions."

"Like the dreams you had when you were a little girl? The blue dreams?"

I blinked. "How do you know about them?"

"Liza told me. She said that sometimes you would dream the same thing as she. She thought you had a special connection to her, that you were telepathic."

I grasped the fence, twisting my fingers around the wire.

"She talked to me about you all the time," Mike said. "She really missed you. I was so sure you'd come to see her."

"Well, I have—finally." I fought back the tears.

From the other side of the fence Mike smoothed the tips of my fingers with his. "Why did you come? Why now?"

I pulled my hand free of the fence. I didn't want to get into that with him. "Does Paul know who I am? Does Keri or Walker? Did you tell them?"

"I haven't told anyone," he said. "Have you?"

"Just Brian. Who is playing the pranks?"

"Until yesterday, I suspected Brian—Brian with some help from Arthur," he added. "Both would enjoy messing up Walker's rehearsals."

"Brian says it's Paul."

"That's possible. The ring that Liza wore for last year's production, the one that rolled across the floor yesterday, was taken by Keri. Kids thought it was misplaced, but she took it last year and gave it to Paul."

"I don't understand. Why would Keri give Paul something connected to Liza when she was so jealous of her?"

He shrugged. "Maybe Keri hoped Paul would be grateful to her, that he would be grateful and notice her."

"That doesn't make sense."

Mike smiled. "I guess you've never been in love with someone who's in love with someone else. You find yourself saying and doing stupid things just to get that person to look at you."

I looked away. "Does Paul know much about sound equipment?"

"He's pretty good with that stuff when he puts his mind to it. Why?"

"The first day of camp, when you were in the theater, up in the balcony, did you hear voices, voices that sounded like Liza's?"

"All I heard was you saying Liza's lines."

"Before that."

"I came in right then," he said.

At least he kept his story consistent.

"Well, I heard voices. The sound, like Liza's perfume and the sudden appearance of her ring, was haunting, but I believe it was simply a recording of Liza's voice overlapping itself."

"So these pranks are directed at you?"

I shook my head. "I don't think so. I'm beginning to think I stumbled into a private rehearsal. It would have been a good time for the person behind the pranks to practice, since everyone was supposed to be busy with check-in at the dorms. If I did barge into a rehearsal, then these hauntings were planned before camp began, before anyone had a chance to recognize me. And I'm sure no one thought I'd be coming."

"I didn't think I would come this year," Mike said. "But

then I found that I had to in order to go on. Is it like that for you? Is that why you came?"

He kept wanting an answer to that question. "It was at first."

"And now?"

"Liza wants me to find her murderer."

His eyes widened.

"She told me, sort of," I added lamely.

"But the serial killer could be anywhere."

"I believe she was killed by someone who knew her, then doctored the crime to make it look like part of the series."

He was silent for a long moment, spinning the tennis racket in his hand. "That's why you were searching my room. You think I'm involved."

"I think more than one person is involved and that more than one person knows something."

"I can't believe you'd think that I—"

"I have to. I can't trust anyone."

"Including Brian?" he prodded.

"Until I know more, everyone is a suspect, everyone but Liza and me."

Seventeen

I LEFT MIKE beating balls against the wall and returned to Drama House. The common room was air-conditioned, but after washing my face, I chose the quiet and drowsy warmth of my own room.

I set my alarm, hoping to nap, but I couldn't fall asleep. My mind was restless, full of questions and suspicions, flicking from one theory to the next, as if I were clicking through a website. *Uncle Louie,* I remembered suddenly, and opened my laptop to check my e-mail.

His reply to my letter came up on the screen. It was typical Uncle Louie.

Greetings, my most beautiful goddaughter!

What a pleasure to hear from you—even if it was not to invite me to the camp performance. I could make all kinds of pleasant chitchat here, but as I know that you are a young lady who keeps to a schedule, let me hasten to the question at hand, the history of Walker Burke.

I cannot be entirely negative toward Walker; after all, he did give Broadway the finest star we have today, inviting your father to America. Walker offered your father his first role in New York, and it was quite a nice showcase for his talents. He found him his second job as well.

The problem with Walker was that even as the years went by and your father's skills far exceeded any opportunities Walker had given him, he felt your father owed him. Perhaps your father felt so, too, for he agreed to star in a new play, a script and production about which I had many doubts. To begin with, the producer was in love with the writer—you know how romance clouds the vision—and he was desperate to please her. Meanwhile, Walker was desperate to establish himself as a Broadway director. He even put in some money of his own—not much by theater standards, but probably his life savings, given his status at that point.

I believe your father knew the play was a dud well before previews. Opening night reviews ran from mediocre to bad.

Nevertheless, Lee performed for another two weeks, and because of his name, they brought in a full house each night. Walker, the writer, and the producer were quite pleased with the production; not so your father, who dropped out the third week. The play sank faster than the Titanic.

Walker, having lost his money and his reputation, was furious and blamed everything on your father. Eventually he left New York and, apparently, beached in Maryland. Too bad he can't let go of the past; old grudges and bitterness always hurt the individual more than the one whom he believes injured him.

So ends today's lesson. (What a dutiful godfather I am, not only answering your question but imparting that last bit of wisdom!) I hope you are finding the camp enjoyable, and I know you are finding it challenging. I am inexpressibly proud of you for taking this on, knowing your reluctance in the past.

Do let this old man know when the performance will be.

Love,
Uncle Louie

I leaned back against the slats of my desk chair, thinking about Walker, realizing that he had plenty reason to hate my father. Uncle Louie told the story from his perspective, the same perspective as my father's, but if I imagined Brian with all his ambition working to make it in L.A., or Mike with his intense love for theater struggling to make it in New York, I could easily understand how Walker had felt. His big chance had come, the theater was full every night, then the whole thing came crashing down. Years of dreams and effort ended with my father's one decision.

Uncle Louie was right about a grudge hurting the one who bore it, but it didn't *always* hurt that person more—not if he acted on it, not if he suddenly got a chance to lash out at someone close to the person he begrudged—say someone as close as a child.

The Merchant of Venice was the film being shown that night. Usually, Lawrence Olivier mesmerized me, but tonight Walker held my attention. I watched him out of the corner of my eye, trying to tell if he was absorbed in the movie or simply sitting through it. At eight-thirty, with another forty-five minutes of film to go, I headed to the ladies' room and continued out the door of the Student Union. My plan was to search Walker's files and return to the darkened auditorium just before the final credits.

I wasn't sure what I was looking for, but I planned to start with student files—mine and, if he still had it, Liza's, as well as anything he kept on Paul, Keri, Mike, and Brian. One little notation made by Walker or one tiny fact from a person's application might shed light on how he or someone else could have the mind and the means to kill my sister.

The back entrance of Stoddard was open as usual. I wondered what time campus security locked the building for the night. I'd have a lot of explaining to do if an officer caught me. I walked silently down the hall toward Walker's office, turned the corner, and tried his door. It was locked.

On to Plan B, the window, I thought, and exited the building as quietly as I'd come. Since Walker's office was at the corner, its ground-level windows would be the first set facing the quadrangle. It was an exposed area, but it was nearly dark now, just a glimmer of mauve showing in the western sky, and Stoddard's outside lights were clustered at its front and back entrances. With all the campers in the Student Union, the quad was deserted.

Then I noticed light coming from a window the next office down—Maggie's. She hadn't been at the movie, and I had hoped that Walker, realizing that she was working too hard, had given her the evening off. Maybe I could tell her I'd left something in Walker's office and ask her to let me in, I thought.

But that wouldn't give me enough time to search. I turned back to Walker's window.

It was paned and half the height of a normal window, its lower sill even with the grass. Gently but firmly I pushed up against the cross braces. The window slid open. I pulled off my shoes, squeezed through, and dropped four feet down to the floor. After shutting the window I pulled the blinds and turned on a desk lamp, figuring that its light would be dimmer than the overhead and draw less attention. I set my shoes by the window so I wouldn't forget them.

There were two large file cabinets in Walker's office. I tiptoed to them and tried one, then the other, but both were locked. I remembered that during the day Walker carried a ring of keys, but used a single key attached to a small leather pouch to open his office. I figured he kept his collection of theater keys here at work and glanced around the room—files, bookcases, pots with dead plants, another bookcase, a cluttered desk. I tried the desk drawers. In the bottom one I found the ring of keys.

It occurred to me that this was how Paul and Keri had gotten into the tower. Walker was always tossing the ring down somewhere. It wouldn't be hard to slip off a key and get it duplicated at a hardware store. Gradually a person could gain access to all kinds of rooms and storage places in the theater, which would be very helpful if one were haunting it.

It didn't take long to figure out which of the slender keys on the ring fitted the locks of the file cabinets. I eased open the top drawer of one and found a set of binders—prompt books for plays Walker had directed in the past. The next drawer down had student records. I tabbed through them, but they were files for students who attended the college, not summer camp. The drawer below that had teaching materials, exams and syllabi. I knelt on the floor to look at the files in the bottom drawer.

The folders contained a curious hodgepodge of stuff, technical drawings of the stage and light equipment, old costume catalogs, old scripts, warranties for coffeepots, hair dryers, and drills, and, at the back of the cabinet, a file without a label. I opened it with one finger, just enough to glance at its contents—newspaper articles, BRIDGE KILLER STRIKES AGAIN a headline read. I plucked out the file and opened it.

The clipping on top was an account of the murder that had occurred in South Carolina, two months after the one in Florida. Filed behind it were shorter articles that had been gathered off the Internet, reports on both the first and second murder. There were a dozen articles about the third killing, the one in Virginia, which confirmed the police's fear that they had a serial murderer on their hands. In all of the articles certain details, like the smashed watches, the position of the bodies under the bridges, and the condition of the victims' clothes were highlighted in yellow, along with various theories about the kind of person who would do something like this. There was nothing about my sister's murder or the one in New Jersey; all the information Walker had wanted was gathered before she died.

I slipped the file under my arm. It proved nothing more than an unusual interest in learning the details and style of these murders; still, it was something to show the police, who were unlikely to believe a teen's visions.

I checked the files in the next cabinet and found this year's campers near the bottom. In mine there was nothing but my application form, essays, and recommendations. I hunted for Paul's, then glanced at my watch and realized that in trying to be quiet I had used up a lot of time. I wanted to get back to the movie before the lights came on. I closed the final drawer and stood up quickly, carelessly knocking over a wastebasket. In the silence of the building the roll of the metal basket sounded like crashing cymbals. I wondered whether to lie low or rush to the window. If Maggie looked out hers, she might catch me climbing out. I clicked off the lamp.

"Walker?" Maggie called. "Is that you?"

I flattened myself against the wall, not sure what could be seen through the frosted glass. I heard her footsteps approaching. "Walker?"

I figured it would be easier to explain my presence to her

than to security. But then, security was so lax around here, it might take an officer forever to get here. Better to go through the window, I thought. Then I heard keys rattling on the other side of the door and knew Maggie was about to open it. I did instead.

"Jenny!" she exclaimed. "What are you doing here?"

She looked tired, not just in her eyes but in the sag of her shoulders.

"I was looking for something."

"What?" she asked, clicking on the overhead light, eyeing the folder tucked under my arm.

I opened the file for her. "I found this in Walker's cabinet. Look—these are articles about the serial killings, the first three, not the one that happened last year. Why would he have something like this?"

She took the folder from me and paged slowly through the articles. "Probably because he wants to try dinner theater next spring, to stage one of those popular murder mysteries that involve the audience. Walker always does research, collecting details from nonfiction accounts of whatever subject or historical period is being dealt with in a play."

I bit my lip. I wasn't convinced.

"Now, Jenny, I have a question for you. Why are you sneaking around in here?"

"I've got a good reason," I said, then paused, trying to decide how much to tell her and where to begin.

"I'm waiting."

"It's complicated."

She glanced at her watch, then handed me the folder. "Put this back where you found it and come to my office. We'll walk over to the Student Union, and you can explain on the way."

I returned the folder to the cabinet, picked up the trash can, and slipped on my shoes. When I rejoined Maggie, I found her standing next to a bookcase, leaning on it, her head in her hands.

"Maggie, are you all right?"

Her head lifted quickly. "Yes, fine."

"You don't look fine," I observed.

She walked over to her desk and sat down wearily. "I'm just hungry. I haven't eaten all day. And I'm a bit down," she admitted.

"You work too many hours," I said. "You need more time for yourself. You can't always be worrying about drama camp."

"My work is my relief," she replied. "If that was all I had to deal with, my life would be wonderful."

"What do you mean?"

She fidgeted with her scarf. "I've discovered that Brian is lying to me."

"About what?" I asked.

"It's a serious matter, not one I can discuss with you."

Was this about the pranks, I wondered, or was there something more going on?

Maggie leaned forward on her desk, resting her face on her hands. She looked gray.

"Is there anything I can do for you?"

"No. Why don't you run ahead. We'll talk later."

"I'll get you something to eat," I offered. "They're serving sandwiches after the movie. I'll get one and be right back."

She glanced up at me, rubbing her mouth against her knuckle.

"Just rest here, okay? I'll be back," I told her, hurrying out of her office before she could protest. When I reached the Student Union, the movie had ended and kids were picking up sandwiches. Brian was talking to Walker, both of them laughing over something Brian had said.

I knew that Maggie was a worrier and, at the moment, exhausted. When people are tired, problems and fears become exaggerated. But what if Brian *wasn't* trustworthy? What if he leaked my identity and my purpose for being here? I remembered his description of the way people worked: in the end, everyone is out for himself, he had said, and sometimes that makes people seem for you, and sometimes it makes them seem against you.

"Where did you go, Jenny?"

I jumped and Tomas looked at me curiously. "Didn't mean to scare you," he said. He had two large sandwiches on his plate.

"I was at Stoddard talking to Maggie. She's pretty upset, Tomas, and hasn't eaten all day. May I have one of your sandwiches to take back to her?"

"Sure. Want me to come with you?"

"No."

He handed me the paper plate with the untouched sandwich. "People keep disappearing," he said. "You, Mike, Paul."

I glanced around. "Did Mike and Paul come back?"

"Haven't seen them. I can't figure out why Walker isn't saying anything about it."

Perhaps, I thought, *because the two of them were doing something for him.*

"Maybe because he leaves that kind of stuff to Maggie," I said aloud. "She's waiting for me back at her office. Catch up with you later, okay?"

Tomas looked puzzled. "Okay."

I hurried back to the theater and let myself in the back door. When I reached Maggie's office, both her door and Walker's were closed, but her light was still on.

"Just me," I said, tapping lightly on the glass.

She didn't respond to my voice or to a harder knock, so I

opened the door. She was gone. I walked over to her desk to set down her food and saw a note lying on the seat of her chair. I picked it up to read.

I'm sorry, Brian. I can't go on.
I can't try anymore.
My will is with the lawyer.
Everything should be in order.

I stared at the short sentences, their meaning sinking in slowly. It was a suicide note.

"Maggie?" I called. "Maggie!"

I rushed out of her office, then stopped, not knowing which way to turn. There were too many rooms in this place for me to check them all quickly. And she might not even be in the building. *Get Brian,* I thought. *No, call security to get people to search the building and send the police to her house.*

I turned back to make the calls, then spotted her scarf on the floor, halfway down the hall. I noticed the door at the far end was open. The tower door! I ran toward it, hoping I wouldn't be too late.

Eighteen

"Maggie!" I shouted from the bottom of the iron stairs. "Maggie, I have to talk to you!"

I thought I heard movement far above me and hurried up the steps. "Maggie, listen to me. Things will get better. I'll help you. I'll find someone who knows how to help you."

I climbed as fast as I could, turning every five steps to rush up the next five, panicking that I wouldn't get there in time. I was out of breath from calling to her. It seemed as if I'd climbed a hundred stories. Just four, I told myself, the four stories of Stoddard. Then the walls began to narrow. I figured I was entering the top of the brick portion of the tower, the area with the shingled roof that was surmounted by the clock.

The stairs became a spiral here, worming their way up through the shrinking space, then on through an area with narrow platforms and square casements containing the clockworks, one facing each direction. The triangular steps were difficult to climb, so narrow on the inside, my feet slipped off. The spiral became a simple ladder to a trapdoor. It was dark, but I felt a splash of night air coming from above. I climbed through the open door and found myself in a space like a covered porch, enclosed by three-foot walls with a pillar at each corner and a roof.

Maggie was sitting sideways inside one of the four bays, her feet drawn up on the sill, her arms wrapped tightly around her knees. Her body shook. I was sure she heard me, but she kept her head turned away from me. If she rolled to the right, she would fall six stories.

"Maggie," I said softly, "I saw your note."

She turned her head jerkily. In the darkness the pupils of her eyes were large. Her mouth trembled.

The tower was no more than five feet across, but I was afraid to move toward her too quickly. If I reached for her suddenly, she might panic and fall.

"I can help you."

"You?" The laughter that spilled from her jangled out of tune.

"I'll find someone to help. Let's go down now."

"No one can help me," she said, her voice pitching high. "I can never get back what I've lost!"

"You mean Brian? You mean your trust in him?"

She laughed again, and this time it was my nerves that jangled. Something was terribly wrong.

"Tell me what's going on," I persisted. "Tell me and maybe I can figure a way—"

"There is no way out for you."

I replayed her disquieting words in my head, confused.

She lowered her feet to the floor and took two steps toward me, extending her arms, reaching to touch my hair. "Such a pretty girl," she said. "And a nice girl, not like your sister."

"Brian told you who I am."

"Such a shame."

She toyed with my hair, making me increasingly nervous. When she touched my cheek, I flinched.

"You shouldn't have come here, Jenny. Liza is gone. What were you looking for?"

"Peace."

Maggie stroked my face with a thumb that felt like cold sandpaper. "Don't you know, there is no peace for those who have lost someone too soon. I still hear Melanie calling me. In the middle of the night I awaken and hear her. *Don't forget me, Mommy. Don't forget,* she says, just as she did when I'd work long hours away from home. In the middle of the night I feel her soft breath on my cheek. Sometimes she tells me what to do."

"What to do—like what?" I asked warily. Maggie was acting strange but not necessarily suicidal. I wondered if she had written the note to lure me up here.

She tilted her head and gazed at me solemnly. "It shouldn't surprise anyone, Jenny, that you became upset at camp. You kept hearing about Liza. You were having dreams about her. And someone was playing pranks, haunting the theater like the ghost of Liza. No wonder you became confused and depressed."

"I am not depressed."

"How unfortunate your parents chose this time to leave you alone." Her voice had shifted from high pitch to low and smooth as syrup. "I'll write a note explaining—in your handwriting, just like that on your application. I'll explain why you had to kill yourself."

I took a step back from her. The strange, sympathetic look on Maggie's face chilled me to the bone. I glanced at the stone sill, then beyond it. Below me the tower roof sloped far too steeply to stop a fall. I began edging toward the trapdoor.

Maggie saw the movement and lunged at me, shoving me back against the wall with such force I couldn't stay on my feet. I slid onto the sill. My head snapped back, as if someone had pulled a chair out from behind me sixty feet up. I reached out wildly for something—anything I could get my hands on— the stone sill, the pillar. My feet touched cement again and I dropped down in a crouch. As long as I was lower than the sill, she couldn't push me over it. I crawled toward the trapdoor.

"Get up! Get up!" Maggie shrieked and kicked at my stomach, bringing her foot up hard into my ribs. Breathless from the blows, I scrambled through the door, dropping down so quickly my foot missed the rung. It caught two rungs down. I descended as fast as I dared. When I reached the spiral stairs, I turned so I could run down them face forward. I heard Maggie's footsteps above me.

At last I was on the regular-size treads. I raced downward. Too fast! My heel slipped over the edge of one. I went sliding down on my back, my left wrist bent behind me. I was stopped by the wall. Pain crippled my left wrist. With my right hand I quickly grasped the railing, pulled myself to my feet, and continued downward.

Reaching the hall, I rushed through it and around the corner toward the back door of the theater. I pushed hard against the double doors. They gave slightly, then stopped. I glanced down at the handle. A chain, someone had chained the doors!

I didn't know what to think. This was the entrance I had come through just a few minutes ago and now it was locked from the inside. Maggie had acted as if she alone was after me, but this door had been chained by someone else.

I heard Maggie's footsteps in the hall and hurried up the steps to the stage. The light above the staircase suddenly went off.

"Who's there?" Maggie called out.

I glanced over my shoulder. The lights in the hall below had also gone off. The uncertainty in Maggie's voice told me she hadn't been the one to cut the power. I tried to remember if I had seen an unmarked door downstairs. If I knew where the electrical room was, I'd have some idea where the other person was, perhaps the person who had chained the doors. But my mind was reeling with fear and the sudden darkness confused me. It must have confused Maggie, too, for I heard doors opening and closing below and soft cries of surprise.

Tiptoeing onto the back of the stage, I saw the emergency exit signs glowing and the trail of tiny floor lights leading up to them. I wanted to make a run for it. But what if the lobby's outer doors had been chained, too? And what if the lights came back on? I'd be cornered with no place to hide.

I tried to recall what scenery and props were in the wings, to think of something that might conceal me. I remembered the extension ladder. I could climb to the catwalk, then kick aside the ladder. I doubted Maggie would be able to get up the wall rungs, and, as far as I knew, she had no weapon.

I thought we had placed the ladder close to the center of the catwalk. Using the exit signs to center myself, I moved slowly downstage, putting both hands out in front of me. I touched the ladder. Placing my foot lightly on the first rung, I reached with my left hand to pull myself up and gasped with pain. I had been too panicked to notice how badly my wrist was hurt. It was useless to me. I took a deep breath and quietly began to climb the ladder using only my right hand.

I heard Maggie at the bottom of the stairs to the stage. I continued on in slow motion. I heard her at the top of the steps, flicking switches. No lights came on. I continued to climb stealthily.

"Stay where you are," Maggie said loudly, as if she were directing campers.

Objects were knocked over. It sounded as if she was looking for something. There was a long moment of silence and I was afraid to move, afraid that just a shift of weight on the metal ladder would give me away. I figured I was little more than halfway up the thirty-foot climb.

A bright light came on. She had found a flashlight.

The light swung slowly over the stage, the beam wavering as if her hand was shaking, touching the ladder, passing below me. Maggie walked toward the apron of the stage. I watched the play of the beam along the rows of seats. It became steadier, then the light spun around and streaked up the ladder, stopping at me.

I scrambled up two rungs.

"Stop!" she commanded, shining the light in my eyes.

I felt as I did under the glare of stage lights. My stomach grew queasy. I began to sweat. I pulled myself up a rung, but my legs felt unsteady.

"One step farther and I will knock over the ladder," Maggie threatened.

I turned my face away from the light. "Why are you doing this to me?"

Maggie circled the ladder, trying to keep the beam in my eyes.

"Please tell me why."

"You still don't remember?" Her voice quivered. "You must! Every day of my life I wake up remembering the fire."

"The one Melanie was in?"

"You were only three when it occurred," she said, "the same age as Melanie, and your parents were careful not to talk about it. But the memory is with you. You're standing in the third-floor window with Liza. The lights of fire trucks and emergency vehicles are shining up at you. A crowd has gathered below."

As she spoke, a wave of sickness washed over me. I gritted my teeth and took a step up. My hands were slippery with sweat.

"Every time you stand on a stage with lights shining up at you, darkened faces in the audience watching you, the memory and the fear come back."

I climbed another rung. My heart pounded in my ears.

I could feel the heat at my back. I saw strange faces three stories below me, people looking up from a dark New York street. There were lights in my eyes, a dizzying pattern of red, yellow, and blue lights on the street below.

"Jenny, come on! Jenny, please!" Liza begged. She reached for my hand, then grasped my fingers. The metal ladder that had inched toward us finally rested against the windowsill, but I didn't want to get on it. It clanked and moved with each step of the firefighter climbing toward us. "Don't be afraid. I'll help you."

"It's coming back, isn't it?" Maggie observed, her voice breaking through the memory.

There was no blue gleam in these images and no blue gleam in those I had seen at Maggie's house. I should have noticed that before. When I'd gazed at Melanie's picture, I had seen the fragments of buried memory, not the images of a psychic vision.

"Brian recognized you the first day of camp from a photo Liza had shown him," Maggie went on, "but he didn't tell me until this morning. He pretended interest in you so he could find out why you were here. It was stupid of him. *I* know why, and you, remembering as you must now, will understand why I had to kill Liza."

"I will never understand!"

"You will!" she shouted back. "And you'll remember every horrible detail and suffer as I have every day since the fire.

"We were neighbors in New York, all of us working long hours, raising small children. Your parents let Brian and Melanie stay with you, even when they hired a sitter. My husband was glad—it saved money—but I should have known better. Liza was a wild child. One February night, when I had Brian with me and had left Melanie with your baby-sitter, Liza played with matches."

I sagged against the ladder, guessing what came next.

"Liza set the fire. Liza killed Melanie!"

Now I understood what my sister had been referring to in her final e-mail, the terrible thing she had done but didn't mean to. "And when Liza saw you and Brian, she remembered it," I said.

"She remembered the fire, but she didn't recognize Brian or me. In New York she knew me as Mrs. Jones. When I divorced, I took back my maiden name. The name Brian Jones is common enough, and Brian is a man now, not a five-year-old boy. I didn't tell her who we were until the day before she died.

"For the first three weeks of camp I quietly watched her shine, dark-haired, blue-eyed, and pretty as my daughter would have been, a bright future ahead of her, the future my daughter should have had." Maggie's voice grew breathless. "Liza talked endlessly about her experiences—experiences that should have been Melanie's—about all her successes—successes my child deserved!"

Maggie turned suddenly. The beam of her flashlight dodged around the stage. "What's that? Who's there?"

"I didn't hear anything."

I figured that someone else was in the building, but if it was someone who wanted to hurt me, I was no worse off. And if it was someone who would help, then better to pretend I'd heard nothing. Maggie wasn't thinking clearly enough to question the cut in electric power; perhaps she thought I had done it.

The beam of her flashlight paused at a table of tools. Maggie walked over to it, and I took two more steps up.

"At the end of the third week someone set a fire in Drama House," Maggie continued as she fingered the sharp tools. "Liza could brag about her experience with fire, too—how she and her sister had escaped with their baby-sitter through a third-floor window, but a playmate had hidden in a closet and died."

Maggie's face looked distorted, her jaw and the deep sockets of her eyes illuminated by the light she held over the table.

"How your parents showed you the fire exits at every theater and every place you stayed, how they taught you what to do. Like I was a bad parent!"

The beam of her flashlight bobbed and glittered off the knives on the table.

"Like it was my fault that Melanie died!"

She picked up a wood chisel, a four-inch point with a sturdy handle. I glanced upward. There were six more rungs to the catwalk, but just one more would allow me to reach up and grasp it.

"Your parents told Liza it was Melanie's fault for hiding when the baby-sitter called her." Maggie's voice kept rising. "They should have told Liza how wicked she was, how she killed someone, how she murdered my daughter!"

"Liza was only four years old," I protested. "She didn't understand the consequences."

"Liza took from me my greatest treasure!" Maggie cried out, then lowered her voice. "Last summer I took back. I wrote the note she thought Mike had sent. I knew Liza would slip out, even wait for him till I could be sure she and I were alone. Finally I had justice. Your parents and I were even, each left with one child. Then you came." She took a deep breath. "I liked you, Jenny. I felt . . . motherly toward you, when I didn't know who you were."

"We can work things out, Maggie," I said. "We can get help for you and me, for our families—"

"Don't you listen?" she exploded. "No one can help me!

No one can end for me that night I watched you being helped down the ladder, watched you and Liza and the baby-sitter. I waited on the street, clutching Brian's little hand." Maggie's voice grew hysterical. "I watched and I waited for Melanie. I'm waiting still!"

The abrupt shift of the flashlight warned me. I pulled myself up one more rung, then felt the impact of her rushing against the ladder. I flung my hands upward, grasping the edge of the metal walk as the ladder was dragged out from beneath me. It crashed onto the stage.

"Flashlight, flashlight," Maggie called from below, like a small child calling a pet—or an adult totally unhinged. "Where are you, flashlight?"

High above her I dangled in darkness. My left hand was useless. I hung by my right. She found the light and shined it up at me. I pulled back my head to study the structure of the catwalk, a suspended strip of metal lace. My shadow flickered over it like a black moth.

"It's almost over, Jenny," Maggie said, her voice growing eerily soft. "Sooner or later, you will let go. Everyone lets go, except me."

There was a ridge along the catwalk's edge, the thin piece of metal my fingers grasped, then a large gap between that and a restraining bar. I knew I had to swing my legs onto the narrow walkway, but my right hand was slick with sweat. If I swung my body hard, my hand would slip off. I hung from one arm, looking down at Maggie.

"Sooner or later."

"Maggie, I'm begging you—"

I stopped midsentence. I had felt the catwalk vibrate. I grasped the metal harder, but my grip kept slipping. My hand rotated, my palm sliding past the thin ridge.

"Hold on, Jenny!"

Mike's voice. He must have climbed the wall rungs. His footsteps shook the catwalk.

The base of my fingers suddenly slid past the edge. I tried to tighten my grip, but felt the rim of the catwalk moving toward the tips of my fingers. I was hanging by the tips—I couldn't hold on. "Mike!"

A hand swooped down.

The theater went black.

I've fallen, I thought; *I've blacked out.* But Mike's fingers were wrapped tightly around my wrist. Maggie had turned off the flashlight.

"Other hand! Give me your other hand, Jenny!"

"Where are you? I can't see."

"Here. Right above you."

"I can't grip with this hand. I hurt it."

"Hurt it where?"

"My wrist."

Mike's fingers groped for mine, then moved quickly and lightly past my injured wrist and halfway down my forearm. Now he gripped hard.

"I'm lying on my stomach," he said, "and have my feet hooked around the walk. I'm going to pull you up."

He tried, but it was impossible from that angle.

"I can swing my body, swing my feet," I told him, "if you hold on tight. Don't let go."

He grasped my arms so fiercely I knew I'd have bruises. I swung my legs and hips as if I were on a high bar, till I caught hold of the walk with my feet. With Mike's help I clambered up the rest of the way.

He pulled me close and wrapped his arms tightly around me. I couldn't stop shaking.

"You're okay, Jen. I've got you."

I clung to him, burrowing my head into his chest. He reached with one hand to touch my face, then quickly put his arm around me again, as if he had sensed my panic when he let go. Instead of his hand, he used his cheek to smooth mine.

"I'm not going to let anything happen to you."

"Where is she?" I whispered. "Where's Maggie?"

"Don't know," he answered quietly. "Stay still. Listen."

There was a long minute of silence, then a sudden banging noise.

"The door," I said. "She's at the door at the bottom of the steps. She can't get out that way. It's chained."

"Chained?"

"From the inside," I told him, "How did you get in?"

"I tried the doors, everything was locked, so I came through Walker's window."

"Did you cut the power?" I asked.

"No."

"Then someone else is in the building."

He was silent for a moment. "Brian?"

"I don't know."

"Stay here," Mike instructed and carefully disentangled himself from me. "I'll see what's up."

When he stood, I grabbed his ankle. "Oh, no, you don't. Not without me."

"It's safer here."

"It's safer two against one," I argued.

"It could be two against two."

"All the more reason." I reached for his hand, pulled myself up, then grasped the restraining bar.

We climbed down the wall rungs, then tiptoed to the steps and paused to listen.

"I want you to stay behind me," Mike whispered.

"No way."

"Don't be heroic, Jenny. We just want to get out."

"Heroic? I'm faster and don't want to get stuck behind you."

He swallowed a laugh, then pulled me back against him. "If we get out of here alive, you've got a date for a race."

I wondered if he thought I was as brave as I pretended. "Did you leave Walker's door open?"

"That's what we're shooting for."

When we reached the bottom of the steps, we crept side by side down the hall. My ears strained to pick up movement. We had to be close to the turn, I thought, close to Walker's office. I prayed no one had shut and locked the door. Finally my hands touched the corner of the hall.

"Almost there," I whispered.

Just as we reached the office door, something fell, something in Maggie's office.

Mike pushed me from behind. "Go, Jen! Go!"

I rushed through Walker's office toward the open window. Mike shoved me through and I pulled him out after me. We sprang to our feet, ready to run, then heard commotion inside the building. Maggie screamed. The blinds in her window were flattened against the glass, as if something had crashed against them. Mike and I waited, holding on to each other, shivering.

After a long moment the shades swung inward ominously, the weight no longer pressing on them. They were pulled up and Arthur peered out. He opened the window, his face shining in the pale light, a dark streak on his cheek.

"I'm all finished," he announced.

Mike's arms tightened around me.

"All done. There's no reason to be afraid."

Mike walked backward, away from the building, pulling me with him.

"I won't hurt you. It was her I had to kill," Arthur said. "She took what was mine. She killed the girl and pretended to be me. You understand, don't you? The watch and the bridge, they were mine. It's not right to take a man's identity. I had to kill her to get myself back."

He rubbed his cheek as he spoke, then studied the blood that had come off on his fingers, sniffing it, rubbing one finger against another. I thought I was going to throw up.

Gazing at us again, Arthur appeared relaxed, almost cheerful, as if a huge burden had been lifted from his shoulders. "You run along and call the police," he said. "I'll turn the electricity back on."

Nineteen

THE CAMPUS SECURITY office was small and smelled of Chinese carryout. I sat on a bench between Mike and Tomas, my wrist packed in ice. Walker stood by a window with a noisy air conditioner, his arms folded over his chest, his eyes puffy and bloodshot. Paul crouched in the corner of the paneled office, leaning against the wall, like a person folded up on himself.

According to Tomas, Mike had returned to the Student Union not long after I left with the sandwich for Maggie. He asked Tomas where I was, then raced off to the theater. When time elapsed and he didn't return, Tomas told Walker he was worried. On their way to Stoddard, they met up with Paul. The three of them found us outside Maggie's window, just after Arthur told us to call the police.

While Walker called on his cell phone, Paul climbed through the window to talk to Arthur, whom he had befriended. Paul had suspected from the beginning that Liza's murderer was someone who knew her and had sought the custodian's help in drawing out the killer by haunting the theater. He'd never guessed that as much as Arthur was helping him, he was helping Arthur find the person who had "taken" Arthur's identity. The haunting had succeeded in unnerving Maggie, precipitating her arguments with Brian, arguments that revealed to the eavesdropping Arthur that Maggie was the murderer.

Paul confirmed for us that Maggie was dead. Maybe he wasn't into violence as much as he wanted everyone to think: it was he who threw up, not me.

The police did not allow anyone else to enter the building. But they wanted to interview all of us, which was why we were gathered at the security office. Arthur was being held separately for the FBI. He had cut the power and chained the doors, planning to kill Maggie that night, realizing too late that I had returned to the building. He explained carefully to the police and us that while he had "killed" Maggie, he had "murdered" only four people. In his deranged mind, Maggie's death was a form of justice, a way of erasing Liza's death from his list. Since Maggie's death "didn't count," he didn't need to kill her beneath a bridge.

The police were still seeking Brian. When security went to fetch him at the Student Union, he wasn't there. I kept telling myself that Brian didn't realize his mother had killed Liza till it was too late. If he had, he would never have told her who I was; he wouldn't have betrayed me like that.

But in my heart I knew otherwise. He had probed to find out what I remembered of the fire because he knew that the fire was his mother's motive for murder; he was trying to discover if I had pieced together the puzzle.

The door to the office opened and Brian walked in with a police officer. All of us looked up. None of us knew what to say.

Brian glanced around. "This is a happy-looking group."

"Where were you?" Walker asked. "I left you with our students. You were supposed to be in charge."

"I was in charge," Brian replied lightly, "until I went home. I had a few things to take care of."

He slipped his hands in his pockets and casually rested one shoulder against the wall, looking as relaxed as a guy waiting for his pizza order. It was as if none of this horrid situation shocked him. I wanted to tell him how sorry I was about his mother, but his coolness quelled my sympathy.

Mike spoke up suddenly: "What did you do with the boat?"

"What boat?" Brian replied.

"The rowboat your mother signed out the day Liza was killed."

"I don't know what you're talking about."

"I think you do," Mike countered. "When Jenny told me Liza had been murdered beneath the pavilion, I wondered how her body could have been transported to the bridge without leaving a trail of blood. Then I realized that if a boat was floated in the shallow water close to the pavilion, a body could be carried out to it, even dragged. The blood left behind would be washed out by the tide. The boat, of course, would be stained."

A small smile curled the corners of Brian's mouth.

"I remembered that just before Liza died your mother had asked me how to sign out a boat from the college. During the movie tonight I met my friend who runs the boathouse. We checked the records as well as every boat in the yard and on the docks. The boat your mother signed out had been signed in by someone, but it was missing, probably has been since that night, which leads me to ask—where did you sink it?"

Brian shrugged his shoulders and spread his hands. "I have no idea what you're talking about."

The local police officer who had escorted Brian and had been listening attentively to our conversation cocked his head.

"What about Liza's bracelet?" I asked. "You urged me to search Paul's room. Did you plant it there? You had time when you returned our lunch trays."

He smiled but said nothing.

"And the fire alarm," I added.

"I'll take credit for that," Brian said agreeably.

Our conversation was interrupted by the arrival of a state trooper.

"Here's your ride," the local officer said to Brian. "I don't know what kind of games you're playing, Mr. Jones, but I suggest you don't play too hard till you meet with a lawyer. You told police that your mother came to you after the murder, and you helped her transport the body by boat. As for the fire alarm, we know who set it off, a local juvenile, not you."

"Just having a little fun with my friends," Brian replied, smiling. Then he turned to me, his eyes alight with amusement. "You look so amazed, Jenny. I told you at the beginning, I'm a better actor than Walker thinks." He flicked a glance at Walker. "Much better. Come visit me in L.A."

A campus security guard brought me back from Easton Hospital at two a.m. with my wrist in a cast and sling. The door to Drama House was open and I let myself in. Walker emerged from the common room, greeted me, then eyed the cast.

"Broken?"

"Yup."

He took a deep breath and let it out slowly. He looked exhausted, and his eyes, which had cleared before I left campus, had become red and puffy again.

"I'm sorry, Jenny."

"I'm sorry, too. Maggie was a very good friend to you."

He nodded, pressing his lips together several times before he could speak. "Your parents are on their way home from London. They caught the early flight out and will be here around one p.m. our time. I've contacted everyone else's parents and told them I'm closing camp." He gestured toward the doorway of the common room. "Everyone is upset. I told those who didn't want to sleep in their own rooms to bring a pillow and blanket here. The kids saved a sofa for you, but sleep wherever you can get comfortable. Did the doctor give you some painkillers?"

"Yes."

He followed me into the common room and sat in a chair with three cups of coffee next to it, where I guessed he was spending the night. Mike, Tomas, and Shawna were asleep on the floor in front of an empty sofa. Paul was sleeping in the corner of the room, curled on his side, his knees drawn up. Keri lay a few feet away from him.

I carefully stepped around the various sleepers till I reached Mike, then knelt and touched his cheek. "Thank you," I said softly, though I knew he didn't hear me.

Turning toward Tomas, I smiled when I saw he was sleeping with his backpack, one of his sketchbooks on top. I took it and returned to Walker.

"I'm going to my room."

"Good girl," he replied, as if I were a child. "You'll rest better there."

"Would you let Tomas know I have one of his books?"

Walker nodded. We said good night and I went straight to my room.

Without turning on the lights, I closed the door behind me and carried the sketchpad over to the window seat. Making myself comfortable there, I opened the book and studied Tomas's newest drawings, dark silky pencil lines on moon-bright pages, sketches of the bridge, the gazebo, and the pavilion. I closed my eyes and let my mind wander. The scenes Tomas had drawn slowly evolved into real scenes, a stretch of tall grass, the concrete bridge, dark wood pilings, the wide creek. A blue gleam surrounded the images, but I felt no fear. The breeze was gentle and the creek lapped peacefully. "I know you are here," I whispered to my sister. "You'll always be with me in my heart. But sleep now, Liza. Sweet dreams now. Sweet dreams only for you and me."

Twenty

SHAWNA AWAKENED ME at noon the next day, telling me my parents had phoned from the airport near Baltimore and would soon be in Wisteria. Most of the other kids had already been picked up by nervous family members, but she had put off her departure so we could say good-bye.

Tomas stopped in after her.

"I've got your sketchpad," I told him.

"I came for a hug," he replied. "You scared me, Jenny."

Before I got a chance to see Mike, my parents arrived and asked me to go down to the creek with them. We spent an hour at the pavilion, standing on the deck, gazing out at the water. We talked about Liza, remembering, laughing, and crying some.

"Well, dearest," my father said, resting his hand on mine, "we should get back to campus. Your mother and I spoke to Walker when we arrived and asked him to join us for an early tea."

"You did?" I replied, surprised. "You met with him and it went okay?"

"Of course," my father said, "we're grown men."

My mother rolled her eyes. "It was as awkward as two old bachelors meeting at their former girlfriend's wedding. I'm the one who proposed tea, and neither your father nor Walker had the nerve to say no."

I laughed and strolled down the ramp with them. When we reached the bottom, I saw Mike standing by the tall grasses that surrounded the pavilion, a dark-haired man next to him. They turned toward us at the same time, the man closing a small black book.

"Hi, Mike. I want you to meet my parents."

My mother quickly patted her blowing curls into place, her hands making little butterfly motions.

The man introduced himself as the Reverend James Wilcox. He had Mike's blue eyes, broad shoulders, and deep voice.

"We were just praying for Liza," Reverend Wilcox said.

I was amused by the way he and my father studied each other. Both knew how to assume a commanding, theatrical presence—and they were giving it their best effort. Mike examined my cast, but we said little, letting our parents do the talking. Then my father, playing one of his favorite roles—famous actor acknowledging an apprentice—asked Mike about his interest in theater.

"I like it okay," Mike replied, "but the real reason I came to camp was to live away from home."

"What?" I exclaimed softly.

The reverend's jaw dropped. "I don't think I heard you right, Michael."

"Well, drama is fun. I'm just not as interested in it as I used to be."

"I can't believe it." The reverend blinked a couple times and his voice resonated with incredulity. "I truly cannot believe it!"

I stifled a smile. Mike's father was as pompous and melodramatic as mine.

Reverend Wilcox turned to my parents. "I have been praying for the last two years that I would accept my son's calling. There is, after all, something blessed in every gift."

"Indeed," said my father.

"I have spent the last two weeks reading Michael's college catalog and the drama books he left behind. And now, just as I near acceptance, he tells me he's not interested."

"Tragic," my father replied.

"Excuse me," I said, "I'd like to talk to Mike alone. Mom and Dad, why don't you take Reverend Wilcox to tea with you and Walker?"

Ministers ought to be good at reconciliation, I thought.

My father looked at me, puzzled. "Aren't you coming, dearest? I had so hoped—"

My mother, having better instincts than he, shook her head at him, then steered him and Mike's father toward Goose Lane.

When our parents were well out of earshot, I turned to Mike. "What was that all about?"

He ignored my question. "How are you feeling, Jenny?"

"Apparently, better than you," I said, and took a step closer.

He took a step back. "I'm fine."

"Except for your minor surgery last night—did you undergo a brain transplant?"

He smiled a little and started walking toward the docks, striding quickly, as if he couldn't stand still and look at me. "No, but I had a lot of dreams—actually the same one over and over."

I struggled to keep up with him.

"I kept searching for you in a dark theater," he said. "I'd find you, but each time I reached for you, you'd slip through my fingers."

"And after that nightmare you decided that you didn't like working in theaters anymore. I get it. Hey, slow down! And look at me, please." I grabbed the edge of his shirt. "You're making it difficult for a one-armed girl."

He stopped. "Sorry."

"Look me in the eye, Mike, and tell me you don't love theater."

He gazed at my hair instead.

"Lower," I told him.

"Your hair is like a burning bush."

"Lower," I repeated, then caught my breath when his eyes met mine.

"All right," I said. "You had no trouble looking in my eyes and saying all those romantic lines during auditions. Let's see how well you can act now. Eyeball to eyeball, tell me you don't love theater."

"I wasn't acting then."

"Mike, I know what you're afraid of. You think that I'll think you're trying to score points with—What did you say?"

"I wasn't acting, Jenny. I didn't hang around Liza hoping to meet her father, but hoping to meet her sister."

"Me?" My heart did a somersault.

"Liza kept talking about you, what you did, what you said, what you thought, how you could make her laugh. She showed me pictures of you. I kept waiting for you to come see her."

"I can't believe it!"

"I realized too late that Liza mistook my interest in you for interest in her. I felt terrible about it, but I didn't tell her the truth because I didn't want to hurt her. I tried to back out, but she wouldn't let go. In the end I think she began to figure it out. The morning she died, she gave me the picture of the two of you."

I closed my eyes and swallowed hard.

"When I learned from Keri that Liza had been lured out of the house by a note she thought I wrote, I felt responsible for her death. If I hadn't been so eager to meet you, if I hadn't hung around so much, she might not have fallen for it."

I shook my head. "You're not responsible, Mike. If it wasn't that, it would have been something else," I said. "Maggie was in so much pain, she would have figured a way to get her no matter what."

"Because of the note I thought that the murderer was someone who knew Liza," he continued. "But when the police decided it was a serial killer, I was so relieved I accepted the theory. I convinced myself that Keri had made up the story—or maybe wrote the note herself—to prove to Paul that Liza didn't like him.

"I didn't want to come back this year, but Walker kept calling me. I decided that to get past what had happened, I had to return. When I arrived I went straight to the theater, because that's where Liza was happiest. I was shocked to see a girl onstage delivering lines exactly as Liza had. I suspected it was you, and when I met you beneath the bridge, I knew for sure."

Mike and I had reached the docks and walked out on one. I followed him down a ramp and onto a floating platform.

"I couldn't understand why you had come, Jenny, or why, after all that had happened I still wanted so badly to know you. I felt wrong for feeling the way I did, and I tried to avoid you, but it was impossible. You weren't a dream girl but a real girl, and the more I got to know you the harder it was to stop thinking of you."

As he spoke he kept his distance, letting only his eyes touch me. His eyes alone were enough to make me feel unsteady on my feet.

"Mike, sometimes when I look at you it's like—" I hesitated, trying to find the words. Now I knew why people quoted plays and poems. "It feels like the ground is moving beneath me."

He laughed. "It is, Jenny. We're standing on a floating dock."

"That's not what I meant."

The words "I love you" were still too new, too scary, but somehow I had to explain to him. "I think there should be no more accidents."

He studied me a moment, his eyes turning gray. "Sure, that's okay, I understand."

"No! Wait! You don't understand. I meant that from now on every kiss of mine is purely intentional."

"Is it?"

I waited for him to take me in his arms, to sweep me off my feet, as dramatic types are supposed to do. He didn't move.

"So, uh, don't you want to kiss me?"

"You go first," he replied. "I did last time."

But I suddenly felt shy.

"If you want to kiss me, Jenny, why don't you?"

I held on to his arm with one hand, stood on my toes, and kissed him on the cheek. It was horribly awkward.

Then Mike leaned down and gently kissed the fingers of my injured hand. He kissed each bruise on my arms, the places he had gripped to keep me from falling. He drew me close to him and cupped my head with one hand, laying his cheek against mine.

"I'll never stop wanting to kiss you," he whispered, then sealed his words with tenderness.

The Deep End of Fear

To Patricia MacDonald, with thanks
for your careful reading, insight, and encouragement.

One

12 Years Earlier

I HUDDLED UNDER the blankets in the backseat of the car. Wind rocked the body of our old Ford. Sharp needles of sleet beat against the windows.

"Mommy?"

"Hush, Katie."

I raised my head, peeking out of the blankets, wondering where we were going in the middle of the night. I could see nothing, not even the headlights of our car.

"Did you fasten Katie's seat belt?" my mother asked.

"She was asleep," my father replied, "so I laid her down on the seat."

"Luciano!" My mother always used his full name when he had done something wrong. "Stop the car."

"Not yet. We haven't cleared the estate. Do you see the main road?"

"I can't see a thing," my mother replied tensely. "Put on the headlights."

"And let everyone know we're leaving?"

My mother sighed. "Quickly, Katie, sit down on the floor. All the way down."

I wedged myself into the seat well, the space between the rear seat and front, where people place their feet. "Why are we leaving?"

There was no answer from the front of the car.

"When are we coming back?"

"We're not," my father said.

"Not ever?" I had liked it at Mason's Choice. "But, I—"

"There's Scarborough Road," my mother interrupted.

The car turned and headlights flicked on.

"I didn't say good-bye to Ashley."

For a moment all I heard was sleet and wind.

"Ashley isn't here anymore, remember?" my mother prompted quietly. "Ashley has gone to heaven."

That was what everyone said, but I had trouble understanding how it could be so. I still heard her and played with her. Sometimes I saw her by the pond, though Mommy said they had pulled her out of it. Ashley always scared me a little, but on the big estate there were no other children to play with, and that had made her my best friend. "I want to say good-bye to Ashley," I insisted.

"Luke! In the mirror, behind us!" My mother sounded panicky, and I stood up in the seat well to see.

"Get down, Katie!" my father shouted. "Now!"

I quickly dropped between the seats. Daddy sometimes shouted at the people who hired him to paint portraits of their pets. He'd scream at his paintings, too, when he got frustrated, but never at me. Our car suddenly picked up speed. I pulled the blanket over my head.

"There's ice on the road," my mother warned.

"You don't have to tell me, Victoria."

"We shouldn't have tried this."

"We had no choice," he said. "Do you remember the cutoff?"

"The one that runs by the Chasney farm—yes. About a hundred meters before it, there's a sharp curve."

My father nodded. "We'll get around it, I'll cut the lights, and he won't see us take the cutoff."

Our car picked up speed.

"But the ice—"

"Katie, I want you to stay on the floor," my father said, sounding more stern than I had ever heard him. I hugged my knees and my heart pounded. The car motor grew louder. The wind shrieked, as if we were tearing a hole in it by going so fast.

"Almost there!"

I wished I could climb up front and hold on to Mommy.

Then the car turned. Suddenly, I couldn't feel the road beneath us. The car began to spin. Mommy screamed. I felt her hands groping behind the seat for me. I couldn't move, pinned against the backseat by the force of the rotating car.

We came to a stop.

"Katie—?"

"Mommy—"

The stillness lasted no more than a few seconds. The next sound came like thunder—I could feel as well as hear it.

"Behind us, Luke," my mother gasped.

"Yes."

"Oh, God!" Her voice shook.

I jumped up to see what was behind us, but my father drove on. All I could see were darkness and a coat of ice halfway up the rear window of the car. We turned onto another road.

"I've got to keep going, Vic. For Katie's sake."

My mother's head was in her hands.

"If we go back and he isn't injured, we'll walk into a trap. If he's badly hurt, there is not much we can do. The gas station farther up has an outside pay phone. It's closed now—no one will see us. I'll call in the accident."

My mother nodded silently. For a moment I thought she

was crying. But she never cried—my father was the emotional one.

"What happened, Daddy? Did somebody get hurt?"

My mother raised her head and brushed back her long yellow hair. "Everything's all right," she said, her voice steady again. "There—there was a herd of deer by the side of the road, and your father was trying to avoid them. You know how they do, Katie, bolting across before you can see them. Some of them crashed into the wood. One went into the little dip next to the road."

"Did the deer get hurt?" I asked.

"I'm not sure," my father answered.

"Of course not," my mother said quickly, giving me the answer I wanted to hear but didn't believe. She unfastened her seat belt and knelt on the seat, facing me, to buckle me into my restraint.

My father drove more slowly now. There was a long silence.

"Victoria," he said at last, "I'm sorry."

She didn't reply.

Sorry for what? I wondered, but I knew they wouldn't tell me.

A chilly loneliness had settled around me, the way a winter fog settles in the ditches along the roads on the Eastern Shore.

The silence deepened as we drove north to Canada and, a few days later, flew to England, my mother's birthplace. My mother and father shared a secret—I had known that from the day Ashley died. It was a secret that I was left to discover twelve years later, after both parents had disappeared from my life.

Two

My dearest Kate,

You are the most wonderful daughter a man could have.
You can't possibly know how much I love you. I fear that
the last few months of my illness have been very hard on
you, and I hesitate to ask any more of your generous heart.
Still, I must leave you with two requests.

First, do not forget that your mother loves you as much
as I. I know you don't believe me—I see it in your eyes
each time I say this—but I was the reason your mother
left. It broke her heart to be separated from you. Below is
the name and number through which you can contact her.
Please do so, Kate.

Right, Dad, I replied silently to his letter, as soon as the sky falls.

Victoria, as I now refer to my mother, had left Dad and me the day after we arrived in England—left without explanation, simply walked out the door while I was sleeping. I was five years old then and needed her desperately. At seventeen, I did not.

I glanced back down at the letter.

Second, in the chimney cupboard, I have left a ring that belongs to Adrian Westbrook of Wisteria, Maryland. I took it the night we left the estate. Please return it.

I frowned and refolded the letter, as I had done many times in the three months since Dad had died. His second request, and the brilliant sapphire and diamond ring I had found in the cupboard, baffled me. In his career as a painter of animal portraits—horses, dogs, cats, birds, lizards, snakes, leopards— my father had worked for fabulously wealthy people, with access to the homes and estates where these pampered pets lived; as far as I knew, he had never stolen anything. I did not look forward to presenting this piece of missing property to Adrian Westbrook or to seeing a place that I connected so strongly with my mother. But I had to honor at least one of my father's final requests.

I carefully returned the letter to my travel bag and paced the room I had taken at a bed-and-breakfast in Wisteria, Maryland. After airport security, a six-hour transatlantic flight, customs, and a two-hour ride in an airport shuttle to the Eastern Shore town, I longed for a decent cup of tea, but the sooner I got this over with, the better. I headed downstairs to a small room equipped with a guest phone and punched in the number I had found in an Internet directory.

My call was answered on the third ring.

"Mason's Choice."

For a moment I was confused, then I remembered that that was the name of the estate where Ashley had lived.

"May I speak with Mr. Westbrook, please, Adrian Westbrook."

"Who is calling?" asked a woman with a deep voice.

"Kate Venerelli."

"Excuse me?"

Aware that years of schooling in England had given me an accent more clipped than Americans were accustomed to, I repeated my name slowly.

"I'm sorry. Mr. Westbrook is not available."

"When may I call back?" I asked.

"You may leave a message with me now."

I hesitated. An image of a person I had long forgotten

formed in my head: a cap of straight gray hair, a pale stone face, a mouth and forehead carved with disapproval. Mrs. Hopewell. It seemed as if the housekeeper should be 103 by now, but of course, when you are five, anyone older than your parents seems ancient to you. She was probably in her sixties.

"Thank you," I said politely, "but I would like to speak to Mr. Westbrook myself."

Click.

I stared at the phone—she had hung up. Quickly I dialed the number again. "May I speak with *Mrs.* Westbrook, please?" I knew from Dad's clients that rich old men always had wives, usually young, pretty ones. "Who is calling?"

"Kate Venerelli." There was no reason to lie—I was certain the housekeeper took note of the number displayed on her phone and realized the same person was calling.

"Mrs. Westbrook is not available," Mrs. Hopewell replied.

"Who is it?" I heard a younger woman ask in the background.

"Someone selling something, a marketing call," the housekeeper said, just before the click sounded again in my ear.

I put down the phone. My reluctance to carry out my father's request had melted in the low heat of Mrs. Hopewell's voice. I strode down the hall, hoping to learn something current about the Westbrooks from the owner of the Strawberry B&B.

I found Amelia Sutter in the kitchen, finger-deep in bread dough. She was very glad to talk, but I discovered that conversation with her was harder to steer than a flock of birds. It took twenty minutes of kneading to learn that Adrian had married a young woman named Emily and now had a little boy. Both of Adrian's grown children, Trent Westbrook and Robyn Caulfield, had divorced and never remarried. Of course, there was much more to those stories, details worthy of a racy novel, but those were the only statements made by Mrs. Sutter that I believed to be facts.

As her stories wandered on to other subjects, so did my attention. I tried to think of a reason to show up at the gates of Mason's Choice, some excuse that would get me past Mrs. Hopewell. Until I understood why my father had taken the ring, I wasn't going to reveal it to anyone but Adrian Westbrook. I stared down at a college newspaper lying open on the kitchen table. CARS TOWED, a headline read. That was an idea—I could pretend I had a disabled car and needed help. I continued scanning the page, my eyes stopping at an ad with a familiar phone number—the one I had just called.

WANTED: TUTOR FOR 7-YEAR-OLD CHILD. DUTIES INCL. TRANSPORTATION TO SCHOOL, HOMEWORK, & SOME REC TIME. EXCELLENT JOB FOR COLLEGE STUDENT. ROOM, BOARD, SALARY DPDT. ON EXPERIENCE.

My ticket in! I thought, jumping up so fast, I startled Mrs. Sutter. I didn't actually want the job—I had plans to tour cross county before attending university—but an interview would get me onto the estate, inside the house.

"Oh, there I've gone and offended you." Mrs. Sutter sighed. "I forgot how proper you English folks are."

"I'm American," I said, bluntly enough to prove it, then remembered my manners. "Would you excuse me? There is something I need to do—to do as soon as possible."

I hurried upstairs and grabbed my coat. I was certain that the vigilant Mrs. Hopewell wouldn't answer a third call from the same number, but I had ditched my old mobile in London. Now I headed out in search of a phone store or pay phone, whichever I came upon first.

At 4:20 that afternoon, about ten kilometers outside of town, Mrs. Sutter—Amelia, as she had asked me to call her—pulled up to the iron gates of Mason's Choice. They swung inward, triggered by an electric eye, an orb less discriminating than Mrs. Hopewell's. My plan had worked. Having used a pay phone at the local college, a bad French accent (I was afraid my American Southern wouldn't convince a native), and a polite request to speak to Emily Westbrook, I had gotten past the housekeeper.

My job interview was at 4:30, but the gloomy weather of early March made it appear later than that. A chilly fog had settled over the Eastern Shore, turning even the small wood that shielded the estate from Scarborough Road into the forbidding forest of a fairy tale. Massive vines and dripping black branches crowded close to both sides of the private road that led to the house. Amelia sped up, as if eager to get through the wood. A broken branch whisked across the windshield. Past the wood was an open area of lawn, bounded by a long hedge, perhaps three times the height of an adult, with a keyhole cut through where the entrance road passed. As a child I had found this living wall rather menacing; it didn't seem much friendlier now.

Then I remembered and turned my head quickly to the right. "Amelia, could you stop for a moment?"

"Yes, of course, dear. What is it?" she asked.

"A cemetery."

She strained to see. Had I not already known it was there, I wouldn't have noticed it—the wrought-iron fence and weeping angels. It had been foggy like this the week Ashley had fallen through the ice. After her funeral, I had visited her grave with my mother.

I remembered gapping my mother's hand as I watched the wisps of mist slip between the leaning stones. Ashley had claimed that the ghosts in the graveyard whispered to her; even when we weren't together, she said, the spirits watched me and told her what I did.

I shook off the eerie memory. Every day had been exciting with Ashley, but she had also frightened me. That summer, autumn, and winter, she and I had had the entire estate for our playground—gardens, pool, docks, play equipment, an old barn, and deserted outbuildings. She had loved daring me to try the forbidden. Spoiled and hot-tempered, and two years older than I, she had known how to scare me into doing what she wanted.

"Thanks, Amelia," I said, turning back. "We can keep going."

Passing through the hedge, we drove through the formal gardens bordering the long drive. The flowering plants were clipped clean to the ground, and the boxwood was perfectly manicured in patterns that looked as if they had been formed by big biscuit cutters. The house lay straight ahead.

Like many homes built in the American Colonial period, it was brick and impressive in its simplicity. The house rose three stories, the third being a steep roof with five dormer windows across. A wing extended from each side of the main house. Structurally, the wings were smaller versions of the house, turned sideways and attached to it by small brick sections that had roofs with dormers as their second story. There were no outside shutters, which made the house's paned windows seem to stare like unblinking eyes. Its red brick was stained dark with moisture.

Amelia stopped the car and craned her head to see the house. "I've changed my mind. I don't want to live here after all," she said, as if she had been seriously considering it. "If I owned this place, I'd sell it and buy myself three cozier homes."

"I think it has a view of the bay from the other side."

"I'd never see it," she replied. "I'd always be glancing over my shoulder. I didn't realize there was a graveyard here."

"Most old estates have them."

"I'd dig it up."

I laughed. "Then you certainly would have something ghastly standing at your shoulder, looking for a new place to rest," I said as we climbed out of the car.

Fortunately, an older gentleman, an employee I didn't know, answered the door. Mrs. Hopewell might have recognized me, at least, recognized a young "Victoria." During the last year I had cut my hair several times, starting with it well below my shoulder, shortening it to shoulder-length, chin-length, and finally having it snipped to wisps of gold that barely made it to the tips of my ears. I told Dad it was "sympathetic hair," for he was bald from the cancer treatments. But actually, it was my resemblance to the woman I remembered from twelve years back, her green eyes and cascade of blond hair, that had motivated me.

Amelia was asked to wait in the library on the left side of the spacious entrance hall, and I was escorted to an office on the right. A few moments later, Emily Westbrook entered. She was a slender woman with strawberry blond hair—probably tinted, for her eyebrows were much redder. She moved quickly, elegantly, as if she had been raised on ballet lessons.

We sat in chairs placed by a large, mahogany desk. While she studied my hastily created résumé, I studied the family pictures displayed on the fireplace mantel, curious to see the people whom I knew only through a child's eyes. I spotted Adrian's children, who were close to my parents' age, now early to mid-forties: Robyn in her horse-show gear, and Trent on a sailboat. Emily Westbrook and a baby—perhaps the little boy in need of a tutor—were in a large photo at the center of the mantel. Brook Caulfield, Robyn's son, who I thought was the same age as his cousin Ashley—two years older than I—sulked in a photo taken during those "wonderful" years of early adolescence. We all have those photos—I burned mine. Adrian, handsome, physically fit, looked nearly the same in all of his pictures, except his hair had turned from black to silver-streaked to pure white.

I checked the pictures on the desk and those placed on

shelves, disappointed that there were none of Ashley. Perhaps the family had found it too painful to display her photos. It occurred to me that the woman interviewing me might not know who I was or that I had lived here once. If her son was seven, she would have been part of the household for at least eight years, but it was possible that what had occurred four years before that was never talked about.

"So, you were educated in England," she said, looking up.

"Yes, ma'am, and sometimes, because of my father's work, we lived on the Continent, but I was born here and am an American citizen. As you can see from my résumé, I completed my A levels and will be applying for university next year. Because I learned through correspondence when we traveled, I was able to finish up a year early," I added as an explanation for my age.

"We have a number of paintings in this house done by a Luciano Venerelli," she said.

"He was my father. He died three months ago."

"Really! Are you an artist? Can you teach art?"

"I—I could teach some of the basic things my father taught me when I was a child."

"Do you play a musical instrument?"

"A little bit of piano."

"So you could teach it?"

"The basics," I replied, with the uncomfortable feeling that she was getting too interested in hiring me. "Of course, I have no experience in tutoring children."

"You say here that you have baby-sat quite a bit."

Yes, I thought, *but that was to get me inside your front door, not fetch myself a job.*

She picked up a desk phone. "Mrs. Hopewell, please send in Patrick."

I had to act fast. "Mrs. Westbrook, I need to explain why—"

"Let me tell you what we are looking for," she interrupted, with the air of someone who expected others to listen to her. "We call it a tutoring job because we want a nanny who is educated and can teach Patrick in a manner that is appropriate to his position in life. We want an employee who speaks English well and can correct Patrick's mistakes, someone who can assist in his studies, and introduce him to other things a well-bred person should know."

There was a light knock, and the door opened. The little boy who entered was definitely a Westbrook—dark hair, blue eyes, fair skin, with a child's smattering of freckles. For a moment I felt like little Katie gazing at Brook. Clearly, Patrick had already been bred in a manner "appropriate to his position in life": His walk and raised chin indicated that he believed he owned the place. I almost laughed.

"Patrick, darling, this is Kate Venerelli."

Patrick surveyed me, not like a curious seven-year-old, but like an adult who was deciding whether I would do. I surveyed him with the same measuring eyes, as if deciding whether *he* would do. He suddenly turned into a little boy, backing up and moving closer to his mother.

"Kate is going to be your tutor."

I swallowed my gasp. "I'm sorry?"

"I've made up my mind," Mrs. Westbrook told me. "You are educated, you are familiar with the arts, and you speak very well."

"But—but don't you think you should have references?" I asked.

"Do you have any?"

"No."

"It doesn't matter," Mrs. Westbrook said. "No one supplies *bad* references. Recommendations don't prove anything about a person."

"But I'm sure Mr. Westbrook would like to interview me too," I suggested. I considered explaining my ruse, but if she grew angry and sent me off, I'd have no excuse to return.

"Patrick's father has been ill. He will be returning Friday from Hopkins, where he has been receiving cancer treatments."

"Oh." I still winced when someone mentioned cancer. I glanced at Patrick, but his expression didn't change. Either he didn't understand, or he was already proficient at wearing a public face.

"When he arrives, Mr. Westbrook will have many other things to tend to," she went on.

"I need some time to think about this," I said, hoping to keep the masquerade going for one more day and hand deliver the ring.

"Perhaps you would like to get to know Patrick a little better," she suggested. "Darling, be a good boy and show Kate your room and the rooms on the third floor. Would you do that for Mommy?"

Darling didn't answer right away. Perhaps he was thinking about refusing or, better still, driving a bargain with Mommy.

I wanted this chance to see the places in which I had once played. "I'm sure you have some smashing toys in your room," I said encouragingly.

Patrick looked at me with new interest. "I'm not supposed to smash them."

His mother laughed. "That's an expression, Patrick. She means wonderful toys, exciting toys."

I think he would have preferred that I meant smashable toys, but he nodded and started toward the door, calling to me over his shoulder, "Come on, Kate."

I followed him out of the office. The entrance hall, which was furnished to serve as a formal reception room, ended at a wide passageway that ran from one side of the house to the other— that is, to the left and right, continuing on to the wings of the house. The living room and dining room, the two large rooms at the "back" of the house, were behind the passageway—facing the water, I remembered. The main stairway rose to our right, running parallel to the passageway.

The house had other stairways, in both the main section and wings, back steps that wrapped around the corners of its many fireplaces. It was a perfect place to play hide-and-seek, with three floors and so many escape routes connecting them. But it had also made me uncomfortable. I never knew for sure where Brook was, because he could sneak up and down stairways without us seeing him. Ashley had loved to leap out from behind a door and make me scream, immediately after my mother, who earned extra money by babysitting her would tell us we must play quietly.

Patrick and I climbed the wide stairway. Halfway down the second-floor hall I paused at a secretary filled with photos. I scanned them quickly, disappointed again to find none of Ashley. Amelia had said that Trent was divorced; perhaps Ashley's mother had taken all the pictures with her.

Patrick reached back for my hand, impatient with me. "It's

this way." He led me to the room at the front corner of the main house, the last doorway on the left before the center hall narrowed to connect the southern wing.

I stepped inside the door of his room and moved no farther. The drapes and comforter were green check rather than Ashley's pink, but the furniture was the same—dark, heavy, too large for a child—each piece in the same place it had occupied twelve years ago. I looked at the bed and thought of Ashley swinging like a monkey on its tall posters. I gazed at the bureau and saw her standing on top of it, performing for me. The two big chairs, if covered with a quilt, were the covered wagon in which she and I had "traveled west." To me, her presence in the room was so strong, I could nearly hear her speak.

Why, given the absence of pictures, would the family have kept her furniture? Perhaps the deep connections with objects that a child experiences are lost on an adult. Certainly, the Westbrooks would have sold it, if they had found the furniture as haunting as I.

"You don't like it?" Patrick asked. He had been watching my face closely.

"Oh, no. It's a very nice room. In fact, it's positively smashing," I added, since he seemed to enjoy that word.

He grinned. "Want to see some of my stuff?"

"Of course."

Patrick opened the walk-in closet, which was filled to the brim with toys. My breath caught when I saw the shelf of plastic horses. They had given him her toys! Then I remembered that these had been Robyn's horses, toys that had belonged to Ashley's aunt. Perhaps the toys and furniture were kept because they were regarded as an inheritance.

I lifted up a prancing dapple gray. *Hello, Silver Knight,* I said silently. That had been the toy's secret name, and I still found myself reluctant to say it aloud.

"Want to play?" Patrick asked.

I set down the horse. "Not now. We had better follow your mother's instructions and see the third floor."

"This stairway goes up to your room," he said, opening the door next to the fireplace.

"You mean if I take the job," I reminded him, afraid that he was starting to think I would.

"You don't like me?"

"Taking the job has nothing to do with whether I like you."

Patrick gazed at me silently, doubtfully.

"I mean it," I insisted.

His mouth tightened into a little seam. He led the way up to the room that had belonged to Ashley's tutor, Mr. Joseph. Directly above Patrick and Ashley's bedroom, it was on the corner of the house, with a dormer window facing the front and a smaller window facing the side. Icy air slipped in through their cracks. The two spindle-back chairs and iron bedstead were painted white. Without blankets, pillows, or any kind of fabric to soften the room, not even curtains, they made me think of bones picked clean.

"Do you like it?" Patrick asked, looking up at me with a hopefulness I wished I hadn't seen.

"It's quite nice."

We exited into the third-floor hall. At the opposite end of the rectangular hall were the main stairs with rooms on either side of them. He showed me the schoolroom first.

"This is where I do my homework."

The piano had been rolled to a different corner in the room, and the computer and printer were new, but otherwise, the tables, chairs, and shelf-lined walls looked just as I remembered them. Perhaps it was simply the dreary lighting and the familiar smells of the house, smells I connected with Ashley, but I couldn't shake the feeling that she was at Mason's Choice, in the rooms Patrick was showing me.

He led me to the playroom. "Want to meet Patricia?"

"Who?"

"My hamster."

I smiled. "It's a lovely name."

"I like Patrick better," he replied, "but she's a girl."

The large room was a kingdom of little-boy toys. Patricia's cage, an aquarium filled with wood shavings and covered by a weighted screen, sat in the corner.

"Hi, Pat," I greeted the silky brown hamster. Ashley had had hamsters and a zoo of other creatures. "Do you have a dog or cat?" I asked Patrick.

"No. I'm allergic to their fur. I'm not supposed to pick up Patricia, but I do. She gets lonely."

It's he who gets lonely, I thought, *though surrounded by every toy a kid could want.*

The walls were covered with sports posters, most of them showing ice hockey players. Patrick watched my eyes, reading every reaction. "You like hockey? We could go see the games. Wouldn't that be fun?"

"You have a team in Wisteria?"

"Of course." He pulled a high school sports program from beneath a pile of crayons. "This is Sam Koscinski," he said, pointing to a guy with a helmet, shoulder pads, and a manic look in his dark eyes. "He's the best. He . . . *smashes* people."

"Sounds like a nice chap. Patrick, do you have some friends? Do you invite them over from school?"

He shook his head. "Tim moved away."

"There's no one else?"

"Just Ashley."

"Ashley?" My voice sounded hollow. "Ashley who?"

"Just Ashley."

I regained my senses. "Is she a hamster too?"

Patrick shouted with laughter. "No. She's a person who plays with me. Would you play with me?" His voice pleaded. "You could visit and play. You don't have to be my tutor. Just come and play."

I sat down by a table overrun by plastic action figures. Patrick walked toward me, then lightly, tentatively, rested a hand on my knee. "We could have lots of fun together. I wouldn't be *real* bad."

I could see the desperation in his eyes and knew the feeling, the loneliness of being the only child among preoccupied adults. Before my father was successful enough to have his own studio, we had traveled from household to household. I had spent a lot of time in the kitchen with the help, who were busy with their jobs, waiting for my father to finish his job—waiting for someone to notice me. For a moment I considered taking the Westbrook position. Only a moment. After years of parenting my loving but inept father, I wasn't about to take on "another" little boy.

"It would be lots of fun, Patrick. But I've been thinking about doing some traveling."

"You can't. I want you here," he insisted. "Ashley likes

you," he added, as if that would persuade me.

"How can she if she hasn't met me?"

"She has. She's watching you."

A tingle went up my spine. I glanced around. "I don't see anyone named Ashley."

"She sees you," he said with confidence.

I took a deep breath. "Why don't we go downstairs."

Had family members told him about her? I wondered as we descended the main stairs. The name was common enough; perhaps he simply liked it and chose it on his own for an imaginary playmate. Given his isolation on the estate, it would make sense for him to create a fantasy friend.

When we reached the landing between the first and second floors, Patrick pulled on my arm to keep me from going farther. Below us, women were arguing.

"It's Mrs. Hopewell," he said. "She's mean. She hates me."

"Oh, I'm sure she doesn't hate you, Patrick," I replied, then cringed at how I had sounded like a typical, patronizing adult.

"Robyn hates me too," he added. "We'll go a different way."

But I had just heard what Mrs. Hopewell was saying, and I wasn't going anywhere. I pulled him back and put my finger to my lips.

"You can't trust her," the housekeeper said. "You would be very foolish to hire that young woman."

"Hoppy is right," said another woman. "I'm sorry, Emily, but I simply won't allow it."

"Really. What makes you think you have a say in this, Robyn?"

"Adrian won't allow it," Mrs. Hopewell asserted. "He sent her family packing twelve years ago."

Sent my family packing? If Adrian had dismissed us, why did we sneak away in the middle of the night? Something wasn't right.

"Her mother was a strange woman, a very angry woman," Mrs. Hopewell went on. "She was supposed to be watching Ashley the day she fell through the ice."

Robyn quickly cut her off. "We don't need to go into that, Hoppy. The point is, Emily, this girl will bring back bad memories and upset Daddy and Trent. I can't allow it."

"Well, you talk to *Daddy* when he gets home," Emily replied, "and I will talk to my husband, and we will see if he chooses to listen to his daughter, his housekeeper, or his wife concerning the welfare of his son." The strength of Emily's words were betrayed by the high pitch of her voice. I guessed that she was intimidated by Mrs. Hopewell and Robyn.

But I wasn't.

"Who are they talking about?" Patrick whispered to me as I took his hand and started down the main stairs.

"Your new tutor."

Three

I CAN'T REMEMBER the last time I did something so impulsively. Curiosity about why my family had left and sheer defiance made up my mind. I had no idea how long I would stay, or rather, how long they would keep me. It worried me that I would be one more person in Patrick's life who didn't stay around, but I didn't know what I could do about that.

The scene at the bottom of the stairway had been brief and tense, Mrs. Hopewell responding to my introduction with one sentence: "I know who you are." Mrs. Caulfield—Robyn—had informed me that the *final* decision on my hiring would be made by Mr. Westbrook.

Amelia had been bursting with curiosity when the door of the library reopened. The ladies had closed it in order to have their argument, but she had heard bits and pieces. I told her several times that the two older women had confused me with someone else, which, not surprisingly, she didn't believe. That evening I stole away from Amelia's questions, taking a walk through town.

The fog, which had rendered the afternoon so dismal, now made the night seem brighter, the mist holding the apricot light of streetlamps and shimmering on the brick sidewalks. Though it was only seven o'clock, most of the shops were closed. Lights shone in the rooms above them and through the fanlights and windows of the old homes that fronted the eighteenth-century street. Somewhere ahead of me, at the end of High Street, was the river, but fog blotted out everything more than a block away. Peering in a shop window, pressing my face close to the glass, was like looking in a crystal ball, the objects inside magically clear.

I stared at a painting of a cat. I knew the artist at once, recognizing his attentiveness to the cat's ears, the expression in the animal's tail, and the tone of the background, carefully chosen to bring out the colors in the cat's coat. It was an early work by my father. I took a step back to read the shop's sign: OLIVIA'S ANTIQUES. That's what you get for dying, Dad, I thought; your paintings are antiques now.

A man was working inside the shop, staring down at his clipboard, a pen hanging out of one side of his mouth like a cigarette—ex-smoker, I thought, recognizing my father's habit. I pushed open the front door, unloosing a flurry of bells.

"Shop's closed," the man said, pointing to a sign.

"I was hoping I might look at the painting of the cat."

"It's not for sale. Nothing here is for sale. I'm just taking inventory."

"It's a Venerelli, isn't it?"

He removed the pen from his mouth, perhaps surprised that a teenager would know something like that. "Unsigned," he replied.

"Even so, it is," I told the man, walking over to the painting to study it more closely.

He put down his clipboard and joined me in front of the painting. "How do you know that? It would be worth a lot more if I could be certain."

"He was my father. I'd recognize his work anywhere."

Now the man tipped forward on his toes to look at my face. "Katie!" he exclaimed softly.

I took a step back.

"I never expected to see you in Wisteria, but still, I should have recognized you. You look exactly like your mother."

"Not *exactly*."

"You don't remember me, do you?" the man continued. "You were only a little girl the last time I saw you."

I waited to see if his face surfaced in my memory as Mrs. Hopewell's had. "No, I'm sorry, I don't."

"Joseph Oakley." He held out his hand. "I was Ashley's tutor."

"Mr. Joseph! I *do* remember you." Though I didn't recall him looking anything like he did now. Ashley's tutor, a college student, had been skinny, with a little knob of a chin. The person in front of me had the shape of a plump, middle-aged man, and sported a full beard flecked with gray. But he was younger than he appeared; the skin on his face was smooth, almost lineless.

"My condolences about your father," he said.

I nodded.

"I know how it is," he went on. "Mother died several months ago."

"I'm sorry.

"That's why I'm back in town, settling her affairs. This was her shop."

I glanced around at the odd collection of things—a beautiful oil lamp, a tacky ceramic of a fisherman, an elegant silver brush set, a purple teapot shaped like an elephant's head—his trunk was the spout. Next to my father's simple painting was a very large canvas: Several robust women with 1920 hairstyles bathed at a pink spring while odd-looking winged creatures darted about.

"Her taste was certainly . . . wide-ranging," I said.

"Her records are even more erratic than her taste," he replied with a grimace. "Of course, Mother was no spring chicken when she had me, and I think she was losing it mentally these last few years. I'm going to be forced to declare bankruptcy."

"Oh, no."

"But I want to hear about you and your mother, Katie. Is she here with you? How long will you be in Wisteria?"

"Well, actually—"

A loud jingle of the bells on the door interrupted us. "Shop's closed," Joseph called out, then turned back to me. "You were saying—"

"It can't be closed." A guy about my age had rushed into the store. "I got here as soon as I could." He looked at me as if I might plead his case for him. "I've got to get a birthday present."

"Shop's closed," Joseph repeated.

"But I know what I want. It's right over there." He strode toward a glass case. "The bracelet with the blue stones."

"The lapis lazuli?" Joseph asked quietly. "It's three hundred dollars."

I think Joseph assumed the high price would immediately get rid of the shopper, but he miscalculated.

The guy cocked his head, as if he hadn't heard right, then bent over the case to get a closer look. "You've got to be kidding. It's not even sapphires."

"And this isn't Wal-Mart."

The guy straightened up. "Okay, okay," he said, rubbing his hands, then glancing at his watch.

I got the feeling he had a very short deadline.

"Let's see." He ran one hand through curly black hair. He was athletically built, a few inches taller than I, and very good-looking—if he would just stand still for a second. The room didn't seem big enough to contain his energy. I wanted to send him outside for a run.

"There must be something else here." He moved down the long jewelry case, playing it like a piano.

Joseph sighed. "Please don't put your fingerprints all over the glass."

"There, that plain silver one. You put tags on your cheaper stuff. Fifty dollars, I can swing it. Wait a minute, I like that one too. Forty-five."

He spun around, turning to Joseph, then me. I was glad there wasn't a shelf of glassware anywhere near him. "You're a woman—sort of," he said.

I frowned at him.

"I mean, a girl. A female. Could you help me out? I hate choosing this kind of stuff."

He had great eyes, eyes like the shiny black stones I collected from my favorite beach on the Channel. That's the only explanation I can offer for helping this last-minute lover in his gift selection.

"Which bracelet do you like best?" he asked. "That silver one, or the gold one with the green paint."

"Green *enamel,*" Joseph corrected him.

I leaned over the case, studying them. "The green and gold."

"But all of her earrings are silver," the guy protested.

"Then why did you ask me?" I replied, exasperated.

He lifted his hands, then dropped them heavily on the glass. Out of the corner of my eye, I saw Joseph wince. The guy had strong hands, square hands, totally unartistic hands. Was it crazy to be attracted to a guy's hands?

"I like the enamel one too," he admitted. "But since she likes silver, I was hoping you'd choose that and make it an easy choice."

"Both bracelets are pretty. It's just that I like to wear green."

His fingers stopped drumming the case, his hands finally becoming still. I looked up and found him gazing at my hair. He met my eyes, then perused my face—just stared at me, making no effort to pretend he wasn't.

"I see," he said. "Because of your eyes. Your eyes are grass green."

Grass green?

"What I mean is pale, bright green—"

Joseph shook his head.

"See-through green, like—like the plastic of a Sprite bottle."

He seemed pleased with the accuracy of that last description. I hoped he wasn't going to compose his own gift card.

"I'll take the silver bracelet," the guy said, turning to Joseph, pulling out his money. "I'm kind of in a hurry."

Joseph must have realized that a sale was the quickest way to get rid of this guy. Moving behind the counter, he took the customer's money. The guy pocketed the bracelet, leaving without a box or bag.

"You were saying," Joseph prompted me, as the bells on the door jingled and fell silent.

"I'll be here for a while. I took a temporary job."

"Wonderful. Where?"

"Mason's Choice."

He looked at me, surprised.

"Do you remember Mrs. Hopewell?" I asked.

"Despite my best efforts to forget her."

"She's still there."

Joseph sat down heavily on a shop stool. "Why did you go back, Katie?"

The tone of his voice made me uneasy. "Why not?"

He thought before he spoke. "Your family didn't leave under the best of circumstances. What does your mother think of this?"

"I don't know. I haven't seen her for twelve years."

His brown eyes grew wider for a moment.

"Victoria left us when we got to England."

He stroked his beard with long fingers—the only part of him that had remained thin. He had been a musician, I remembered. Poor man, studying music, having to listen to Ashley and me banging on the schoolroom piano.

"I had no idea, no idea at all. Do you know why your mother left?" he asked.

I shook my head.

"What did your father tell you about the Westbrooks?"

"He wouldn't talk about them. All I know is what I remember from when I was five. For instance, Mrs. Caulfield, Ashley's aunt, couldn't stand Ashley and got along better with horses than people."

"Still does. I heard Robyn just came back from the Florida horse-show circuit."

"Mr. Trent," I said, using the name for him that I had used as a child, "was very serious."

"Yes. He runs the business for Adrian."

"What *is* their business?"

"Furniture and art. They began with a handful of local

auction houses, like Crossroads, the one here on the Eastern Shore. In the last two decades they've been doing a lot of importing. Have you seen Adrian? I heard he's getting cancer treatments and they haven't been successful."

"They haven't?" I wondered what the Westbrooks had told Patrick. "He's coming home Friday."

Joseph pressed his hands together and rested his mouth against his fingertips, thinking. "Which means the vultures will be gathering. You'll have to deal with all of them, Katie." He reached for a store receipt and scribbled down a number. "This is the phone at my mother's house. The number printed on the top is the store's. I'll be in Wisteria for the next few weeks. Call me if you need anything."

"I'll be all right," I said, smiling. "You know, I've spent a lot of time in other people's households. I've seen it all."

"I'm sure, but why don't you check in with me now and then."

"I don't check in with anyone," I said, then added quickly, "What I mean is that I'm used to being on my own. When Dad was alive, *he* checked in with me."

Joseph shook his head. "The Westbrooks are not nice people, Katie. You can't trust them."

"Don't worry," I replied. "I haven't trusted anyone in a very long time."

The next afternoon the Westbrooks' groundskeeper who introduced himself as Roger Hale, picked me up from the Strawberry, then drove to Patrick's private school, which was at the far end of High Street, backing up to Wist Creek.

No street in Wisteria was far from a piece of shoreline. The town, a parcel of land jutting into the mouth of the Sycamore River, was surrounded on three sides by water, the river and two wide creeks named Oyster and Wist. The next point of land outside of town and moving in the direction of the Chesapeake Bay was the Scarborough Estate, and the point after that was Mason's Choice, where the river flowed into the bay.

"Do you think you can find your way?" Roger asked me, when he had driven from the school to the estate. He parked in a multi-car garage that was to one side of the house. From now on it would be my job to transport Patrick to and from in a staff car.

"Yes, thanks." It wasn't the route I was concerned about, but trying to drive on the right side of the road, which was opposite from the way I had learned in England. It's just a matter of concentration, I told myself, and decided not to bring up the matter.

"I'll leave a map in the car," Roger said, as he pulled my bags from the back of it, "and one on your bureau when I take your luggage to your room. You get on to the house now—Mrs. Westbrook is always anxious to see Patrick."

Patrick had chattered cheerfully in the car, but as he and I approached the house, he grew quiet. He turned his head suddenly, looking at the tall windows to the left of the main entrance. Someone gazed out from the library, but the weather had cleared and the bright reflections on the glass made it difficult to see who.

"I always go in through the kitchen," Patrick said.

"Sorry, but your mother told me to bring you in the front."

He hung back.

"Come on, Patrick. She wants to see you straightaway."

He stood rooted in the grass. If we hadn't just met, I would have worried that he had learned that ugly, defiant look from me.

"All right," I said. "I'll go in. When you're ready to join me, knock on the door. But I'll answer only the front entrance."

"Our doors aren't locked in the daytime," he informed me.

I continued walking.

"You're mean."

"But I was being so much nicer than usual," I replied.

He stared at me and I winked. "Come on, the sooner you see your mother, the sooner we can go outside and play."

When he and I entered the main hall, his mother emerged from the library.

"Darling, how was school?"

"Okay." He edged away from the library door.

She held out her arms. "Are you forgetting something? Patrick!" She sounded hurt.

He dutifully went back and kissed her.

"Trent has just arrived from Philadelphia. Come say hello to him and Robyn. You as well, Kate."

Through the door I could see Robyn pacing back and forth, pressing a cell phone to her ear. Years in the sun had aged her skin. The vertical creases between her eyebrows had deepened noticeably, and her black hair had streaks of silver. She still had the bone structure of a beautiful woman, but Ashley's suggestion that she was the bad queen in *Snow White* didn't seem that farfetched. As Patrick and I entered, she glanced at me, then turned her back.

Trent was sitting at a desk, dressed in a business suit, reading some kind of document. He was still slender, with thin, almost colorless hair. He had adored Ashley but had been hopeless at playing. She and I had had a much better time with my father, who, though I hadn't realized it then, had the imagination and heart of a child.

"Trent," Emily said, "here's Patrick, and his new tutor, Kate Venerelli."

Trent's blue eyes looked up over his reading glasses. He rose from his seat. "Good God!"

I had thought Mrs. Hopewell and Robyn would have warned Trent about me, but the small, satisfied curve of Robyn's lips suggested they hadn't. The little color Trent had in his cheeks disappeared completely.

"You're a double for your mother."

Patrick gazed up at me. "You have a mother?"

"Everyone has one at birth," I replied.

"How old are you now?" Trent asked me.

"Seventeen."

I could see him doing the mental calculation. Ashley would be nineteen. As children, both of us had strongly resembled our mothers. What would Ashley have looked like now—another Corinne, his wife when he first met her?

"I was sorry to learn about your father's death," he said.

I nodded, but Trent didn't see it, sitting down again, his eyes returning to the paper he'd been reading before he had even finished his sentence.

"Here's Patrick," Emily said, sounding a little peeved that her son had not been acknowledged by Trent.

"Hello, Patrick," Trent responded, without looking up. When Patrick didn't reply, Trent added crisply, "Children speak when spoken to."

And when *looked* at, I thought.

"Hi," Patrick said, his lips barely parting. He had learned

from his half brother how to greet a person coldly.

"So when will *your* charming son arrive, Robyn?" Trent asked.

"By now, I thought." She returned the cell phone to her pocket. "I'm worried."

"You don't think he stopped by a few parties on the way up from Beach Ball University, do you?"

"No, Uncle Trent, I did not," replied a deep voice, "because I knew how delighted you would be to see me."

"Brook," his mother greeted him with relief. He kissed her, his lips barely brushing her cheek.

Ashley's cousin and "best enemy" had inherited the Westbrook look, a handsome, large-featured face, dark hair, and blue eyes.

"I can't tell you how happy I was to leave sunny Florida and come back to this cold, damp place," Brook said sarcastically. "Exactly when is dear Grandfather coming home?"

"Tomorrow, Brook, and I'm counting on you," his mother responded with a meaning-filled look.

"As always," he replied casually, and sprawled in a chair, one foot up on the low table in front of him. His skin was deeply tanned. "And who are you?" he asked, eyeing me.

"Kate."

"Kate Venerelli," his mother said.

Brook blinked. I could see the change in his eyes. "Katie!"

he exclaimed softly, sitting up straight. His eyes traveled down and up me in a way that made me squirm inside, which wasn't much different from the way I reacted to him when I was five. I had steered clear of a boy who played hard enough to hurt, kicked nests of wild kittens, and threw rocks at a pet when he thought no one was looking.

"Kate is Patrick's tutor," Emily said.

Brook glanced at Patrick. "Hey, little jerk." There was no fondness in his greeting.

Patrick simply stared at him, which made Brook laugh.

"You know, Patrick, I always thought you were stupid. But maybe you're not as dumb as I figured—maybe you've been faking it so you could get a pretty tutor."

Emily took a step toward Brook.

"Just teasing," he added quickly, unconvincingly. His gaze skipped around the room. "Something's missing," he said. "Ah! The old dragon."

Trent immediately turned toward the fireplace mantel behind him.

"I guess she's in the kitchen chewing out Cook," Brook added, pleased with his little joke, which apparently referred to Mrs. Hopewell.

"Where *is* the Chinese dragon?" Trent asked, still surveying the mantel.

"Robyn took it," Emily replied, like a child happy to tattle. "She claims your father promised it to her."

"You are truly amazing, Robyn," Trent said to his sister. "One day I'm going to come home and find the main house stripped. But I'll know where to find everything—in your wing."

"Not if I sell it first," Robyn retorted. "Besides, Daddy did say he would give it to me."

Trent rose, lifted a small bronze from the mantel and carefully turned it in his hands, as if appraising it, then placed the figure in his open briefcase. "Guess what? Dad promised this sculpture to me."

Brook threw back his head and laughed. Emily got the same tight-lipped look as I had seen on Patrick's face. I had been right about her: She was intimidated enough by her husband's children not to insist that these things still belonged to Adrian.

"So Grandfather is on his last legs," Brook said. "That's hard to imagine."

"I find your lack of respect appalling," Emily said to Brook, apparently not cowed by a college student.

"Oh come now, Emily, why else would you have married an old man?" Robyn challenged her.

"It's called love, Robyn, but I doubt that word is in your vocabulary."

"You are wrong! I have loved him all my life," Robyn

replied, with such intensity that her voice sounded strange. "I have loved him, lived with him, and taken care of him longer than you have."

"The prognosis is less than a year," Trent told Brook.

Joseph was right, I thought. Adrian was dying and the vultures were gathering, each one afraid that the next person would get a larger slice of the inheritance. What a lovely group for a child to grow up around!

"I'm taking Patrick outside," I said.

He bolted for the door, and I followed.

"Play clothes," his mother called after us. "Put on his play clothes, Kate."

I didn't know a little boy could peel and dress so quickly. He ended up with his mittens on the wrong hands, which we fixed when we got outside. We walked silently for a few moments. I let him lead the way and guessed that we were going to the pond.

"What does it mean, 'on his last legs'?" Patrick asked me when we were a distance from the house.

I hesitated, then lied. "I'm not sure. It must be an American expression. Sometime when you and your mother are alone, ask her."

We walked beyond the formal gardens and through a bare orchard that ended at paddocks and a horse barn. As a child I had thought I was luckier than Ashley because my parents and I lived in one of the employee cottages, which was near the horse barn and, better yet, an empty cow barn with lofts and ladders, where Ashley and I had liked to play. Between the horse and cow barns was Ashley's favorite place, the pond.

Surrounded by a thick ring of trees, mostly cedar and pine, it was reached by a narrow path. Round, about half the size of a soccer field, the pond looked as it had twelve years before, but the collar of vegetation had tightened around it, the circle of evergreens growing inward, encroaching on its edge, casting long shadows on its half-frozen surface. Dying things and living things mixed together here. A rush of feelings came back to me with the distinctive smell—a smell that was both fresh green and thick with decay. Alone with Ashley, knowing no one could see us, I had found the pond a frightening place. Ashley could think of a hundred forbidden things to do.

"Want to play hockey?" Patrick asked.

"Here?" After what had happened to Ashley, surely someone had taught him. . . .

"We can pretend we're on skates and use branches for hockey sticks."

"Patrick, the ice is too soft! When it's dark and slushy, you can't skate. It will never hold your weight."

"Yes, it will."

"Sorry, but—"

"Ashley said so."

The breath caught in my throat. "What did you say?"

"Ashley told me it's okay."

I felt a finger of ice along my spine. "Well, she's wrong." I crouched next to Patrick. "Are you listening? She's dead wrong."

I looked out at the thin ice, at the hole in it, a circle of black water lying off-center in the pond. There is a scientific reason that area doesn't freeze well, I told myself. Perhaps the pond's spring was located beneath it, or the temperature was warmer because of the amount of sun it received. Though even now, it wasn't hard to believe Ashley's explanation. I had seen the brown and black water snakes basking on the shore and could easily imagine other creatures with serpentine limbs, which Ashley had said hid beneath the pond's dark surface, waiting to pull us under.

I turned to Patrick, who was gazing toward the watery circle. "I guess Ashley is your imaginary friend," I said.

He nodded. "Only she's not imaginary."

"Oh? What does she look like?"

"She has brown hair. It's very pretty, brown and curly. She wears a pink coat. She always wants to wear her purple shoes."

Another chill went through me. Ashley had loved her

purple sneakers and had worn a pink snowsuit. But most little girls love pink and purple, I reminded myself, and a lot of people have brown curly hair. And though I had seen no pictures of her displayed in the house, it was very possible someone had shown him one.

I debated whether to tell him that I had played with a little girl named Ashley, then decided against it. It was a big leap to think he was talking about the child I had known. My job would be simpler if I didn't admit to him that I had once lived here.

Four

FRIDAY MORNING I drove to Wisteria Country Day School, muttering to myself all the way.

"Why do you keep saying, 'To the right'?" Patrick asked as we motored along.

"So I remember to drive on that side of the road."

"Why would you drive on the other side? There are cars coming."

"Good point."

After dropping him off, I arrived back at the house in the middle of a family quarrel, the subject of which was money— who was spending how much on what. I paused in the hall, picking out the voices of Trent, Robyn, and Emily. Two women carrying cleaning equipment, part of the estate's day help, nodded to me as they passed. They either pretended not to notice the raised voices or were so used to it, they weren't interested. I headed upstairs, glad that I had eaten breakfast earlier and that my room was two floors above those where the family gathered.

The bright day made the white room cheerier than it had seemed two days ago, and the slanting roof made it snug, though no warmer. Outside the wind was gusting up and the temperature dropping. The plaster walls of the room were cold to the touch, the old glass panes in the windows frigid. Mrs. Hopewell had provided me with a wool blanket, quilt, rug, and what appeared to be old kitchen curtains—thin panels of yellow fabric with red teapots all over. I stuffed towels at the base of both windows, pulled a chair closer to the radiator, and settled down to read. My only company was the photo of my father that I had set on my bureau.

About eleven o'clock I heard a car drive up to the house and a flurry of activity downstairs, indicating that Adrian Westbrook had arrived home. An hour later, though I had not asked for lunch, I was informed by intercom that it would be delivered. My offer to fetch it myself was rejected. Henry, the older gentleman who had first answered the door for Amelia and me, served me in my room and instructed me to leave the dirty dishes outside my door. I wondered if the situation downstairs was tense.

Over lunch, I studied my U.S. atlas, focusing on the Maryland area, calculating the distance from the Eastern Shore to

Washington, D.C. It appeared short enough for a day trip. I finished my soup and sandwich, turned up the volume on my iPod, then flipped through another book, looking for sites both Patrick and I would enjoy; after all, I was supposed to be introducing him to things that "a well-bred person should know."

I didn't know how long Mrs. Hopewell was standing inside my room, observing me read. With my music on, I hadn't heard her open the door.

"Mr. Westbrook will see you now."

I removed my earbuds. "I'm sorry, did you knock?"

She ignored the question. "He hasn't a lot of time to waste."

"Please tell him I'll be down in five minutes," I said, wanting to wash my face and retrieve the ring from my drawer unobserved.

"He will see you *now.*"

Interpreting this to mean I was to follow her, I stood up, making a motion to do so. She preceded me out the door, and I closed it behind her. "I won't be long," I called.

A few minutes later, I found Mrs. Hopewell waiting for me on the second-floor landing.

"I hope that Mr. Westbrook has been told about me," I said, as we descended the stairs. "Mr. Trent seemed rather startled yesterday."

"He has been informed," the housekeeper replied coolly. "He knows who you are."

"Good."

It was curious, I thought, that Mrs. Hopewell had made the long trek up to the third floor to fetch me rather than employing the intercom, or Henry, or the young man I had noticed at her beck and call in the kitchen earlier. Of course, that is the problem with wanting to be in control—it requires a great deal of personal effort.

"Mrs. Hopewell, do you still live in the house?"

"Yes."

"If I remember correctly, you are in the section that connects to Mrs. Caulfield's wing, the second floor of it."

She glanced sideways at me. "You must remember a great deal from your time here."

"Just bits and pieces," I replied. "I don't think I could draw a map of the house or the estate, but I do seem to know how to get from one place to the next."

She waited till we reached the bottom of the steps then turned toward me, blocking my path with her foot. Her muddy brown eyes had a peculiar shine to them. "I am sure your mother filled you in on many things."

"No, after we left Mason's Choice, she and I never talked about the place." I saw no reason to inform Mrs. Hopewell that we never talked at all.

The woman's nostrils quivered, as if she could sniff the truth, then she ushered me to the office and gave a quick double rap on the door.

"Thank you, Louise," a voice called from within.

She opened the door.

"Katie Venerelli," Adrian Westbrook greeted me, rising from behind the desk as I stepped inside the room. "All grown-up! What an enchanting sight you are! Welcome back, Katie," he said, taking my hands warmly, then cocking his head slightly to the right, as if looking over my shoulder. "That will be all, Louise."

Mrs. Hopewell turned abruptly and exited.

"The door, Louise," he called after her.

It was closed. I imagined her listening through the keyhole.

"Hello, Mr. Westbrook."

"*Mr. Westbrook?* Have we suddenly become formal? Must I now call you Miss Venerelli? Don't you remember, child, you insisted on calling me Adrian, no matter how many times your parents corrected you. You said you liked the name much better. You're not going to change that, are you?"

"Well—"

"I'd be insulted—I'd feel like a doddering old man if you called me Mr. Westbrook. I'm already old and will be doddering soon enough, as I'm sure they've told you. They're all abuzz about my impending demise. It's a wonder they haven't put tags on the furniture, claiming their loot. But don't *you* make me a relic before I have to be."

His blue eyes had lost none of their spark, and his white hair, though shorter than in his pictures, was still thick. He hasn't had radiation recently, I thought. His color was poor, as was my father's, but despite illness and age, he was a handsome man, having the large, even features Robyn had inherited, plus a sense of humor, which she hadn't. The lines engraved in his face traced amusement rather than frustration and anger.

"You look wonderful," I said honestly.

"You've worked one day and you want a raise?"

"You know that isn't true. And you know that what I said, is."

He smiled. It was nice to feel at ease with someone in the house. I had liked Adrian as a child and found that I still liked him now.

He gestured for me to sit down, then took a seat himself. "My condolences on the loss of your father."

"Thank you."

"And your mother, how is she?"

"I haven't seen her since I was five."

For the second time in two days, I had someone gazing at me incredulously.

"I knew she and Luke had separated, but I assumed . . ." He didn't complete his sentence. "So you are on your own," he said. "That can't be easy."

"I can handle it."

One corner of his mouth turned up slightly. "I have no doubt."

"I do have one matter relating to my father, which I need to take care of," I went on. From my pocket I pulled out the ring. "He asked me to return this to you."

Adrian stared at it. "Good Lord."

"You recognize it?"

"Yes, of course. It was my grandmother's."

"I don't know why my father took it," I said, shifting in my seat uncomfortably. "All I know is that I am supposed to return it."

I laid it on the table next to Adrian, since he didn't seem inclined to take it. There was a faraway look in his eyes.

"It would really help me," I continued, "if you could tell me why Dad had it. I never knew him to be a thief."

"Oh, Katie, of course he wasn't a thief," Adrian said, picking up the ring, then placing it in his desk drawer. "Luke was an artist, with an artist's temperament, as I am sure you know."

"Yes. . . ."

"I'm equally sure I wasn't the only client your father accused of failing to appreciate his genius."

I smiled a little. "You weren't."

"He left here in an artistic huff. I suppose he took the ring, fearing that I wouldn't make good on the work he had completed for me. I did, eighteen months later, when he surfaced in England, painting for an old college chum of mine."

I frowned. "He should have returned the ring then."

"Oh, don't be hard on him. He was young with a little girl to support and no money saved. It is a testament to your father's honesty that he kept it all these years with the plan of returning it."

I wanted to believe him—to believe the best about my father—but stories weren't matching up. "Mrs. Hopewell said that you sent us packing."

Adrian looked surprised. "That's odd. Her memory has always been good," he replied. "Of course, that is how she would have perceived the situation. As you may have noticed, she is loyal to a fault, especially to Robyn and me. She would assume I fired your father rather than think I was jilted by an unestablished artist."

That made some sense. But then why did we leave so secretly in the middle of the night? Perhaps because my father had stolen the ring.

"You look unconvinced," Adrian observed. "What did your father tell you?"

"Nothing. He never wanted to talk about our time here."

Adrian shook his head. "I hope your time with us left you with a few good memories. Ashley loved having you for her little friend. You were a very happy part of her life. I'm glad that Patrick will have that opportunity now. How do you find him?"

"Lonely."

Adrian sat back in his chair. "You are blunt, just like your mother."

"I hardly know Patrick, but it is obvious that he needs other children around him."

Adrian sighed. "You are probably right. Give me a few days to set my affairs in order, then we shall put our heads together to see what can be done for him."

I nodded.

"I am delighted you are here, Katie—Kate, I suppose I should call you, now that you are a young woman. We'll be getting you a cell phone, which I'd like you to keep with you at all times. I don't know why the microwave and small refrigerator were removed from your room, but Mrs. Hopewell assures me they will be put back. You are welcome to eat in the kitchen anytime, of course, but most people want some privacy."

He rose, signaling the end of our meeting.

"Thank you . . . thanks—" I hesitated, not ready to address my employer by his first name.

The lines of amusement deepened in his face. "And what did we agree you would call me?" he asked.

"Adrian."

"Your father has come home," I told Patrick when I picked him up from school that day.

His face lit up. "Is he all better?"

"He still has cancer, but he is better right now," I replied, glad that I had asked Emily what they had told Patrick about Adrian's health.

"And he is very happy to be home," I added, as Patrick struggled to get his stuffed backpack in the rear seat of the car. "He can't wait to see you."

"I wish they could make Daddy's cancer go away." Patrick's voice sounded small, wistful.

I rested my hand on his shoulder. "Me too."

He climbed into the car.

"Fasten your seat belt," I reminded him, then got into the driver's seat and started the car. "So how was school today?"

"Okay . . . sort of . . . I got a fifty on my spelling test," he blurted suddenly, as I pulled out of the school lot. "It has to be signed."

"A fifty." I glanced in the mirror and saw his tense little face. "How many words were on the test?"

"Ten."

"So you can spell five. That's a start. We'll work on the other five tonight."

He looked relieved that I hadn't come down hard on him. "Will you sign the test?"

"No, your mother or father has to, but I will tell them we're working on those five words and learning new ones too."

"Okay," he said, sounding cheerful. "To the right, to the right," he chanted, recalling my mantra earlier in the day.

"I'm driving fairly well now, Patrick. I don't think I need prompting."

"Yeah," he agreed, "only you came out of the parking lot where you are supposed to go in."

"I did?"

"That's why our crossing guard was blowing her whistle at you."

"She was?"

I glanced back in the rearview mirror. "Oh, well. You help me drive and I'll help you spell."

"Home is the other way," he informed me.

"Oh. Right." I needed to turn the car around. "Don't worry. All we have to do is—whoops! DO NOT ENTER. So . . . so, we'll take a left, then another left." I made the first turn. "We'll get there eventually."

"When we do, can we play with my plastic horses? Ashley said you can ride Silver Knight."

"Ashley said—what?"

A horn blared at me as I turned the corner.

"To the right!" Patrick cried.

There was no time to veer away from the oncoming car. I slammed on the brakes. Our car screeched to a stop, nose to nose with the other vehicle. I wrenched around to look at Patrick. "Are you okay?"

He bobbed his head. "That was close."

There had been no thump, no crushing metal sounds, no shattering of glass. I sank back against my seat. "I'm sorry, Patrick. I hope I didn't scare you."

"Nope," he said. I saw him looking past me, and I turned to see the guy who had been driving the other car leap out of it. He shouted at me, waving his arms like a lunatic.

"What are you doing, lady? Are you trying to kill me?"

We could hear him though our windows were rolled up.

"You ever driven a car before? Are you driving with your eyes closed? Do you know left from right? Do you want both sides of the street to be your side?"

"I think he's mad," Patrick observed.

"Perhaps a bit," I said calmly. "You stay here." I got out of the car to speak to the guy and make sure no damage had been done. Cars moved slowly around our two vehicles, people craning their heads to see what had happened.

"Didn't you see me coming?" the guy asked as we strode toward each other. "What does it matter if you saw me?" he answered himself. "You're on the wrong side of the street!"

"I'm sorry. I made a mistake. But there's no reason to get dramatic about it."

"No reason! My entire life flashed before my eyes."

"Really. I hope it was interesting," I said, then checked over both cars, though clearly they had not touched. "I didn't even jostle your bonnet."

He looked at me funny, and I remembered that American cars had another name for the front of the vehicle. "I mean your cap."

He squinted at me and ran his hands through his hair, big hands through dark and wavy hair. I suddenly recognized him—the guy in the antique shop, the one who had been buying a last-minute gift.

"What I mean is that whatever that big metal thing is"—I pointed to the front of his car—"I didn't touch it."

"I remember you from the store," he said. "You're English."

"Not exactly."

"That's why you're driving on the wrong side of the road."

"It's only the wrong side in America," I pointed out.

He took a step closer, perhaps wanting another look at eyes that were like green plastic pop bottles, but I couldn't step back. The obedient little boy I had told to stay in the car was standing on my heels, peeking around me.

The guy rested his hand on the front of his car. "This is called a hood."

"I'll try to remember that," I replied crisply. "And I'll try to stay on the right side of the road." *Oh, those dark, brilliant eyes!* I thought. "Let's go, Patrick."

"Wait, Kate." Patrick yanked on me, wanting me to bend down so he could whisper. He spoke loud enough to be heard in the next shire. "It's Sam Koscinski, the hockey player. Don't you remember? I showed you his picture."

Hearing the awe in Patrick's voice, the guy smiled. *No guy,* I thought, *should have both eyes and a smile that could melt steel. His ego was probably insufferable.*

"I do remember. The manic-looking one."

The guy laughed. He didn't care—he knew girls found him attractive.

"Can I have your autograph?" Patrick asked.

"Sure," Sam replied in his soft American drawl. "Do you have something I could sign?"

Patrick glanced up at me.

"Get a piece of paper from your book bag. *Not* your spelling test," I added, watching him to make sure he stayed on the left side of the car, walking safely between it and the sidewalk.

"Are you his baby-sitter?" Sam asked me.

I turned back to him. "His tutor," I said, "his nanny, au pair, whatever. I live with the family."

"Oh, yeah? Where?"

"Outside of town, an estate called Mason's Choice."

"The Westbrooks' place?" Sam's smile disappeared.

"Yes."

"That kid is a Westbrook?" Sam's eyes narrowed. "How is he related?"

"He is Adrian Westbrook's son."

"Nice father," Sam remarked, his voice thick with sarcasm.

"What do you mean?"

"I mean a lot of things. For one, his father yanks people around."

"Well, his father isn't the one who wants your autograph," I reminded him.

"I tore off two pieces of paper," Patrick announced as he rejoined us. "Can you sign both? I'm going to mail one to Tim," he explained happily. "Tim's dad took us to your games."

Sam signed both of the ragged pieces quickly—carelessly, I

thought. I hoped that Patrick was too enamored to notice the sudden chill in the air.

"Are you playing here this Saturday?" Patrick asked him.

"Yup. Got to go," Sam said brusquely.

"Can we go to the game, Kate? Can we, please? Please?"

"If we can't find anything better to do," I said.

Sam, who had started off, glanced back a moment.

I couldn't tell him off, not in front of Patrick. I wasn't going to tear down a child's hero, even if he was a royal jerk.

Sam waited for me to back up and drive past his car, perhaps thinking it was safest if he didn't move while I was on the road. It wasn't until we turned into the gates of Mason's Choice that I remembered what had distracted me from my driving.

At the thought of it, the skin on my arms rose in little bumps. According to Patrick, Ashley had said I could "ride" Silver Knight. The toy's name had been a secret shared by us—how did Patrick know it? Since the horse was my favorite among Ashley's toys, it was also the bribe she would use when she wanted me to play with her. I found it spooky that twelve years later, Patrick, wanting me to play, was making the same offer.

Five

"AN EXCELLENT IDEA, Patrick," Adrian said that evening, touching his son's cheek, smiling at him. "Mrs. Hopewell, set a place at the dinner table for Kate."

Eating dinner with the family was the last thing I wanted to do. "Thank you very much, but—"

"You may place her between Trent and me," Emily interrupted.

"I've told you before, Emily," Robyn said, "you don't need to give Hoppy instructions. She is quite capable at her job. Besides, the order for seating people at the table was set long before *you* arrived here."

"By you, I suppose," Emily replied, "before I was born."

Robyn sent her a withering look.

In the last fifteen minutes, with the family gathered in the beautiful, high-ceilinged room that overlooked an expanse of darkening water and sky, the petty comments had run nonstop.

Robyn, who had chosen the armchair closest to her father's, showed considerable skill in undermining Emily's authority in the household. Emily, responding by positioning herself even closer to Adrian, perching on the ottoman that matched his chair, displayed her own talent for small put-downs, such as reminding Robyn of her age. Both women continually glanced at Adrian, like schoolgirls waiting for an adult to notice and take sides.

Across the room, next to the fireplace, Trent and Brook had their own game going.

"I don't care where anyone sits," Brook said, lounging on a striped silk sofa, his muddy feet on the upholstery, "as long as I get fed."

"Spoken like the well-bred gentleman that you are," Trent remarked. He sat on a matching sofa, but his feet were flat on the floor and his back straighter, stiffer than the furniture.

Adrian, apparently unfazed by these small exchanges, watched Patrick with obvious pleasure. Tearing through the pile of gifts his father had purchased for him in Baltimore, Patrick was acting like a spoiled brat, tossing down each box after seeing what it contained, wanting the next one.

He paused, holding a sleek red car. "I want Kate next to me."

"No," Robyn said. "The matter is settled."

"But I want to sit next to Kate! I want to! I have to!"

He yanked tissue from the box and threw it at Robyn.

"Patrick," I said softly, unsure whether I should correct him when his parents were present.

Robyn's tan face darkened with anger. "Children who have been raised properly do not insist on getting their way."

"He's only seven," Emily protested.

"And he has such a fine role model in your own son," Trent added from across the room. "With Brook around, whatever would give Patrick the idea that he can have everything he wants?"

Robyn glared at Trent, but Brook smiled, as if he thought his uncle's jab was a compliment.

"Daddy, really," Robyn said, "Patrick must learn his place."

"Louise," Adrian said calmly, "seat Patrick on my right and Kate next to Patrick."

Mrs. Hopewell nodded, her face expressionless as a wig stand.

Robyn blinked her eyes rapidly, as if fighting back tears, which I found a bit weird. She was too old to become unhinged at losing a battle over seats.

Emily pouted beautifully, like a model in a lipstick ad. "Darling, Patrick was with Kate all afternoon and will be with her again this evening. I want him next to me at dinner."

Adrian ignored his wife and turned his gaze on Robyn and

Trent. "Inviting guests for dinner is part of Patrick's training if he is to be the next head of this household. He may invite and seat his guests as he wishes."

A sullen silence followed. Trent toyed with a paperweight on the table next to him. Robyn flipped furiously through a horse magazine, not pausing long enough to read a headline. Brook scowled at the ceiling, and Emily developed a sudden fascination with Patrick's model car. I excused myself to get ready for dinner, eager to get away from them all.

Was Adrian really planning to make Patrick the head of the household, his principal heir, I wondered; or was it simply his way of silencing the nasty group? It was certainly a good way to create antagonism toward Patrick. To Robyn and Trent, Patrick was a newcomer surpassing them in the amount of attention they received from their father, and perhaps in the amount of money.

Surely Patrick sensed the jealousy among the members of his family and felt their intense dislike for him. Most children, I thought, aware of others' hostility, either acted out or retreated. Perhaps Ashley, created out of snippets Patrick had heard from members of the household, was his retreat. In effect, he had made himself a new relative, one he could play with.

When I returned to the first floor, dinner was ready to be served. Adrian took his seat at the head of the long table, and

Henry, the elderly employee, seated Emily on the left side of Adrian, across from Patrick. I, of course, was to sit next to Patrick. Brook stood behind me as if courteously waiting to push in my chair. I felt his finger, the tip of it, making small circles on the bare skin at the back of my neck. I would have preferred being touched by a lizard. I glanced across the table at Robyn, who pulled in her own chair with a grim look.

"Now, Mother," Brook told her, "guests must be seated first. According to Patrick, Kate is a guest. And, as we all know, Patrick is the one who calls the shots around here."

"Sit down, Brook," Adrian said, his voice quiet but carrying like thunder.

Brook sat next to me, with Trent across from him. A girl not much older than I assisted Henry in serving the soup. Mrs. Hopewell stood in the doorway and watched. For a few minutes all you could hear were spoons scraping against china and the wind coming off the bay. A fire had been made in the dining room hearth; it hissed and sputtered.

"You know my dump truck?" Patrick asked, breaking the silence.

"The one you unwrapped this afternoon?" Adrian replied.

Patrick nodded. "I gave Patricia a ride in it."

"Oh, Patrick," Emily said, "your hamster should stay in her cage."

"But she liked it, she really liked it—didn't she, Kate?" he said, appealing to me.

"She didn't actually say so, but yes, I believe she did."

Patricia, being old as well as plump, had showed no inclination to scurry around. I didn't see any harm in letting her out of her cage. Children need to touch animals.

"The hamster must remain in her cage, Kate," Emily said.

"Yes, ma'am."

"You were informed that Patrick is allergic to cats and dogs."

"Yes, ma'am. Is he also allergic to hamsters?"

Brook laughed, which made my question seem flip.

"No," Robyn answered, before Emily could. "His mother is. She has a severe reaction to anything that walks on four legs."

"So, Trent," Adrian said, "I had counted on meeting with you this afternoon. I've been going over last year's earnings, and I can't say I am pleased."

Trent nodded. "I assumed you would need a day to settle in, Father, so I dropped by Crossroads. We've received another complaint from the Gleasons, the family who lives next to it."

"The shack people?" Brook interjected. "The family who doesn't know when to stop having kids? Though that's okay with me. The oldest girl is pretty hot."

"Stay away from her, Brook," his mother said. "She's not our kind of people."

"It's good of you to remind me, Brook," Adrian added dryly. "Mrs. Hopewell, with Brook home, you must remember not to set the house security system at night. We don't need the alarm going off at four in the morning."

"This time," Trent went on in his businesslike, colorless voice, "the Gleasons have contacted the county animal control people and have asked them to examine the fencing on the kennels. They believe the dogs are a danger to their children, who play next to them."

Adrian shrugged. "I believe their children are a danger to my dogs."

Robyn laughed, a bit too loudly. "The Gleasons have contacted the right person in our family," she observed. "Did you pet the dogs, Trent, to convince the family that they are friendly?"

"No, he stuck his head in one of their mouths," Brook said, making his mother laugh again and even winning a smile from Adrian.

I remembered how timid Trent had been around Ashley's collection of animals, especially the wild creatures she was always feeding—featherless birds, baby raccoons, and her favorite, a battle-scarred orange tabby.

"The point is," Trent said, "we will need to comply with suggestions by the county. If the dogs got out and something happened, we could be sued."

"The dogs know their job," Adrian replied. "They will maul anyone who enters the building after hours, just as I trained them to do. Case closed."

The soup was removed and the next course brought in, steak with vegetables. Patrick was silent, his eyes flicking from one member of the family to the next, like those of a wary animal.

"Did Louise give you a phone message, Trent?" Emily asked. "Someone from the Queen Victoria called today."

"The hotel?" Robyn cut in. "You're not still seeing that woman, Margery whatever."

"Gilbert," Trent said, pronouncing the last name distinctly.

"I would think, Trent," Robyn went on, "that somewhere in New York or Philadelphia, you could find a woman more suitable than a hotel manager who went through the Wisteria public school system."

"And I would think," Trent responded, "that if you had a worthwhile way to spend your life, you wouldn't be so concerned about mine."

"Perhaps if she had her own romance," Emily suggested slyly. "How many years has it been since you've had a man in your life, Robyn? I mean, besides your father."

Robyn's eyes bored through Emily.

A sudden gust of wind rattled the dining room's old windowpanes. The flame in the fireplace sputtered and blew out.

"Where—where did that come from?" Trent asked softly.

Everyone turned, following his eyes to a window. The sky was completely black now, but the outside floodlights had come on, lighting the window casements like small stages against the darkness. There wasn't a sound at the dinner table—not a sip from a glass or a clink of silver. In the window farthest to the right sat a battle-scarred orange tabby.

Without a word, Patrick pushed back his chair and walked toward the window. He laid his palm flat against the glass. The tabby arched its back, rubbing against the pane, as a cat rubs against the leg of some one it knows.

"Can I let him in, Daddy? Can I keep him?"

"Darling, you have an allergy," Emily said.

"But—"

"He's a feral cat," Adrian replied. "You can't own a wild animal like that. They are never happy staying inside."

"But he likes me," Patrick pleaded.

Brook glanced from the cat to his mother. She shifted uncomfortably in her chair. Trent gazed at the shabby cat, as if entranced. Orange stripes, a bitten-off tail, half of its left ear missing—it was identical to the one Ashley had loved.

Ashley's cat could still be alive, I reasoned, for cats could live twenty years or more. It seemed too much a coincidence that another animal would have the exact same coloring and scars as Ashley's and would choose the same window he had liked to occupy twelve years before. But if this was Ashley's feral cat, how much more a coincidence was it that he would show up now, now that I had returned to Mason's Choice, now that Patrick saw something in the air he called Ashley?

I was dreaming, unhappy, five-year-old dreams, having cried myself to sleep in the cottage bedroom. Ashley had taken Lilly, my golden-haired baby doll. She had shelves full of her own dolls, but she wanted mine. When Ashley snatched Lilly, I screamed for help, but since I did a lot of shrieking while playing with her, the adults ignored me until it was too late. Now Ashley had hidden my doll where no one could find her.

I sat up suddenly, awakened from my afternoon nap by the sound of something crashing through the cottage window. Broken glass flew inward. I jumped out of bed, then saw my doll lying on the floor among the sharp pieces.

"Lilly!"

"You can have her back."

Surprised by the sound of Ashley's voice, I looked up. She was supposed to be punished, not allowed out of the house till she gave back my doll, but she sat on the limb of an old maple outside my bedroom window.

"You climbed the tree," I said in awe.

She shrugged. "We can climb anywhere." The orange cat she loved, the wild one with the torn ear, was perched two branches higher, staring in at me.

"You can have Lilly. I don't want her," Ashley said. "She's ugly now."

I looked down at my baby. Her teeth had been colored black with a marker. Jagged black scribbles had been made all over her beautiful face.

"Mommy!" I howled. "Mom-my! Mommy, I need you."

Hands tugged at me. Small hands held my face. "Kate? Kate!"

I sat up, no longer in a cottage bedroom, but in the main house at Mason's Choice. The clock read 2:05 A.M. Patrick stood next to my bed, his eyes big and frightened.

"Patrick, what is it?" I asked, struggling to free myself from the threads of my dream. "Is something wrong?"

"It's Ashley," he said. "She keeps talking."

"What?"

Patrick chewed on the sleeve of his pajamas. "I told her to be quiet, but she won't. She won't let me sleep."

I climbed out of a bed and knelt in front of him. Resting my hands on his thin shoulders, I could feel him shivering beneath his flannel top. "You were dreaming."

"No, Kate, she's there. She's in my toy closet, playing with my horses."

I glanced toward the stairway between his room and mine. What did it mean—both of us dreaming of Ashley at the same time? Nothing, I told myself. Returning to her home, it was only natural I would dream of her. But perhaps not so naturally, Patrick did.

I slipped my arms in my dressing gown, then took a jacket from my closet and put it on Patrick. He looked small and vulnerable in it, its cuffs dangling well below the ends of his arms.

"Let's go have a look," I told him, then headed down the steps. He trailed behind, reluctant to go back to his room, but equally reluctant to be left alone in mine. At the bottom of the turning stairs I stopped. The door of his toy closet was ajar; light emanated from within.

"Who turned on the light?" I asked quietly.

Patrick looked unsure. "Ashley," he answered at last.

Though my mind kept saying these were nothing but dreams, my hands were shaking. I stuffed them in the pockets of my gown, then crept toward the door of the walk-in closet. Without touching the door, I slowly moved my head forward, till I could peer through.

In the slice of lit closet I could see two horses on the floor, Silver Knight and Whirlwind, facing each other as if someone had been playing with them. A light prickle ran along the back of my neck. Ashley had loved to put together these two horses, to make them "talk." I wriggled my shoulders, wishing I could slip out of the eerie grip of another coincidence.

"I don't see her," I said, opening the door wider.

Patrick, who had stayed on the bottom step, crept over and peeked in. "She left. But she'll come back. She'll come back as soon as you leave. I want to sleep in your room, Kate."

If I let him do it once, he'd want to do it again and again.

"Where do you think Ashley went?" I asked, hoping to prove she wasn't in the room. I needed some convincing myself.

He glanced around. His eyes paused at the tall mirror above the bureau, full of gray night shadows that came alive each time he or I moved. He glanced up at the wardrobe with the massive top that seemed to make it tip forward, then studied the drapes that hung to the floor. Ashley used to hide behind drapes, waiting for her chance to jump out at me.

"Would you look under my bed?" Patrick asked.

"All right," I said, opening the closet door all the way, allowing more light in the room. I didn't turn on the large bureau lamps, for their brightness would make it difficult for him to fall asleep again. Getting down or my knees, I lifted layers of bed clothing. "Nothing there. Want to see?"

He dropped down next to me, his side pressed against mine. We checked the inside of his wardrobe, behind the curtains, and every other place into which Ashley might fit. At last I closed the closet door, leaving a narrow strip of light shining, in case he wanted to check it again, then I turned on a soft night-light by his bed.

"Come on, Patrick, let's get you under the covers where it's warmer." I fluffed the quilt, then placed a chair next to his mattress. "I'll stay with you for a while and make sure Ashley doesn't come back. Into bed now. You must be freezing—I am," I said, lifting one bare foot, then the other off the cold floorboards.

He took one last look around and joined me. "Can I wear your coat, Kate?"

"I don't think you'll need it with all these blankets."

"I need it," he said, his voice quivering.

"All right then." If he thought the coat would protect him from Ashley, I wasn't taking it away from him. "In you go, under the covers, head on your pillow."

He climbed in and stared up at me, his nose just above the edge of a quilt. Impulsively, I leaned down to kiss his forehead. Two arms in very long sleeves reached around my neck and hugged me hard.

"Close your eyes," I said, "left then right. Good night, starlight." I pressed my lips together, surprised at how easily it had come back to me, the saying my mother had used when putting me to bed.

Patrick rolled onto his tummy. While I rubbed his back, I thought about the things he had said and their connections to the past. Something strange was going on in this house. I wasn't a person who believed in ghosts or devils; traveling with my father, I had seen enough to convince me that human beings alone were sufficient to account for the frightening and evil things that happened in the world. Still, the coincidences of the last few days were spooking me.

There was a meanness at Mason's Choice, a quiet kind of menace that lived below the level of petty quarrels. Whether it originated from household members, one of whom might be preying on Patrick, planting ideas that would frighten him, or from something far less tangible, I didn't know. I was sure of only one thing: The source of Patrick's fear was dangerous— dangerous and sly.

Six

SATURDAY MORNING PATRICK rose rested and eager to go to the hockey game. I wondered if he remembered the events of last night, but I was reluctant to mention Ashley by name, not wanting to reintroduce fears that sleep may have erased. While we painted a sign saying GO, SAM! I told Patrick that I had had a strange dream last night, giving him a chance to talk about whatever he might remember.

"Do you think Sam will see my sign?" was his response. "Maybe we should make it bigger."

Apparently, ice hockey was the only thing on his mind today.

We arrived late at the game, which began at noon. The high school team played at Chase College's athletic center, with the college's JV and varsity teams scheduled later in the day. Either ice hockey was big in this small town or there was nothing else to do in Wisteria in early March; the place was packed with teens, adults, and bands of little boys and girls in hockey garb. Patrick wanted to sit close to the rink and team bench. I had forgotten about the American love for cheerleaders and watched with fascination as the girls bounced around in the aisles. One of them thought Patrick was cute and told him that Sam was her favorite player too.

Even without Patrick screeching in my ear, I could have picked out Number 23 of the white jerseys. Most of the guys looked the same with their huge pads and helmets, but 23 was clearly manic. When his team scored, he punched the air and any teammate available with such ferocity that he'd knock down his own players. When a sub was put in and he was supposed to be resting on the bench, he was up and dancing, screaming at the players and the officials. I saw the referee giving him the eye when he hollered at a call he didn't like.

"Icing? Icing!" Sam cried out. "Did you forget your glasses, ref? If thirty-three had moved his big butt, he'd have had that!"

Whenever Sam took a penalty shot, a one-on-one situation with the goalie, the crowd would chant, "Sam, Sam, Sam's the man!" He was good, much better than the other players—even I could tell that. And though I didn't know the sport, I was very familiar with his style. I knew that sooner or later emotion would get the better of Sam, and then he'd look at the offending party with disbelief, even hurt. If he didn't quickly get a grip on his emotions, the passion that made him so good would work against him. I'd seen that happen repeatedly with my father.

"Tripping?" Sam screamed at the referee, as his opponent went flying headfirst across the ice.

The official struck his leg with his hand, which must have been a signal for the penalty call.

"But I touched the puck! I touched it first."

The referee jerked his head toward the penalty box. From the look of utter disbelief on Sam's face, you would have thought he'd been accused of playing with four arms. He skated over to the box, then stewed in there for two minutes.

"Stupid ref," Patrick said.

"A penalty is a penalty," I replied.

After three long periods of athletics and theatrics, Sam and his teammates won. They spent a lot of time hugging one another.

"I want to get Sam's autograph," Patrick said.

"You have two already."

"I want him to autograph my sign," he explained. "Let's go. I know where the players come out. Please, Kate. It's the last game."

For a moment I didn't reply. "It is?"

"The announcer just said so."

I quickly turned my back to the rink and snatched up our coats. "All right."

"Can we get tickets to the play-offs?" Patrick asked.

"I thought you said it was the last game."

"Before the play-offs. Didn't you hear the announcement?"

A moment ago? No, I hadn't heard a word, for Sam had taken off his helmet and gloves, and I had stood like a moron staring at him, attracted again by his strong hands. I had gotten a strange feeling inside, one that I quelled fast. A tough jock with damp curly hair, which made him seem childlike, muscle and sweat, but a badly bruised hand—maybe that was it, the mix of macho and vulnerability. I had turned away, but it was a second too late. He had caught me gazing at him, and worse, had gazed back with the dark eyes that were unsafe to look into.

I was relieved to find a large group of people outside the players' dressing room, waiting to congratulate their team. I took a seat some distance away, where a group of adults were waiting, keeping my eye on Patrick as he bobbed around the teens and kids gathering by the players' entrance. I counted on this group of admirers to keep Sam from being too cold to Patrick.

The woman next to me saw Patrick waving to me and gesturing with his sign. "Are you a fan of Sam's?" she asked.

"Hardly."

She tilted her head, and I realized that my response sounded rude. "What I mean is that I'm not much of a hockey fan, but that little boy is. He thinks Sam Koscinski is the greatest thing since the Queen's hats."

The woman laughed, a silvery laugh that seemed to go with her prematurely silver hair. She had beautiful skin, and dark eyes with a touch of merriness.

The players started coming out and were surrounded by friends and fans. Sam got swallowed up. I watched Patrick hopping like a bunny, trying to get his hero's attention. If I helped him I'd have to fight my way into the group, which had a rather high percentage of cute girls. I glanced down at my jeans, then my heavy boots, which were still coated with mud from yesterday's trek to the pond. I felt like a sheep farmer. Patrick was on his own.

Sam's group moved slowly in our direction. He hugged everyone on the way—girls, guys, parents, somebody's grandmother. Patrick trailed behind. I was probably going to have to do something.

"Hey, Mom!" Sam called. "We're number one!"

"Hey, Sam," replied the woman next to me, the one who had asked me if I was a fan. "Good job."

I turned to look at her and she smiled a little.

"There's a short guy behind the other kids, Sam," she added, "who would really like your attention."

Sam craned his head to see Patrick, then glanced back at me.

"No, *she's* not a fan," his mother said, laughing as she had when I'd told her "Hardly." "Don't let the short guy down, Sam."

I wondered if Mrs. Koscinski already knew who Patrick was and how Sam had responded to him yesterday. Did she know I drove on the wrong side of the road?

"Thank you for helping Sam pick out my bracelet," she said to me, jingling the silver chain on her wrist. "It's beautiful."

A guy who talked to his mother—I would never have guessed it. A guy who remembered his mother's birthday—not his girlfriend's—not that it meant he didn't have a girlfriend, and not that it mattered, of course.

Sam was surveying Patrick's sign. Patrick was thrilled, chattering away. Sam listened and responded, acting much nicer to him than before.

"Thank you for saying something," I told Mrs. Koscinski. "This means a lot to Patrick."

She nodded graciously.

Sam knelt down to sign the poster. Seeing Patrick's hand resting on Sam's wide shoulder, his earnest little face close to Sam's attentive one, I felt a lump in my throat.

I shook off the feeling, just in time, for Sam rose and carried the sign over to me.

"I guess you couldn't find anything better to do today," he said, reminding me of yesterday's remark.

"Patrick wanted to come very badly," I replied, keeping the focus on my charge. "He really enjoyed the game."

"Yeah, he just gave me the play-by-play. Thanks for making the poster. I noticed it between periods. It's great!"

"I really didn't have anything to do with it," I said. "Patrick painted it all."

Sam smiled a little, then very lightly touched my fingertips with his. Saying nothing more, he moved on.

His brief touch traveled all the way through me. My skin felt warm, my cheeks hot. I gazed down at my hands: Incriminating poster paint was stuck beneath my fingernails.

"Come on, Patrick." I rose from my seat. "Let's get going."

"Nice meeting you, Kate," Sam's mother called after me.

I turned back to her and saw that Sam had inherited her wonderful smile. "Nice meeting you, Mrs. Koscinski."

"Store's closed."

"Maybe you should lock the door, Mr. Joseph," I replied, entering Olivia's Antiques, Patrick trailing behind me. We had left the car in the college parking lot and walked to High Street.

Joseph looked up from a worn-looking ledger. "Right. And

then when shoppers insist on coming in, because they are either ignorant or illiterate—"

"Or stubborn?" I suggested.

"I have to stop what I'm doing, go to the door, unlock it, and tell them what is already posted on the sign. But I'm glad to see you, Katie. And please leave off the 'Mister' part. Who is this fine young man?"

Patrick looked behind him.

"You, sport," Joseph said.

I made the introductions and explained that we had just come from the game.

"Hockey, that's a nice violent activity. Well, Patrick, do you know what I have for you in the back?" Joseph asked.

"How can I if I've never been there?"

"Cute," Joseph remarked.

"Patrick, your manners," I chided. Whether he was being flip or reacting to a patronizing adult tone, I wasn't sure.

"Sorry."

"I have a pile of cartons that need to be broken down flat," Joseph continued. "Nowadays, they not only want you to recycle, they want you to fold your boxes like laundry before they haul them away. Do you think you could help me with that?"

Patrick looked up at me. He knew when someone was trying to get rid of him.

"It will give you something to do while Joseph and I talk," I said.

Joseph led the way to the back storeroom. After about thirty seconds, Patrick found it too much fun stomping on the cardboard boxes to care if he was being kept busy.

"So how is it going?" Joseph asked quietly, when he and I had passed through the doorway to the front of the store.

"When it is just Patrick and me, fine. I am to pick him up from school at three o'clock every day, and in the afternoon and evening, I'm going to do my best to keep him away from other members of the household—except his parents, of course."

"I was afraid you would find them a rotten lot."

"Trent is cold and barely acknowledges him. Robyn is mean and, if you ask me, a bit strange in the way she still competes for her father's attention. Brook teases—pretends he teases— but there is no love behind it, and Patrick isn't fooled. Mrs. Hopewell is the same as ever—I think she flies on a broomstick at night."

Joseph laughed.

"Patrick's parents aren't helping any. Emily clings to him, which drives him away. Adrian loves him and makes it far too clear that Patrick is his favorite, which fuels the others' resentment of him."

I recounted the scene at dinner last night and Adrian's

statement about the possibility of Patrick being the next head of the household.

"Good old Adrian," Joseph said. "He knows how to push people's buttons."

"Maybe. Even so, I like him better than the rest."

"Most people do," Joseph replied, sitting down on a piece of store merchandise. The old chair wobbled beneath his weight. "But don't trust him, Katie. He can turn on you. Do you still have my number? Did they give you a phone?"

"A mobile—cell," I added, switching to Americanese, and wrote down my new number. "Joseph, why did my parents leave Mason's Choice?"

"Didn't your father tell you?" he asked.

"No. He would never talk about it." I walked around an assortment of tables and lamps, running my finger under the fringe of one of the shades. "Mrs. Hopewell said that we were sent packing by Adrian. Adrian said my father left in an artistic huff. I remember leaving late at night in the middle of a terrible storm. My father drove without headlights, as if he didn't want anyone to see us, and I don't recall any other time in which my father got in an artistic snit and sneaked away. When he was angry, he wanted everyone to know. He had a knack for melodrama."

Joseph smiled, as if remembering that aspect of his personality. "Of course, your father was quite young then, and not very sure of himself. He may have been afraid of Adrian."

Or afraid that the ring would be discovered missing, I thought. *Maybe it really did make sense.*

"You know, Adrian has a history of using people and discarding them," Joseph continued.

I glanced toward the storage room to make certain there were no little ears listening in. "What do you mean?"

"When you can offer Adrian something he desires, he's delighted to make a deal and acts as if he is your best friend. But once he has gotten what he wants, he is inclined to toss people away—he'll run over you if it suits him."

Sam had indicated as much.

"So, Mrs. Hopewell assumed that he was tossing us away, that he sent us packing."

"I'm guessing that. There are some things you should understand about Mrs. Hopewell. She is very loyal to Adrian, and perhaps even more so to Robyn. She raised Robyn—Trent, too, after Adrian divorced, but it's Robyn that Hopewell sees as her daughter. She'll do anything for her."

"Kate, c'mere," Patrick called from the back room.

"In a minute," I called back, then lowered my voice. "Joseph, do you remember the orange cat that Ashley loved?"

"The feral one?"

"He showed up last night."

"The same cat?" Joseph asked, his head bent forward as if he hadn't heard me correctly.

"One with a bitten-off tail and torn ear. It was the cat's left ear, wasn't it?"

He nodded thoughtfully. "There was something . . . unsettling about that cat, the way he responded to Ashley—did what she wanted with just a look from her, without her saying a word."

"There are a lot of unsettling things at Mason's Choice," I replied. "Patrick has Ashley's furniture and Ashley's horses—he knows her secret names for them. He has Ashley's books and Ashley's outdoor play set—or I should say mine—you remember the old metal swings and bars by the workers' cottages. He prefers them to the new equipment the way Ashley did and—"

"Kate?" Patrick stood at the storage room door. "We'd better go home. I'm supposed to play with Ashley this afternoon. She'll get mad if I'm not there."

I turned back to Joseph, whose eyes had just grown larger. "That's the other thing I wanted to tell you about."

Seven

WHEN PATRICK AND I arrived home, he ceremoniously carried his autographed poster to the third-floor playroom, where we hung it on the wall.

"It looks spectacular," I said, then glanced past him. Something was missing. "Patrick, where's Patricia?"

He turned quickly and saw the hamster's empty cage. The screen, which should have covered the glass tank, was propped against its side. "Patricia?" he called softly.

Emily was going to have my head.

I remembered seeing Patrick replace the weighted screen after feeding his pet. Sometime after that, there had been five minutes, maybe less, when I had left him alone. "Were you playing with her after she ate?" I asked.

"No."

"You're certain of that? I'm not angry. I want to know because it makes sense to look wherever you last saw her."

"I last saw her in her cage."

A hamster could hide in a million places in the playroom and schoolroom, not to mention the rest of the third floor—my room and the two large storage rooms.

"Maybe Ashley let her out," Patrick suggested.

"Don't blame her," I said shortly.

"I'm not blaming her. If Ashley did it, it was an accident. She probably just wanted to play and I wasn't here."

I bit my lip. He wasn't using his imaginary playmate as an excuse—he really believed it.

We searched the playroom, schoolroom, and my bedroom. When I opened the door to one of the storage rooms, I saw that the task was overwhelming. Clothing, furniture, old athletic equipment, books—there was no way we could find a three-inch bit of fur unless she willingly came out. I hated lying to Patrick; still, I wondered how hard it would be to buy an identical hamster and pretend that a hungry "Patricia" had come home while he was in school Monday.

We searched the storage room for a while, and I saw Patrick's eyes fill up several times.

"Let's go outside," I suggested. "Since Patricia ate all of her food this morning, she won't be hungry enough to come back yet."

"But she may come back because she misses me."

"Of course. Of course, she misses you, but she's having a little adventure right now. We'll check for her later."

I had hoped we could make it outside without seeing anyone—I needed time to decide how to handle this—but when we reached the kitchen, Brook was there. Patrick's concern for his pet made him desperate for help.

"Patricia is gone," he confided. "She's not in her cage. Have you seen her?"

"Patricia," Brook replied, popping open a can of Coke. "Is she a hamster? Kind of brown?"

"Yeah! Real brown!" Patrick looked hopeful.

"Brook," I warned.

"I did see her. She was carrying a little backpack, heading to the orangerie."

"Cut it out, Brook."

He shrugged at me. "I'm just telling you what I saw," he said.

Patrick rushed toward the kitchen door.

"Brook was teasing," I called, then hurried outside after Patrick. He rounded the corner of the house and ran toward the orangerie.

The orangerie, tennis courts, outdoor pool, and docks were laid out in a line along the northern edge of the estate, which bordered the river mouth. The orangerie was a long building with a row of tall Palladian windows, more glass than brick. Citrus trees and other tropical plants grew inside.

"Do you think she went in?" Patrick asked me.

"Not unless she can reach the door handle," I replied. I knew that hamsters could burrow and slip through cracks in foundations, but I assumed Patricia was holed up in some warm, snug spot on the third floor of the house. "Brook was joking. He made up that story."

"But she might really be here," Patrick insisted.

"All right. Walk around the building and see."

He did, calling Patricia's name softly, woefully. Then he hollered suddenly from the other side, "Hey, Kate. C'mere!"

Rounding the corner, I found him standing five feet from the orange cat that had perched in the window last night. The cat dismissed my appearance with the briefest of looks, then ventured toward Patrick, rubbing against his leg.

"He likes me," Patrick announced happily, momentarily forgetting about his hamster. "I told Daddy he liked me."

The cat flicked his tail, then broke into a quick trot in the direction of the tennis courts.

"I think he knows where Patricia is," Patrick said.

I hoped not, given that this wild tabby was used to catching his own dinner. Patrick followed the cat past the screen of evergreens that shielded the house from the courts, and I hurried after him. He and I caught up with the tabby near the in-ground swimming pool. The cat crossed the concrete deck and began to pace along the pool's edge, as if he had quarried something. As we walked toward him, the cat stopped and peered into the deep end. Curious, we did the same.

The water had been removed from the pool, but leaves clotted the drains and rain had formed a half-frozen crust beneath the diving board. I thought I was seeing just another brown leaf, then Patrick started screaming, "Patricia! Patricia!"

I grabbed him by the collar as he took off for a set of metal steps. "I'll get her."

I descended the steps at the shallow end of the pool. Patrick kept wailing his pet's name.

Perhaps if she hasn't been outside too long . . . I thought, hoping against the odds. The first seven meters of the pool were dry, but there was a steep drop down to the diving section, and there the footing became treacherous. My feet slid out from under me. I flew down the concrete slope on my back, my feet crashing through the layer of ice and water covering the bottom of the deep end. The freezing mix sloshed over my shoes. I walked as quickly as possible toward Patricia, then scooped her up in my gloved hand.

"Is she okay?" Patrick called.

"I'll know better when I get out of the pool."

The hamster was dead, but I wanted to be close to Patrick when I told him. I had to scramble to get up the pool's slope with only one free hand. Patrick was waiting for me by the steps at the shallow end, anxiously beating his mittens together. The cat lurked a short distance behind, interested in what I was doing, staring the way cats do, as if they can see so much more than people.

I knelt down in front of Patrick, opening the hand that cradled the hamster. "I'm sorry."

He gazed down at her. "Her eyes are open," he said. "She's alive!"

"She's not. I'm really sorry."

"But her eyes are open, Kate. Look!"

I shook my head. "Animals die with their eyes open. See, she isn't moving. She isn't breathing."

"Maybe she's just frozen," Patrick said. "Let me hold her, I'll warm her up."

I laid the hamster in his cupped hands. Tears brimmed in his eyes.

"Come on, Patricia. Come on," he pleaded. "Wake up. We'll take you inside. We'll get you warm enough. We'll make you okay."

"Patrick, listen to me," I said softly. "She's frozen, and when a hamster freezes, its heart stops. Patricia is dead. There is nothing we can do."

"You're wrong!" he shouted, then lowered his eyes.

His dark lashes were wet against his cheek. He buried his chin in his chest. Tears rolled silently down his face, then he started to sob.

I wrapped my arms around him and pulled him close. "I'm so sorry. If I could make her be alive for you, I would."

He cried hard. The cat watched us for a moment, then slipped away, as if he had fulfilled his mission.

At last the sobs grew quieter. Patrick rested his head against me, his hands still cradling his pet between my chest and his. I reached for some tissues in my pocket. Patrick sneaked a peak at the hamster, probably hoping that she had warmed up and come back to life.

"Would you like to bury her?" I asked, handing him the tissue.

He nodded mutely, more tears rolling down.

"There's probably a shovel in the orangerie," I said.

Patrick wanted to bury Patricia in the family cemetery. I could have called Adrian on my cell phone and asked permission to dig there, but the hole for Patricia would be small and I counted on him to understand how fragile his son was at that moment. We fetched a shovel from the orangerie, then cut across the formal gardens to the main drive, and passed through the keyhole in the tall hedge.

Who did this? I wondered as we walked silently toward the graveyard. It seemed unlikely that the lazy Patricia would have so quickly made her way down three stories of the large house. But even if she did, I could not believe that a home-bred hamster would venture far in the cold, certainly not as far as the pool, an open area without vegetation, where no animal would seek refuge.

It was possible the orange cat had caught her close to the house and dropped her in the pool, for the cat had led us there. But why hadn't he eaten her—surely, hunting rodents was how this wild cat survived. And if he wasn't hungry, why didn't he do what a domesticated cat would—keep its prey in a cozy place where it could play with it. More curious still, how did the cat know what Patrick was searching for?

I caught myself in the middle of that wild leap of an idea. The cat was just a cat, despite what Joseph had said about the silent communication between the tabby and Ashley. People who are good with animals often seem to have an intangible connection to them. The only unnatural, abnormal thing on Mason's Choice was Patrick's heartless relatives; for, no matter what the chain of events, the crisis started when the hamster was let out of her cage.

Most adults wouldn't believe a child who said he had put the top back on a cage. I knew if I started making accusations, that's how Patrick's family would respond. But I believed him. Someone had let Patricia out, someone enjoying a bit of cruel entertainment at Patrick's expense. Brook was the most likely suspect.

We had reached the cemetery. The large plot, surrounded by an iron fence, was barren of trees. The obelisks and statues, some standing upright, some leaning, cast long shadows in the late afternoon light. No winter birds stirred here, no squirrels scurried through. The only animals inhabiting the plot were the carved stone creatures placed around Ashley's grave. There was quiet but no peace here—I had felt it as a child, and felt it again now.

Ashley had said that the ghosts in this graveyard spoke to her. She had said they watched me when she and I were apart, that they told her what I did. Even now it was hard to shake off the feeling of being observed.

"Where should we bury her?" Patrick asked.

"Sorry? Oh. How about here?" I suggested, pointing to a patch of grass behind the gate that was unlikely to be used for anything else.

He knelt, solemnly watching as I dug into the hard earth. I wrapped Patricia in my scarf and laid her in the hole. Patrick helped me cover her with dirt.

"She'll rest warm and happy now," I told him, and wiped the tears from his face.

"Kate, when you're dead, do you have bad dreams?"

"No, only good ones." How I ached for him!

He glanced toward the new corner of the cemetery.

"That's where Ashley is resting," I told him. "Do you want to say a prayer for her and Patricia?"

"Ashley's not there."

"If you go over to the stone with the little animals around it, you will see her name."

"I know. But she's not there," he insisted.

"What do you mean?"

"She's in other places," he said.

A chill spread over my shoulders and the back of my neck. My feet, having been soaked in the pool's frigid water, felt like lumps of ice.

"Patrick, who is telling you these things about Ashley?"

Someone had to be, someone trying to frighten him. Whoever it was wouldn't dare hurt him physically and risk the wrath of Adrian. But the person knew how to do just as much damage psychologically.

"Is it Brook?"

"Ashley doesn't like Brook," he said.

"Is it Robyn? Trent?"

"Do you think Ashley let out Patricia?" Patrick asked me.

"What?" I stood up, took Patrick's hand, and quickly led

him out of the graveyard. "Why won't you tell me who is talking to you about Ashley?"

"Nobody is but you," he said.

I didn't know how to reason with him. "Why do you think she would let out Patricia?"

"Because I didn't get home in time. She was mad. She wanted to play and I wasn't home and she got mad."

"Patrick, Ashley would never hurt an animal. She loved them."

"So you can see her now?" he asked.

"No! No," I repeated in a softer voice. "It's just that everyone knows she loved animals."

"But she gets mad," he pointed out. "Sometimes she really screams when I don't do what she wants."

It was eerie how similar his Ashley was to the one I had known. But these were just imaginings, I reminded myself, and if I could not reason him past them, I could, at least, shape them for him.

"Did you ever see the movie about Casper the ghost?" I asked.

"I have the video."

"Remember how he's a nice ghost? Ashley is like that. Oh, sometimes she screams and puts up a fuss, but she's just lonely. She's just looking for a friend."

Patrick gazed up at me, his face scrunched. "Are you sure?"

"Yes."

So, it has come to this, I thought, as we trudged toward the house. I, who hated the way adults lied to children, was telling tales to Patrick. I'd do anything to make his fear and hurt go away.

As soon as Patrick and I returned from the burial, I spoke to Emily. She chastised me for not coming to her immediately—at a time like that, Patrick needed his mother, she said—though I had trouble imagining her trekking out to the cemetery in her Ferragamos. Since it was Saturday night and everyone was headed out, Patrick had dinner with me in the kitchen. Happily for us, Mrs. Hopewell was off Saturday evening through Sunday, so though she was still on the premises, she wasn't breathing down our necks.

The one thing that took Patrick's mind off Patricia was talking about ice hockey. After dinner, I remembered I had seen old sports equipment in the third-floor storage rooms. We searched and found a pair of battered hockey sticks. While Patrick ran up and down the hall, pushing an imaginary puck and dodging opponents, I went on to the schoolroom computer and downloaded information about children's hockey leagues. Logging on to Chase College's Web site, I discovered that the rink where

Sam played had an open skating session from 5:30 to 7:00 every weekday evening. I promised Patrick I'd take him.

After all the emotion of the day, he fell asleep early. I didn't close my eyes till late that night, my mind continually sifting through events, trying to find logical answers for the questions that had been accumulating in the last few days, most of them circling around Ashley.

It was possible that Brook, who had liked to spy on Ashley and me, had overheard and remembered the secret names of Ashley's toy horses. And given that, when he got jealous, he used to let out Ashley's pets, it was reasonable to think he had taken Patrick's. But he was mature enough now to see the plan through, and if his goal was to upset Patrick, why would he leave the hamster in the pool beyond the orangerie? He couldn't have counted on us to find it there. Perhaps he had simply tossed the hamster outside, never meaning for it to be found, but the cat had caught it. Or perhaps his plan was to torment Patrick with a fruitless search, and then, a few days later, pretend to have discovered it himself.

Despite my suspicions, I decided it best not to accuse him or anyone else. After denying they had any part in it, Patrick's loving family members might use the pet's death for their own cruel pleasure, discussing it, distressing him even more.

When I finally closed my eyes, my sleep was made restless

by dreams, a series of images, past and present, one melting into the next. I saw Patrick's hamster struggling to escape the ice at the bottom of the pool. I rushed toward her, trying to reach her in time. When I leaned over to scoop her up, I saw Ashley's face, Ashley trapped beneath the ice of the pond, staring up at me. Her mouth moved, but I couldn't understand her words.

I took a step back, afraid. The surface broke and Ashley rose up through the dark water, her eyes sparkling like blue ice.

"I dare you, Katie."

The edge of the round pond straightened and it became the pool again. I was on the diving board, walking its length slowly, my legs shaking.

"Go all the way to the end," Ashley instructed.

I did what she said. I tried not to look at the bottom of the pool far below me, but the icy crust covering the drain drew my eyes like a sore.

"Now jump up and down. Jump and land on the board again. I dare you, Katie!"

"I—I can't."

"Scaredy-cat, scaredy-cat," Ashley taunted. "Jump, Katie, jump!"

But what if I missed the board coming down? What if my feet slipped off?

"Mom-my!"

I awoke shivering, sat up, and glanced around. When I went to bed, I had closed the door to the hallway; it was open now. I pulled my blanket and quilt around me, but they were useless. The cold came from within, an anxious cold crawling in my belly.

I slipped out of bed and crept toward the door, listening. A small night-light, plugged into the wall outside the third-floor bathroom, provided the only light in the hall. I glanced over my shoulder toward the steps to Patrick's room. I should check that he is there, safely asleep, I thought. Then I heard a noise from the other side of the hall, close to the main stairs, a rustling soft as cloth brushing against cloth. I reached for the light switch in my room.

My overhead light illuminated a wide swath of the rectangular hall. If anyone was there, he or she clung to the shadows. I stared into the dark corners, listening. My muscles tensed. From the other end of the hall came a thin, scratching sound. *Rodents,* I thought, calming myself. Then the main stairs creaked.

I moved forward silently. They creaked again—it sounded as if the noise came from the bottom of the stairs. Someone had tread on them, someone had descended from the third floor before I turned on the light. I rushed across the hall.

Reaching the top of the stairs, I stopped suddenly, surprised to see Patrick alone in the schoolroom. He was writing on the blackboard, his chalk making the scratching sound I had heard. Distracted, I lost precious seconds on the person trying to get away.

I hurried down the steps. The night lamp in the second-floor hall suddenly went out. I stumbled, caught hold of the railing, and continued on. But with the night lamp extinguished and bedroom doors closed, the darkness on the second floor was thick as velvet. I paused at the bottom of the stairs. I couldn't remember which side of the hall the lamp was on or the location of the wall switches. All I could do was listen and try to hear where the person was going. There were a number of exits from the second-floor hall: the bedrooms, the stairs down to the first floor, and the hallways to each wing.

My ears ached to hear the slightest movement. Then a faint crack of light showed. It came from the direction of Robyn's wing. The sliver of light darkened for a moment, all but at the top, then shone again just before it disappeared completely. I replayed the sequence in my mind, trying to figure out what I had just seen: Someone had opened a door into a softly lit area, passed through it, then closed it.

I remained still, fixing in my head the exact way the light had shone. From where I was standing in the second-floor hall, the door into Robyn and Brook's quarters opened straight on. But Mrs. Hopewell, with rooms in the connecting section between the main house and their quarters, would have a door along the hallway—not straight on, but to the right. I was fairly sure the light had been angled from that direction. I wriggled my shoulders at the thought of the housekeeper silently opening my bedroom door and looking in while I slept. Had she roused Patrick? Was she the one talking to him about Ashley?

I hurried upstairs, making no effort to be quiet. Patrick was still at the blackboard, writing one sentence beneath the next, like a child who had been kept after school and made to write one hundred times "I will not talk in class." But his message was far more chilling: *You can't hurt me.*

I stared at the repeated lines, then entered the room. "Patrick, what are you doing?"

He kept writing.

"Patrick, stop."

When he didn't, I reached out and turned his face toward me. He blinked, but there was no recognition. I uncurled his fingers and took away the chalk. He gazed at me blankly.

"Wake up, Patrick. You're not in bed. Wake up." I gently shook his shoulders.

He blinked again and turned his head away from me to look around the room. He was awake now.

"Patrick, how did you get here?" I asked.

He continued to look around. "I don't know."

"Do you remember climbing out of bed?"

He shook his head.

"Did you hear something? Maybe you heard a noise and got curious?"

He thought for a moment and shook his head again.

"Were you talking to Mrs. Hopewell?"

His eyes grew wary. "Where is she?"

"She's in bed now. I thought you may have seen her earlier."

"No."

I pointed to the sentences on the board. "You wrote this. Who wants to hurt you?"

He rubbed his eyes. "I don't know. I forget."

I took a deep breath. He was exhausted, and he really might not remember. I reached for his hand. "Do you think you can walk with me back to your room?"

"Yes."

We went by way of my bedroom and the back steps. He climbed into bed willingly.

"Would you say it?" he asked as I tucked him in.

"Say what?"

"Left and right and starlight," he prompted.

I swallowed hard. "Of course." I leaned down to kiss him on his forehead, and then, as my mother used to, placed a kiss on each eye, saying, "Close your eyes, left then right. Good night, starlight."

Eight

SUNDAY MORNING I checked on Patrick as soon as I awakened. He didn't remember the events of last night—I asked him directly. A few minutes later, Emily came into his room and chatted about what they were going to do together that day. When Patrick realized that it was my day off and I wouldn't be spending it with him, he put up a fuss. Emily's mouth drooped, her feelings hurt. Patrick's fuss turned into a tantrum, and I exited quickly, knowing he would keep it up as long as I was there.

I had planned to show Adrian the writing on the blackboard, but he wasn't available. Uncertain about how Emily would react, I decided to talk to Adrian alone when I returned. I didn't want the others to see the board—they might be inspired with new ways to upset Patrick—so I wiped the slate clean before leaving Mason's Choice.

At Amelia's bed-and-breakfast I had seen an ad for Tea

Leaves, a bakery and café on High Street. I drove into town and parked at the top of the street, where I found two spaces together, making it easier for me to slip in from the "wrong" side of the road. As I walked down the town's main street, my heart grew lighter than it had been since I'd arrived at Mason's Choice. Everything was so normal and cheerful. People walked dogs and carried fat Sunday newspapers under their arms. On the steps of a church, families poured out, adults and children bursting to talk, their breath making clouds in the cold air. Shops were closed, so pedestrians strolled the sidewalks like patrons at an outdoor museum, pausing at store windows to see what they framed.

As I neared the café, I caught sight of a familiar figure across the street. Trent stood at the door of an old hotel, the Queen Victoria, talking with a woman dressed in a businesslike red suit—the hotel manager, I thought, the one Robyn deemed beneath Westbrook standards. The woman and Trent were so intent in their conversation, they didn't notice me. I studied them as I walked, my head turned sideways.

"Umph!" My ear banged against somebody's chest.

"You walk worse than you drive," Sam said.

I stepped back quickly. "Sorry. You might have stepped out of the way," I added.

"And let you crash into that tree?"

I glanced at the sycamore behind him, part of the row that lined the brick walk.

"Okay, next time," he said agreeably, then gestured toward the café. "They make the best doughnuts in the world. You should try some, Kate."

It was the first time he had called me by my name. I heard the way he said it—and I felt it, too, somehow.

"That's where I was going," I said, taking a step toward the door.

"Me too."

I hesitated and he laughed.

"I think there is room enough in there for both of us," he said, "even if you can't stand me."

That wasn't why I'd hesitated. Now that he had been nice to Patrick, it was doubly dangerous to be around him. I didn't want to meet his dark eyes and nurture this lunacy inside me.

He reached for the door and held it open, waiting for me to go through.

"I can open my own door."

He walked through and let it slam in my face.

I took a deep breath and entered. There was a mob around the glass cases, so I didn't have to stand next to him. He took a number, then I took a number. We went to opposite ends of the bakery shelves, but both of us gravitated toward the center, to a seductive tray labeled "cheese pastries." There were six left.

"I hope there are more of those in the back," Sam said, glancing sideways at me.

"How many do you eat?"

"Six."

When his turn came he bought all six, then turned around and offered me three.

"Thanks, but I prefer doughnuts," I lied.

I saw the twitch of his mouth and the light in his eyes. I looked away, annoyed. I was doing my best to be prickly and off-putting, and he found it entertaining.

I ordered cinnamon doughnuts to go, paid, and headed for the door, looking neither left nor right. It was a relief to step into the brisk air. I turned toward the riverfront, then heard footsteps behind me.

Sam strolled next to me, chewing a pastry.

"What are you doing?" I asked.

"Eating. Walking. Being friendly. I would have left with you, but I was waiting for you to do your door thing," he explained. "Trade you a cheese Danish for a doughnut."

"No thanks." I wasn't going to be seduced. "But you may have a doughnut."

His hand dove into the bag. "Do you act like a cactus with everyone?"

I didn't respond. We crossed the street and continued down another block.

"Maybe you kind of like me and are just pretending."

"That's an interesting theory," I replied.

"So, where's the short guy today?"

"Patrick? With his mother and headed for a concert. It's my day off."

"I owe him an apology," Sam said, "but since I don't think he realizes it, I'll apologize to you. I'm sorry I was a jerk. It's stupid to judge people by their parents. It's not like we get a choice."

We walked on silently, he seeming much more at ease than I.

"So," Sam said, "can Patrick and you come to the play-off game next Saturday?"

"We're planning to. It will be good for him."

"And for you?"

"It's entertaining," I said.

We had reached the public dock, a large wooden platform that jutted over the river, with pilings for temporary docking. On a cold day like this, it was deserted. I sat down on a bench facing the river and Sam sat next to me. Maybe it was just the roughness of the water and the way the wind came off it and wrapped around us, but I was very aware of Sam's closeness and warmth. Part of me wanted to move even closer to him; part of me wanted to move away.

He was staring at me again.

"Didn't your mother teach you not to stare at people?"

"She tried, but it didn't take," he said. "I don't pretend, Kate. I look where I want to look, except when I'm playing hockey. Don't your ears get cold?"

"Because my hair is short? No colder than yours."

"They're bright red. You look like you've got a rose stuck on either side of your head."

I covered my ears with my hands. "You have such a way with words."

He took a wool hat out of his pocket and put it on my head, pulling it down too far, then adjusting it, carefully rolling back the edge around my face. His big hands were surprisingly gentle. His thumb brushed my cheek. It felt warm where he touched me.

What was happening to me? How could I find a guy who said my eyes looked like green pop bottles and my ears poked out like roses in *any* way romantic?

His dark eyes swept my face. *That* was how.

I couldn't think of anything to say. I turned my face away from his, pulled my shoulders in, and folded my arms in front of me, as if I were cold. Out of the corner of my eye, I could see him smiling, as if he guessed I wasn't doing that to stay warm.

"So how old were you when you learned to play hockey?" I asked.

He tilted his head slightly, perhaps trying to decide whether I was truly interested or simply making polite conversation.

"I started skating when I was four. My dad taught me. He had grown up near a rink in Brooklyn and loved to skate." Sam's voice grew warm. "When we moved here from New York, they had just built the rink at Chase—it's an old college, and they keep trying to be like Harvard. Anyway, Dad would take me there every chance he got. He taught me a little about using a hockey stick. Then, well, then, a year or so after Dad died, when I was six, my mom enrolled me in lessons and then a league."

"Your father died?" I repeated quietly.

He nodded. "After his death I became an angry little kid. Mom hoped sports would help me channel that. It did more—it earned me a college scholarship. Nothing too impressive—to Chase—but it's full tuition for four years."

"Congratulations. Your father would be very proud."

"Yeah."

I heard the wistfulness in his voice.

"I'm sorry." I thought of telling him that my own father had died recently, but sometimes, when people respond to your sadness by immediately telling you their own, it's as if they take away the importance of yours. We sat quietly, watching the gulls, which had discovered us and were circling close, hoping for a handout.

"I want to get Patrick started in hockey," I said at last. "He's a kid with some problems, and it would help him to get involved in a team sport."

"What kind of problems?"

"It's a long story."

"I have three more Danishes and can chew very slowly."

I told Sam about the situation at Mason's Choice, the quarreling and resentment, and the way Adrian's cancer and the favoritism he showed Patrick made a bad situation worse. I recounted how the others treated Patrick, ending with my suspicions about the loss of his hamster.

"They'd kill a little kid's pet? Don't they have anything better to do with their time? I can't believe it—though I don't know why!" The anger in his voice surprised me.

"I have no proof that it was deliberate, but I'm suspicious. Brook used to do the same kind of thing to Ashley, let out her pets, though we usually found them."

"Ashley—the girl who was murdered?"

"Drowned," I corrected. "She fell through the ice."

His eyes narrowed. "You said, *'we* usually found them.' Who is *we?*"

"My mother and I. My father was an artist hired by Adrian, and my mother sometimes took care of Ashley. We played together."

"You're—you're Venerelli's daughter!" He spoke it like an accusation.

"That's right."

He hurled the pastry straight out in the river. The gulls dove.

"Is that some kind of problem for you?" I asked.

"You might say that." When he looked at me, his eyes were cold black glass. "My father was a detective for the N.Y.P.D. We moved here because the violence he saw every day was getting to him. My mother grew up on the Eastern Shore—it was the only other place they knew. But Dad had trouble getting work in Wisteria—all his training and experience were in detective work—so he hung up his shingle as a private investigator. He was hired by Adrian Westbrook to investigate Victoria Venerelli."

"Investigate . . . my mother—why?"

"For killing Westbrook's granddaughter."

For a moment I was speechless. It was like being in a dream, trying to scream, wanting desperately to tell him he was wrong, but unable to make a sound.

I rubbed my throat. "No one killed Ashley. She fell through the ice."

"Or she was pushed."

"She was looking for her rabbit!"

"Okay, she was lured," he said.

"By my mother? You're mad, you're completely mad!"

"By whoever took the rabbit, then placed it on the ice."

I was outraged. Victoria wasn't capable of murder. She was too motherly a person—before she ditched her only child, I reminded myself. How could I presume to know anything about the woman who had abandoned me?

Still, what motive was there? I regained my composure. "She had no motive."

Sam stood up and paced back and forth behind the bench.

Joseph was right, I thought. I couldn't trust Adrian, telling that tale about my father's artistic temper tantrum. No wonder he was nice to me now. He was responsible for my parents' sudden departure, frightening them, hiring a private detective to find evidence against my mother. My father probably stole the ring because he knew they'd have to lie low for a while, but when my mother left us, it became possible for him to work in the open again.

My thoughts took a surprising turn: Maybe my mother hadn't really wanted to leave us. Maybe she had had no choice. But if she was innocent, why would she have run scared? Perhaps she was guilty—at least, of neglect.

"She had no motive," I repeated to Sam. "Didn't you hear me? What is your problem?" I asked angrily.

"Dad was following your parents the night they left Mason's Choice. Later the sheriff received a call about a possible accident. They found Dad's car upside down in a ditch. He was dead."

I mouthed Sam's words silently, trying to understand them. I felt sick, the taste of cake going sour in my throat. I remembered huddling between the seats of our car, terrified of the storm and the speed at which my father was driving. The car had taken a sharp turn, then spun out of control. I remembered the crashing sound that came almost immediately after our car had stopped. It was deer, my parents said, a herd of them rushing across the road and crashing into the brush on the other side. Farther on, at a dark petrol station, my Father had made a telephone call. He never told me that someone had been following us that night, that someone had been killed on the road.

I rose, the liquid in my stomach threatening to come up. Steadying myself, I walked past Sam. A distance away, I stopped to look back. He was kicking at the blanks in the dock, jamming the toe of his shoe against the uneven edges.

"Feeling sorry for yourself?" I asked.

He looked up. "I don't expect you to understand. Your parents and Westbrook are responsible for my father's death. Hating them helped me get through it."

"At least you have your mother," I replied, "which is one more parent than I."

"What do you mean?"

I continued walking, heading toward my car, wanting to get away from him. I, too, was good at feeling sorry or myself. Like Sam, I had dealt with the pain of losing a parent by turning it into anger and resentment. I had funneled my hurt into an effort to hate—hate my mother. And I suspected that, in the end, the effort had wrought as much peace and happiness to Sam as it had brought to me, which is to say none.

I spent the rest of the day on the road and in stores, driving as far as a popular shopping mall in Delaware, but it was impossible to drive away from my thoughts. It occurred to me that Joseph had been no more forthcoming than Adrian regarding the investigation of my mother. He must have known about it, yet he had gone along with Adrian's story about my father's artistic temper tantrum, indicating that was the reason we had left Wisteria. About 7:30, angry at everyone, I returned to Mason's Choice.

"I warned Mr. Westbrook you would bring trouble," Mrs. Hopewell greeted me as I came in the kitchen door.

"It's lovely to see you, too, Mrs. Hopewell."

"I knew it from the moment you telephoned."

"And you made it quite clear," I said, continuing toward the hall. I guessed that something had happened while I was gone, but I would not take her bait and ask what was wrong. I walked quickly, anxious to find Patrick.

"Kate," Robyn called.

I stopped reluctantly at the dining room door. The supper candles were still burning, and several chairs had been pushed back from the table at odd angles. She and Trent sat nursing their coffee.

"Yes, ma'am?"

"Come in," she said.

I took one step inside the door.

"When I give you an instruction to come in, young lady—"

"Let it go, Robyn," Trent interrupted. "Kate, have you been talking to Patrick about your time here as a child?"

"No, sir, I haven't said a word about it."

"Don't lie," Robyn hissed between her teeth.

"I don't," I replied.

"After you left today," Trent went on, "Patrick climbed a tree growing close to a cottage, the one where your family lived."

"Children climb trees, they have for centuries," I pointed

out. "And, unless *someone else* told him, he has no idea where I used to live. He doesn't know my family stayed at Mason's Choice."

"He was trying to climb in the bedroom window," Trent pressed on, his eyes sharply observing me. Ashley had climbed that tree the day she threw my doll through the window—he remembered that as well as I.

"Were the windows and doors on the first floor locked?" I asked.

"Shuttered and locked," said Robyn.

"So then, it makes sense that he tried to get in through the second floor."

Trent took a sip of coffee. "When questioned, he told us he was playing with Ashley." Trent's voice was steady, but I heard the china cup clatter in its saucer. "Ashley and the orange cat."

"He has been talking a lot about Ashley," I admitted.

"Since you arrived," Robyn said quickly. "Emily told us that this talk started when you arrived."

"Did it?" I replied. "Then I can't help but wonder why someone would choose that moment to start telling ghost stories, for that is what I'm hearing from Patrick. Does someone want to frighten him, or is this directed at me? Perhaps it's an effort to get rid of me by upsetting others. What do you think?"

Trent and Robyn exchanged glances.

"Who found Patrick doing this?" I asked.

"Roger, the groundskeeper," Robyn replied.

"I thought he was off today."

"He lives in the cottage next door. He heard Patrick cry out when he fell."

"Fell! Why didn't you tell me? Is Patrick all right? Where is he?"

"This discussion isn't over," Trent said as I turned to exit.

"Then you will have to finish it yourselves," I replied, and rushed toward the steps.

I found Patrick in bed, wearing his sailboat pajamas, making action figures climb over the little mountains that were his knees under the quilt.

"Kate, you're back!" he said, his face lighting up. His right cheek was bruised, and there was a slight cut over his eye.

"Hel-lo, you're looking colorful! What happened to you?"

Patrick immediately pulled up his pajama sleeve to show me a bruised arm.

"Impressive. How did you do that?" I asked.

"I fell out of a tree."

"That doesn't sound like a fun thing to do."

He cackled. "I didn't *try* to, Kate."

"Glad to hear it. So why were you climbing the tree?"

"Ashley dared me."

The breath caught in my throat—dared him, the way she had dared me. But daring is something children like to do, I reminded myself, and it provided a good excuse.

"We were playing with November," he said, "and he climbed the tree."

"November?"

"The orange cat. That's his secret name."

My skin tingled. Ashley would never tell me the cat's name—she had enjoyed tormenting me with it, as she had tormented Brook with the names of her horses. November was an unusual name for Patrick to have chosen on his own—but not for Ashley, I thought suddenly. The cat had first appeared at Thanksgiving, which would have been November.

"From now on, Patrick, when someone dares you to do something—I don't care who it is—say no."

"I told her I didn't want to go any higher, but she kept daring me."

"Ashley can't tell you what to do," I said, sounding eerily like my mother.

His legs moved restlessly under the quilt. "Kate, are you sure she's like Casper?"

"You mean a friendly sort of ghost?"

He nodded.

I sat on the edge of his bed. "Perhaps she is like children

you've met before, sometimes a good friend and sometimes not. But I'm certain of one thing: Ashley can't tell you what to do. If she tries, you come tell me."

"So," said Emily, entering the room, "you do talk to him about Ashley."

"I didn't start it," I said.

"You know, Kate, I defended you in front of the others."

"We talk about Ashley when Patrick wants to," I explained, "when he feels uncomfortable about things."

She looked more tired than angry, her usual pink lipstick worn off, her fair skin showing gray under her eyes.

"Patrick, this kind of talk has to stop," she said. "It makes Trent and Robyn very unhappy. Daddy doesn't like it either. And Mrs. Hopewell is angered by everything you do. There can be no more mention of Ashley."

Patrick pressed his lips together, locking his thoughts inside.

Emily asked if I would help her put Patrick to bed. Ten minutes later, when we emerged into the main hall, with Patrick's door closed behind us, I turned to her. "What does Adrian think about this Ashley talk?" I asked quietly.

"He says that it is nothing, that it's just a stage Patrick is going through"—Emily glanced toward their bedroom door—"but I know that it, along with some other things happening in this house, is upsetting him. This evening he looked as bad as the last time he went into the hospital." Her whisper grew ragged with anger. "His children are heartless. Heartless! You would think, after all he has given them, they'd try to make his last year a happy one. But all they can think of is themselves and what they would acquire if Adrian hadn't married me. If it were up to me, they'd find themselves out on Scarborough Road without a cent."

Eyes burning with tears, she turned her face away from me, then slipped into a hall bathroom, the small one Patrick used. She probably wanted to cry without Adrian seeing her. Knowing better than to offer sympathy to an employer who was sensitive about authority and position, I took the main stairs up to my room

I felt badly for Emily and worse for Adrian, but his serious illness made it all the more necessary that I talk to him as soon as possible. Someone was preying on Patrick's mind, and if he was the designated heir, the greedy, vicious members of this household had plenty of motivation to go after him. It occurred to me that Ashley had also been Adrian's favorite. What if Sam was right and she was murdered?

Impossible, I thought. And yet Adrian thought it possible enough to investigate my mother. Why? Things were being hidden from me. What didn't I know about Patrick's situation? What didn't I know about my own?

Nine

THE PHONE CALL came early Monday morning while Patrick and I were eating breakfast. Mrs. Hopewell looked incredibly annoyed. "These are your working hours," she said to me. "Socializing is to be done on your own time."

I took the phone from her hands without asking who it was. I would have chatted with someone selling real estate at the North Pole. "Hello?"

"Kate? Sam. I know this is a bad time, but it seemed too long to wait all day. I'll make it quick. I'm sorry about your dad. I'm sorry about his cancer and death and all."

That certainly was quick—a sudden jab to the heart.

"My mother said she saw the obituary a couple months ago," he continued. "It must have been hard for you. I'm really sorry."

I had received many condolences and had responded graciously to people ranging from Princess Ann to the postman, but all I could do now was stare at my toast.

"Are you there?"

"Yes."

"I'm sorry about your mother, too," he said. "I didn't know anything about that. I can't really understand what it's like to be in your shoes, but it's got to be tough."

After several months, what *I* couldn't understand was why I was suddenly close to tears. Sam was no poet, but it was as if I heard his words deeper inside me, as if they reached some part of me that other people's words did not.

Patrick tugged on my sleeve. "Who is it?" he asked.

"Sam."

"Sam! Can I talk to him?"

"Thanks for calling," I said. "Patrick wants to talk to you." I handed over the phone with relief.

"Hi. We're eating breakfast," Patrick told him cheerfully. "Toast with grape jelly . . . Yeah . . . yeah." As Sam spoke to him, Patrick began to study my face. "Well, she's just sitting there. . . . No, she hasn't eaten anything yet."

I stuffed a piece of toast in my mouth.

"Now she has—why is that funny?" Patrick asked. "I think she's okay. Okay, I will." He hung up. "Sam said I should be good today and try to make you smile."

"That's nice," I said, and swallowed in lumps the rest of my breakfast.

Immediately after I dropped Patrick at school, I drove to Olivia's Antiques, hoping to find Joseph in early. I could have called him, but I wanted to see Joseph's face when I questioned him. His reaction would guide me in how to proceed with Adrian.

"Just the person I was hoping to see," Joseph greeted me, when I opened the shop door, making the bells jingle.

"Aren't you supposed to say, 'Shop's closed'?"

He smiled. "I'm on my way to Crossroads, to see what prices some of these unforgivably ugly objects are fetching at auction. Would you like to come along? Someone told me they have a painting that looks like one of your father's—a retriever with a goose. It seems strange that he would leave such a number of paintings unsigned."

"He signed only those he was satisfied with," I explained, "and he had very high standards. I'd like to have a look."

"My S.U.V. is around back."

Joseph drove to Crossroads and I bided my time, wanting a clear view of his face when I told him what I had discovered. He was in a good mood, chatting about his public relations job at the conservatory in Baltimore, fussing about the prima donna attitudes of the visiting musicians.

Crossroads was outside of town, but on the other side of Wisteria from Mason's Choice, north of Oyster Creek. The large building sat at an intersection of Eastern Shore routes, roads that provided easy connections west to Baltimore and Washington, and north to Wilmington, Philadelphia, and New York. Joseph said that it was one of the three major auctions serving Mid-Atlantic dealers, each one running just one day a week. But it had also kept its old role, having an outdoor auction where local people and flea-market enthusiasts bid on "the ugly and the useless."

We parked in an open field, and I soon saw what he meant. Spread on a sandy lot next to the auction house were rows of items that should have been taken to the dump—worn Christmas decorations, old propane tanks, paintings of rock stars on velvet, rusted appliances covered with flowered Con-Tact paper, and furniture that one couldn't imagine buying when new. A motorized cart, manned by an auctioneer, rolled up and down the rows, trailed by bidders.

Joseph and I followed at a distance. "Maybe Mother left me more than I realized," Joseph said. "I'll bring her things here, though I'm going to have to wear a disguise. I wouldn't want anyone to think they're mine."

We moved slowly in the direction of the auction house, then turned at the head of the next row. I stopped to look at a batch of sports memorabilia, which included a hockey stick.

"You're really into the sport," Joseph remarked.

"No, Patrick is," I replied, "and he needs someone to be

into whatever he's into. Joseph, do you remember the guy who came to Olivia's to buy a bracelet last week?"

"The eloquent one who left his fingerprints all over the glass counter?"

"That's right. He plays hockey for the high school. His name is Sam Koscinski."

I watched for a reaction. Joseph's beard and mustache hid most of his mouth, and the skin around his eyes stayed as smooth as before.

"Do you know the family?" I asked.

"I knew of a man who might have been his father, Mike Koscinski."

"A private investigator," I prompted.

Joseph nodded slowly.

I lost patience. "Why didn't you tell me my mother was a murder suspect?"

Joseph pulled a pen from his pocket and stuck it in his mouth. "Because I was afraid you'd ask the next question."

"I'm asking it. Why did Adrian suspect her?"

Joseph chewed on the pen, then drew it out of his mouth like a cigarette and started walking.

"Adrian suspected a lot of people, Katie. He was desperate for someone to blame. People get that way when there has been a terrible accident." We stopped at the edge of the auction lot, next to a large placard pointing to the building entrance. "He suspected me, even Mrs. Hopewell. Anyone who wasn't family was looked at askance."

"Perhaps, but it was my mother whom Mr. Koscinski was hired to investigate—Sam told me. It was my mother who was being chased by him the night we left."

Joseph clicked the pen in his hand.

"Tell me what you know," I insisted. "I'm talking to Adrian this afternoon and I'm going to ask him about it. I will get to the bottom of this, you can count on it."

He rubbed his perpetually damp brow. "Katie, let me explain something to you and perhaps you'll understand why I didn't want you to ask too many questions. There was—uh—a connection between your father and Corinne, Trent's wife."

I steeled myself. "What kind of connection?"

"You know what I mean—you're almost an adult. They were lovers. It happened before your father met your mother, when Corinne first came to Mason's Choice as Trent's bride and your father came as a very young, very handsome artist. I wasn't around then, of course, but people don't change. Trent is quite intelligent, and probably the most boring, uptight person on the face of the earth. Your father was dashing, dramatic—"

I wasn't interested in excuses. "When Dad came back with my mother and me, did he keep it up?"

"Yes. And he discovered he had fathered *two* little girls, Katie and Ashley."

"Ashley!" It was like looking into a convex mirror—I recognized all the objects shown, but everything looked different, their spatial relationships changed.

I wanted to deny what Joseph said, to deny any pain my mother might have felt because of my father's unfaithfulness, which would then require me to feel sorry for her. But I remembered how my father loved to see Ashley and me playing together, how he would do little sketches of us with our arms around each other, how he wept when he was told of the accident. And I remembered the times when Ashley and I came upon my father and her mother together. We were too innocent to figure it out—at least, I was.

"Did my mother know?"

"She found out two weeks before Ashley died."

I leaned against the sign.

"I didn't want to have to tell you that," Joseph went on. "Of course, it was just a coincidence, but you can see how Adrian, needing to blame someone, would turn on your mother."

"And feel remorseful about it now—perhaps that is why he is so nice to me. Perhaps he spun that story about my father's artistic tantrum because he thought the reality would be too painful for me."

"Or for him," Joseph said bluntly. Even with the beard, I could see one side of his mouth draw up. "Adrian hates to be wrong."

"He *was* wrong, wasn't he?"

"Katie! How can you think otherwise?"

Easily. My parents had told me half-truths. So had Adrian and Joseph. Why should I believe any of them now? I jammed my hands into my coat pockets.

"Are you all right?" Joseph asked, after a long moment of silence.

"Just cold," I replied crisply. "Let's go in."

The building, covered with pale siding and a new tin roof, showed its age inside. As long as an athletic field, it had a concrete floor and a loft that ran along three sides. The loft area was crammed with furniture, and a sign on the stairway that led to it said, NOTE TO CUSTOMERS: YOU CARRY IT UP THE STEPS, YOU CARRY IT DOWN. I guessed it was used for items that were waiting to be picked up by the buyer.

Joseph and I walked along one side of the building, scanning the merchandise. We passed a door with a sign prohibiting entrance and warning that dogs were inside—the ones Trent had spoken of, I assumed.

An auction was going on at either end of the building, two motorized vehicles moving along the floor trailed by crowds of interested buyers. Joseph decided to follow the furniture auctioneer at the far end, while I wandered the rows of tables spread with smaller items—glassware, china, mirrors, statues, and paintings, looking for a portrait my father might have done, the retriever carrying a goose. But I barely saw what was in front of me, for memories were running inside my head like old films, cinema that I was watching with older, more knowing eyes.

Was my mother capable of killing out of revenge and hurt? Could she have done something less deliberate than murder, such as ignore the safety of a child she could no longer endure?

I found the painting that was thought to be my father's and knew immediately it wasn't. I realized that, with regard to my father, the only thing I could be certain about was whether he had done a particular painting. Since he had been the one constant in my life, this new uncertainty made everything I thought I knew seem questionable.

I turned away from the painting, aware of someone's eyes on me. Trent, with file folders tucked under his arm, gazed at me through a half-glass wall that sealed off the auction's business office.

I looked back. Did he know who Ashley's real father was? Since that fact had generated Adrian's investigation, he must have.

"Ah," said Joseph, who had materialized at my elbow, "you have found the painting."

"It's not my father's," I told him. "That goose not only looks dead, it doesn't look as if it were ever alive."

Joseph laughed.

"Trent is watching us from the office," I added.

Joseph glanced up and the two men nodded at each other.

"I don't understand, Joseph, why wouldn't Trent have been a suspect? He had the same motivation—he'd been cheated on. And why wasn't Robyn considered a possibility? She was jealous of Ashley—even as a five-year-old I was aware of that. I can see how she deals with Patrick now, with anyone whom she thinks is competition for her father's attention and money. Trent, Robyn, Brook—all of them were home that day. All of them knew Ashley loved to go to the pond. Why didn't Mr. Koscinski investigate them?"

"Because he was hired by Adrian." Joseph replied, he and Trent turning their backs to each other at the same time. "The Westbrooks will claw one another's eyes out in private, but in public they are loyal and strive to keep up their fine family image. Those kinds of suspicions are something Adrian couldn't even consider."

"Well," I said, "he *should* consider them—for Patrick's sake."

"All right, Kate," Adrian said, three hours later, "what is this business that is so pressing you got past Cerberus, my three-headed dog—otherwise known as Mrs. Hopewell," he added in quieter voice.

There was a sharp rap on the office door.

"Almost got past," he corrected himself. "Yes, Louise?"

She opened the door. "I told the girl she could not see you."

"Thank you," Adrian replied. "I'm quite sure you did."

Mrs. Hopewell waited, as if he might ask her to escort me out.

"What do you have in your hand, Louise? May I see it?"

She stepped into the room, but walked no farther than the credenza, depositing the FedEx envelope there rather than carrying it to Adrian. I believed it was her small way of protesting the fact that he had granted me a meeting.

After the housekeeper left, Adrian rose from his chair a bit stiffly, closed the door, then picked up the envelope. "Some days are good and some days aren't so good," he said, returning to his seat across from me. He gave me a wry smile and sat down wearily.

"So, Kate, I trust that you have the phone, the microwave, the refrigerator, and whatever else you need."

"Yes, thanks. It's Patrick I want to talk about."

"His loneliness."

"That, too," I said.

"Oh dear, there's a list."

I was silent for a moment, ordering my questions and points.

Adrian leaned forward, smiling. "I'm kidding you. I am interested in all that you have to say."

"Patrick definitely needs friends," I began. "We should encourage him to invite other children to the house. I would be happy to supervise them. I think it would be good if we could get him to join a team. He likes hockey, but that season is almost over. Any kind of sport would do—just something that would place him with a group of children. He is too isolated at Mason's Choice."

"I agree."

"But there's something more to consider," I rushed on, "and that is the reason why he doesn't have friends. Tim moved away, and Patrick doesn't talk about any other children."

"Except Ashley," Adrian remarked dryly.

"When I pick him up from school, I see the boys playing together and him standing alone."

Adrian sighed. "I've been too caught up in my ridiculous therapy."

"Many children have only one parent and do fine," I assured

him. "If you want my opinion—and I'm going to give it to you whether you do or not—I think the problems he has here at home are affecting his ability to get along with other children. I suspect he is acting like an impossible brat at school or withdrawing entirely. Either would be a natural response, given the hostile treatment he receives from those who are supposed to be loving family members—Robyn, Trent, and Brook. Mrs. Hopewell doesn't help any."

"You're quite blunt, just as your mother was."

"They're quite nasty, just as they were to Ashley."

I saw the brightness in his eyes—whether it was surprise or amusement, I wasn't sure.

"True enough," he said. "And so you want me to put the leash on them."

"Yes."

Adrian pulled the tab on the FedEx package and shook out a blue-striped envelope, which he slit with a letter opener.

"I can't do that, Kate, though I wish more than anything I could spare Patrick the pain. But it is better for him to go through this while I am still here to keep an eye on it.

"See this?" he waved the blue letter at me. "Someone wants money. They all have heard the enticing news of my cancer." He grimaced. "Every college on the East Coast, every charitable institution, a flock of former employees, and relatives I haven't heard from in years are suddenly interested in making contact with me.

"Perhaps you can understand then that Patrick, as my heir, will need to become tougher, to grow a much thicker skin. He will spend his life dealing with greedy people, many of them his own relatives. He has got to learn how to keep them from getting to him."

"In time," I agreed. "But he's only seven years old."

"And he is doing well enough for a little boy," Adrian replied, "keeping them at bay with this Ashley nonsense. Eventually he will learn to do better than that: He will intimidate them when necessary. And trust me, it *will* be necessary for Patrick's survival."

I felt helpless. Adrian understood what I was saying, but he believed it called for a different response.

"In the meantime," I said, "why don't you speak to the school counselor? I'm a little surprised the counselor hasn't asked to speak to you."

"She has, but I have no use for her prying and suggestions. One has to look no further than psychologists' children to see that these people don't know what they are doing. Patrick is in a very special situation, one his teacher and the counselor could never understand."

"I think you are wrong," I said.

"Rarely," he replied. "Is there anything else you wish to discuss?"

"Yes. Why did you lie to me about the reason my parents left? You were having my mother investigated for the death of Ashley."

Adrian leaned back in his chair for a moment, as if catching his breath, then moved forward, leaning on the carved arm, looking me directly in the eye. "As I said, I am rarely wrong, but I was that time, and it shames me. It shames me each time I look at you. Anything else?" he repeated, this time more softly.

"Just one thing. I am very afraid for Patrick."

"So am I, Kate. So am I."

Ten

"But Kate, I *kno-o-ow* it's frozen," Patrick protested Monday afternoon. He looked longingly out of the schoolroom window. "I can see the ice."

I laughed. Surrounded by tall evergreens, the pond wasn't visible from any window of the house.

"The ice isn't thick enough. Besides, we made a deal. We'll skate at the college rink this evening, but only if you finish your homework."

Patrick sighed. He was failing math and had brought home remedial work from his teacher. It was taking him a long time to complete his subtraction problems. His focus would wander, and he would forget what he had borrowed from the adjacent column. My reminder to write it down only made him angrier.

"All right, shall we work on the next problem?"

He stared at the numbers.

"Can you take seven from five?" I prompted.

He pushed his pencil hard against the paper. The point broke.

"Think it through," I said, calmly handing him a fresh pencil.

He threw it down. "I hate this!"

He pushed back his chair, looking pleased when it fell over. Striding around the room, he poked at things, his hand skipping from books to art supplies to a plastic globe, knocking them over. He'd already fidgeted his way through one "time-out"; I doubted another one was going to help, but I also wasn't going to give in to playtime. He needed an activity that was physical as well as mental to work off some energy and help him concentrate. "Let's take a break and try piano."

"Piano?" He sounded interested.

"Yes, but don't forget that we're going to have to finish these problems if you want to skate."

For the first ten minutes, he seemed intrigued. I taught him the way I remembered Joseph teaching Ashley and me. After numbering the fingers on his right hand with a marker, I called out one to five, and he would practice wiggling them. When I mixed up the order, it became a game for him. Then I assigned five black piano keys to his fingers and called out the numbers again, this time for him to play.

He made a mistake. His jaw clenched.

"You're doing well. Everyone makes mistakes when learning, and afterward, too. Let's try again. Ready?"

He made another mistake, and I suppose it was one too many that day. He slammed both hands down on the piano. "I hate this!" he screamed, jumping off the bench. His arm swept across the top of the piano, knocking off a pile of music books. They were Ashley's, their bindings old and dry. Sheets of music flew everywhere.

"Stop it, Patrick!"

A second pile was thrown to the floor.

"You can forget about skating," I said angrily.

"I hate it! I hate you!" he cried.

Leaning over to pick up the books before he damaged them further, I noticed a pair of black shoes in the doorway. Perfect timing. I straightened up. "Hello, Mrs. Hopewell."

She nodded stiffly.

"Is there something I can do for you?"

"You can control him," she said. "And if you can't, you should resign."

Patrick gazed up at her wonderingly. For a moment I was speechless. "Well, thank you for clarifying the situation."

Mrs. Hopewell stepped into the room and gazed down at the music sheets, her face grim. Patrick backed against me—I was his best friend again.

"Pick them up," she ordered.

He jutted out his jaw, trying to look defiant, but I could see his little hands shaking. "I will if Kate tells me," he said.

I almost laughed. Just as she followed Robyn's orders over Emily's, he followed mine over hers. It angered her. A vein on the side of her head, a small blue one close to her hairline, pulsed.

"Let's do it together, Patrick," I suggested.

"He'll do it himself," Mrs. Hopewell said. "You and I have something to talk about."

"I can talk and pick up at the same time."

"You were at the auction house with Joseph Oakley." She spoke it like a challenge.

"Yes, this morning," I replied. "Here, Patrick, I think this page goes with the book you're holding."

"I am telling you for your own good, you cannot trust that man."

"Thank you for the advice, Mrs. Hopewell, but I learned not to trust people a long time ago."

"It would be foolish to make any deals with him regarding your father's paintings."

I glanced up from my handful of sheets, surprised. Why would she care? What was it that really vexed her?

She walked over to the window and looked out, her chin

raised, surveying the property. "To Joseph Oakley, a fair deal is anything that works out well for himself."

"That's not unusual in business."

She faced me. "Joseph hasn't the brains to be a businessman. His only skill is whining. He sees himself as a victim of circumstances who deserves whatever he can get his hands on. I hope his view of the Westbrooks will not pervert yours."

"I make my own judgments of people," I said, then turned to Patrick. "Let's put these on top of the piano and order them later. Why don't you finish up your math problems, so we can get to the skating rink by five-thirty?"

He set aside the papers and dutifully sat down at his worktable.

"Five thirty . . . today?" Mrs. Hopewell asked. "He is scheduled for dinner."

"I spoke with Emily. She gave me permission to take him skating from five thirty to seven."

"But you must clear it with me," the woman insisted. "Everything that goes on in this house is cleared through me."

"It is? How long has that been the rule?"

"Since Mr. Westbrook divorced his first wife."

"I see. Then perhaps you can help me."

The firm line of her mouth told me that she had no intention of helping, but I gestured toward the hall, counting on her desire to know what everyone was doing. After a moment she followed me, and I closed the door behind us.

"Mrs. Hopewell, what do you remember about the day Ashley died?"

Her short eyelashes flicked. "Good employees do not gossip about their employers' personal business."

"It's my business too," I pointed out, "since my mother was investigated for the death."

"This sounds like Joseph's nonsense. You're a fool to believe him."

"Adrian confirmed it."

Not a muscle moved in her face, but her hands tensed.

"Where were you that day, when we were looking for Ashley's rabbit?"

"What an absurd question to ask! How would I remember?"

"How could you forget?" I replied. "It was a rather dramatic day. Where was Robyn?"

The woman's thick fingers curled into her palms. "There is no reason I would know that."

"You just told me everything is cleared through you. Even if you didn't know beforehand, I am sure you pursued the details afterward."

The blue vein again, pulsing like a warning light before a structure blows.

"That's why you came here, isn't it," she said, "to stir up the past, to pry into matters that were settled long ago. I knew you meant trouble."

"Then you're prophetic, Mrs. Hopewell, for I came simply to return a ring to Adrian."

"What ring?"

"But you gave me such a difficult time," I continued, "I had to devise an excuse to get inside the house and see him. I decided I liked my excuse—it would be interesting to work here. Since then, I have discovered some unsettling things about the time when Ashley was alive. I have remembered a few things as well."

"Things such as what?"

"You didn't like Ashley," I went on. "Why? Were you jealous, as Robyn was? Perhaps it bothered you that you couldn't control Ashley."

"I controlled that child better than anyone," she said between her teeth.

"You tried," I replied, "but she wasn't afraid of you. She wasn't afraid of anyone or anything."

Mrs. Hopewell's flat voice chilled. "Only the foolish and the dead have no fear."

"As proven by Ashley, who ended up dead," I replied.

I knew she was warning me, hoping that fear would keep

me from prying into family secrets. Unfortunately for Mrs. Hopewell, when I become afraid I find it unbearable to pull the covers over my head. No, I am the kind who, when frightened, must open the closet door.

My rental skates had blades as blunt as butter knives. Not that it mattered—Patrick and I weren't going to be ice dancing anytime soon. He had been given a beautiful pair of skates at Christmas, but the time to take him skating was something no one in the family could seem to afford. He had never been on the ice, and his legs went every which way but forward.

After ten minutes of brave effort he hung on to the side of the rink like an exhausted swimmer hanging on to a pool wall. "This is kind of hard, Kate."

"I know. Everything is at first. Rest a moment and, when you're ready, we'll try again."

I needed the break as much as he. I had made Patrick wear thick pants, knee pads, and a padded snow jacket, which had protected him from the tumbles we had taken. But I, dressed in thin yoga pants and a sweater, was starting to feel like a mashed frozen vegetable.

Fortunately, there were few people using the rink that evening. The guy who had stamped our hands had said the college was on spring break. The high school team moved off the ice at 5:30, and the college team didn't practice until 7:15. I had dawdled a bit, reading athletic plaques aloud to Patrick, to make sure we didn't run into Sam. My anger had faded with the phone call this morning. Having learned since then that Mr. Koscinski had had a legitimate reason to suspect my mother, I was embarrassed.

"Ready," Patrick announced.

"Take my hand," I said. "Remember, push, glide, push, glide."

He faltered, then surprised me, all at once figuring it out. He had his balance, and we were moving steadily forward.

"I'm doing it!" he shouted.

"Good! Keep it going. Push, glide. Easy now. Easy!" I warned.

With a burst of confidence, Patrick took off, dragging me by the hand. Suddenly, he discovered his feet weren't under him. His arms rotated like propellers. I reached forward to steady him, and we went down in a heap.

"Are you all right?"

He nodded. "I guess I went too fast."

"You guess right."

He scrambled halfway up on his feet, then fell back down. "The wall's too far away," he complained. We had been using it to pull ourselves up.

"Okay. Let me stand first."

But before I was all the way up, he pulled on me, eager to get going. I lost my footing and came crashing down with him.

Others skaters laughed.

"Patrick, you must wait," I said, attempting to rise again.

Something in him just couldn't. We landed on the ice once more.

"Patrick!"

"I didn't mean it!"

"I know, but you must listen to me." I rubbed my backside and glanced around the rink. At that moment, my body hurt a lot more than my pride. "Why don't we crawl to the wall," I suggested. "Come on, make like a dog."

Patrick thought that was funny, and barked and crawled. I reached the wall first and pulled myself up.

"Hello, Kate."

Sam. He was sitting in the first row, his arms draped casually over the seatbacks, his school pack on one side, his skates and sports bag on the other.

"Sam, you're here!" Patrick said joyfully, using me and the wall to pull himself up. "Guess what, I'm skating!"

"Is that what that is. And what is Kate doing?" Sam asked.

"She's teaching me. Want to skate with us?"

Sam glanced at his watch.

"I'm sure he's too busy, Patrick"

"Are you?" Sam replied. "Do you know my schedule?"

"Well no, of course not," I sputtered. "I simply didn't want you to feel as if you had to."

"I never feel as if I *have* to do something," he said, then laughed at himself. "I'm cool. Here's the situation. I've got a pile of homework, but I'm waiting for Dion." He pointed to a guy skating backward on the ice. "He was late today. Coach assigned him laps. So, maybe I can give you a few pointers, Patrick"—he glanced at me uncertainly—"or maybe not."

For Patrick, this was better than Christmas. "That would be very nice," I said.

Sam slipped the plastic guards from his skates, then pulled them on. His sweater sleeves were pushed up, revealing the muscles in his forearms. I watched his strong fingers as he quickly laced his skates. He glanced up, and I turned away.

"Do you want me to stay around for the lesson?" I asked, when Sam had stepped onto the ice. His shoulders were huge, even without the hockey padding. Patrick gawked up at him.

Sam studied my face. "You don't want to."

"I thought it might be easier without me."

Sam smiled; he didn't believe the excuse.

"Call if you need me," I said, pushing off quickly, aware of the heat in my cheeks.

For the first five laps I skated looking straight ahead, but when I thought they had forgotten about me, I stopped to watch from a distance. Patrick listened intently to Sam, taking in every word. I laughed to myself when his little-boy arms gestured the same way Sam's did, imitating even the nonskating moves. How could a guy resist a child who so adored him?

Sam squatted next to Patrick and adjusted the position of his feet for the hundredth time. Patrick skated, began to turn, and took a spill. Tears started—from frustration, I thought, rather than hurt. Sam crouched down again. He talked to Patrick, holding his face in his hands. How could a girl resist a guy who was so tender with a child?

Skate, Kate, I told myself, and moved my legs faster, as if I could give my thoughts and feelings the slip. Dion, making his laps, caught my eye and flashed me a smile. I wondered about Sam's friends, who they were, what they did, what kind of girls he dated. I skated on and tried to think about other things, focusing my attention on the talk show that was being broadcast over the college's radio station.

"Is there anyone here named Kate?"

I looked quickly to the right. Sam had caught up with me. "Sorry, were you talking to me? Where's Patrick?" I asked, spinning on my skates, looking for my charge.

"He's okay. Dion's taking care of him."

I skated more slowly, checking out the situation across the rink.

Sam matched my strides. "So how's it going?"

"I think he's catching on. You're a good teacher."

Sam sighed. "I was asking about you."

"Oh. Everything is, uh, going well."

"Everything like what?" Sam asked.

I felt confused, by his presence more than his question. "Like . . . whatever it is you were asking about!"

He laughed, and the back of his hand brushed the back of mine.

"About Patrick," I began.

"A safe subject," he remarked, "especially given the others we share."

"Do you know where they sell hockey sticks for little boys?"

"Yes. I can go with him when he's ready to buy. But don't rush him. Let him get his confidence as a skater first."

Sam's hand brushed my hand a second time.

"In the meantime I should get him some kind of crash helmet," I said.

"Definitely."

"About your hat, the one you lent me yesterday, I'll get it back to you."

"No hurry." His hand touched mine a third time. "Kate, when a guy skates with a girl and brushes her hand, she is supposed to take it."

"I know that."

"But you choose not to. Okay," he said, laughing. He skated ahead, then turned around quickly, skating backward, facing me.

"I really appreciate your spending the time with Patrick."

"It's fun." Sam skated closer to me, his legs matching the movement of mine like an ice dancer's.

"I can't see past you," I told him.

"You don't need to. Just follow me."

"Follow a guy who is skating backward and can't see where we're going?"

"I know when someone is behind me," he replied. "It's a sixth sense."

He skated closer still, as close as he could without actually touching me.

He's doing this on purpose, I thought.

"You'd skate better if you didn't look down," Sam said. "You don't have to worry, my feet will move out of the way of your feet."

"I'm not worried," I insisted.

"Look up. Keep your eyes on my eyes. Trust me," he said.

I glanced up, briefly meeting his eyes, then tried to look past his left shoulder.

"Trust me, Kate," he said softly.

"I can't."

"Give it a try. It's not hard. Just skate and look me in the eye."

I did, and it wasn't hard. In fact, it was far too easy. There was no music, but we were in perfect rhythm. We didn't touch, but his dark eyes held me, his intense gaze keeping me there, his body tantalizingly close.

Then suddenly, that sixth sense of his failed. Sam was stopped as if he'd backed into a brick wall, and I flew into him. His arms wrapped around me. We spun off the rink wall and he held me tightly against him. His face was a breath away from mine—he could have kissed me. His eyes lowered, and I thought he might, then Dion's laughter burst the moment. Patrick cackled.

Sam and I released each other slowly.

"Dion, you jerk!" Sam said, grinning at his friend, who had skated into us.

I laughed, trying to act like a normal teen girl with school friends, but nothing seemed normal to me. How can it, when your heart is beating absurdly fast and you feel a person's fingers like heat under your skin?

Dion looked pleased with himself. Patrick tried to laugh with a deep voice like the older boys, which made them laugh more. I got through the moment by focusing on Patrick, playing my nanny role.

Sam reminded Dion about their pile of homework, and the two of them left. Patrick and I skated a little longer. When we emerged from the college athletic center, a soft snow was falling.

Patrick swung his skates, kicking up the thin frosting on the grass. "No school tomorrow, Kate! They'll have to close school."

"I think we'll need a few more flakes than this," I said, though it was falling in the quiet, steady way that is the beginning of big snows.

At home, Patrick told his parents of his glorious night, then fell asleep almost immediately. I sat for a while by his bed, listening to his soft breathing and watching the snow. I wished the peace of that moment was mine. But everything was stirred up inside me, questions and suspicions running wild. And through it all I kept thinking about the feeling of being in Sam's arms, being there longer than necessary. Which one of us had been reluctant to let go?

Eleven

I SAT UP in bed with a start and glanced around my room, wondering what had awakened me. My sleep had been dreamless. With the heat turned back for the night, the house was cold and silent, not even the banging of old pipes to break the quiet. Shivering, I climbed out of bed and tiptoed to the window. By the light of the garage lamps I could see that it was still snowing, a windless, silent snow.

Check Patrick, I thought; *perhaps he cried out.*

I donned my ski jacket, which was warmer than my dressing gown, and started toward the stairway that connected our rooms. Halfway there I turned around. Music—piano music—was coming from the schoolroom. The simple tune sounded familiar, like a nursery school song one had sung repeatedly as a child but had long since forgotten.

"Patrick?"

I hurried into the third-floor hall, then stopped. It couldn't be Patrick—he wasn't capable of playing songs on that level for another two months. My skin prickled. Each note played was like a ghostly finger touching my shoulder. A wrong note was struck, and the hair on the back of my neck rose. Ashley had delighted in playing that note incorrectly; she had played it repeatedly to frustrate Joseph.

The song ended. I held my breath, waiting for what would happen next. The music started again, the same piece. I hummed the melody, anticipating, dreading that one wrong note.

It was struck. My back grew rigid.

Fearing what I might see—fearing what I might not—I crept toward the schoolroom. I'm not crazy, I told myself; I have to be hearing it. But I couldn't imagine anyone currently living in the house playing that song. The schoolroom door was partway open. The nerves in my fingertips tingled as I laid them lightly against the wood, then pushed the door all the way.

Patrick sat on the piano bench. With no moonlight and just a pale triangle cast by the hall night-light, I could see only his silhouette and the rectangular shape of the piano. A feeling of deep uneasiness seeped into me, a sense that something hidden in the dark was watching me, and it didn't want me there.

"Patrick?" I called softly, approaching the bench. "Patrick." I spoke it with more insistence, but he didn't turn around. "Patrick, stop playing!"

He didn't move his head, didn't show any sign of hearing me.

His failure to listen made me bolder. I placed a hand on his shoulder, then leaned over to look at him. Though his hands moved, his face was still, strange, inanimate as a molded puppet's. His eyes were partially closed, the pale irises and whites of his eyes like half-moons, his mouth slightly open.

"Can you hear me?" I asked.

He continued to play.

"Patrick, stop!" I grabbed his hands and held them still. After a moment, he raised his chin to look at me. His eyes slowly opened to full size. He didn't speak.

"What are you doing?" I asked.

He glanced down at the keyboard. "Playing."

"What song was that?"

He thought for a moment. "'Little Red Rooster.'"

I could picture the page in Ashley's songbook, for she had crayoned a waxy red rooster next to the title. How could he have learned it? What made his hands suddenly able to play the song? "Who taught you that?"

"I just know it," he said.

"I think you may have played the song incorrectly. One note was wrong."

"I played it the way *I* play it."

I let go of his hands and backed away from him. The words

were the same, the intonation exact, his child's voice no deeper than Ashley's. Each time Joseph had corrected her, that had been her response.

My mind groped for explanations. Brook might have remembered the song, but it seemed unlikely, given that he had avoided the schoolroom as much as possible. Robyn had rarely come to the third floor. Perhaps Trent or Mrs. Hopewell knew the song and remembered how Ashley had played the incorrect note, but how could they have taught it so quickly to Patrick, who had shown no piano skills the previous afternoon? And why wouldn't Patrick admit that one of them had taught him? There were so many eerie similarities between the playmate Patrick called Ashley and the little girl I had known. It was growing increasingly difficult to pretend there wasn't something haunting this house, haunting this child.

Patrick sat with his hands in his lap, shivering.

"It's cold and late," I said. "You should be in bed."

"I wasn't cold till now," he told me, then slipped off the bench.

As he did, something leaped from beneath the keyboard. I screamed, then muffled the sound with my hand.

"It's just November," Patrick said.

The feral cat stopped short of the doorway.

"November! Why is he here? Did you let him in? You know

you're not supposed to go downstairs by yourself at night."

"He was outside my bedroom window."

"Patrick, there is no way a cat can leap up to a second-story windowsill."

"My window by the roof."

I remembered that one of his side windows faced the extension that joined Robyn's wing to the house. Perhaps there was a trellis or some other structure that gave the cat passage to the low roof, then up to the window.

"There was snow on his fur, so I let him in to get warm."

"I'm sure the snow made him look cold," I said, "but he's a wild cat and used to being outside. He has a thick coat of fur. He's probably happier out there."

"No, he'll freeze. He'll freeze to death like Patricia!" Patrick's voice grew panicky. "He'll die!"

"Shh! You'll wake the others. November may stay here tonight, just tonight," I said, hoping I could close the cat in the schoolroom till Roger helped me put him out. I knew better than to fool with a feral animal that hadn't had its shots. "We'll talk about it further in the morning. Now let's get you in bed."

As soon as we moved, the cat ran out the door and disappeared down the main stairs. I sighed. There was no point in my bumbling around the dark house trying to find him. Patrick and I crossed the third-floor hall to my room, then took the back steps down to his. When I turned on Patrick's small night-light, November slunk out from the shadows and leaped onto the bed. Patrick was charmed; I found it creepy. Ashley used to bring in the cat and hide it till bedtime so she could sleep with it. After a lapse of twelve years, what had suddenly drawn this wild animal back to her room?

"He can't stay with you, Patrick."

"But he likes me."

"You have allergies," I argued. "You're already starting to sniffle. Come on, November. Scoot!"

I waved my hand at the cat. He hissed. Determined to get rid of him, I moved closer. He hissed again and swung a paw, claws extended. He meant business.

"I don't think November likes *you,*" Patrick observed.

"Can you get him off the bed—without touching him, I mean."

Patrick shooed him halfheartedly, and the cat moved down to the foot of the bed. Patrick happily climbed in at the other end.

"I'm running out of patience," I said. "Listen to me. The cat hasn't had his shots, and if he bites you, you could get rabies. You are *not* to touch him. Do you understand?"

"Yes, but he won't bite me."

I wouldn't admit it and encourage petting the cat, but I sensed the same thing. I decided I could leave them alone long enough to fetch some bait and get the cat out of the room. "Stay in bed and don't touch him. I'm going downstairs for a can of tuna and will be back in a minute."

The hall door had been knocked ajar by the cat. I opened it all the way.

"Someone has turned out the rose lamp," Patrick observed.

"It probably burned out."

With all the bedroom doors closed but Patrick's, and his night-light casting no more than a dim glow inside his room, the hall was black as night itself, its walls and corners invisible. Knocking over an antique rose lamp in a clumsy attempt to find and light it seemed a bad idea. Lighting the bright over-heads in the hall might wake up Emily and Adrian. The more fuss there was, the harder it would be to get Patrick back to sleep, especially after Emily had strung me up for allowing the cat in his room. The best plan was to walk straight ahead till I reached the steps at the other end of the hall. There I could turn on the stairway sconces.

Holding one hand out in front of me, I walked slowly, slower still as I reached what I thought would be the wall next to the stairway. I finally touched it, but I must have veered slightly to the left while crossing the hall, for there were no switches there.

I slid my foot to the right, feeling the wooden edge of the step. I moved farther to the right, my hand searching for the heavy wood banister and the wall with the light plates. I heard a noise behind me, a sound as light as padded feet. Something rushed against my legs. I stifled a scream. *The cat,* I thought, teetering on the step. *Just the cat. Relax, Kate.*

The next moment something hard and flat, the size of a hand, slammed between my shoulder blades. I cried out and pitched forward. I reached out desperately for the banister—the wall—anything that could stop my fall. My bare feet slid, my arches rolling over the hard edge of the step. I began to tumble—headfirst into the darkness—and yanked myself backward. For a moment I touched nothing, then suddenly I made contact, my right shoulder and hip banging down against the steps. I could count the steps I was sliding down, each one a blow against my upper arm.

At the landing, I stopped. I couldn't move. My ski jacket had padded the fall, but the right side of my body ached, and the feeling of tumbling helplessly had taken my breath away. So simple, I thought, so simple and effective—it didn't take much effort to hurt a person.

I sat up slowly, hearing movement in the hall above me. It was Patrick's light footsteps running across it. "Stop, Patrick! Don't run. You'll fall down the steps."

Lights came on, all of the ceiling lights, flooding the hall with whiteness. The door to Adrian and Emily's room opened.

"Kate!" Adrian exclaimed as he reached the top of the stairs. "Are you all right?"

Emily grabbed Patrick's hand, and Adrian started down the steps.

"What happened? Emily, you had better call 911."

"No," I said quickly. "I'm fine—a little shaken up, that's all."

"I'd rather be on the safe side," Adrian replied, arriving on the landing, bending over me.

"No, really, please don't. I didn't hit my head. I didn't break anything," I said, flexing my arms and legs, hoping to convince him. "I'm bruised, nothing more."

A door on the second-floor hall banged open.

"Why are the lights on, the emergency lights in my hall?" Trent asked, coming from the wing behind the stairs. He cleared the corner, looked down, and saw Adrian standing over me. "Good God! What has happened?"

"Kate fell," Patrick said.

"When we heard the noise out here, Adrian pushed the master switch," Emily explained.

A door at the opposite end of the hall opened, and quick footsteps crossed it. Robyn and Brook joined the others at the top of the steps.

"Hey, a family reunion at three A.M. What a great idea!" Brook said. "Let's open a keg."

"You're ridiculous in the middle of the day," Trent told Brook. "Don't push your luck in the middle of the night."

"No more ridiculous than you in your red silk designer robe," Robyn responded in defense of her son. "I wonder who gave you that?" She gazed down the steps at Adrian and me. "What happened, Daddy?"

Adrian sat down two steps above me. "Apparently Kate tripped and fell down the stairs."

"What was Kate doing?" It was the steely voice of Mrs. Hopewell, who had silently joined the others.

Adrian gave me a sly wink. "Meeting her sweetheart for a romp in the snow. Or perhaps, Louise, sneaking a piece of that delicious pie you made."

"Was November with you?" Patrick asked. "He left my room."

"Who's November?" Brook asked.

"The cat," I replied. "The orange tabby. Patrick said he found him outside his window, the one by the roof and let him in. I was going downstairs to get some bait to coax him out of the room."

"Oh, wonderful," Trent observed, "we have a rabid cat in the house."

"Just lock your bedroom door, Trent," Robyn responded

sarcastically, "and you'll be safe from all ten pounds of him."

"Darling," Emily said to Patrick, "that cat is dirty. It has diseases."

"Where is it now?" Mrs. Hopewell asked.

"I don't know. It brushed past me at the top of the steps."

"And tripped you," Adrian said.

"No. It wasn't the cat." I looked him in the eye and spoke loudly enough for everyone to hear. "Someone pushed me from behind."

Adrian's blue eyes narrowed. I gazed up at the group standing at the top of the steps, but with the ceiling lights shining brightly behind their heads, I couldn't see their faces.

"Someone pushed me. I felt a hand against my back."

Adrian's face became grim. Whether it was because he thought that a member of his household was capable of the act or that I was getting paranoid, I didn't know.

"Certainly you would have seen someone," Robyn said, breaking the silence.

"The night lamp is off," Brook observed.

"Louise?"

"I turned it on before retiring," the housekeeper assured Adrian, "just as I always do."

I heard the light click of a switch, someone testing the rose lamp. "Well, the bulb isn't burned out," Trent said.

"Perhaps you were dreaming, Kate," Emily suggested. "Perhaps—"

"Ashley pushed you," Patrick interjected.

His words chilled us to silence. The house itself was quiet, as if the walls and floors were waiting to hear more from him.

"Ashley didn't want you to put November outside," Patrick went on. "She was afraid he'd freeze. So she pushed you."

The flesh along my arms rose in tiny bumps. Standing in the schoolroom I had felt as if something were watching me, something that didn't like me. For a moment I actually believed Ashley was responsible.

You're losing it, Kate, I told myself; *it was the cat watching you.*

"Father, Patrick has got to stop this crazy talk," Trent said.

"He's your brother," Adrian replied quietly. "If it bothers you, you may ask him yourself."

"Daddy doesn't do what Daddy doesn't want to do," Robyn said, her hips switching. She sounded like a little girl enjoying her brother's discomfort.

Trent turned abruptly and returned to his wing.

"This isn't as good a party as I thought," Brook observed. "I'm going to bed."

Robyn gazed down at Adrian and me, then shook her

head, more like an adult now. "Things are getting out of hand, Daddy." She followed her son.

"If you don't need me, sir . . . "

"No, Louise, good night," Adrian replied.

Mrs. Hopewell started off, then turned back. "About the cat."

"If all of us keep our doors closed, the cat will find a cozy spot by itself," Adrian told her. "We'll put it out tomorrow."

"I shall put Patrick to bed," Emily said.

"No, I want Kate," Patrick protested.

"Darling," Emily replied, "I'm your mommy."

"But Kate puts me to bed."

"Go with your mother," Adrian said sternly.

When the two of them had disappeared, Adrian turned to me. In the harsh lighting he looked years older; for once, he looked like a man who was seriously ill.

"Be straight with me, Kate, and I will keep what you say to myself. Is there any chance you were partially asleep? Is there a chance that you were sleepwalking—dreaming?"

"No."

"You're certain?"

I recounted to him how I was awakened by the sound of Patrick playing the piano, the strangeness of hearing the song Ashley used to play, and what had followed after that. "I was awake for at least fifteen minutes."

"Is there any possibility that it was an accident—that in the dark, someone came up behind you and knocked into you, then didn't want to admit it?"

"It's possible, but I don't think it happened that way. I believe it was intentional."

"Then you must be very cautious," Adrian said. "I'd like to tell you there is no reason for you to fear, but I know my family too well."

"Then you know why I am worried about Patrick," I replied.

"No one will hurt him. My family will hiss and howl, scratch and nip, but they will not seriously harm one another."

"But what about Ashley? What if—"

"Kate, I, more than anyone, understand your suspicions." He took a deep breath. "After all, I blamed your mother, unable to accept that an event so horrible could have been chance. But it was. It was an accident."

I wasn't convinced, and he saw that.

"Of course, you know you may leave your employment here at any time and I would fully understand. I would make sure you are compensated and help you find another job."

"I'm not leaving."

He studied me for a moment, then nodded. "I'm glad, but be cautious and keep in close touch with me, Kate. Promise me that."

"I will."

Adrian stood up slowly, then held out a hand for me. We climbed the steps together. "Sleep well, if that is not a totally preposterous hope," he said.

"You too. Good night."

I returned to my room and listened to the muffled voices of Emily and Patrick in the room below me. She had closed the door to the stairway that connected our two rooms. A few minutes later, all was quiet. I crept down the steps to check on Patrick. He was already asleep, the night-light casting a pale glow on his face, creating a deceptively peaceful portrait of a child.

Back in my room, I couldn't sleep. I stood at the window, resting my forehead against the freezing glass, my hands on a lukewarm radiator. I ran through the list—Robyn, Brook, Trent, Mrs. Hopewell—trying to figure out who had pushed me. I could have been seriously injured—even killed—if I had broken my neck. I was afraid.

Only the foolish and the dead have no fear. Had Mrs. Hopewell made good on her warning about the danger of prying into family secrets? Clearly, she and Robyn wanted me out of the house, but perhaps Trent and Brook did too. Why? So they could get to Patrick—or was I, myself, perceived as a threat?

I was starting to believe Sam's theory that Ashley had been

lured by a murderer onto the ice. What if Patrick's constant talk of her and the questions I had been asking were beginning to fray the nerves of the killer? Then both Patrick and I were in serious danger, and I was the only one who could do something about it. But what I should do, I had no idea.

Twelve

A BRILLIANT BLUE sky and fringe of glittering icicles was the first thing I saw the next morning. The sun was high, too high. I wrenched around in the bedcovers to look at the alarm clock and felt a stab of pain in my right shoulder: 8:45. Then I saw the note next to my clock: "School has been canceled because of snow. Mr Westbrook gave instructions to let you sleep. Patrick is with his mother."

I could imagine the thick fingers of Mrs. Hopewell forming the short, square letters, then turning off my alarm clock. The thought of her creeping into my room and watching me while I slept made me wriggle my shoulders—a painful mistake. When I climbed out of bed and checked myself in the mirror, I saw what looked like a purple map of Norway and Sweden on the right half of my back, Finland on my arm.

Putting on a turtleneck and sweater took some care and time. I pulled on a pair of jeans, figuring that Patrick would be eager to go out in the snow. When I pushed back my lower set of curtains, the brightness made me blink. Everything below was white, evergreens and hedges dolloped with snowy meringue. After the shadows of last night, the pure light seemed almost unreal.

I descended the steps to Patrick's room, then entered the second-floor hall, pausing to study its layout. It would have been easy enough for Robyn, Brook, or Mrs. Hopewell to follow me across the hall last night to the top of the stairway, since the exit to the wing where they slept was just beyond Patrick's bedroom door. But Trent, whose wing was on the opposite side of the house, also had easy access. The exit to his wing was on a short hall that ran next to the main staircase. Of course, Emily and Adrian's room was on the main hall, its doorway fairly close to the steps.

Preoccupied with the immediate problem of putting out the cat, I had made it easy for whomever had come up behind me. I tried to remember if I had seen the night lamp shining on the landing between the two floors when I was still on the third floor, walking toward the schoolroom. But I had been so caught up in the eeriness of hearing the song Ashley had once played, I hadn't noticed anything else.

The raised voices of Emily and Robyn drew me back to the present. When I arrived on the first floor, I saw them face-to-face outside the laundry room, near Robyn's wing. Patrick stood next to his mother, holding his hands a distance behind him. Brook leaned against the frame of the laundry door, drinking a cup of coffee, surveying his mother, who was dressed in her barn clothes.

"This is outrageous." Robyn's voice shook with anger. "He's a horrid child, a wicked boy. You should be ashamed."

Emily didn't respond; apparently, she wasn't.

"If it makes you feel any better, Mother," Brook said, *"I'm* ashamed—that I never thought of such a prank," he added, grinning. "And I'm sure Emily will be very ashamed—as soon as she stops laughing. Patrick, you're a little turd, dumping the manure through the hay chute. Of course, Mother is now a big turd."

Robyn shot her son a look.

"What's 'turd' mean?" Patrick asked.

"It's a piece of manure," Emily told him.

I surmised that Robyn had been tending one of her horses, standing beneath a stall's hay chute, when Patrick dropped down a smelly pile from the manure heap. It was tempting to laugh, but if Patrick thought the prank was funny, he might try it again. At the moment he wasn't looking very contrite.

"I don't know what possessed you to do such a thing, Patrick," Emily said. "I don't want it to happen again."

"Oh, it won't," Robyn responded, her eyes flashing. "If I catch him near the barn, I'll rub his face in a pile till he suffocates."

Brook cheerfully saluted me with his coffee cup. "Good morning, Kate. Come join our family fun."

Patrick turned around, but Emily reached for his arm and held it tightly. She and Robyn, locked in glares, didn't acknowledge me.

"That child needs a strap across his backside," Robyn continued. "I'm going to talk to Daddy. He will straighten out Patrick."

"Forty-two years old and still tattling," Emily observed scornfully. "When are you going to stop pretending that you're Daddy's girl? He has a wife now and a little boy."

Robyn's lips trembled. She turned on her heel, entered the laundry room, and slammed the door behind her.

"I'll get your robe, Mother," Brook called, then leaned toward me. "I wonder how long she would stay there if I forgot?"

I didn't reply, and he headed through the door to their wing.

"Come, Patrick, we should wash your hands again," Emily said.

He sniffed his fingers, then nodded in agreement.

She still hadn't acknowledged me. Perhaps she was miffed that I hadn't been at the barn to stop Patrick, but I wasn't the one who had turned off my alarm clock.

"Sounds as if there's a problem," I remarked quietly.

"She's the problem," Emily retorted.

I walked with them toward the kitchen.

"Daddy said I shouldn't wake you up, Kate."

"That was kind of him, and of you, too," I replied. "Speaking of kindness, that was a rather mean thing to do to Robyn."

"I was just playing," he said, then glanced at his mother, as if expecting her to defend him.

"Would you have liked Robyn to dump the manure on you?" I asked.

He grinned. "I wouldn't care."

Of course not—I was talking to a little boy.

I pushed open the kitchen door. "The point is, adults don't like it, and you know that."

"He's just a child," Emily protested.

She would be saying that when Patrick was thirty-five. I felt as if we were replaying a drama that this house had witnessed before: Corinne had always defended Ashley, undercutting Joseph when he would discipline her.

"You had better use the utility sink," I told Patrick. "Did you clean up the mess you made in the barn?"

"No."

"The grooms can do it," Emily said. "I'm sure they already have."

A nice thing to teach a child, I thought: Misbehave, make a mess, and others will clean it up for you. I wasn't letting Patrick off the hook so easily. "Then you owe both Robyn and the grooms an apology."

Patrick's brow furled, just like his mother's. "It wasn't my fault!"

"Whose fault was it?"

"Ashley's. She told me to do it."

Emily sighed. "I thought we weren't going to talk about Ashley anymore."

Patrick stretched his hands over the sink, and I pushed back his sleeves—Emily didn't want to touch anything that might stink. "When someone tells you to do something that you know is wrong, Patrick, you should say no."

"I did," he whined, "but she dared me."

"If Ashley dares you again, come and tell me—or your mother," I added quickly, for the color was rising in Emily's cheeks. I wasn't trying to take over her role, but he was only a child, and someone had to teach him.

Patrick scrubbed and dried his hands. I turned to Emily. "Do you think it would be a good idea if Patrick wrote notes of apology to Robyn and the grooms?"

"You're asking me?" she snapped. "Why bother? You'll have him do whatever you want. And if I question it, Adrian will defend you." She picked up a copy of the morning paper and walked off, her flat snakeskin shoes clicking.

"All right, Patrick, let's go upstairs and start those notes."

He looked at me defiantly. "No."

"Sorry?"

"I won't."

I studied him for a moment. His blue eyes shrank as he stared back at me, their lids tightening. The skin on my face felt cold. He looked like Ashley when she'd bore into me with one of her looks. No, like any child—I told myself quickly—it was simply the way children's round eyes appear when they become defiant.

"You have made a lot of extra work and trouble for Robyn and the grooms," I told him. "You owe them an apology."

"You can't make me do it."

I gazed at him until he turned his face away.

"No, I can't," I agreed. "And if you want to remain upstairs for the rest of the day, that is fine with me. My shoulder hurts. I don't want to play in the snow that much."

He turned back, the defiance gone from his face. "Did you hurt it when you fell down the steps?" He laid his hand lightly on my arm. "Does it hurt a lot?"

"It's not too bad."

"Maybe you should put your arm in a sling," he suggested.

"No, nothing is broken."

"You could take some aspirin," he said. "It's locked in the cupboard in my bathroom. I'll get you a soda to drink with it."

"Thank you, but no," I replied, puzzled by Patrick's sudden concern for me. A turn of his head and his mood had shifted dramatically. It was as if he were two people in one.

Shaking off an uneasy feeling, I started up the steps. He followed quietly and, when we reached the schoolroom, sat down to write.

Later that morning I carried the notes of apology downstairs. Ideally, Patrick should have hand delivered them, but I didn't want to push our luck with a second trip to the barn and perhaps another confrontation with Robyn. I gave the grooms' notes to Roger, who was heading toward the barn to finish plowing. I placed Robyn's note in her mailbox outside the office door. As I turned away from the mahogany boxes, a woman emerged from the office.

"You must be Kate," she said, then held out her hand in greeting.

The woman was pretty, in her late sixties, I thought, with pale blond hair that had the molded and sprayed look of someone who went weekly to a salon.

"I'm Elaine, Adrian's personal secretary. I work part-time now, once or twice a week."

"It's nice to meet you."

She reached into a folder she was carrying. "I have a phone number that was requested by Patrick."

I glanced down at the square of paper she handed me, surprised. "Sam Koscinski?"

"He said Sam was his friend." Her eyes brightened with amusement. "Patrick has the same demanding way as his father when he wants a phone number pronto."

"He demanded it?" I wasn't amused at the idea of a seven-year-old talking to an adult as if she were his employee. It was so easy to turn a sweet kid into a brat.

"Well, thank you. Thank you very much." I slipped the paper in my pocket and climbed the steps to the third floor.

I had left Patrick playing a game on his computer and, upon reaching the last flight of steps, expected to hear pinging sounds against a background of music. When I heard an electronic voice asking repeatedly *Hey, want to play?* I quickened my pace toward the schoolroom. He wasn't there.

"Patrick?"

I checked the playroom, then hurried to my room and downstairs to his. He was nowhere in sight. I listened for footsteps above my head, in case he was hiding, then returned to the third floor to search the two storerooms.

"Patrick? If you're hiding, I want you to come out now."

Nothing in the two rooms appeared to be disturbed. The old hockey sticks, deflated basketball, and other sports equipment lay in the same places as before. The furniture was coated with dust and bore no fingerprints or streaks.

I wavered between anger and fear.

He is playing games with me, being a brat, there is nothing to worry about, I told myself. But after the incidents of the last few days, all I could think of were the dangerous things Ashley had dared me to do when Joseph and my mother weren't around— jumping off a shed roof, wading into the bay during a storm, making a fire by the pond. I debated whether to go immediately to Adrian. If Patrick was simply playing a hiding game, and I created a ruckus by having everyone search for him, he and I would both regret it.

I hurried downstairs to check the coat closet. His snow jacket was gone, though not his boots. I rushed to the kitchen door and saw a set of small footprints leading away from it. Without pausing to put on a coat or boots, I raced out, following the prints. When I got to the orangerie, Patrick's path suddenly veered around a bush, and a second trail appeared. The snow was above my ankles, so it was difficult to see the actual paw prints, but I was sure they were a cat's.

"Patrick?" I shouted.

I couldn't tell if the cat led the boy or the boy led the cat, but both routes were headed toward the tennis courts and the pool beyond it. The evergreen screen around the courts and pool obscured my view. I rushed on, passing the wall of spruce close to the pool, then stopped short.

Patrick stood on the diving board, at the very end, looking down. Far below him was the concrete floor of the pool, covered by a layer of snow and ice. The cat sat by the steps, watching him.

I called softly to Patrick, afraid I would startle him. He didn't look up. Continuing to call his name, I walked toward the deep end. For a moment I thought he saw me—clearly, something had caught his attention. He lifted his head. Then he began to jump up and down on the end of the board.

"Patrick, don't! Stop!" I screamed.

He continued bouncing. If he fell and struck his head or neck, he'd kill himself.

I rushed around the corner of the pool and climbed up on the board. The sun glared off the ice below, nearly blinding me as I made my way along the board. Patrick kept jumping, swinging his arms to propel himself higher, landing precariously on the edge. I felt seasick, the flexing board dropping and rising beneath my feet.

I had to think fast. If I caught him from behind, he might lose his balance and throw mine as well. But calling his name drew no response. As soon as I reached him I sat down on the board, straddling it, for the lower my position, the easier it would be to stay on the board. I reached up and grabbed him by the waist. Pain shot through my injured shoulder as I jerked him back against me. "Patrick! Don't fight me."

He pulled forward to get away from me. I yanked him back. "Be still!"

At last he stopped resisting.

The easiest way to get back to the pool's deck was to crawl, but I wasn't about to let go of him and tell him to follow. Who knew what instructions he heard besides mine?

"Don't fight me," I warned, then slid back on the rough surface of the board, pulling him with me. I continued to slide back and pull him toward me, slowly making our way to the pool deck. As soon as my feet touched the cement, I climbed off the diving board, then struggled to remove Patrick. On solid ground again, he wrenched away from me.

"You can't hurt me!" he said.

"Hurt you? What are you talking about?"

He turned his back to me, hunching his shoulders. "You can't hurt me."

"Patrick, you know that I won't. What is going on with you?"

"November hates you," he said.

"I'm not fond of November, either, after what happened last night."

Patrick turned his head to look questioningly at the cat. "Why? What did he do?"

"He came in the house, don't you remember? He wouldn't leave your room. I was going downstairs to get some bait, when I fell and hurt my shoulder."

Patrick turned all the way around to face me. He eyed my shoulder. "Does it hurt a lot?"

"No." I studied him, perplexed, trying to read the expression in his eyes. "We talked about it already this morning, remember?"

He bit his lip and nodded, but I wasn't sure that he did.

"Patrick, you could have killed yourself falling off the diving board. Why did you do that?" I had to ask, though I knew before he answered what he would say.

"You'll get mad," he replied. "You won't believe me."

"Because Ashley dared you?"

He nodded.

Twelve years ago, as in my dream the other night, she had dared me to do the same thing—to jump up and down at the end of the board, to entertain her with a stupid, risky game.

"I do believe you."

I believed in and feared something at Mason's Choice that was as dangerous as the people currently living here—a mind and force that I had never known how to handle: angry, vindictive, careless Ashley.

Thirteen

WHAT DID ASHLEY want, I wondered, as Patrick and I ate lunch. Justice? The company and friendship of another child? Friendship that would ultimately mean death?

Patrick was quiet during the meal, not like a child enjoying a school holiday, nothing like the little boy who had danced in the falling snow the night before. I feared that Ashley was changing him, and I didn't know how to stop her. Though Adrian would listen, he wouldn't believe me if I told him Patrick was haunted. I could tell him that I had found Patrick playing on the diving board, omitting my own experience with Ashley and fears about what was happening, but that wouldn't keep Patrick safe from her.

And it might backfire. I sensed that Emily was turning against me, jealous when Adrian supported me, upset when Patrick wanted to be with me. She could charge me with incompetence for letting her son wander off to the pool alone.

If she had me dismissed, Patrick would have no one to watch over him.

I set down my half-eaten sandwich. At the same time, Patrick pushed back his plate. "I'm not hungry."

I immediately picked up my roll again and took a hearty bite. "Try just a little more. You want to have energy to play in the snow."

He didn't respond.

"Do you want to play outside after lunch?"

"I guess."

"We can make a snowman. How about a snow fort?"

He shrugged. "Okay."

The Eastern Shore was mostly flat, and there were no hills on Mason's Choice for sledding. The drop of land down to the bay was too steep. "Do you know of a place around here where children like to sled?"

"No. That's okay."

I took a long sip of tea and made up my mind. "I'll be right back. Don't go anywhere. I want to see three more bites out of that roll."

I didn't want to make the phone call in front of Patrick and build up his hopes only to crush them. Standing close to a window in the dining room, hoping I'd hear or see him if he decided to slip out the kitchen door, I pulled out my cell and punched in Sam's number, the one Elaine had given me.

Someone picked up at the other end.

"Hi," I said after a moment of silence.

"Hi, Kate," he replied.

"How did you know it was me?"

"The way you said hi, as if you weren't sure you wanted to, as if you might hang up."

Was I that obvious? "You have Caller ID," I guessed.

"That too. What's up?"

I issued an invitation to play in the snow. "Patrick would love to see you," I added. Realizing that I was pacing nervously, I made myself stop.

"Can't do it."

"Not at all? Not even for a half hour? Twenty minutes?"

"Would *you* love to see me?" he asked.

"Uh,"—he had caught me off guard—"yes, I'd like it, of course."

"Okay, then. I don't want to hang out with two people when one of them doesn't want me there."

"I didn't realize your ego was that sensitive," I said.

"Neither did I," he replied with a sigh.

"So . . . we'll see you in a bit. Do you know how to get here?"

"I can find the gates."

"They open automatically. Come straight up the road to the house."

"By the way, I have to leave by three o'clock," Sam said. "Even though school is canceled, we have hockey practice."

"Lovely. I mean, it's lovely that you're coming, not that you have to leave at three o'clock."

He laughed and I signed off quickly, wishing I could stop the burn in my cheeks. At least we'd be out in the cold where my cheeks always got pink—and my ears looked like roses stuck on either side of my head, I remembered.

When I told Patrick the news, he perked up. We found Emily in her sitting room, working on sketches for an art course she was taking, and received official permission for Sam to visit. Twenty minutes later, as Patrick and I headed to the kitchen to pull on our boots, we passed Brook in the hall.

"Anybody you know drive an old heap?" Brook asked. "One just pulled up in front of the house."

Patrick ran to the front window. "He's here!" he cried, as if Father Christmas had just arrived.

Mrs. Hopewell called down sternly from the top of the stairs: "There is company, and I wasn't informed."

"She has a boxful of eyeballs," Brook whispered to me. "She puts one in each window of the house."

I walked to the foot of the stairs and spoke loud enough

for both him and Mrs. Hopewell to hear. "The guest is a friend of Patrick and mine. We had permission to invite him." There was no need to say permission from whom or that we secured it after I issued the invitation.

Patrick yanked open the front door. "Hey, Sam!"

"Hey, buddy. How are you?"

"Good! Come in. I'll be right back. I have to get something upstairs."

Sam stepped inside and Patrick raced past me. When he spied Mrs. Hopewell at the top of the stairs, he put on the brakes and headed in another direction, choosing a set of back steps.

"Hello, Kate," Sam greeted me.

"Hi." I tried not to notice his rough beard—he must not have shaved—or his dark hair or his intense eyes, or the softness of the sweater he wore beneath an open jacket.

Sam walked toward Brook and held out his hand. "Hello. Sam Koscinski."

Brook nodded without taking his hand. "Westbrook Caulfield," he replied formally.

Mrs. Hopewell had descended half the flight of steps and stood staring down at Sam. I assumed she recognized the name and knew he was related to the man who had investigated Ashley's death.

"Hello, Mrs. Westbrook," Sam greeted the housekeeper.

She pulled back her head with surprise. Brook burst out laughing.

"This is Mrs. Hopewell," I said.

Sam didn't blink. "Hello, Mrs. Hopewell."

Without a word, she descended the remaining steps and strode down the hall toward Robyn's wing, probably to tell her who was here. Brook asked about the condition of the roads, then headed out.

Sam turned to me. "I knew who the old gargoyle was," he said. "She's a legend in town. Besides, I know how a house-keeper dresses—I've seen movies."

"So why did you pretend not to?"

He shrugged. "To get her to stop staring. To remind her that she is not the owner of the house." He glanced around. "Nice place."

"I've got my boots in the kitchen," I said, leading the way.

Patrick joined us there, carrying two battered hockey sticks, the ones I had seen in the third-floor storage rooms.

"Whoa! Look at those," Sam said, taking one in his hands, running his fingers up and down it. "This must have been used in the Revolutionary War."

"No, I think my dad used it," Patrick answered seriously. "We can play on the pond if you want."

"You can *what?*" I exclaimed.

"Kate says it isn't frozen hard enough to hold us," Patrick quickly confided to Sam, "but I know it is."

"Yeah? How do you know that?" Sam asked.

"Ashley told me."

That answer didn't surprise me anymore, but Sam hadn't expected it, and he glanced at me before responding. "Well, here's the problem. Since, far as I can tell, Ashley is lighter than air, and you and I are not, I'm going by what Kate says. But we can bring the sticks outside," he added. "They'll be good for batting snowballs."

Though disappointed, Patrick was agreeable. He and I tugged on our boots, and the three of us headed to the grounds behind the house, where there were no gardens hidden by snow that we might damage. The stretch of lawn was a white downy quilt against the long, blue horizon of bay and sky.

We took turns tossing snowballs, walloping them with hockey sticks, and running madly around the bases, which were mounds of snow.

"Are you sure you're a leftie?" Sam asked, when the balls I threw kept falling short of home plate.

"Are you implying I can't pitch?" I didn't want to tell him my right shoulder hurt.

Everything Sam did, Patrick did: winding his arm to pitch, sliding dramatically into base, bellowing that he was "safe." Afterward, we made a snowman as tall as Sam and gave him a hockey stick to hold.

"We need eyes and a nose," Patrick said. "And I want to make a number for him to wear."

"You're supposed to use a carrot for his nose," Sam replied, "but I always used broccoli, used it for everything—even had broccoli hair—that way, there wouldn't be any left for dinner."

Patrick laughed. "Green hair. Cool!"

"How about you, Kate?" Sam asked.

"It didn't snow much in England, not where we lived, but once we had a big storm and my father gave me loops of undeveloped film to make curly hair, then he and I dressed up our snow lady in paint rags and a drop cloth spattered with colors. She was elegant."

I hadn't thought about that for years. I blinked before the unexpected tears got beyond the corners of my eyes.

"Cool!" Patrick repeated.

"Very cool," Sam said, his voice unusually gentle.

"So what do we use now?" I asked, glancing about, trying to look as if I'd already forgotten about the snow lady.

"Beach stuff," Patrick said. "Let's go down there."

"Can we?" Sam asked.

"I suppose so." There were steps, steep wooden ones that ran down the side of what Ashley and I used to call "the cliffs," eroded banks of sandy soil and clay that dropped about eight meters to a narrow shoreline of sand, shells, and stones. "We should be careful on the steps. They may be rotted in places. Let me go first, Patrick."

"I'll go first," Sam offered.

"I said I would."

He raised an eyebrow. "Is this like the door thing?"

It was, and it was stupid, but I wouldn't admit it. "Fall through the steps if you want to," I said. "You're the one who has a play-off game on Saturday."

"Good point. You go first."

"Kate fell down the steps last night," Patrick volunteered, "down the big stairs, and woke everybody up. Daddy wanted to call 911."

Sam turned to stare at me.

"It wasn't as bad as it sounds. I stopped at the landing."

"Mommy said she could have killed herself."

"I bruised my shoulder, that's all," I told Sam. "Come on. This snowman needs eyes and numbers." I started walking.

"Race!" Sam shouted suddenly, and took off. The snow made it harder for Patrick to pick up his short legs and run. He looked like a bunny hopping after Sam. I waited till Sam slowed down to let Patrick catch up, then shot past the two of them.

Snowballs pelted the backs of my legs. I stopped to taunt the boys, and Sam rushed past me. He stood grinning at the top of the steps, then started down them, kicking off snow as he went. As it turned out, the wood was in good shape; I should have known that Adrian would keep his property perfectly maintained.

At the bottom, strips of snow lay like shimmering froth left behind by waves. It was low tide, and stones sparkled at the edge of the sand. The banks above us looked streaky, red clay and yellow sand sugared over with snow. The fresh smell of snow mixed with the tang of salt.

Patrick skipped along the shore, searching for materials. "We'll use clams for his ears," he called over his shoulder.

"Perfect!" I said, starting after him, but Sam caught me by the sleeve.

"What happened last night?"

"What do you mean?" I asked.

"How did you fall down the steps?"

"I just fell."

"I don't think so," he said. "I think you called me because something has happened to upset you."

"I called because I was worried about Patrick."

"Did you trip?" he persisted.

"No."

Sam waited for an explanation.

"I was pushed."

"Pushed! By who?"

"I don't know. It was dark—someone turned out the night lamp."

"Who do you think it was?"

"Ashley."

He grimaced. "That answer works only when you're seven. Be honest, who do you think it was?"

"I don't know," I told him.

"Why do you think you were pushed?"

"I don't know!"

"You can trust me, Kate."

I bit my lip.

"I went on the Internet," Sam said, "and read the obituaries about your dad."

I glanced at him, startled. He was doing research on me.

"One of the articles said he and your mom had been separated for twelve years."

"That's right. She left us after we got to London. I haven't seen her since."

"That must have—" Sam broke off, seeing Patrick walking toward us.

"I found eyes and ears for the snowman," Patrick said, studying the treasures he carried. He dropped mussels and clamshells into my hands.

Sam admired them. "Great! Now we need a lot of stones, so we can write out the uniform number."

Patrick went off again.

"That must have been pretty tough, your mother suddenly disappearing," Sam said, continuing our conversation.

I shrugged. "The tough part was having to raise my father alone."

He smiled a little, but his eyes were serious. "Do you know how to contact your mother?"

I looked out at the bay, at the cold blue-gray waves, their jagged glitter. "Yes, but I won't. Ever. Can we change the subject?"

He didn't answer right away. "Okay. What do you want to talk about?"

"Patrick." I watched him at the edge of the water, picking up stones. There were others on dryer land, but he wanted the wet ones, the shiny ones. "I am really worried about him."

"Has his loving family killed any more pets?" Sam asked.

"He doesn't have any other pets, unless you count November."

I told Sam about the strange reappearance of Ashley's cat

and recounted the other odd events: the way Patrick had played the song Ashley had played, with the same incorrect note; the dare on the diving board—the same dare Ashley had made to me. Once I started, I couldn't stop and I told him everything, though I avoided using the word "ghost."

"Sam," I said, finding my nerve at last, "what if Patrick sees and hears something . . . something real?"

"Like what?"

"I don't know—a force, a spirit, the mind of Ashley. I think you may be right about her being murdered. What if Ashley is seeking justice?" I rushed on. "Or what if she is lonely and wants Patrick with her, in her world, forever?"

"Get a grip, Kate!" Sam exclaimed.

"I had one, till someone pushed me down the steps. Maybe it was someone in the family. Or maybe it was Ashley. I can feel Patrick resisting me now when I talk to him, closing his mind to me. What if Ashley is trying to separate us, so she can put him in a deadly situation?"

Sam bent down, picked up the shells that had slipped through my fingers, and put them back in my hand. "We don't need supernatural events to explain what is happening."

I had guessed he would say that.

"Patrick is lonely and hurting," Sam went on. "What do kids like that do? Create imaginary playmates for company and get attention however they can. He's been very successful at getting it—his dares have rattled you, his talk of Ashley has rattled his family."

"That's what I thought at first," I said, "but too many eerie things have happened. Patrick knows too much about Ashley. He knows things I didn't think anyone else knew but Ashley and me."

"Kate, all little kids have secrets they think adults don't know. Not only do *they* know, but so do the brothers and sisters who spy on the kids—or, in this case, cousins, like Westbrook Caulfield." He said the name as haughtily as Brook had.

I shook my head, rejecting his suggestion.

"Okay, let's say you're right," he said. "Then you should be able to solve the mystery of Ashley's death pretty easily. Learn ghost talk and ask her who killed her."

I felt mocked. "That's what I get for trusting you."

He took a step back. "Excuse *me*! Trust doesn't mean you'll get the response you want from someone, but that you'll get an honest response, and that the other person will stick by you even when you can't agree."

Stick by you for how long, through how much? I wondered. What is the expiration date on trust?

I watched Patrick tiptoeing toward a gull, leaning forward,

calling to it, trying to befriend it. He was a kid desperate for companions—people, animals, ghosts. I kicked at the stones beneath my feet, then crouched down. "I should collect some of these. Patrick has been distracted."

Sam crouched next to me. "I'm telling you again, Kate, you can trust me."

Saying no more, he quietly gathered stones with me till I called to Patrick.

We climbed the steps and found our snowman sweating, its surface shining in the warm afternoon sun. We pressed the shells in place, then worked on the number for his "jersey." Patrick chose 23.

"Twenty-three!" Sam exclaimed. "Are you saying my ears look like clamshells and my hair like dry seaweed?"

Patrick cackled. "Yup."

When our hockey player was complete, we went for a walk. Patrick wanted to show Sam and me his tricks on the monkey bars. As we passed the garage, November sauntered out of the bushes and followed us to the workers' cottages, where the old play set was. Sam glanced sideways at me, as if to ask if this was the cat I'd told him about.

When the play equipment was in sight, Patrick raced ahead.

"It's not exactly state-of-the-art," Sam remarked, observing the large metal structures.

"It was built by a groundskeeper from equipment he salvaged. Patrick has a new set beyond the pool, but the swings aren't half as tall, and the plastic slide is slow. He prefers this one."

I caught my breath as I watched Patrick swing himself around a bar and narrowly miss whacking his skull. "Don't forget where your head is."

"I guess it's genetic," Sam remarked. "Guys just have to show off."

"Watch this! Is everybody watching?" Patrick shouted.

"We see you."

He leaped from a high bar to the ground.

"Good jump!"

"Want to see another?" he called, and didn't wait for our reply.

Sam leaned over and brushed snow off a bench, then gestured for me to sit down. "Which house did you live in?" he asked, turning to gaze at the cottages behind us.

I turned with him. "The one on the end with the green trim.

"And that's where your dad painted?"

"No, Adrian gave him part of the orangerie—the light was better there. Sam, since you mentioned Dad, there's something"—I swallowed in mid-sentence, still awkward with the truth—"something I need to tell you about. Yesterday

I learned that Dad was the father of Ashley and that my mother discovered it two weeks before Ashley died. That doesn't mean she killed Ashley," I added quickly. "I'm telling you only because I said your father went after her without a motive. The truth is, your father had a good reason to chase us that night."

Sam nodded.

"You're not surprised."

"No, I knew about your father and Corinne."

"You what? Why didn't you tell me? How long have you known?"

He shrugged. "I guess I was eleven or twelve when I asked my mother to tell me everything she knew about the case. My father left behind some notes. He always typed separate notes for the client—he never handed over his personal notebook. She had kept it and told me what was in it."

I was outraged. "You knew all along about my dad. Why didn't you tell me? Why didn't you correct me when I said my mother had no motive?"

"I didn't want to hurt you."

"I'm tired of people lying to me!"

"I didn't lie," he answered calmly. "I just didn't tell you everything I knew."

"Omitting important facts is the same as lying—it's the kind of lying my father specialized in."

"Maybe *he* didn't want to hurt you," Sam suggested.

"Or maybe he was ashamed," I said. "Tell me this: If you discovered my mother was guilty, would you go to the police with that information?"

He looked me steadily in the eye. "Yes."

"So if you would do it then, why save me the grief now?"

"Because I don't want to hurt you unnecessarily."

"Don't you understand? It hurts twice as much when you finally discover the truth."

He was silent for a moment. "I guess I never thought about that. I was trying to do the right thing for you."

"Stop trying. I don't need you to look out for me."

"Why does it bother you if I do, Kate?" he asked, his anger surfacing. "What's the big deal?"

The big deal was that it made me vulnerable, ripe for abandonment. But that was telling him too much. "You can't ask me to trust you and, at the same time—"

A shout froze the words in my throat. Sam and I turned.

Patrick hung from a metal bar high above the snow. He had climbed to the top of the swing set, onto the beam from which the swings were suspended, halfway between the tall A-frames that were meant to support it. One end of the beam had broken loose from its frame.

"I can't—I can't hold on," he cried.

Sam and I rushed forward. The ten meters between Patrick and us seemed to stretch as long as a playing field. Patrick dangled helplessly, kicking his legs. I saw his mittens slipping on the bar. He lost his grip.

"Patrick!"

He fell, landing on his back in the snow. I heard a low, grinding sound and looked up quickly. The long bar above him was pulling loose from its connection to the other frame.

"Roll away!" I screamed. "Roll away—the bar's going to fall!" But he lay there stunned.

Sam reached him first. Grabbing Patrick's feet, he dragged him away from the swing set. Seconds later, the end of the heavy bar broke free. Chains clanked as it dropped on top of the swings and plunged into the snow.

"Patrick," Sam said, breathing hard, "are you all right?"

I knelt on the other side of Patrick. He stared up at Sam, then turned his head to see me. There was something strange about the look in his eyes—a distance, a coolness in their blue light.

"Say something," I begged.

He gazed at me for a long moment, then frowned. "You're crying."

"Of course I am," I said, hastily wiping my cheek. "You could have been seriously hurt."

"I'm not."

He didn't appear shaken, didn't seem to understand how close he had come to harm. November ventured near, making a circle around us, continually sniffing.

"What were you doing on the top bar?" Sam asked, his voice rough.

"Playing."

"That's a support for the swings, not a bar to climb on," Sam scolded.

Patrick's eyelashes lowered, then he looked up again. "It was Ashley's idea."

"It was a very bad idea."

"She dared me."

"Then she's an idiot," Sam replied gruffly.

Patrick's eyes widened. "You had better be careful what you say. She can hear you."

Sam shook his head, then rose and walked over to examine the bar that had fallen.

"Can you wriggle your fingers and toes, Patrick?" I asked, gently brushing the snow from his hair.

He pushed my hands away and sat up. "Leave me alone."

Bewildered by his response, I left him sitting in the snow and joined Sam.

"How could this have happened?" I asked. "How could the swing set have fallen apart like that?"

"Looks like some bolts are missing," he replied, then turned toward Patrick. "You were awfully lucky, buddy."

"I'm lucky Ashley is my friend. She watches out for me."

Sam ignored the comment. "We had better take you back to the house. You look okay, but we should make sure, and we should tell your father about the swing set."

"But I want to go the pond," Patrick insisted. "Ashley is—"

"Later," Sam said, his voice stern.

This time, crossing the snowy grounds, Patrick trailed behind us. November wandered off. Sam and I walked silently side by side.

"The equipment is old," Sam said at last, "and bolts rust and loosen."

"On both ends at the same time?"

He shook his head. "I don't believe it was an accident. I think someone got out a ratchet and worked on the bolts. I'm just telling you what the others might say."

I glanced over my shoulder to make certain Patrick was with us. He trudged, head down, so I couldn't see his face.

"Kate, this is getting dangerous," Sam said, "dangerous for both of you. Killing a hamster is one thing. Pushing a person down a flight of steps and causing a swing set to collapse is something else. I think the last two incidents are related. What kept Patrick from being hurt just now? You warned him, and I pulled him away before the bar fell. You're Patrick's protector. Someone wants you out of the way so he or she can get to him."

"Maybe," I said, "or maybe someone is getting nervous because Patrick and I are talking about Ashley. I still think this is connected to her death."

"But not to a ghost," Sam replied quickly.

I shrugged. "I don't see why murderous relatives preclude a ghost."

"They don't," Sam said. "But if what you see accounts for what is happening, why bring in what you can't see? It just muddies the situation. It is people, not ghosts, who murder. I think someone has murdered here before and is willing to do it again."

I tried to quell my growing fear. "Maybe these incidents are meant as nothing more than warnings," I said. "If I was serious about killing someone, I wouldn't fool around with attempts that may or may not work, warning the victim."

Sam laughed. "Then you'd make a lousy murderer, Kate. Think about it. The more direct the attempt—the more certain the outcome—the less chance it has of being considered an accident. As long as a murderer has the time to try a few 'accidents,' why not?

"Why not take the safer route, as long as the victims are available?" He turned toward me, grasping my wrists, making certain I was listening to him. "And you are, Kate. You and Patrick are way too available."

Fourteen

AT FIRST, SAM and I thought Adrian wasn't listening. We found him in the office, pacing the floor, deep in thought. As we recounted what had happened, he glanced at Patrick, then drifted over to a pile of opened mail and fingered through it. Sam grew irritated—I could hear it in his voice—but, of course, Adrian had heard every word. When we were done, he checked over his son as thoroughly as we had, then sat down facing him.

"Well, Patrick, did you thank Sam? You owe him a great deal for pulling you away from the swing set."

"Thank you," Patrick said softly.

"And did you tell Kate you are sorry for scaring her?"

"I'm sorry."

Adrian rested his hand on Patrick's shoulder. "We have a problem, son. If we tell your mother about this, she will become quite worried and will wonder what else you might get into."

Adrian lowered his head and peeked at Patrick. "You're not getting into any other trouble, are you?"

"No, Daddy."

A wry smile formed on Adrian's face; he knew better than to believe it. "Then why don't we keep this a secret between you and me, so we don't upset your mother. Can you do that?"

Patrick nodded silently.

Sam had to leave for practice, but took a few minutes to accompany Patrick to the third floor to see the playroom, where his hockey picture was enshrined. I remained behind.

"About this secret," I said to Adrian when we were alone, "are you protecting Emily from worry, or me from being disciplined?"

He smiled. "I can always count on you to be forthright. Both, actually. I know it's not your fault, Kate. As for Emily, she worries excessively and sometimes smothers Patrick with her affection, but don't think poorly of her. This is my third child; he is Emily's only."

Then he called Roger on his cell phone, asking him if he had noticed anyone around the metal play equipment and telling him to dismantle it immediately.

When he hung up, he looked tired.

"Do you think someone tampered with the swing set?" I asked.

"It's possible. Stay as close as you can to Patrick," he said, gesturing toward the door, indicating that our discussion was over. I knew Adrian wasn't the kind of person who felt obligated to tell others how he intended to handle matters. Family reputation was important to him; he would address the situation quietly. I left and met Patrick and Sam on my way upstairs.

"I've got to run," Sam said. "I'm picking up some of the other guys for practice."

"Thanks for coming, thanks for everything," I replied. "I know Adrian is grateful too."

Sam grimaced. "I did my best to be polite to him. It wasn't easy."

"Why?" asked Patrick.

Sam glanced down at the questioning face. "Because sometimes I'm a little rude. Don't do anything stupid, buddy, I don't care who dares you. Understand?"

Patrick nodded.

"Yeah-yeah," Sam muttered, and raised his eyes to me. "Keep in touch?"

"Sure." I met his eyes for half a second, then looked away.

He reached out, resting two fingers lightly on the back of my hand. "Keep in touch, Kate."

After Sam left, Patrick and I put on dry clothes and spent the rest of the afternoon upstairs. Because he was doing poorly in his schoolwork, we used the extra time to work on spelling and math. He was unusually quiet and agreeable. Perhaps I had imagined him pulling away from me, I thought; I was getting like Emily, overreacting when he didn't want to be a cute, cuddly little kid.

Patrick and I endured another family dinner, though Trent was absent from this one—in town with the "kitchen-sink blonde" who managed the hotel. I learned from Brook that Robyn's description meant the woman colored her own hair, which meant that she was a middle-class working type who didn't have much money to spend on herself, which *meant* she wasn't up to the Westbrook standards.

With one less participant, I had hoped the mealtime squabbling would be less, but instead it became a cat fight between Robyn and Emily. Adrian ignored them, occasionally addressing Patrick and me. Brook assigned points to the ladies' jibes, keeping score. Patrick withdrew as soon as the quarreling began, raising his head now and then to gaze at the flickering candles.

After dinner, when we were alone, he remained withdrawn, wanting to go to bed early that evening. His behavior was beginning to worry me. I asked him if he was ill, if he was sore from his fall, if he was afraid of something, if he was sad—I posed every conceivable question about how he felt, but was told nothing.

I asked Emily to come in and read a book with him, then

requested that Adrian do the same, hoping to reassure him with their love and attention. Neither of them appeared to be concerned, for Patrick seemed like a quiet, sleepy child, the ideal seven-year-old at bedtime, but I knew something was wrong. He barely responded when I said the little rhyme he liked and kissed him good night. It was as if he had fallen deep inside himself, into a world I couldn't reach.

I slept poorly that night, awakening at every sound, checking on him at midnight, 2:15, 3:55. I awoke again a few minutes after five, tired and cross, but there was no getting back to sleep until I checked him again. Once more, I crept downstairs.

He was gone. I couldn't quite believe it, and yet it was what some part of me had been waiting for all night. I checked the rooms on the third floor, then quickly dressed and hurried down to the kitchen. The door to the outside was locked, but the deadbolt undone, indicating that Patrick may have exited from there. I debated whether to wake the family. A search party might find him faster, but creating that kind of scene would make things worse for him. I thrust my feet in my boots. I would find him myself. I had to.

Checking my pocket for keys, I opened the door and stepped into the brittle cold. A day of March sunlight had melted the surface of the snow, but the dipping temperatures of the clear night had frozen it again, making an icy crust that glimmered in the moonlight. Hanging low in the west, the moon cast long shadows and darkened the craters of footprints, confusing the paths that converged at the back door. Had he gone to the pool? Taken the steps down to the bay? No, it was the pond that drew Patrick. I took off.

The hardened snow made it difficult to run, my feet sinking in at odd angles, my toes catching in the crust. Having circled to the front of the house, I cut across the gardens and suddenly found a fresh trail, Patrick's prints—at least prints small enough to be his. Reaching the drive that ran between the house and the main road, I saw another set of prints in the slushy, cindered snow. A cat's. November. It was as if the cat had instantly appeared and disappeared, leaving no trace of where he had come from or where he had gone on the other side of the plowed road. Then I realized that the animal was light and had probably walked on top of the frozen snow.

Patrick's tracks ran through the orchard and around the barn. I raced across the last stretch of snow toward the pond. The tall ring of evergreen trees that surrounded the pond rose up dark and silent, a forbidding circle. I entered the trees, following the short path that wound through the cedar and pine and emerged several meters from Patrick. He knelt at the pond's edge. A collection of small branches lay piled in front of him like an offering. The cat, sitting close to him, turned his head to see who had come into their circle.

My teeth chattered, not from the weather, but from the cold, otherworldliness of the scene. Shadows cast by long fingers of pine stretched across the pond's dull white ice. Near the center, the circle of dark water that never froze shone like a black moon. Patrick seemed a part of this unearthly place, as if he had stepped over the line that divided the colorful world of the living from the stark shades of death.

I walked quietly toward him. "What are you doing?" He didn't turn his head, didn't act as if he had heard me. He was striking matches, one after another; they must have been wet, for none of them would light. I could see the thin flannel of his pajama pants beneath his snow jacket. He wore shoes rather than boots. His head and hands were bare.

I knelt next to him. "What are you doing?" I repeated.

"This will keep us warm," he said.

I touched the pile of sticks. "Are you making a fire?"

"Don't be afraid. It won't melt the ice."

His voice sounded both strange and familiar. It wasn't the slightly high pitch Patrick used when he was trying to convince me of something, but the low, demanding tone of Ashley when she had insisted that I believe her.

"You can't believe what the grown-ups say," he went on. "They tell you things just to scare you."

The tingle started low in my spine and ran to the base of my skull. I had had this conversation before.

"They lie to you."

"Who does?" I asked.

"Everyone. They lie because they want you to do something."

"Not always," I argued.

"They want to hurt you."

"Who does?"

"They hate me, Katie!"

I pulled back. Patrick's fists were clenched with fury. He was no longer just hearing a ghost—he was speaking her words, he was feeling her emotions.

"Patrick, look at me."

He abruptly turned his back, then rose and walked over to November. "They don't know your name," he whispered to the cat. "No one knows it but me. No one can touch you but me." His fists relaxed as he pet the animal, then he glanced in my direction. "We'll get warm, and then we'll go skating."

"No, Patrick." I said, walking toward him. "It isn't safe."

Kneeling again, I took his face in my hands and turned it toward me. His eyes were open, but I felt as if I were looking into the eyes of a plastic doll—unblinking, glittering circles, eyes that did not physically see me.

I shook him lightly. His eyes rolled back in his head, then his lids closed. Panicking, I pulled them open with my fingertips. All I saw were the whites. "Patrick!" I cried. "Wake up!"

I let go, and his eyelids closed. I shook him, terrified that I was losing him. "Come back, Patrick! Stay with me—stay awake!"

I shook him again, harder than I meant to.

He opened his eyes, gazing blankly at me for a moment. Then his eyes widened. He wrenched away from my grasp. "You can't hurt me!"

He scrambled to his feet, stepping on the cat. November squealed. Patrick rushed toward the path through the woods.

I stood up, bewildered, and glanced around the pond. "Show yourself, Ashley!" I cried out angrily. "I dare you!"

I ran after Patrick and caught up with him outside the ring of trees. I followed at a short distance, wary of getting too close. I would wait till he stopped, I thought, wait till whatever frightened and drove him away from me ceased in his mind. But when we reached the road he veered suddenly, turning away from the house toward the cemetery. At its iron gate, I grabbed him and held him tightly against me.

"Stop, Patrick."

He fought me.

"Patrick, be still."

His resistance lessened.

"It's Kate! I'm trying to help you."

At last he sagged against me. I was almost afraid to let go and look in his eyes, afraid I'd set him running again. I slowly eased down next to him. "How are you doing?"

He looked ghastly in the pale moonlight. "I don't feel good."

"I know you don't." I removed my jacket and put it over his. "Climb on my back. I'll give you a ride."

He climbed on and placed his arms around my neck. "Where's November?" he asked.

"I think he stayed back at the pond. He'll be all right."

I stood up, holding on to Patrick's legs, massaging them as I walked toward the house, trying to warm them. I carried him piggyback all the way up the main stairs. When we reached his room, I laid him on his bed. I quickly pulled off his wet pajamas and gave him a dry set along with a woolly pair of socks.

"Better?" I asked as I tucked his quilt around him.

He nodded. I gently rubbed his cold cheeks and ears. He lay there for a long time with his eyes wide open, his body absolutely still. When his eyes finally closed, I turned off his alarm clock, then tiptoed to the stairs connecting our rooms, planning to turn off my own alarm and fetch my quilt. It would keep me warm while I sat by Patrick's bed. At the top of the steps, I found the door to my room shut. Opening it, I felt a rush of frigid air. I quickly closed the door behind me, cutting off the draft so it wouldn't blow closed the door to Patrick's room. Then I saw my window and backed up. The upper half was shattered, jagged pieces of glass hanging from its wooden frame. Shards glittered like ice on the floor.

I walked toward the window, glass crunching beneath my boots. I knew what was outside the dormer, but I couldn't believe what I was seeing and I had to be certain. At the cottage there had been a tree for Ashley to climb when she'd thrown my doll through the bedroom window, smashing it inward. Here— just as I had thought—there was nothing more than a strip of steep slate roof. Still, the window had broken inward, the glass scattering on the floor rather than on the roof outside.

"I dare you to show yourself, Ashley," I whispered.

In the thin moonlight I caught the reflection of a rounded piece of glass. The framed picture of my father—and *hers*—lay as my doll had among the rubble.

Fifteen

I DIDN'T CLOCK it, but I would say that ninety seconds after Patrick was due downstairs, dressed for school, Mrs. Hopewell arrived outside his room to inquire why he wasn't. I was waiting for her by the door and told her that Patrick hadn't felt well during the night, so I was letting him sleep. I also informed her that my window had been broken. She asked how and why I had broken it—as if people routinely break their own bedroom windows in the middle of freezing winter nights. Twenty minutes after she departed, Emily tiptoed in to see the sleeping Patrick. Adrian showed up more than an hour after that, when the others were downstairs at breakfast. I left Patrick in his room getting dressed and accompanied Adrian to my room so that he could inspect the window.

"How is Patrick doing?" he asked, closing my door behind us.

"Physically, all right, I think."

"And emotionally?"

"Not well at all." I quickly told him what I hadn't told the others, where I had found Patrick last night and what he was doing.

Adrian paced my room, and for the first time I saw the color of barely repressed anger in his face. "Someone is planting these ideas in his head." He kicked at the shards of glass. "And someone is playing pranks. I'm going to find out who." He took a deep breath. "I suppose you know there was some opposition to hiring you."

"Yes. I overheard Mrs. Hopewell and Mrs. Caulfield talking the day I was interviewed."

"Trent wasn't happy about it either. As for my grandson, while he has never objected to you, I believe he has a double major in partying and pranks. It is a terrible thing to say about one's own household, but any of them could have done it."

Including Ashley, I thought. "I found it odd, the way the glass broke inward," I ventured aloud.

"What do you mean?"

"Well, it would be easy to knock it out and onto the roof, but—"

Adrian walked over to the window and looked out. "I see what you're saying." After studying the shattered upper half of the window, he lifted the lower half a few inches and slid his arm under the sash. "I suppose any number of objects could be adapted to break the top inward, something like a pole with a hook at the end. A golf club."

Or a hockey stick, I thought. We had left one with the snowman and the other in Patrick's playroom. I should have thought of it last night.

He withdrew his arm. "Obviously, by scattering glass on your floor, someone meant to be nasty. I have given Mrs. Hopewell orders to vacuum several times, then wash the floor. We'll get you a new rug. In the meantime, don't go barefoot."

"Adrian, would it be possible to turn on the alarm system at night? It's too easy and too dangerous for Patrick to slip out alone. Can't the others come in and reset the alarm?"

"Brook doesn't know the code." In response to the surprise on my face, Adrian smiled a little. "No, I don't trust him, but you are right, I need to set the alarm. Brook will have to abide by a curfew until this nonsense is over."

He started toward the door, then stopped. "You know how grateful I am to you, Kate. You also know I could hardly blame you if you decided to find a less . . . dysfunctional family to work for."

"I'm not leaving Patrick."

He opened the door, a grim smile on his face. "I always seem to like the ones who aren't my own," he said, then descended the steps to talk with Patrick.

I drove Patrick to school about 10:15. He was willing to go, and I thought it better for him to spend time away from his family. I walked him to the office and, when he had departed for his classroom, asked if I could meet with his school counselor. I was told that, as caretaker rather than family member, I had to have his parents' written permission to discuss him with her. Adrian had already made it clear that he did not want the counselor's involvement. Frustrated, I headed for High Street, hoping to catch Joseph at the store.

"Shop's closed," I greeted Joseph as I entered.

He looked up from behind the counter and smiled, then got a curious look on his face. "Don't take this personally, Katie, but you look wretched."

"I haven't slept much lately."

"Pull up a piece of antique and tell me what's been going on," he invited.

I lugged an old chair over to the counter. Joseph picked up the tarnished necklace he had been examining and poked through a case of jeweler's tools. He worked on the clasp while I filled him in on the events at Mason's Choice.

"I don't know what to do, Joseph," I said at the end. "How

can I protect Patrick if I don't know where the danger is coming from, if I can't even decide if it is human or not?"

I waited for him to respond. So far, he had shown no reaction to my idea that there might be something other than flesh and blood haunting Patrick.

"I can discuss only half of my fears with Adrian," I went on. "He would think I am mad, talking about a ghost. Sam is already convinced of it. I myself think I'm going mad, and yet . . ." I stopped and shrugged my shoulders.

"And yet?" Joseph prompted, setting down a tool.

"Ashley seems so real to me. Go ahead, you have my permission to laugh."

"I wish I could, but I find what you have told me too disturbing. I'm sure the family does, too, even if they don't admit it. There's nothing like guilt to make you worry there might be a hereafter."

I laughed out loud, though the idea was sobering. "So you think Ashley might have been murdered."

"I don't know, Katie. I've spent the last twelve years believing that Adrian acted stupid and mean when he tried to blame someone for an unfortunate accident. It's a struggle now for me to admit he may have been right."

"I'm going to the college library today to see if I can find a book about ghosts, the kind that takes seriously the paranormal, if they have anything like that. I don't know what else to do," I said, sounding defensive. "I asked to talk to the counselor at Patrick's school, hoping she could help me understand what Patrick is feeling. She can't see me without permission from his parents."

Joseph gazed at me thoughtfully, "I think I can help you," he said, then set down the necklace and rummaged beneath the counter. At last he pulled out a ragged looking phone directory. "Obviously, Mother believed that when you own an antique shop, it's in poor taste to have anything current. Still, this old book may do. James wasn't the type to move around." He paged through the directory, wrote a number on a store receipt, then searched some more and scribbled another one.

"'Dr. James Parker,'" I read aloud, when Joseph handed me the paper.

"He's an old friend of mine—we went to college together. He works at the high school as a psychologist, so he must know about family problems. But he has a hobby—at least he used to—paranormal psyche. Two for the price of one, Katie, and I believe he is discreet. Why don't you give him a call? He's probably at the school now, the first number there."

I called from the store, then left my cell phone number. I was on my way to the college campus when Dr. Parker returned the call. I told him that Joseph Oakley had referred me and described some of the problems Patrick was having with his family; he said he could see me next week. Then I told him about Ashley; he suddenly had a free period that afternoon and gave me directions to the high school.

It was a brick building with two stories of long windows. Inside, the lockers and speckled floor looked new, but the beige tiled walls definitely were not. A big sign advertising the hockey team's championship game hung in the lobby.

I signed in at the school office, where the psychologist met me.

"I'm Dr. James Parker," he said. "Call me Jim."

I nodded and planned to call him Dr. Parker.

Fortunately, I had been warned by Joseph not to let the psychologist's "fashion sense" put me off. He wore a short-sleeved flowered shirt and pink tie with a long gray sweater vest. I estimated that the sheep that had produced the sweater had been dead for at least seventy years. Perhaps the same sheep had produced the wool socks that puffed out under his sandals. But the man had inquisitive eyes, and a cheerful smile peeked through his beard; I suppose the world looked very rosy to him, given his tinted glasses.

He led me to his office and soon proved himself a skillful reader of people. He gestured to the sofa first, then quickly changed his mind and pointed to a stiff-backed chair, which was fortunate, because I had no intention of getting comfortable. He chose a wheeled chair for himself, which he pushed back a half meter, putting a little more distance between us. For a moment we simply looked at each other.

"So you are a friend of Joseph Oakley."

"I knew him twelve years ago, when he and my mother took care of Ashley Westbrook. This is the first time I've been back to the States since then. I met up with him last week and he has been helping me, listening mostly."

"I hope he hasn't been telling you tales from our college days," Dr. Parker said.

I suspected he really hoped that Joseph *had*. "No, sir."

"Joseph and I were two locals—'farmers' are what the dorm kids called us. We were hopeless—neither of us jocks, both of us lousy at cards. Joseph was good at music, but he didn't listen to rock. We were about as uncool as you could get, until he got that great car—a used Jaguar. Even used, it cost him a bundle, but it was worth every penny." Dr. Parker laughed. "A lot of kids wanted to ride around in that Jag."

I smiled, trying to imagine Joseph and this late-blooming flower child cruising in a British sports car.

"So tell me what has been happening, Kate."

There was a lot to recount. I was grateful that he didn't interrupt me, though I wondered from time to time whether he was thinking with his eyes closed or taking a short nap.

"Interesting," he said, when I had finished. "Extremely interesting." He opened his eyes and took off his glasses, glancing around as if surprised to see the world less pink, then put the spectacles back on. "Tell me, Kate, how do you account for these events?"

"As I said a few minutes ago, I have two theories. Either someone in the family is setting things up and seeding Patrick's fears, or there is an actual ghost—but I don't like either theory. I don't believe in ghosts, and the fact is, I don't see or hear something that might be considered the ghost of Ashley. But when Patrick speaks of her, when he speaks the same words she did and does the same things she was daring me to do, she feels so alive. In the beginning he claimed that she liked me, but that is changing. Patrick is distancing himself from me, sometimes acting afraid of me, and I think it is she who is causing this. It is as if he is possessed by her. I don't know how to protect him."

"And you feel as if you need to."

I stiffened. Was he turning this into a psychological analysis of me? "When it results in something as dangerous as standing on a diving board over an empty pool or walking on thin ice—yes!"

"There is nothing harder to do than to protect another person from himself."

From himself? I thought. "If you are saying Patrick is making this up, I don't believe it."

"I'm not suggesting that he is making it up, but that he is making it possible."

The psychologist stood up and walked around. The two deep-silled windows in his office bloomed with plastic flowers, a contradiction to the bag of "All Natural" health food sitting by his briefcase. He picked up a bouquet of faded roses and shook it, creating a cloud of dust.

"Based on what you've told me, I would be very surprised if Ashley is a ghost the way we normally define ghosts, i.e., a spirit from the other side, the personality and soul of someone who is dead. For one thing, no one else has seen her. Now, you might be particularly insensitive—"

"Excuse me?"

"Insensitive to the spiritual world, but I doubt that everyone on Mason's Choice is that way. And yet no one has admitted to seeing her. I would very much like to talk to Patrick."

I bit my lip. "I don't think I can arrange that. I am certain Adrian would not give his permission, and while I, myself, can come here without telling Adrian, I don't have the right to bring his son without him knowing it."

"I understand, but I can't offer you an opinion on Patrick without an evaluation of him. I don't venture opinions on what I haven't examined myself."

I thought quickly. "I don't want an opinion, just a hypothesis I can test out. I'm not asking for a diagnosis of Patrick but a theory about Ashley, whom *no one* can examine."

I was trifling with words, for it all amounted to the same thing, but I needed Dr. Parker's help. Perhaps he saw my desperation. I found it interesting that this man, who studied the mind and other unseen things, looked so carefully at my face and hands, depended on the physical to give him clues. He returned to his chair.

"Theoretically," he said, "it is possible that Patrick is tuning in to a psychic imprint left behind by Ashley."

"A psychic imprint?"

"A record of her thoughts and emotions. He is the same age as she was when she died, correct?"

"Yes. Seven."

"He lives in the same house, in the same room, and in the same emotional environment, spoiled by his parents, aware of the hostility that members of his family bear toward him."

Dr. Parker's wheeled chair edged forward. "It is possible that what Patrick perceives is not something happening now, but something that happened twelve years ago. Being on the same wavelength as Ashley, he may have access to the psychic trace of her thoughts and feelings—some very powerful ones—

and is perceiving them as if they are occurring in the present.

"In a way, it is like reading an autobiography in which you strongly identify with the hero. The events happened in the past, but you, when involved in the book, experience them as if they are occurring now. Or, it is like perceiving stars that are light-years away. That light was shining eons ago, but you see it now—at least, those people with the right equipment and focus perceive it now. Others cannot. Do you understand?"

"I think so . . . but then—then there is nothing I can do to change what he is perceiving. It was set twelve years ago."

The doctor nodded.

I rubbed my arms, chilled by the idea. Ashley's childish perceptions, selfishness, and quick anger were not a world inside which I wanted Patrick trapped.

"What about the cat?" I asked. "How do you explain that?"

"I don't explain anything. I offer theories, possibilities, nothing more."

"And one theory is?"

"Of course, you cannot rule out coincidence. A cat's life could easily span the twelve-year period, and cats, especially half-wild ones, will wander in and out of people's lives. Still, the timing is striking."

I made my fingers still, though they wanted to tap with impatience.

"In folklore, cats have long been associated with the paranormal—with witches, for instance. They may have a certain sensitivity to psychic elements. If Patrick is experiencing Ashley's thoughts and feelings, the cat may be sensitive to those it recognizes as belonging to a little girl who cared for him."

"So November won't hurt Patrick."

"I don't guarantee anything. I offer theories, possibilities—"

"Yes, I know." I stood up, weary of his theories now, wanting answers, needing to know exactly how to help Patrick. I walked over to one of the windows filled with artificial flowers, then picked up a box of plant fertilizer.

"Just a little joke," Dr. Parker said.

I set it down. "What can I do to help Patrick? You have to understand—Ashley was a daredevil. She was often angry and mean-spirited. If your theory is correct, it scares me to think of Patrick being imprisoned inside her thoughts and feelings. Isn't there some way to get him free of her?"

"Well, if Patrick did not have the same family problems and situation as Ashley had, his connection to her psychic imprint probably wouldn't be as strong. I believe it would fade completely with time. Can you convince the Westbrooks to get him and themselves some therapy?"

Even if I could convince Emily, the others would never

agree to it. I doubted that Adrian's opinion of psychologists was the only obstacle; ugly and personal things would come out, precisely the kind of things that no one in the family wanted to admit.

"I'll try again, but I think it's impossible," I said, frustrated. "I'm afraid I don't like your theory any more than my own."

He smiled. "Good. It's when we like our theories too much that we should be wary."

Dr. Parker gave me his card and told me not to hesitate to contact him. I emerged from his quiet office deep in thought and found myself in sudden bedlam. Classes were changing. A river of people flowed down the hall. I hesitated, then took the plunge, trying to make my way to the front door.

"Kate!"

At the sound of Sam's voice, I turned around.

"Over here."

I struggled to make my way toward him but was swimming upstream. He reached out and grabbed my hand, towing me to a wall of lockers.

"Looking for me?" he asked, smiling, propping an arm against a locker, framing me with his body. He was so good at it—getting close without touching.

"No."

He dropped his arm. "Well, maybe you could pretend."

ELIZABETH CHANDLER

"Sam, we're going to be late," a girl called to him.

"Go on, Sara," he answered. "Tell Campbell I'm finishing a test."

"Tell him yourself," the girl said, sounding annoyed.

Sam turned back to me. "So why are you here?"

"I was talking to Dr. Parker."

Sam grinned. "No, really."

"*Really*. Why would I make that up?"

"Because the man is flake-o, Kate."

I shrugged.

"You went to see him—like a counselor?"

"Yes. Joseph suggested him." The bell rang; the hallway cleared and grew quiet. "Dr. Parker has not only a background in psychology, but an interest in the paranormal."

Sam hooted softly.

"Just because you are unwilling to keep an open mind and consider all the possible causes—"

He interrupted me. "The problem with keeping your mind open to *im*possible causes is that it distracts you from chasing down the real ones, from talking to the people who can definitely help you."

"Like who? If you have a suggestion, tell me. I'll follow up on it."

"Your mother."

I took a step back.

"I want to talk to her, Kate. I need her phone number or e-mail address."

Five years ago, my father had given me the contact information that she had sent for me. I had attempted several times to tear up the slip of paper but never succeeded. As if he had guessed I might do that, he'd also left the information with his attorney.

"Do you have it?" Sam asked.

"Not with me," I said brusquely.

"When you get back to your room, call and leave it on my voice mail, okay?"

"I don't remember hiring you as a private investigator."

"You didn't."

"What makes you think you have the right to interfere with my family?"

His eyes narrowed. "You forget, this involves my family too."

"So you're picking up where your father left off, solving his case—"

"Maybe."

"Proving my mother did it."

"No! That's no fair, Kate. You're jumping to conclusions."

"But it's a possibility, isn't it? Isn't it? And as much as I may despise my mother, I am not going to help you hang her."

I turned quickly to walk away. He grabbed my hand.

"Let go!"

He did, but he stood very close. "Listen to me, Kate. I am definitely interested in solving my father's case, and it *is* possible your mother is guilty, but that's not my main reason for pursuing this. You've gotten yourself mixed up with a vicious group of people, and I'm not going to stand by waiting for something to happen to you. You know that Patrick is in danger, but when it comes to yourself, you just don't get it."

The intensity of his eyes and voice made me feel shaky inside. There wasn't a nerve in my body unaware of him. "I get it. I'm scared."

"Then let me help."

"Help Patrick, okay?"

He threw up his hands. "You just can't trust, can you?"

"Not easily," I said, and left.

Sixteen

When I picked up Patrick that afternoon, he handed me a note from his teacher addressed to his parents. I quickly parked the car and brought him and the sealed note back into school, hoping I could speak with the teacher. While Patrick stood in the pet corner of his classroom, silently watching a hamster in its cage, Miss Crichton explained that the rule that applied to counselors applied to teachers as well. Without permission, she could speak only to the parents.

By the time I got Patrick home and into his play clothes, I could guess what was in the note that I had placed in Adrian's mailbox: Patrick showed no interest in what was around him. I didn't know if it was Ashley or the hostility of the others that was draining him of his energy, but I found the seeping away of his spirit more frightening than the recent dares and danger he had encountered.

Since he didn't appear to be physically ill, I gave him a snack and took him outside, hoping the sunlight and fresh air would help. The melting snow was ankle-deep now. To my relief, when Patrick spotted his snowman, he ran toward it, kicking up the sloppy snow, acting like a normal kid. He snatched up the hockey stick and gave it a swing.

"Goal!" I shouted. "Westbrook scores!"

He raised his arms in triumph, as Sam and the other hockey players did, then froze in that pose, his mouth opening with surprise. He dropped the stick. "November! November!" he cried.

He raced forward, then crouched in the snow. I saw the strip of orange fur lying still on the ground. My heart tightened. Don't let it be, I thought.

"November, wake up! Wake up! Move! Come on, you can."

I hurried forward and knelt next to Patrick. The cat lay motionless, his eyes staring ahead, his mouth open. Piles of vomit had gelled in the snow around him. I glanced about for an empty food dish; no evidence had been left behind, but I suspected that someone had poisoned the cat.

I put my arms around Patrick. "I'm so sorry."

His small frame felt rigid.

"I'm so terribly sorry."

His bottom lip quivered, but his eyes were dry. "Why did

they do it?" he asked. "Why do they want him dead? Was it because of me?"

"Of course not. November was very old, and old cats die naturally," I replied, unwilling to admit the truth, wanting to spare Patrick as much pain as possible. I sounded like my mother when she'd told me the "deer" weren't harmed.

Patrick wasn't fooled. "When Tim's cat ate weed killer, he threw up and died. November ate poison."

"Well, yes, he could have. It does look that way."

Patrick's fists tightened. "He killed him. He killed November!"

"Who did?" I asked, taken aback by the certainty in his voice.

"Daddy."

"What?"

Patrick trembled with anger. "He didn't like him."

"But your father loves animals."

"He didn't want me to keep him."

"Because wild cats can't be pets," I said.

Patrick's shoulders sagged, his sorrow greater than his anger. He took off his mittens and gently touched the cat, petting around his torn ear, softly stroking the whiskers. Large tears rolled down his face.

I wanted to rip into whoever had done this. I wondered if

Brook had graduated from tormenting Ashley's pets to killing Patrick's. Or was it Trent? I thought. He had disliked and feared the cat when Ashley had loved it, and it would be a painful reminder to him now. Because of Robyn's love for animals, I had trouble imagining her doing it, though perhaps Patrick's animals didn't count to her, or perhaps she had asked her son to handle it. Mrs. Hopewell also could have done it—it wasn't hard, it wasn't messy, putting poison in food.

I watched as Patrick ran his fingers down the back of the cat. He rubbed around its ears again. "November didn't like to have his paws touched," he said, honoring that even in death.

I ached for him.

"Did he hurt a lot?" Patrick asked. "Did his stomach hurt bad?"

I could hide behind a half-truth and say that I didn't know how it felt to be a cat.

"Does your stomach hurt you when you throw up?" I asked back.

"Yes. But sometimes I feel better after I do."

I nodded. "I would think it's the same. If there is a cat heaven, November feels much better now."

The cat needed a larger and deeper hole than the hamster, so I asked Roger to help us bury it in the cemetery. Afterward Patrick and I took a back route up to the third floor, successfully avoiding the others. He didn't want to talk and didn't want to play. I put on a video, a superhero story that, as far as I could remember, didn't have any animals in it, then went downstairs to speak to his parents. Emily was still at the college that afternoon, working on an art project, so I talked to Adrian alone.

Perhaps because I was shaking with anger, he remained very calm when I told him about the cat's death. But when I warned him that Patrick believed he had poisoned it, Adrian looked incredulous, then hurt.

"Why would he think that?" he exclaimed, like a stung child. "Because I wouldn't let him keep it as a pet?"

"Patrick has blamed me for things, as well. Sometimes he pulls away from me and tells me that I can't hurt him. Did you read the note from his teacher?"

Adrian nodded.

"I don't know what she said, but I would guess he is withdrawing at school, too. It's dangerous, Adrian. He is separating from those of us who care most for him and want to help him. I haven't told anyone but Roger about my suspicion of poisoning. I can't handle it yet. I'm furious that someone would do this, knowing how deeply it would hurt Patrick."

"Don't worry, I'll see to the others. And I will fill in Emily as soon as she gets home."

"Adrian, what about having a vet do an autopsy?"

He shook his head. "It would do nothing more than prove what you and I already know."

An hour later, Emily arrived and came upstairs. I left her alone to talk with Patrick, telling her I'd be in my room if she needed me. "Stay upstairs," she advised me. "Adrian is having a word with the family and staff."

Fifteen minutes later she came to my room, her face drawn. "He would barely talk to me."

"To anyone, it's not just you," I assured her.

She twisted a handkerchief in her hands. "You see, Kate, this is another reason why Patrick should not have pets. They can break a child's heart."

"It's people who are breaking his heart," I replied.

"He refuses to eat dinner."

"I'll have my dinner up here and maybe he will discover he is hungry."

Two trays were brought up, but Patrick didn't touch his. I retrieved a pack of crackers from my purse, and he ate two. Henry came upstairs to clear our dishes, then brought back dessert.

"Just one piece?" I asked, as he handed me the fruit pie.

The old man looked embarrassed. "Mrs. Hopewell says that Patrick cannot have dessert until he eats his dinner." He glanced at Patrick. "I'm sorry. She makes the rules."

She doesn't make them for us, I thought. When Henry was gone, I offered Patrick my pie, but it didn't tempt him.

We sat side by side on the sofa in his playroom, watching the telly. I edged closer to him and finally put my arm around him. For a moment he gave in, leaning against me, then he pulled back, as if suddenly remembering a reason to keep his distance. I hated the thought of all the pain bottled up in him. I decided to call Sam. Though we had parted on a bad note, I counted on him to ignore that when it came to Patrick.

"Stay right here, Patrick," I said, then fetched Sam's number from my room. I stood in the hall, where I could keep my eye on the door to the playroom, and punched in the digits.

"Hello?"

"Mrs. Koscinski? This is Kate, Kate Venerelli."

"Oh, hello, Kate. It's nice to hear from you."

"Is—uh—Sam there?"

"Well, no, dear, not at the moment. May I take a message?"

She sounded so cheerful, so normal. I hadn't realized how cold and oppressive life seemed at Mason's Choice.

"Do you know when he'll get home?"

"It may be late. You sound concerned, Kate. Is something wrong?"

"No. Yes. I'm worried about Patrick. A cat that he loved"—I hesitated—"uh, died today. Patrick is upset."

"Oh, poor child! I'm very sorry."

"Sam is good with him. I thought maybe he could drop by, tonight or tomorrow."

"I have the number where he can be reached—it's somewhere here—give me a moment to put my hands on it. Practice should be over now. Afterward, Sam was going to study at Sara's house."

Sara, the girl who had called to him in the hall; I got a hollow feeling in my stomach. "Never mind. We'll talk tomorrow."

"Wait. Here it is." She read the number to me. "Did you get it?"

"Yes, thanks."

"Be sure to call him, Kate," Mrs. Koscinski added. "Sara's parents won't mind. They're very nice."

"Right. Bye."

He must go there often, I thought, if Mrs. Koscinski knows the parents don't mind being called. Well, even Sam couldn't make Patrick's pain go away tonight. I'd try to reach him tomorrow—perhaps take Patrick to the ice rink so he could talk to him after practice.

When I returned to the playroom, I saw that Patrick had taken a bite from the pie.

"It smells delicious," I said encouragingly. "How does it taste?"

"Good. I think it's raspberry."

"Have some more."

He ate another spoonful.

"Eat all you want. Raspberries are good for you."

He took one more spoonful, then pushed the pie away. I sat next to him again and watched the cartoon. Just when the hero was about to storm the castle belonging to the evil wizard, Patrick announced, "I want to go to my room."

"Don't you want to see what happens?"

"No."

I looked at my watch. "Patrick, it's not even seven o'clock. Let's try another channel."

"I want to go to bed."

"How about this—we'll put on your pajamas and read a while."

"I want to sleep."

He was probably exhausted from the accumulation of things that had been happening. But what if he planned to slip out and see Ashley as soon as his bedroom door was shut? Perhaps he imagined that she alone could understand how he felt about November. Adrian had promised to turn on the alarm system before retiring, but I wasn't taking chances; I planned to spend the night in Patrick's room.

We took the main stairway down, Patrick walking ahead of

me. I carried the piece of pie, hoping I could coax him to eat a little more. As we crossed the second-floor hall to his room, Patrick suddenly stopped. He looked back at me, then quickly turned away.

"What's wrong?"

His body shuddered violently, then he bent over and threw up. I quickly set the pie on a side table and put my arm around his waist, supporting him. He heaved and heaved, but nothing more came out after that first sickening puddle of reddish purple.

"My tummy hurts, Kate. It hurts bad."

Even in the warm light of the hall lamps, his face was pale as milk. He clutched his stomach, his fingers digging into his clothes. I laid my hand over his, then rubbed his tummy gently, trying to soothe him.

"Do you think you can make it as far as your bathroom?" I asked. It was the next door down the hall, just before his bedroom. "We'll rinse your mouth and wipe your face, then get you in bed."

We had taken only five more steps, when he began to shudder again. I dropped down next to him. He strained forward in my arms and wretched a second time.

"I can't help it. I can't stop it."

"Oh, Patrick, I know that. You're ill."

"Mrs. Hopewell is going to be mad."

"I'll clean it up before she sees it. It's hardly anything," I said, glancing at the second puddle, less red this time, with a lot of clear liquid.

He has nothing in him to vomit, I thought, probably less than the cat had, just crackers and three bites of raspberry pie. Then a chill went through me. The crackers were plain soda wafers, packaged in cellophane. I doubted they had caused the problem. But the raspberry pie had come from downstairs. Had someone dared to taint his food? I was ready to believe it. If Patrick hadn't been so miserable, I would have rushed down the steps, screaming at the lot of them.

"I guess I shouldn't have eaten your pie," Patrick said.

My pie. I was so focused on protecting him, I had forgotten—the piece was intended for me.

"Come on, Patrick, a few steps more. Let's get you cleaned up."

From the bathroom I buzzed the intercom for assistance.

"Henry is coming," Mrs. Hopewell responded, then clicked off before I could tell her what I wanted.

I buzzed again. "Mrs. Hopewell, please send up Emily and Adrian. Patrick is ill."

"I will tell them after dinner is over." *Click.*

I pushed the button a third time.

"You will tell them now. The pie may have been tainted," I said, avoiding the word "poisoned" for Patrick's sake.

A long silence followed. "I don't understand," Mrs. Hopewell replied at last. "What exactly is the problem?"

"He ate a few bites of the pie. He has thrown up twice."

"That wasn't his dessert!"

Was she irate because a plan to poison me had gone awry or because her rule about dinner before dessert had been ignored? It was difficult to tell with her.

"Mrs. Hopewell, send Adrian up before I make my own decision to phone for medical assistance." I clicked off.

She, Adrian, Emily, and Brook arrived upstairs shortly after, meeting Patrick and me in the bedroom. I made him comfortable under his quilt and quickly recounted what had happened. Patrick was no longer holding his stomach, and his color had started to return. Still, when Emily wanted to call a paramedic, I pressed Adrian for the same thing. "At least his doctor," I said.

"The child is already recovering," Mrs. Hopewell observed. "You can't call a pediatrician every time a child sneezes or throws up."

"My mother did," Brook remarked. "Though sometimes she got confused and called the vet."

"The last time the doctor was called, all of Wisteria knew it," Mrs. Hopewell reminded Adrian.

He nodded. "It was most unfortunate. Call the doctor, Louise."

While Emily sat by Patrick's bed holding his hand, Adrian paced back and forth in the room. The expression on his face was calm, his hands steady, but I had observed his son enough to recognize the stiffness in his shoulders and the set of his jaw. He was upset and steeling himself against something.

Brook lounged against the bedroom door. Since he had no affection for Patrick, I wished he had stayed downstairs with Trent and Robyn. "Thank you, Brook," I said quietly, "but I have all the help I need."

He gazed at me, surprised. "I'm not here to help. I'm bored."

Adrian flicked him a look.

I handed Patrick's favorite old picture book to Emily, hoping he would find it comforting to read with her. Outside in the hall, Henry cleaned the Oriental rug. Mrs. Hopewell returned to say the doctor was coming. When the housekeeper told Adrian she wanted to speak to him in the hall, I followed them uninvited, as did Emily, who closed the bedroom door behind us. The door opened and Brook darted out from Patrick's room, then hung like a roach on the wall, listening.

"No one informed me that Patrick had an allergy to raspberries," Mrs. Hopewell said to Emily. "Not that the dessert was intended for him," she added, glancing at me.

"How could I inform you if I wasn't aware of it?" Emily replied, sounding defensive. "You know as well as I do, he has never had a reaction before, not to berries or to any other kind of food."

"And he didn't now," I said. "He was poisoned."

"Poisoned," Emily echoed faintly.

Adrian turned to stare at me. "Do you mean deliberately?"

"I believe the tainting was deliberate—though it was meant for me, not Patrick. If I hadn't been concerned about him, I would have eaten the entire serving myself. What do you think"—I looked from one face to the next and tried to keep my voice steady—"was the pie meant only to make me ill, so I couldn't care for Patrick, or did someone want to kill me?"

"That's a ridiculous question," said Mrs. Hopewell.

"It is somewhat melodramatic," Emily observed.

"But interesting," Brook added. "In my opinion, the pie was intended to do the same thing that pushing you down the steps was intended to do."

"And what was that?" I asked angrily.

No one answered.

"We'll sort this out, Kate," Adrian assured me. "I want the pie wrapped up," he instructed Mrs. Hopewell. "We'll have it tested." He turned toward Patrick's room.

"That won't be possible," the housekeeper said.

Adrian swung around. "And why not?"

"I have cleared it away."

"Then take it out of the trash, Louise." He said each word distinctly.

"I do not put spoiled food in the trash. It may develop a bad odor and attract wildlife. I ground the dessert in the garbage disposal."

"What about the rest of the pie?" Adrian asked.

"The rest!" I cried, frustrated. "Tainting can be done after a piece is cut, done to just one serving. A test will prove nothing."

Mrs. Hopewell went on as if I hadn't spoken. "I thought it best, sir, to dispose of the entire pie."

Adrian grimaced. "Have the doctor speak to me first when he arrives. In the meantime, inform Trent and Robyn of the situation. And take Brook downstairs with you. Kate, I want you to stay with Emily and me." He led the way into Patrick's room.

Patrick was turning the pages of his favorite book, looking at pictures of Max and "the wild things," paging forward and backward. Emily resumed reading aloud. I couldn't tell if Patrick was listening; his eyes followed me around the room as I mechanically straightened things that didn't need straightening.

Adrian sat in the rocking chair, motionless, deep in thought.

When the doctor arrived, Adrian met with her briefly in the hall to explain the situation, then introduced her to us as Dr. Whelan, informing Patrick that she was covering for his pediatrician. Emily pointed out the door to Patrick's bathroom, so that the physician could wash her hands before examining Patrick. She returned to the bedroom with an odd expression on her face. As she checked Patrick's eyes, mouth, and ears, she questioned him.

"Tell me what you ate," she said softly.

"Some of Kate's crackers."

"A package from a vending machine," I told her.

"And some of Kate's pie."

She got out her stethoscope. "What kind was it?"

"Raspberry."

"What else did you eat?"

"Nothing."

"Take a big breath for me. Good. Take another. You ate nothing else?"

"No."

"He had an after-school snack around three forty-five," I said, "a piece of buttered toast and a small glass of apple juice."

"Any tremors, convulsions, labored breathing?" she asked.

"No, ma'am," I replied.

"Patrick, did you have anything to drink later?"

"No."

"Why don't you whisper the answer to me?" the doctor suggested.

"He didn't have anything else!" I said, frustrated that she wasn't keying in on the pie. "Why do you keep asking him?"

She turned to me. "Because there is a bottle of cough syrup lying open on the bathroom sink."

I stared at her dumbfounded.

Emily's red eyebrows pulled together. "His medicine cabinet is kept locked." She looked at me accusingly. "At least, it's supposed to be."

"I keep it locked, just as you told me to," I said, starting out of the room to see for myself. "Besides, there was nothing on the sink when I washed up Patrick."

I stopped at the bathroom's marble transom. There was now—a half-empty bottle. I had been in a hurry to clean him up and get him in bed, but surely I would have noticed it.

I returned to the room. "I don't know how that bottle got there."

"How much of the medicine did you drink, Patrick?" Adrian asked wearily.

"None."

"Tell the truth."

"I am!"

"Did Ashley dare you to take some?" I asked.

"Kate," Emily pleaded.

"Who is Ashley?" Dr. Whelan asked.

Emily sighed. "Patrick's imaginary playmate."

"Did she?" I persisted.

Patrick shook his head no.

I turned to Adrian. He met my eyes, but I couldn't read his gaze—he didn't want me to.

"Dr. Whelan," I said, "is it possible that Patrick ate something that was poisonous enough to make him sick and, if he had eaten more, could have killed him?"

The physician studied me, the lines in her softly weathered face deepening. "There are an endless number of poisons, some more potent than others, some more deadly in a higher dosage. Why do you ask?"

"Are some tasteless?" I persisted. "Some odorless?"

"Yes. Why?"

"Because I don't think Patrick drank any cough syrup. And as it happens, that raspberry pie—the entire piece, not two bites—was intended for me."

Dr. Whelan glanced at Adrian.

"When you have finished examining Patrick, we will discuss matters downstairs in my office," he said.

"I'm done," she told him.

"Emily?" He held out his hand for his wife. "Kate, would you mind staying with Patrick until he is asleep?"

He was not allowing me to talk further with the doctor. What was he afraid of—that I would give her even more reason to question the situation she found at Mason's Choice?

"I'm staying with him all night," I replied.

The doctor rewashed her hands and accompanied Adrian and Emily downstairs. Patrick resumed looking at the illustrations in his old book. I sensed he didn't want me sitting on his bed reading to him, so I pulled a chair next to it and sat quietly.

"I didn't have any medicine, Kate," he said, looking up from the book. "And Ashley didn't dare me."

"I know, Patrick."

I knew that flesh-and-blood hands had tainted the pie and unlocked the medicine cabinet. Whether by poisoning or by framing, someone was desperate to get rid of me. After twelve years, someone's nerves were starting to fray, and I was pretty sure it was Ashley's killer.

Seventeen

I SPENT THE night on Patrick's bedroom floor, getting more rest when I wasn't asleep, for in my dreams I ran continually, searching for Patrick, all the while being chased by someone or something I couldn't see. It was a relief when the alarm clock rang.

Patrick ate all of his breakfast and wanted to go to school. Emily was uncertain about sending him, but Adrian was pleased and praised him repeatedly for being "a strong boy," which made me wince. While Patrick waited for Emily to finish a note to his teacher, I went out to get the car. I stepped into a soft gray day, the warm air and melting snow blanketing the land with fog.

"Good morning."

"Sam!" I exclaimed, startled to see him leaning against his car in the Westbrooks' driveway.

"I got home too late to call you back," he said.

"Your mother told me you were out."

"She told *me* that she gave you Sara's number." He cocked his head. "Why didn't you call?"

"I didn't want to interrupt anything."

"Anything like what?" he asked, laughing.

"Anything."

He moved closer, examining my face, his own becoming more serious. "You don't look like you got a lot of sleep."

"Right you are, Sherlock."

"What happened?" He opened the front door on the passenger side of his car. "Have a seat here in my office. Talk, Kate."

I sat sideways, keeping my feet outside the car, and told him about the poisoning of November, the dessert intended for me, and the sudden appearance of the cough syrup.

"I think Adrian is losing faith in me," I concluded, lapsing into silence. I was more tired than I had realized.

Sam's verbal explosions woke me up. His eyes flashed and he kicked the tires of his car. "You've got to leave, Kate. Do you hear me?"

"I hear you. I can't."

"You've got to!"

"I will not abandon Patrick," I said firmly. "I know how it feels to be left as a child."

"Like I don't? You keep forgetting about my father."

"That's different," I argued. "Your father didn't *choose* to leave. Something happens, Sam, happens to your heart, when you know a person has chosen to leave you. You keep waiting for the next person to go."

He kicked bits of dirty snow out from under his car's tires. "Okay, maybe I don't understand that part," he said. "But here's the thing: If your goal is to help Patrick, I'd like to know how you are going to do that dead."

"Dead?" I shook my head. "Is there something you know that I don't?"

"The steps were a warning—I *think* they were just a warning. The pie, if you had eaten the whole piece—"

"Think about it," I interrupted. "It wouldn't have been very smart for someone to kill me with a piece of pie. An autopsy would have shown I was poisoned." It was the argument with which I had been trying to reassure myself since last night.

"Some poisons show up, some don't."

"All the same, I think you are getting a bit melodramatic," I said, borrowing Emily's line.

"You haven't yet seen melodramatic," he replied, suddenly pulling me out of the car. He held me tightly in his arms. I could feel the blood pulse beneath my skin each place where his body touched mine.

"Why can't you drop the act, Kate?" He pulled back his

head to look at me. His black eyes burned and became liquid with tears. "Don't you get it?" he asked, his voice trembling. "I will go crazy if something happens to you. Don't make me any crazier than you already have."

"Hi, Sam."

At the sound of Patrick's voice, Sam released me. We both sagged against the car. I felt as if I'd had the wind knocked out of me. My eyes burned, my throat was dry.

I had thought your heart was supposed to break when someone left you, not when someone wanted in, but I felt as if Sam were chipping away, putting deep cracks in mine.

He rubbed his mouth. "Hey, short stuff. How's it going?"

"Okay," Patrick replied.

"Yeah? Is it?"

Patrick dropped his book bag next to the car, then shrugged.

"You think you might like another lesson in ice skating?"

"Okay," he said, with only a touch of enthusiasm.

Sam knelt in the snow. "I'm going to be straight with you. I heard that yesterday wasn't okay. I heard it was tough when you got home."

Patrick didn't reply.

Sam put his hand under Patrick's chin, gently lifting it. "I'm sorry about November."

Patrick took deep, sniffly breaths.

"It hurts bad, huh?"

Patrick nodded, and Sam put his arms around him. "It's okay to cry. When my dog died, I cried my eyes out. I cried when my friend's dog died. Heck, I cried when my friend's grandmother's cat died!"

I laughed quietly, but the kindness in Sam's voice and the tender way he held Patrick made my own eyes warm with tears. Patrick suddenly gave in, sobbing against Sam's shoulder. Sam stayed quiet till he was done.

"Feeling better now?"

"Yes," Patrick said softly.

"So, here's the bad news: You might want to cry again. And that's okay. Sometimes crying comes and goes."

Sam took out a package of tissue to wipe Patrick's tears, then handed him one. "Big blow," he said. "We don't want no boogies hanging out. *No boogies for you, no boogies for me,*" he chanted, then blew his own nose.

Patrick giggled. "I like boogies."

"They *are* interesting. But girls don't like them. I bet Kate thinks they're gross."

"You bet right. Need more tissue?"

"What'd I tell you," Sam said to Patrick, and stood up. "Have a decent time at school today. Don't do anything I wouldn't do." He leaned closer to him. "That still leaves you with a pretty long list.

"I'll call you tonight, Kate," Sam went on, turning to me. "Do you have a direct line?"

I wrote down my cell phone number. As he slipped it in his pocket, he glanced toward the house and gave a casual wave. "Just saying hello to the nice people watching us—someone upstairs, someone down."

I turned quickly, but all I saw was a blur as a figure withdrew from the library window.

Sam drove off, leaving greasy black snow where his car had been parked. Patrick and I trudged silently toward the garage as if we were already at the end of a very long day.

I think I woke up Joseph. He sounded a bit cross when I phoned him from the school parking lot, but recovered quickly when he realized I was the one calling. We agreed to meet at Tea Leaves. Twenty minutes later he arrived at the bakery and café, looking like a rumpled schoolboy who had overslept.

"I shouldn't have called you so early," I said as we placed our breakfast on a table by the window and sat down. "Middle button," I added, and he fastened his shirt.

"No, no," Joseph replied, "I had planned to be at the shop by now. I should be wrapping things up faster than I am and getting back to my job in Baltimore. Ah, coffee." He took several sips, then examined the china mug. "I wonder if Jamie would buy off any of my mother's collection? Nothing else here matches."

The owner had painted the café's furniture in a rainbow of hues, making no effort to match the sets of tables and chairs. With the fog enveloping the town, pressing against the café's street-front windows, the room was a cheerful island of color and warmth. I watched Joseph eat his muffin with a knife and fork. I bit into mine, messy but content.

"Did you talk to Jim Parker?" he asked.

That single moment of ease evaporated.

"Yes. He was very helpful. He doesn't think Ashley is a ghost."

I explained the psychologist's theory.

"Well, I find that easier to believe than the walking dead," Joseph remarked when I had finished, "though not much easier."

"But you see the possibilities," I said.

Joseph took a long sip of coffee, "I—no, I don't think I do."

"If Patrick can tap into the record of Ashley's thoughts and feelings, all I have to do is get him on the right page."

"The right page?"

"Get him to connect with Ashley's thoughts on the day she was murdered."

He slowly set down his cup. "I see."

"I'm taking him down to the pond as soon as we get home from school today. I'll talk to him about the day she died, try to get him to think about it, and hope that he taps into her memory trace. If Ashley saw someone when she was lured out on the ice, saw just a piece of clothing through the trees—someone's jacket, for instance—it could be an important clue. Maybe she noticed footprints or heard a familiar voice. I don't know what exactly I'm looking for, but there may be something in her thoughts and feelings from that time that could tell us who killed her."

Joseph chewed thoughtfully. "*If* someone killed her," he said at last. "Katie, I'm not telling you that she wasn't murdered, but I do worry that, without realizing it, you have turned a possibility of murder into a fact."

I picked up my juice glass and swished it around, watching the little particles of orange swirl.

He went on. "I think that—don't be offended—in a way, you want it to be murder. I understand why. It would explain a lot of things that are happening now to Patrick."

I thought about Dr. Parker's warning: It is when we like our theories too much that we should be wary.

"The day Ashley died," Joseph went on, "she was distraught over her missing rabbit. And she was always an impulsive child.

If anyone would have run across dangerous ice to catch her pet, Ashley would have. Remember, they found the rabbit when they drained the pond. And when the coroner examined Ashley's body, he found no sign of trauma."

"That doesn't prove anything," I argued. "No one had to touch her. All they had to do was lure her onto the ice. It would be easy enough to kill a rabbit and slide it out on the ice with a pole, leaving it there for her to see. A rabbit is light; ice that was soft enough to give way beneath Ashley could have held a rabbit."

Joseph chewed some more, thinking, then set down his knife and fork, picking the crumbs off his plate with his fingers, licking the tips.

"What you're saying makes sense. Just remember that if you start out with the wrong assumption, you may misinterpret whatever follows."

I nodded.

"So take Patrick to the pond," Joseph advised. "It can't hurt, and maybe it will help. See what he tells you. I admit, I'm getting curious." He glanced down at his plate, which was now crumbless. "Would you like another muffin?"

"No, but get one for yourself. I have some tea left."

Joseph shoved back his chair. "Wouldn't want to get thin," he said.

As he headed toward the glass cases that ran along the back of the café, I gazed at the buildings across the street. In the fog, the Queen Victoria, with its second- and third-story porches, looked like a faded photograph of a nineteenth-century hotel. The illusion was broken when someone in a bright green business suit emerged from the entrance. She reached back and the man behind her put his coat over her shoulders. It was Trent—and the woman from the other day, the hotel manager, I assumed. They crossed the street and entered Tea Leaves.

Walking to the cases at the back of the café, they passed Joseph on his return to our table. I thought Joseph hadn't noticed them, but when he sat down he leaned forward and said in a hushed voice, "Trent is seeing Margery?"

"I think so."

He offered a toast with his coffee. "Here's to women who know how to latch on to money."

Trent glanced over his shoulder at us.

Unfortunately, the only table in the café available to them was close enough to ours to limit our conversation to Joseph's progress in organizing his mother's estate. "I hope her soul was in better shape than her finances," he kept saying.

He finished his muffin, and we rose to leave. I smiled and said hello to Trent as we passed his table. Just as Joseph and I reached the café door, Trent called to me.

"I had better see what he wants," I said.

Joseph looked irritated and glanced at his watch. "I've got to keep going. I have an appointment with Mother's no-good lawyer."

"Thanks for listening, Joseph."

"Sure, Katie," he said. "You know I'm just an old grouch and don't mean anything when I fuss."

He left, and Trent rose from his seat, meeting me halfway across the room. "We'll go outside for a moment," he said, taking my arm lightly and steering me in that direction.

I pulled my arm free, then glanced toward Margery. She showed the training of a discreet hotel manager, acting as if she hadn't noticed me and had come to the café to eat by herself.

When Trent and I were standing on the brick walk, he started right in. "That's the second time I've seen you with Joseph Oakley."

"And it's the second time I've seen you with her," I replied, nodding toward his companion inside.

"I hope you are not involved with Joseph."

"Involved? Don't you think he is a little too old for me?"

"I wasn't speaking romantically," Trent said stiffly. "I feel it is my duty, Kate, to tell you that Joseph is a dishonest man, an unreliable person. When you are young and naive, it is sometimes difficult to see people for what they are."

"Oh. Well, since you are old and wise, what do you think about Sam Koscinski?" I asked. "You were looking out the library window this morning, weren't you?"

"Yes."

"You know he is the son of the private investigator your father hired after Ashley died, the man who was killed when pursuing my family."

"Yes," Trent replied, his lips barely opening.

"Why was Mr. Koscinski chasing my mother? Why wasn't he pursuing you as well?"

Trent's eyes shifted away from me.

"Both you and my mother were cheated on."

Trent's face washed white. Some people redden with anger; he paled with it.

"You would have the same motive," I continued.

"Motive for what?" he asked.

I ignored the question; we both knew its answer. "Why do you think Ashley keeps talking to Patrick?"

"Patrick is an exceptionally spoiled and confused child," Trent said. "His behavior is easy to understand. It is yours that baffles me. On the surface you appear to care too much for the boy to want to make things harder for him."

"*I'm* making things harder?" I exclaimed, so loudly that a person passing by turned around to look at us. I waited until the man had moved on. "I'm not the one who—"

"You," Trent interrupted, "are the only one in the house who still has a choice in the matter. You can choose to let go of the past and encourage Patrick to forget about Ashley. Let sleeping dogs lie, Kate."

"They've lied too much already," I said.

He shook his head. "Don't make Patrick pay the price for your curiosity about the past. I'm warning you, Kate, and I'm not going to warn you again." He pivoted and reentered the café. I stared through the window at him, but he had sat down and turned his attention to his lady friend.

I walked away, upset by his words. Was I pursuing the truth for Patrick's sake or my own? I had thought I was doing it for Patrick—at least, it had started out that way. But I had learned that the past was tied up in lies, lies that had changed my own life. I was doing this for both of us now, though it was only myself I had the right to endanger. The question was, which was endangering Patrick more: pursuing the truth or letting it go?

Eighteen

WHEN I PICKED up Patrick at school that afternoon, he seemed happier than he had earlier in the day. He had done well on a spelling test and had discovered another boy in his class who liked ice hockey. But the little bit of brightness in his face faded by the time we reached the end of the long road up to Mason's Choice. A few minutes later, when I offered him an after-school snack, he took a tiny bite out of the peanut butter cracker I had fixed, then set it down.

"What's wrong?"

He looked at the plate of crackers warily. "I don't want a tummy ache."

"They won't hurt you. I fixed them myself."

"I'm not hungry."

Trust me! I wanted to say, but even I could recognize the irony of that coming from me.

"Do you want to go for a hike?" I asked.

"No."

"Not even down to the pond?"

"The pond?" He was interested.

"Why don't you change into your play clothes? I'll put your crackers in a bag, and we can take them along for a picnic."

His face lit up, then he reconsidered. "No, thanks. I'm not hungry."

"Then we'll skip the picnic part, but go change your clothes."

Mrs. Hopewell entered the kitchen as soon as Patrick left. I had the feeling she had been eavesdropping.

"Patrick and you will eat with the family tonight."

"Is that what Adrian wishes?" I asked.

She hated it when I called him by his first name. "Yes."

I nodded, put an unopened bag of crackers in my coat pocket, and headed upstairs. When I got to Patrick's bedroom, I saw that he had taken out his ice skates.

"Patrick, can you see how foggy it is outside?"

"Yes."

"When warm air comes in contact with the cold of the melting snow, it makes fog. The air is very warm today, the temperature well above freezing. The ice on the pond will be too soft for skating."

"No, it won't."

"I'm sorry, but it will."

"It won't!" he said, swinging his skates, banging them against his closet door.

"It will," I said firmly.

He dropped his skates and threw himself on the bed. "Then I don't want to go."

"All right. You stay here and do your homework. I'm going on a hike to the pond." I strode across the hall, wondering how far I could go before having to give up the bluff. He followed me down the main stairs, keeping about ten steps behind. Out of the corner of my eye I saw that he was carrying his skates.

When I reached the first-floor hall, I heard voices in the library—more fighting. I walked quietly toward it, trying to decipher Robyn's words. Trent cut her off, then Emily's high-pitched voice interjected something. Patrick caught up with me just as the library door opened. At the sound of their angry voices, he cringed.

"It's okay," I whispered.

Brook emerged. Seeing Patrick and me, he grinned as if he knew a secret. "The cat's away," he told us, "and you know what happens then." He pointed to the library.

"My cat is dead," Patrick replied solemnly.

"Oh yeah, I forgot about that old thing."

"Close the door, Brook," I said.

He reached back and pulled it shut, muffling the sound of the raised voices, then walked toward us. "Do you think your cat ate some raspberry pie?"

I glared at him. "Sometimes, Brook, I can't tell if you are exceptionally mean-spirited or simply stupid."

"I've never been exceptional at anything," he replied, shoving his hands in his pockets, "so I must be stupid. Grandfather thinks so." He shrugged, as if it were unimportant, but there was an edge in his voice. "He has gone into town to see his attorney. Grandfather's personal attorney always comes here, of course. I guess the old man wants some privacy while deciding how to divide up his loot. Anyway, when the cat's away—"

"The mice will play," I finished for him. "It's just a saying, Patrick."

"Oh, it's more than that," Brook said. "It's advice. Be on your guard. The mice can play rough, especially when the cat frustrates them."

The library door opened again. Trent emerged, his face the color of vanilla ice cream, his brow pinched. With barely a glance in our direction, he headed toward his wing. Robyn came out and stared straight at us, but I wasn't certain she saw us. Her cheeks flamed with anger. Emily was still in the library, her fists clenched, tears running silently down her face. Hoping Patrick didn't see his mother, I quickly turned him in the direction of the kitchen, where we kept our boots, and gave him a little push.

"So where are you going, Patrick?" Brook asked.

Patrick didn't reply.

"To the pond," Brook guessed, noting the skates. "What a great idea, ice skating on a nice warm day like this!"

"I told him the pond was too soft. He wants to see for himself. Excuse me."

Patrick was halfway down the hall and I took long strides to catch up with him. In the kitchen, we pulled on our boots, then exited out the back of the house. Patrick walked swiftly, wordlessly toward the snowman we had built two days ago. Our hockey player had shrunk into a troll.

"He's melted," I observed.

Without replying, Patrick picked up the snowman's hockey stick and circled the house to the front. I could have stopped him there and given him the choice of dropping the skates and stick or going to his room, but going back inside that angry house was too stiff a penalty for any child to pay. We'd settle the matter when he could see the ice for himself.

We walked silently down the main road, then cut across a garden and orchard, Patrick leading the way, making a wide circle to skirt the horse barn. The stand of trees around the pond looked eerie in the fading afternoon light, like an island floating in the snow and mist. We entered the ring of cedar and pine, following the short trail through dripping branches. Fog darkened the wood and hung over the pond, turning the straggly trees near the shore into ghostly figures. The ice was leaden gray. Off-center, larger than before, was the circle of black water.

Patrick picked up a stick and threw it on the ice. "See? It's frozen."

"Patrick, sticks float on water."

"But it's not floating," he replied. "It's just sitting there."

"The point is that sticks are so light, they can float on water. You are much heavier."

"I float," he argued. "I float on my back."

Struggling to keep my temper, I took the skates and hockey stick from him. "You can't go on the ice. I don't want to hear any more about it."

I put his things at the entrance to the path, then dragged two heavy limbs to the narrow margin between pond and trees, and pushed them together.

"Do you want to sit on my new bench?" I asked, taking out the bag of crackers. I had brought the buttery ones, his favorite. "You may open them if you like."

The sulk could be sustained for only so long. Patrick sat down next to me. After a moment, he tore open the crackers and gobbled up several of them. As he did, I thought about how to facilitate his contact with Ashley's thoughts the day she died. I knew the first part of the story; perhaps all I had to do was get it started, and let Ashley finish it.

"I never mentioned this, Patrick," I said, "but I used to play with Ashley—"

My cell phone rang, startling both of us. I reached in my pocket to turn it off, but before I could, the three-note ring sounded again.

"It's your phone," Patrick said.

I sighed and pulled it out. "Hello."

"Miss Kate?"

"Yes."

"It's Jack, one of Mrs. Caulfield's grooms."

"I'm sorry?" The voice sounded low and raspy, the connection unclear.

"Jack, from the barn. We got a kind of problem here. I found some painting on the barn, spray paint, low down on the west side. Don't know how long it's been there—no one goes around that way. I had to call Mrs. Caulfield about it. She's mad and coming down to see herself."

He paused.

"So?" I asked, but I could guess what was coming.

"She said you should be here waiting to explain."

"Did she now."

I reminded myself that it wasn't the groom's fault that Robyn had leaped to this conclusion. And, to be fair to Robyn, Patrick had earned her suspicion.

"Would you hold for a moment, please?" I pressed the mute button. "Patrick, did you spray paint the outside of the horse barn?"

"No."

"Are you sure?"

His face grew anxious, his mouth moving silently before he spoke. "I don't have any spray paint."

I mentally ran through the forty-eight hours since he had dropped the manure through the hay chute. He had slipped off that afternoon when I had found him on the diving board, and had slipped away again at dawn when I had found him here at the pond, but I doubted he had gone anywhere other than the pool and pond. Of course, the vandalism might have been done before that and not noticed till now. "Have you had any dares from Ashley that I don't know about?"

"No. Am I in trouble?" He had taken off his mittens to eat the crackers. I saw the tense way he curled his hands, leaving his knuckles bony white.

"Not if you didn't paint the barn." Someone else could have, I thought, someone hoping the blame would fall on Patrick.

I released the mute button and spoke into the phone again.

"Please tell Mrs. Caulfield that I have questioned Patrick, and that it would make more sense if the person who *did* it was there to explain."

"Uh, yeah, I know what you mean. But she's my boss and told me to get you, so I have to do it. Maybe you, uh, want to leave young Mr. Westbrook behind and talk to her yourself first, just until she cools down. She's a little—you know. You know how she is."

"I know very well. Neither Patrick nor I will be there." I clicked off and slipped the phone in my pocket.

"I don't go too close to the barn now," Patrick said to me. "Really, I don't."

I heard the tremor in his voice.

"I believe you."

"Do you think Ashley did it?" he asked.

"No. I think someone else in the house is playing pranks."

"They don't like me."

It was pointless to deny it. "It's their problem, Patrick, not yours. I want you to remember that I like you very much. So does Sam. Tim did—he was your good friend, and I bet the boy at school who knows about hockey likes you."

"Ashley, too," he suggested softly. "She doesn't say it, but I think she does."

"I believe so. You know, Ashley was my friend too."

He took another cracker from the pack, then gazed up at me, frowning slightly. "Ashley usually plays with Katie."

I nodded. "That's right. That's what Ashley called me. We used to play in many of the same places that you like. One of them was the play set by the cottages. Ashley was an excellent swinger. She could go really high."

"And sing," he added.

A shiver went through me. "Yes, she always sang when she swung. We liked to climb trees. She and November could climb all the way to the top of some of them. I wasn't as brave."

Patrick stared out at the pond, no longer worried about the barn, in another world now.

"I thought she had the best toys. Often we played with her horses—Silver Knight was my favorite."

"I like Silver Knight too," he confided.

"Ashley's favorite was Banner."

He nodded. "She likes his mane, the way the plastic looks ripply, like it's blowing in the wind."

I was talking in the past tense, he in the present, but we knew the same girl.

"Ashley had lots of pets—puppies and rabbits, some chickens she kept in the old cow barn, hamsters and fish. But her favorite pet was her brown and white rabbit, the one named Silly."

"Because he has one floppy ear," Patrick said knowingly.

"Yes. One day, when the weather was foggy, like it is now, Silly disappeared from his cage."

Patrick looked surprised for a moment. "Like my hamster?"

"Yes. Ashley was very angry, and afraid, too. My mother, Joseph, and I tried to calm her and help her find Silly."

Patrick thought for a moment, then nodded, as if he knew that now, as if he had caught up with the story told by the trace of Ashley's mind. "Silly isn't in the house," he said quietly.

"No, no, he wasn't. We thought someone might have let him outside."

"She thinks Brook did it," Patrick said.

"Yes. So my mother and I and Ashley and Joseph went out to look for the rabbit."

"Ashley is crying."

"She . . . is," I said, shifting tenses. "She . . . loves Silly very much."

Patrick nodded and continued to gaze out at the pond.

"The four of us are looking for him. Each of us goes a different way. Though my mother tells us to stay close, we don't. Ashley runs here to the pond. The ice looks as if it might be frozen." That was as much of the story as I knew for sure. "She— she thinks she sees Silly on the ice," I ventured.

"She *does* see him."

"So—"

"Kate!" Robyn's shrill voice broke into our story. Patrick's body went rigid.

"I've had all I can take of that hellion!" Robyn shouted, sounding as if she were on the path, coming toward the pond.

Patrick turned to me, his eyes wide. "She found us."

With Brook's help, I thought, for he knew we were going to the pond.

"Don't worry, I'll handle her. I want you to stay quiet, Patrick, and let me talk to her. Stay on these logs. Don't move a millimeter, all right?"

He nodded.

I rose to intercept Robyn at the end of the path, keeping an eye on Patrick and, at the same time, blocking her access to him. In the last twenty-four hours he had become too fragile to withstand her explosions.

"Kate," she cried as she rounded the final bend of trees, "I'll have you fired for this!"

Her barn jacket sat crookedly on her shoulders, buttoned incorrectly, its mismatched front flapping open. Long strands of hair had come loose from the clasp that held it at the back of her head. The fury on her face was far out of proportion to a spray-painted patch of barn.

"We can discuss it later," I said, "when you have your temper under control."

"We'll discuss it now. Brook told me what that monster did."

"I was talking to Brook before we left the house," I said, glancing back at Patrick. He was still on the logs. "Why didn't he say something then?"

"He just received a call from the barn and relayed the message to me. That child is a juvenile delinquent," she hissed.

"Patrick or Brook?"

"By the time he is ten, the police will be picking him up."

"That's absurd, and you know it. In any case, Patrick didn't go near your barn."

"It's a child's work," she insisted. "The groom said so."

I glanced back again at Patrick, then turned to her. "Most people could imitate a child's painting. Even Brook would be capable," I added, unable to keep the sarcasm out of my voice.

"He's a hateful child. Hateful!" Her fingers flexed with anger.

I found myself staring at her hands, her bitten-off nails. One of them was bloody.

"Adrian should take a strap to him," she said. "If he doesn't, I will."

"You touch Patrick, and I'll have the authorities here in a flash."

She smiled. *"If* you're still here."

"I will be."

Robyn looked past my shoulder. "Not the way you're tending to Patrick."

I spun around. He was on the ice, hurrying across it. "Patrick! Patrick, stop!"

I rushed toward the pond and halted at its edge. He was already ten meters from shore. "Help me," I called to Robyn. "Patrick, come back!"

At last he stopped and glanced around warily. Though he looked straight at me, he didn't act as if he saw me. We had been talking about Ashley: Was he seeing the present or the past? I wondered.

"Don't move."

I quickly surveyed the ice, trying to see which sections appeared most solid. My weight might be too much for the area he was on. I needed a long branch, one I could extend to him.

I glanced over my shoulder. Robyn was gone. She didn't care if he drowned—she was crazy, truly mad with jealousy. I continued to look for something that could be used as a pole. The logs were too heavy; the lighter branches and hockey stick were shorter than I wanted.

Patrick had turned his whole body around now and was watching me.

"Walk toward me," I called.

He stood still.

If I moved toward him, he might retreat onto thinner ice. *Oh, God,* I prayed, *tell me what to do, tell me how to get him back.* Aloud, I said, "Patrick, you need to get on shore. Come here."

He gazed at me, but his mind was elsewhere. He was like a person on a phone, listening to a voice I couldn't hear.

"Patrick, come here!"

He didn't blink.

I picked up the longest branch within reach and started across the ice. Its surface was soft, uneven. My heart pounded. If he fell through, it would be hard to find him in the black depths. He might panic and swim under the ice.

I wanted to race to him. Even so, I forced myself to move slowly, steadily, afraid the impact of running steps would break the ice.

I was seven meters from him and getting closer. "I want you to grab hold of the branch," I said.

He edged away from me. He looked afraid.

"Grab the branch and—"

He took a step back. I heard the soft crunching, then the sickening sound of fractures running through the ice. Patrick tumbled into the water. I screamed and raced forward. For a moment his snow jacket buoyed him up, and I thought I could reach him before his head went under. Then he flailed his arms, compressing the air pockets that kept him afloat. He was still on the surface, but barely. I trained my eyes on him, memorizing his position relative to the shore.

I was caught by surprise when the ice gave way beneath me. Frigid water rushed over me. I gulped it, then thrust my head upward. The pond water ringed my throat, but I could touch ground—both feet touched ground. I pressed forward.

"Float! Turn on your back and float!" I cried.

Patrick was terrified and choking down water.

I couldn't move fast enough. It was like walking against a wall of mud, the heavy pond water feeling solid to my neck.

Patrick's clothes, weighted with water, sucked him under. I could still see the top of his head, his hair floating near the surface. Two steps more—I moved in slow motion. *Help me God, please.*

I reached out and grabbed him. My cold hands felt as lifeless as shovels, my fingers so numb they were unable to grasp. I held him against me with just the strength of my arms. He was breathing, still breathing—and coughing.

I waded toward shore, continually pushing against an edge of ice. The upward slope of the pond's floor seemed steep as a mountain. As I struggled, I thought about what to do next—call 911. Get him to the warm barn.

The water grew shallower and Patrick heavier. When the water was at my hips I struggled to hold him and reach for my cell phone. The sooner I called the paramedics, the sooner they would get here. It shouldn't have been hard to push 911, but my fingers couldn't feel the buttons. The phone slid into the dark water and disappeared.

Keep going, you have to keep going, I told myself.

Patrick felt twice his weight, but it was easier now to kick at the ice and push my way through it. At last I was on shore. He breathed heavily, sounding congested. I debated what to do. "Mrs. Caulfield?" I called out in the desperate hope Robyn had stayed to watch. There was no answer.

If I laid him on the ground, I might not be able to pick him up again, and I didn't know how to administer the medical care he needed. I kept going, finding the trail through the wood, amazed that my feet could walk with no sensation of ground beneath them. When I got to the end of the path, I stopped and screamed for help, hoping someone in the barn would hear me.

From the road that led to the employee cottages, Roger shouted back. He streaked toward me, calling to the barn as he did. Someone responded. With Patrick still in my arms, I dropped in a heap, unable to do one thing more.

Nineteen

ROGER CALLED 911, then contacted Emily, who rushed down from the house followed by the others. The paramedics from the volunteer fire department arrived. I didn't know whether to laugh or cry when Mrs. Hopewell informed them that their assistance would not be needed after all—the boy was nothing more than cold. They looked at her as if she were quite mad, then followed Emily's instructions. Emily insisted that I, too, be checked at the hospital, and I agreed because I wanted to be with Patrick.

Adrian called the hospital from his attorney's office and was assured by the E.R. staff that Patrick was stable. An hour later, when Adrian arrived at Easton Hospital, Patrick's body temperature and other vital signs were normal. The doctor informed Adrian that I was unharmed and Patrick would be ready for release in another hour, as long as an X-ray for aspirated water proved negative. When the physician departed, Adrian asked me for an exact account of what had occurred, reminding me to keep my voice low.

How many strange stories could I tell Adrian, I wondered, before he stopped believing me? I began with the phone call from the barn and was quickly interrupted. "There is no groom named Jack."

"But there has to—" I didn't complete my sentence. Maybe not, I thought. I believed Brook was responsible for the vandalism; maybe he was also responsible for the call. Had he disguised his voice and manner of speaking? I had thought the connection was poor, but I hadn't expected the call, so I wasn't trying to detect a ruse.

"Did you look at your Caller ID?" Adrian asked.

"I didn't think about it at the time," I admitted, "but I don't remember seeing a listing. You should ask Brook the same question. His mother said he received a call about the barn and passed on the message to her. Perhaps he did, or perhaps he or one of his friends was playing a prank. Brook enjoys family fights—they make his life less boring. You should question Mrs. Caulfield, as well. She saw Patrick on the ice and didn't stay around to help."

I couldn't read Adrian's reaction to what I had said, but Emily's face was transparent: She held me responsible; she believed I was negligent and pointing a finger at others to cover myself. Each time I moved within the curtained area around Patrick's bed, she moved, positioning herself between her son and me, making it clear she didn't want me near him.

"Why did you go on the ice, Patrick?" Adrian asked. "Kate told you not to."

"I saw November."

"What?"

The answer caught both Adrian and me by surprise.

"I saw November."

"The orange cat," I told Adrian.

"He was running across the ice."

Adrian shook his head.

"Patrick, November is dead," I said. "We buried him in the cemetery, remember?"

Patrick turned his gaze on me. There was a look in his eyes that I had never seen before—defiance masking fear. "You killed him."

"Me? Why would I do such a thing?" I asked, taken aback.

"You don't like him."

"Patrick, I would never kill an animal, not intentionally."

"I think this is just a decoy, Kate," Adrian interjected. "He's trying to distract us from that fact that he ran out on the ice when you forbade it."

"The other day he accused you of killing the cat. Now he's accusing me," I replied, exasperated.

"I was mixed up," Patrick said calmly.

"You're mixed up now," I told him, but he had turned away.

An hour later, when Patrick was released, Emily insisted that I ride back to the estate with Roger. I knew I shouldn't blame her for keeping Patrick away from me. In her eyes, her son had nearly died because of my negligence. How did I appear in Adrian's eyes, I wondered—like another Victoria?

On the way home I questioned Roger but learned nothing. He hadn't noticed anyone lurking about; of course, with the fog, it would have been easy to slip unseen from the woods along Scarborough Road to the pond and barn.

"I don't have a good feeling about this," he said. "Too many funny things have been happening lately."

"Do you have any idea what is going on?" I asked.

"No idea, no idea at all, just a bad feeling that we haven't seen the last of it."

That evening, Emily told me she would take care of Patrick herself. I nibbled on a late dinner alone in my room, wondering why she was letting him stay up. Finally, when it was well past his bedtime and I hadn't heard anything below, I took the back steps down to his room. I discovered that the door at the bottom had been locked from the other side. Taking the main stairs down, I found Patrick's door to the hall wide open, his room empty.

I was about to return to my quarters when I heard a ruckus downstairs. Someone was knocking on the front door and repeatedly ringing the bell.

"Henry, I told you not to answer it," Mrs. Hopewell called out.

I hurried across the second-floor hall and down the steps, then paused at the landing. Henry, retreating toward the kitchen, met my eyes for a moment.

"What the devil is going on, Louise?" Adrian shouted. He sounded as if he was emerging from the office.

"It's a trespasser," she told him. "I was just about to call the police."

"Do you know who it is?"

"A local boy."

Sam, I thought. He was supposed to call after practice.

When I heard Adrian's heavy footsteps moving toward the front door, I hastened down the last set of steps. Having lost her battle, Mrs. Hopewell marched off to the kitchen.

"Hello, Sam," I heard Adrian greet him. "I hope you haven't been waiting too long."

"Where's Kate?" Sam replied, in no mood for pleasantries.

"I do apologize," Adrian continued. "Mrs. Hopewell protects us a little too well at times."

"I want to talk to Kate," Sam saw me crossing the hall toward them. "Why didn't you answer your phone?" he demanded.

"Because it's in the bottom of the pond."

"I tried the house number. The old gargoyle wouldn't let me through."

I saw the flicker of a smile on Adrian's face at Sam's reference to Mrs. Hopewell. "Kate," he said, "I'm working in the office, and Emily has Patrick with her. She wants to keep him in our room tonight. The others have gone to their wings, so use whatever room you want here on the first floor. I will tell Mrs. Hopewell to remain in the kitchen." He turned toward the office, then turned back. "I'm afraid I'm somewhat old-fashioned when it comes to young men and ladies," he added with another wisp of a smile, "and must ask that you keep the door open wherever you are."

I nodded and led Sam into the library because that was the warmest room. I could still feel the pond's cold in my bones.

"I thought something had happened to you," Sam exploded, once we were inside the paneled room. "If you knew I couldn't get through, why didn't you call me?"

"I—I forgot about my phone. So much was happening."

"You make me crazy," he said, turning his back on me, banging the palm of his hand against the fireplace mantel.

"I'm sorry. I really am sorry."

"Yeah-yeah . . . So what's been going on?" he asked, his voice moderating, sounding almost flat.

"Patrick fell through the ice in the pond."

Sam spun around.

"Could we sit down? It's been a long day"

"Not near the fireplace," he said. "Sound travels through flues."

We went to the corner of the room. Sam tried the Westbrooks' deep leather chairs, then sprawled on the rug. I sat on the floor facing him, hugging my knees, and recounted what had happened, backtracking to Dr. Parker's theory to explain why Patrick and I were at the pond.

At the end, Sam sighed. "I don't believe in that kind of stuff. And I especially don't believe a theory by a guy who wears pink glasses. Even so, it's creepy the way Patrick senses things when they are dead."

"I've been thinking about that," I replied. "Orange tabbies are common, and November has probably fathered a few litters. Since little kids don't always grasp the finality of death, Patrick may have seen an orange cat and thought—or hoped—it was November. He may even have imagined the whole event. He's been very upset since the cat died."

"You said Brook knew you were at the pond."

"We talked to him as we were leaving the house. He could

have painted the back of the barn long before and been waiting for the right moment to set his prank in motion. Adrian had an appointment with his lawyer today, supposedly about his will. I think Brook found himself with the perfect opportunity to stir an already boiling pot."

"And then he got lucky," Sam went on, "because Patrick decided to cross the ice? I don't think so. Kate, hasn't it occurred to you that, according to Patrick's story, he was lured onto the ice, lured by a favorite pet, just as Ashley was?"

I shifted uncomfortably and stretched my legs out in front of me. "I thought of it, yes."

"And have you thought about the fact that you were supposed to be watching him, just as your mother was supposed to be watching Ashley? And that if he had drowned, you would have been blamed, just as your mother was for Ashley's death?"

I had thought about *that* quite a bit.

He leaned toward me. "I'm telling you again, you have to leave this place."

"And I'm telling *you* I'm not."

He rubbed his head. "Maybe your mother will talk some sense into you."

At first I thought I hadn't heard him correctly. "Sorry?"

He rested his back against the base of one of the big chairs, seeming a little too pleased with himself, I thought. "I found your mother online. It wasn't hard—I had a hunch she wasn't hiding the way she did twelve years ago. I got her maiden name from her birth records, poked around some, and found her."

I stared at him.

"I told her what was going on, just about everything I knew, including how pigheaded you are. She said you inherited that from her."

I swallowed hard.

"She said she had to get her passport updated, but would come as quickly as possible."

"Here?" I could barely get out the word.

"Yeah," he said casually, but he was faking. He had seen my reaction and was trying to downplay things. "She can stay with Mom and me."

"I can't believe you did that." My words came out in a hoarse whisper. "How dare you!"

His face colored. "You need her, Kate, whether you want to admit it or not. You need someone on your side, and you won't let it be me. So I asked her."

I was speechless.

"I want you to lock your bedroom door tonight," he said.

"It doesn't have a lock."

"Then push some furniture against it. You've seen movies,

you know what to do. I'm serious, totally serious." He stood up. "Call me tomorrow. I'll keep trying to reach you, but Stone-Face probably won't let me through. If I don't hear from you, I'm coming here—understand? I'll park in their driveway and stand outside and howl if they don't let me in. I'm sure they won't appreciate another visit," he added. "My car's dropping a lot of oil on their drive. Call me."

I nodded mutely. My mother was coming. I felt as if I couldn't move from where I was.

"It's okay, I can see myself out," he said, and left.

Twenty

I IGNORED SAM'S advice to barricade my bedroom doors that night. Though Emily kept Patrick with her, I wanted to be available if he wandered off and needed me. I should have listened to Sam, for as it turned out, exhaustion took over and I didn't hear a thing. The next morning I awoke ten minutes before I was scheduled to drive Patrick to school. I knew I had set my alarm to ring an hour and a half earlier; someone had entered my room and turned it off.

I hurried down the steps to Patrick's room. His pajamas were flung on the bed, which meant he was already dressed. I returned to my room, pulled on my clothes, and arrived on the first floor in time to hear a motor rumbling in the driveway. Peering through the hall window, I saw Emily buckling Patrick into the back of Roger's Jeep. She was keeping him away from me.

"Good morning."

The greeting was cold, and I took my time turning from the window.

"Good morning, Mrs. Hopewell. Why was my alarm clock turned off?"

"Mrs. Westbrook said that she was tending to Patrick today. I saw no reason for you to rise."

"Thank you, but I'll make my own decision about rising."

"Breakfast is being served," she went on, without a trace of emotion on her face or in her voice.

"I'm not hungry."

"Mr. Westbrook has asked that you see him in the office—after you breakfast," she added.

"I'll see him now."

"He is not prepared to see you until after you breakfast."

"Fine," I said. "Shall you prepare him for a change in plans, or shall I?"

She pressed her lips together, then walked stiffly toward the office door and knocked.

"Yes, Louise."

"Miss Venerelli has refused breakfast and insists on seeing you now."

"Come in, Kate," he called.

I took a deep breath and entered. I knew this wasn't going to be a pleasant conversation. Adrian rose and nodded at Mrs.

Hopewell, who, for once, departed willingly, closing the door behind her.

Adrian gestured for me to sit down. "How are you this morning?" he asked.

"Fine." I folded my hands tightly in my lap.

He chose the chair nearest to me. "Kate, I am not going to beat around the bush, except to say you don't know how much I hate doing this."

I met his eyes. "That's all right. I can take correction."

His hands opened and closed with frustration. "There is nothing about your work to correct. Nevertheless, I have to let you go."

"Let me go? You mean fire me?" I should have seen it coming, but I didn't.

"In business," he said, "we call it resigning. You resign before I terminate your position. It looks better on your record."

I thought about it for a moment. "The problem is, I'm not resigning."

He raised an eyebrow.

"If you want me to leave, you will have to fire me," I said.

He leaned forward in his chair, moving his head closer to mine, as if we were friends discussing a problem. "I am counting on you to understand. This isn't my choice. You have done a wonderful job with Patrick. Unfortunately, on some issues, I need to defer to Patrick's mother, and this is one of them. I have stood up for you against Robyn, Trent, and Mrs. Hopewell, as I'm sure you know. But too many things have happened now—things that are not your fault, of course. Still, for the sake of family cooperation and my wife's peace of mind, I need to let you go."

"Who is going to look out for Patrick?"

"I will. I promise you I will take a more active role. I should have done so long ago."

"I don't trust any of them," I said. "Robyn, Brook, Trent, Mrs. Hopewell—I don't trust anyone with him but Emily."

"I understand what you are saying," Adrian replied, "and I will heed your warning." Then he offered me a preposterously large amount of money for only a week's worth of work, calling it severance pay.

I rejected the offer. "I'm not resigning."

So he fired me, handing me the large check anyway, and promising to write a stellar recommendation for whatever job I wanted in the future. Roger would drive me where I needed to go; I was to let him know when I was packed.

"What are you going to tell Patrick?" I asked.

"I'm not sure yet."

"May I stay till he comes home from school?" I saw in Adrian's eyes that the answer was no. I felt tears in my own. "Can't I say good-bye to him?"

"His mother is going to pick him up from school today and take him to Easton. They will have dinner there, which will give me some time to talk to the rest of the family. I am afraid that Emily doesn't want you to have further contact with him. I'm sorry, Kate. I can see that this is painful for you."

I stood up shakily, grasping the check, feeling it crinkle in my hand. I would keep it until I had transferred bank funds from England to insure that I could get by for several weeks more. Then I'd return the check to Adrian, just as I had returned the ring my father took.

Roger dropped me at Tea Leaves Café, as I requested. After two cheese pastries, I decided to call Amelia Sutter, who was kind enough to pick up me and my luggage, though returning to the Strawberry Bed and Breakfast may not have been the wisest of moves. Amelia was bursting with curiosity about the Westbrooks. Fortunately the weather that day was mild, only a tattered blanket of snow remaining on the small lawns of the town, its sidewalks clear and dry. I escaped her questions and spent the afternoon wandering the back streets of Wisteria, avoiding Joseph's shop, feeling too raw to talk.

I left a message on Sam's home phone telling him that I had been fired and asking him to keep an eye on Patrick. I didn't mention where I was staying, for I was even less ready to talk to him. I knew he might go to Mason's Choice that evening to ask where I had gone but I decided that was a good thing because he would check on Patrick while he was there. And perhaps Joseph, curious to know if I had learned anything at the pond and unable to reach me by cell phone, would call the estate. All the better. Attention from outsiders might persuade those at Mason's Choice that it would be risky to harm Patrick.

I wanted to think that Patrick was safe and that Sam was right: The real goal of the recent events was to get rid of me. I, with my interest in Ashley's death, was the true threat, and all that had happened to Patrick was staged to make me seem irresponsible, to frame me so that I would be fired. But each time I reached that logical conclusion my gut told me that much more was going on.

I awoke Saturday morning ready to deal with what had occurred. I waited till ten o'clock, when the weekend guests at the Strawberry had left on their excursions, then called Joseph from the tiny room equipped with the B&B's guest phone. I found him at his mother's house.

"Katie!" He breathed into the phone. "Thank God! Where are you? I've been worried. Why didn't you tell me you resigned from Mason's Choice?"

"I'm calling to tell you now. And I didn't resign, I was fired."

"Yes, yes, but where are you? Adrian has been trying to reach you. And Sam Koscinski, both last night and this morning. . . ." Joseph blew hard into the phone. "I know you like him, Katie, but he's a lunatic."

"I won't argue that. Why is Adrian looking for me?"

"Patrick's missing."

"What! When did this happen?"

Amelia, who was passing by the small phone room, paused outside the door.

"Sometime between last night and this morning." Joseph made his voice calm, perhaps to counter the panic rising in me. "According to Trent, Patrick was gone from his bed when Emily went to awaken him."

"He got outside the house unnoticed? Adrian didn't set the alarm?"

"If he did, someone turned it off. Trent said there was no forced entry."

I turned my back on Amelia, whose mouth moved as if she were silently repeating my words, trying to milk their full meaning.

"Did they—did they check the pond? Did they look for signs of—" I couldn't complete the thought. "Did they look for some sign of him there?"

"Yes. Trent said they have looked everywhere on the estate."

"The empty houses and the hayloft? The pool, the orangerie—"

"Everywhere on Mason's Choice."

"The old barn, the beach, the cemetery, the docks—" I couldn't stop thinking of places that were full of danger for a child like Patrick.

"Everywhere, Katie."

"Trent told you this?"

"He left here about twenty minutes ago. Adrian sent him as his envoy. He thought you might be staying with me."

I glanced over my shoulder at Amelia. There was a door to the room, but it was propped open by an iron doorstop. "Excuse me a moment," I said to Joseph. "Amelia, would it be all right if I moved that doorstop and closed the door?"

"No need," she said cheerfully. "There's only me here."

"I understand, but this is a private conversation."

"Oh. I wasn't really listening." She moved on, walking rather slowly.

"What do the police think?" I asked Joseph, keeping my voice low. "Adrian *did* call the police."

"No, not yet."

"What is he waiting for!" I exclaimed.

But, of course, I knew why he hadn't contacted the authorities and why he would put if off as long as possible. "He suspects someone in his family removed Patrick."

"Katie, I don't like telling you this, but Trent came here because Adrian suspected you."

"Me! Why would I do such a stupid thing?"

"Revenge," Joseph suggested. "Anger at being fired."

"But it makes no sense," I argued. "It would confuse and upset Patrick and, in the end, where would it get me?"

"You keep believing that Adrian is as rational and compassionate as you," Joseph replied.

"Perhaps. I need some time to think. Are you going to the shop?"

"I was just about to depart."

"I'll meet you there in a half hour," I told him.

As soon as I hung up, I punched in the numbers for Adrian's cell phone. I reached his voice mail and left a message saying I knew nothing about Patrick's disappearance and could be reached for a limited time at the antique shop, leaving that number as well as Amelia's. I saw no point in speaking to anyone else in the household. I didn't trust Emily to keep a clear head and relate accurate information; as for the others, I didn't trust them at all.

Finally, I called Sam's home. I thought I was calm and collected, but as soon as I heard Mrs. Koscinski's voice, I felt the moisture in the corners of my eyes. She said Sam had gone on an errand. "He received your message last night and has been trying to find you, Kate. Is everything all right?"

"Yes." My voice shook. "No."

She waited patiently till I found the words to tell her that Patrick was missing.

"Why don't you come here and wait for Sam," she said. "He should be back soon. Come over and I'll fix you some breakfast."

"Thank you, no."

"A cup of tea," she offered. "Tea or coffee or juice."

I blinked back the tears. It was tempting to run to her, sit in her kitchen, drink her tea, and have a good cry, but I wasn't that kind of girl. At least, I hadn't been till now.

"Thank you, but another friend is expecting me," I said, then gave her the name and number of the bed-and-breakfast. "I'll try to call back. It's Sam's play-off game tonight, isn't it? I know he has to get ready for that."

"First, he has to know you are safe," she said. "If he could talk to you, Kate, he'd feel better. If he saw you, he'd feel more assured. Me too."

"I—I'll be in touch," I said, and hung up. It was bad enough to fall for a guy, without liking his mother, too.

I grabbed my coat and headed out, glad for the long walk to the shop on High Street. The stiff March breeze blowing up from the water helped clear my head. It seemed to me there were two possibilities: Patrick had run away, or he had been abducted.

If he had run away, where would he have gone? A seven-year-old couldn't walk far and would head for a place familiar to him. I remembered when I was eight and had run away from home—all the way to our next-door neighbor. Perhaps Patrick was just beyond the estate boundaries. Perhaps he had tried to walk to school; given the tension and fighting at home, school may have become a safe haven for him.

It seemed odd, however, that no one had spotted a young child walking alone and questioned the situation, though he could have fallen asleep beneath some bushes, somewhere out of sight. When I got to the shop I'd leave another message for Sam, asking him to gather a group of friends and search the area around the estate as well as the route between the estate and school.

If Patrick had been kidnapped, it had to be by someone who had easy access to him, someone on the estate who could silently remove him from the house. Had the anger and envy within the family finally boiled over? It seemed absurd for any of them to think they could get away with harming Patrick, but then, murder had happened before at Mason's Choice and no member of the family had been charged. I refused to think about that possibility—Patrick had to be alive. I made myself focus on the question of where he might have been taken.

The Eastern Shore, with its large rural stretches, had a million places to hide a child. If Robyn had done it, someone she knew through the horse business might have a barn or shed, some isolated building that could be easily secured. If Brook, a friend might have his own place now and hide Patrick there. I didn't know where to begin if Mrs. Hopewell had taken things into her own hands; I couldn't imagine her having friends or family. If Trent had done it? It came to me when I turned onto High Street: Why not the Queen Victoria, the hotel where his friend, Margery, was manager?

I mentioned this as soon as I saw Joseph, who was standing before a table of hardware, preparing to work on a lamp.

He shook his head. "Too many people would recognize Trent and would wonder why Patrick was with him."

"Not if he showed up at three A.M.," I argued, "wrapped in a winter scarf, hidden under a hat, and carrying a sleeping child bundled against the cold. He could have sedated Patrick and brought him in a back entrance with the help of Margery."

Joseph played with the lamp's switch, then sorted through his tools. His deliberate movements calmed me. "Trent is too cautious to take risks like that."

"It's unlike him," I admitted. "He isn't first on my list, but it won't hurt to check the hotel while I figure out where else to look."

After leaving another message with Sam's mother about searching the area between Mason's Choice and Patrick's school, I paged through the shop's phone book, then rang up the Queen Vic.

"Mr. Westbrook's room, please."

"I'm sorry," the desk clerk replied, "that room is not accepting calls. May I take a message?"

I stared at the phone's mouthpiece, surprised at succeeding. Joseph, noticing my silence, set down a tool and took several steps closer.

"I said, may I take a message?" the clerk repeated.

I thought quickly. "I have a delivery for Mr. Westbrook at the Queen Victoria Hotel. What room is that, please?"

"I'm sorry, we don't give out that information. You may leave the delivery at our front desk, and we will be happy to take it to his room."

I thanked the woman, then set the phone back in its cradle.

"He's there?" Joseph asked, incredulous.

"Someone named Westbrook is, but the person isn't accepting calls."

"I guessed wrong. I never would have thought—"

I interrupted him. "It could be that Trent keeps a room

there simply to be with Margery. In any case, we are supposed to leave our delivery at the front desk, and they will be happy to take it up to his room."

"What delivery is that?"

"Something large enough that, when they see it, they won't really be happy to take it up themselves. Something ugly enough that they won't be much happier about keeping it in the lobby."

Joseph smiled. "So they will give us the room number, wanting us to deliver it." His hand swept the air, indicating all the merchandise in the shop. "So much to choose from."

I surveyed the items around us, then spotted it in the corner. "Yes, oh yes!"

Twenty-one

AN HOUR LATER, Joseph and I, breathing hard, leaned a large painting wrapped in brown paper against the hotel's front desk. Carrying the artwork, which had the awkward size and proportions of a long sofa, through the elegantly furnished lobby of the Queen Victoria hadn't been easy. The desk clerk greeted us coolly and, at our request, studied the store tag from Olivia's. The date and time of delivery, as well as the name of the hotel, were printed clearly on it; the customer's "signature" was unreadable. Joseph and I, afraid a delivery for Mr. Westbrook would raise too many questions, had decided on a different strategy.

"The writing on this tag is illegible. I can't possibly help you," said the clerk, a twenty-something man with a fake British accent. He looked past us, as if he thought we might go away.

I rested both arms on the counter, not planning to go anywhere but upstairs. "I remember the customer coming into our store. We spent quite a bit of time discussing Olivia's fine selection of paintings. I am certain I would recognize the name if I saw it again."

The clerk pursed his lips and refused to take the bait.

"Perhaps if you looked at the registry," Joseph suggested.

"No one," said the clerk, "is allowed to look at the list of guests. May I help the next in line, please."

"I think it began with 'S,'" Joseph continued, propping his elbow on the counter, occupying more space. "I hope it's Superman. This masterpiece must weigh a hundred fifty pounds."

"'S'? I thought it was 'M.'"

I could hear the people who were waiting behind us shifting their belongings.

"I must ask you to step aside," the clerk said to us.

"But we have to deliver this," I replied.

"Step aside, please. You may use the public phone if you would like to contact the store for the necessary information." He cocked his head, indicating that he was addressing the guest behind us. "Yes, sir. Thank you for waiting *so graciously.*"

I stepped aside—slightly. "Perhaps we should leave the painting here, Joseph. Surely the purchaser will recognize it."

"I'm sure of only one thing," Joseph responded, "I'm not lugging it back to the shop."

Though this was part of our script, Joseph wasn't acting; he had sweat profusely during our effort to get the painting in and out of his S.U.V.

We carried the painting toward a mahogany pillar, a prominent position in the tastefully restored lobby. Working quickly, we peeled off its wrapping. The huge gilt frame, which had enough dips and waves in it to make a person seasick, caught the light and made the perfect border for a painting of very plump women bathing in a pink, soda-pop spring with strange winged creatures darting about.

Three middle-aged ladies who entered the hotel saw the painting, glanced at one another, then laughed out loud. The desk clerk looked up. When he saw what the patrons were staring at, a look of horror crossed his face. "What are you doing?" he demanded.

"We thought we'd leave it here till the owner claimed it," Joseph replied.

"You must be joking!"

More people entered the lobby. "Mommy, those ladies don't have any clothes on," a child observed.

A quiet buzzer sounded behind the desk. The office door opened and I held my breath, hoping it wasn't Margery, who might recognize me. To my relief, a dark-haired woman emerged.

"What's the problem, Francis?" she asked the desk clerk, but she spotted it as she spoke.

Francis explained how this "unfortunate painting" had materialized in the lobby, then boldly suggested that it be stored in her office.

The woman, whose name tag indicated she was the assistant manager, studied the canvas. "Not while I work there," she said.

"If I could look at the registry," I interjected, "I think I would recognize the customer's name."

She nodded. "Come behind the desk. It's on the computer."

I did so, scanning the list, making sure to search beyond Westbrook, Room 305.

"Got it. McCutcheon. Room 313."

Joseph scribbled the number on the tag.

"She's expecting us, but we'll use the house phone to tell her we're coming up," I said, hoping to keep Francis from making such a call.

"Thank you, we are rather busy," the woman replied, smiling, then disappearing into her office, leaving behind a pouting desk clerk. A few minutes later, after faking the call, Joseph and I discovered that the antiquated guest elevator was too small for transporting the painting. Francis exacted his revenge by informing us that only employees were allowed to use the service elevator. I could have demanded to speak again to the assistant manager, but I was afraid she would tell an employee to accompany us.

"Looks like it's the steps," I said to Joseph.

Wide enough for a dozen people to climb shoulder to shoulder, the Victorian staircase swept up to a large, stained-glass window, then split into two stairways that doubled back, rising to the second floor. After pausing at the split, Joseph went left and I went right. We nearly dropped the painting between us. Then he went right and I went left, both of us grunting as we slammed our foreheads and shoulders against the ornate frame.

"Which way?" he asked, mopping his brow on his sleeve, puffing hard.

"You choose, I'll follow." Usually, the stronger person follows, bearing the weight of an object when climbing stairs, and that was me.

We carried the bathing ladies down to room 313, in case someone checked on our delivery. "Sallie McCutcheon," I said, remembering the name on the registry, "is going to be very surprised."

Joseph, who had lost his sense of humor, simply dried his hands on a handkerchief and walked back to Room 305. I caught up with him at the door and pressed my ear against it. At first I couldn't figure out whose voices I heard, then I squeezed Joseph's arm. "It's the telly," I whispered, "tuned into a children's program. Patrick's here!"

"Do you think Trent is with him?"

I listened a moment longer. "I doubt it. He's probably back at Mason's Choice, pretending he has nothing to do with this." I knocked on the door.

When no one answered, I rapped harder.

"Patrick may be bound or drugged," Joseph said, then slipped from his pocket a case of small tools. In the last few weeks he had become skilled at opening locked boxes and bureaus, both in the shop and at his mother's house. What he lacked in muscle, he made up for with dexterity. A minute later, he turned his head toward me, smiled a little, and softly opened the door.

The room was dark and stuffy, its heavy drapes pulled across the windows. Patrick lay on the bed, sunken into the pillows. I ran to him. "Patrick, are you all right?"

His glassy eyes slid away from the cartoon he was watching. He turned his head slowly, his eyes gradually focusing on me, then he pulled the bedcovers around him.

"I'm so glad to see you!" I said, hugging him. I felt him recoil, though his drugged body didn't have enough strength to pull away from me. I let go. "Patrick?"

"He's been given something," Joseph said, standing on the other side of the bed.

"It's more than that," I replied bitterly. "Someone has been telling him things about me. They've been lying about me."

I reached for Patrick's hand. He flinched.

"Patrick, listen to me. I didn't want to abandon you. I was fired. I was forced to leave."

Patrick moved closer to Joseph.

"You may be right," Joseph observed.

"We're here to help you, " I continued. "We're going to take you back to your father."

Patrick didn't respond.

"We should call Adrian," I said to Joseph, "and tell him where we are, in case something prevents us from jetting Patrick out of here."

"The front desk may be able to monitor hotel phones," Joseph replied, pulling out his cell. "What's the number?"

I gave him Adrian's private line.

"Should we leave a message if he isn't there?—Wait, I have him. Adrian, hold on for Kate." He handed me the phone.

"Kate? Where are you?"

"At the Queen Victoria," I answered. "Joseph and I have found Patrick. He has been sedated, but he seems all right. He was here alone."

"At the hotel? Do you know how he got there? Did he say who took him?"

"I suspect Trent, since he is friends with the manager. We slipped into the room with the help of Joseph's tools from the store. Patrick is awake, but hasn't spoken yet. I think he's afraid of me, Adrian."

"Let me talk to him."

I handed the phone to Patrick. "It's your father."

Patrick listened for a minute or two, then handed back the phone.

"Was he there?" Adrian asked, sounding both irritated and anxious.

"Yes. He's just not speaking. We'll bring him home."

"Not yet," Adrian said. "Get him out of there—Trent just left the house and may be headed in your direction. But don't bring Patrick here. Emily is hysterical, and I want to talk to him before she gets him upset and confused. I don't think Trent is alone in this, and Patrick may be the only one who can tell us the details we need. The hotel must have a back way out, a fire exit."

"We'll find it."

"I'll meet you at the auction house. It's closed today. No one will be there, and we can talk. I'll go in the back way to turn off the alarm and lock up the dogs," he continued. "Then

I'll meet you at the front. You should make it in twenty minutes. If you're not there in forty, I'll call the police. What vehicle are you taking?"

I gave him a description of Joseph's S.U.V. When I hung up, I told Joseph the plan, then checked the hall for a fire escape. A set of inside steps was designated as the fire exit, but I thought I had seen the stairway's door near the front desk. Having entered the lobby with a large, ugly painting, we'd surely be remembered and questioned if we exited with a drugged child.

There was an old iron fire escape, a zigzagging ladder, attached to the outside of the building. The problem with that route was that Patrick, in his doped-up state, couldn't be counted on to climb down safely by himself. Returning to the room, I told Joseph that I would carry Patrick piggyback down the outside steps.

But Patrick refused to let me touch him. With unexpected energy, he kicked at me, then punched me with balled-up fists. I caught his wrists, but he continued to kick.

"Patrick! What is going on?"

"I won't go with you! I won't!"

"You have to."

"You're pig snot," he said. "You're a bucket full of pig snot."

I let go of him. It was one of Ashley's expressions, a description she had used for Joseph.

"Why don't you ask him what color it is?" Joseph remarked dryly.

I had asked Ashley that more than once.

"Green swirled with pink," Patrick said.

Joseph grimaced at the "correct" answer. "It *is* creepy, Katie. It's as if she's inside him."

"I know." I reached for Patrick again. He squirmed away and lurched toward Joseph, who caught him. "Will you let Joseph carry you?" I asked.

Joseph's eyes widened. "You're trying to give me a heart attack, aren't you."

"At least, this time, you're headed down."

Patrick finally agreed, and Joseph helped him put on his shoes, since he wouldn't allow me. We used Joseph's belt and a sheet to tie Patrick onto Joseph's back, in case he let go.

"Now he's secure, but my pants aren't," Joseph complained.

Opening the room's door, I looked both ways and led them down the hall. I climbed down the fire escape first, testing it for safety. When I reached the bottom, Joseph slowly descended with Patrick on his back. Each time Joseph's foot felt for a rung, I held my breath. I kept checking the back windows of the hotel to see if anyone was watching us. So far so good.

The fire escape ended several meters off the ground. I argued with Patrick about letting me catch him. Finally, I pushed a pile of garbage bags and boxes over to the spot to soften his fall, then stepped in and caught him at the last moment.

He wrenched himself away from me. "I hate you!" he said. "You're goose poop."

I bit my lip. It was another of Ashley's descriptions of Joseph, inspired by our experience of walking through fields fouled by Canadian geese. As funny as the expression sounded, Patrick was deadly serious, his eyes angry—angry and scared.

"All right, take Joseph's hand. Let's walk as quickly as possible."

Patrick's behavior didn't make sense, I thought, as we hurried up the alley then backtracked down the front street. If Patrick was tapping into the record of Ashley's thoughts and feelings, why didn't he act this way toward Joseph?

Suddenly I realized my mistake. At the beginning, when Patrick had described Ashley's hair and clothes, I had thought that he was seeing a talking image of her, seeing her the way people are supposed to see ghosts. But Dr. Parker had said that he was experiencing her emotions and thoughts, nothing more. Ashley had been proud of her curly hair and had loved the coat and shoes that Patrick described. He knew what she looked like not by seeing some kind of image, but simply through her thoughts about herself.

Even after talking with Dr. Parker, I had imagined that

Patrick "heard" Ashley's thoughts the way one might hear a ghost—as if Ashley were narrating her story, as if she were an actress delivering lines for his benefit. But he was experiencing her thoughts and feelings as if she were inside his head. Perhaps the more he connected with her psychic trace, the less able he became to distinguish her thoughts from his own. Immersed in her thoughts, he had transferred her feelings about various people to people in his own life.

Patrick wouldn't recognize Joseph by Ashley's *thoughts* about his physical appearance, for Joseph looked nothing like he did twelve years ago. But if Patrick experienced her negative thoughts about "my tutor," he might apply those thoughts and feelings to his own tutor—me. If Patrick "heard" Ashley's thoughts as if they were his own, then his belief that his father had killed November made sense: Ashley would have thought, "Daddy hates November. Daddy wants to get rid of him," meaning Trent; but to Patrick, "Daddy" was Adrian.

"This is it, Katie," Joseph called out to me, trying to catch my attention. "You're not leaving me alone with this kid, are you?"

I turned around and saw that I had walked past the S.U.V. "Sorry."

Patrick got in the back of the vehicle and I in the front. When I checked to see if his seat belt was fastened, he glared at me.

Joseph must have read the pain on my face. "Don't take him so seriously, Katie. His brain has been scrambled by whatever Trent gave him."

But I knew it wasn't the effect of the sedative. Patrick had begun to pull away from me the night I discovered him playing the piano the same way Ashley had played to annoy Joseph. And the look on his face now—defiance and fear—I had seen that two days ago when rescuing him from the pond.

A new thought occurred to me, one so strange and chilling, goose bumps rose at the back of my neck. At the pond I had been trying to get Patrick to tap into the moments when Ashley was lured onto the ice, hoping she saw who was responsible and that he could learn the murderer's identity from her. What if he had learned that it was "my tutor"?

I turned slowly toward Joseph and watched him drive, popping Life Savers into his mouth, wiping the sweat off his brow, looking like a normal, overweight guy on a warmish day in March. Joseph? Impossible.

But he had been there the day Ashley had died. And he knew I was taking Patrick to the pond after school in an effort to learn about her death. He knew about the reappearance of November, but I hadn't told him the cat was killed—our conversation at Tea Leaves was cut short when Trent and Margery arrived. It wouldn't have been hard to find an orange tabby that resembled

November from a distance. Had Joseph hidden among the trees that day? Had he called me on the cell phone, disguising his voice, baiting me, knowing the one reason I'd leave Patrick for a moment was to protect him from a furious Robyn?

"What is it?" Joseph asked, suddenly aware that I was gazing at him.

We were stopped at a red light, and his brown eyes looked steadily into mine, a small frown forming above them. "Is something wrong?"

I shook my head and looked away. "No, I was just thinking."

How well did I know this man? No better than I knew Trent, or Robyn, or Brook—I only thought I did because he seemed to be on my side.

The light changed, and Joseph drove on.

He had no reason to kill Ashley, I told myself. He had no reason to bait Patrick. People, sane ones, don't murder people they simply don't like. And even if there was some motive sufficient for deadly revenge against the Westbrooks, something I knew nothing about, why would a person who hated them *that* much suddenly help me rescue Patrick? It didn't make sense.

I wished I could talk to Sam. I could count on Sam to say what he thought, to argue with me till we were blue in the face, till we got to the truth. Sam was the only one I could really trust.

Twenty-two

JOSEPH PULLED INTO the empty lot at the front of the auction house. The long building was closed up tight. "I don't see Adrian," he said, sounding a little miffed.

"He's probably in the back. He said he would take care of the alarm and the dogs, then meet us at the front door."

Joseph glanced in the rearview mirror, then climbed out and opened the door for Patrick. Dizzy from the ride, Patrick grasped Joseph's hand as he walked toward the building's front entrance. I watched them a moment, then checked the driveway that circled the building for fresh tire tracks. As mad as my suspicion of Joseph seemed, I didn't want to be here alone with him.

Two sets of tracks scarred the sandy road. *Someone has followed Adrian,* I thought. *Trent?*

The auction house door opened. Relief shone on Adrian's face.

"Patrick!"

Patrick ran to his father, but his feet were clumsy and his balance off. He tripped and fell. Adrian rushed out the door, picked up his son, and carried him into the auction house. Joseph and I followed, Joseph quietly closing the door behind us.

Sitting on a bench, Adrian held Patrick close to him. "I was so afraid for you," he said, his voice cracking. He touched his son's face lovingly. "Who did this to you? Who took you from me?"

Patrick pulled back to gaze at his father, then looked around the cavernous building, as if searching for an answer among the jumble of furniture. His eyes stopped at me and he pointed.

"What?" I exclaimed. "That's not true! Joseph and I rescued you." I met Adrian's eyes. "You must believe me."

"I do, Kate," Adrian replied. "Patrick, who was in the room with you, before Kate and Joseph found you?"

"Trent."

Adrian's mouth stiffened. "Anyone else?"

"Miss Margery."

"And who else?"

"Nobody."

"Are you sure?"

Patrick thought for a moment, then nodded.

"Who took you from your bedroom last night?"

Patrick gazed about him, and I expected to be accused again.

"I don't remember."

"Who drove you to the hotel?"

"I was asleep," Patrick said. "When I woke up, I was in a big bed. I wasn't home anymore."

"Before you went to bed at home, did someone give you something to drink? Perhaps a little treat?" Adrian asked.

"Kate did."

I shook my head.

"Kate wasn't there," Adrian reminded him.

Patrick thought again. "Mommy did."

Adrian sighed. "All right. We'll talk some more when you're feeling better." He stood up, still holding his son. "I'm taking Patrick out to the car."

"He can walk if you hold his hand and move slowly," I said, for Adrian seemed out of breath. Patrick wasn't light, and the building was as long as a playing field.

"I can carry him," Adrian replied. This was his little boy, and he didn't want to let go.

I walked with him, and Joseph followed.

"I don't want Kate to come," Patrick said. "Please, Daddy, don't let her."

Adrian turned to Joseph and me. "I would like both of you to remain here so we can talk. It's time to get to the bottom of this foolishness."

"You can't leave Patrick alone in the car," I protested.

"I've brought someone else who will take him to a safe place."

The second set of tracks, I thought.

"Still, Adrian, I'd like to—"

"If you care about Patrick, you will stay here," he said firmly. "I don't want him frightened any more than he already is."

I swallowed hard and nodded.

As soon as the door closed behind Adrian and Patrick, Joseph began to pace. He paused to finger merchandise, picking up and putting down stemware, teacups, soup bowls, dinner plates. I wanted to blurt out my suspicions. I wanted Joseph to look stunned, then explain to me how it couldn't be so. I couldn't stand thinking there was a chance he had murdered Ashley. Nervous and cold, I rubbed my hands together, then folded my arms across my chest.

Beneath the thin soles of my shoes, the building's concrete floor felt like a block of ice. Emergency lights were on at each exit, and two ceiling lights lit either end of the rectangular structure, but in between the space was a confusion of objects and shadows. The balcony receded into darkness. This was no place to be alone with a murderer—no place to ask if he was one. Still, I had to know. "Joseph?"

He was immersed in his own thoughts.

"Joseph?"

He turned suddenly to look at me. "What?" he asked, his voice sharper than usual.

"Sorry. Never mind."

To my relief, I heard the back door open again and Adrian's footsteps. "Now," he said, when he reached us, "we have some matters to settle."

"We do, indeed," Joseph agreed. "You owe me, Adrian. Who knows what could have happened to Patrick if Katie and I hadn't found him."

"I admit, this last bit of shenanigans has caught me by surprise," Adrian said. "I believed that Kate had taken him, and that Trent would find him at your house, Joseph."

"How could you?" I asked. "How could you not trust me after all that has happened?"

Adrian rested a hand on my shoulder. "I underestimated how true blue you are. My apologies, Kate. I've made some— some rather poor decisions lately." His voice sounded tired. In the thin fluorescent lighting, his skin looked pallid. "So, Joseph, what exactly is it that you want?"

"You know. FedEx delivered."

"Twice," Adrian answered. "Twice a waste of your money and my time."

I remembered the package Adrian had opened in front of me, the one with the blue-striped envelope inside—Olivia's stationery. I had seen it earlier today, when Joseph was looking for a store tag. The slim hope I had clung to, that Joseph wanted nothing more than reward money, faded.

"If you think I will pay you a dime," Adrian went on, "you're even more ridiculous than I thought."

Joseph's neck turned pink.

"I realize you were disappointed by your mother's estate. She left you with quite a mess, didn't she?"

His face grew mottled.

"But I thought you were earning an honest living now, you know, writing about the Conservatory, rubbing elbows with more talented musicians."

"You'll live to regret this," Joseph whispered.

"Will I?" Adrian laughed. "Perhaps you forgot—with so little time to live, there is not much I fear anymore."

"You should fear for Patrick," Joseph replied quickly. "You know what I'm talking about—you received my warnings. You must have guessed who loosened the bolts on the swing set."

I cringed. I had told Joseph how Patrick preferred the old play equipment.

"And then there was the little accident on the ice," Joseph added.

I had given him that opportunity, too, telling him I was taking Patrick to the pond that day.

"I didn't think I could pull it off, not when Katie wouldn't take the bait and go to the barn," Joseph continued in a boasting voice. "I had to think fast. Brook's phone number was listed. And I was sure he didn't pay enough attention to his mother to know the names of her stable boys—that part was easy. But the timing . . ." Joseph smiled to himself. "The timing was delicate."

"You were there in the trees, watching us," I said accusingly.

"It was a wonder you didn't smell me out with my collection of fish and a rank old tomcat in a cage," Joseph replied, obviously enjoying his own story.

He turned to Adrian. "My window of opportunity was small for tossing the fish on the ice and releasing the cat. Even if Katie had gone to the barn, I counted on her to return quickly to check on Patrick. Oh, I didn't plan to kill Patrick," Joseph added. "No, no, I didn't miss my mark, Adrian. I executed perfectly—getting him on the ice just before Katie could notice and save him, sending a warning I knew you'd understand. After all, I had to let Patrick live long enough for one more chance at a deal. But not next time. Next time is for keeps."

"You're a pathetic man," Adrian said, and began to walk away. "You're sick, you're delusional, thinking this game will work."

"Adrian!"

He turned at the shrill sound of my voice.

"Joseph means it. He killed Ashley."

Adrian's eyes moved quickly to Joseph, then back to me. Joseph said nothing. I couldn't bear to look at him. In my mind, his face was that of a friend, and I couldn't stand to see the betrayal on it.

"Joseph is nothing more than pathetic, Kate," Adrian said. "He is a wimp, a whiner, a person who blames others for his own failings. He hasn't the guts or skill to do anything challenging, much less murder."

"But he killed her," I insisted. "Patrick has been tapping into a trace of Ashley's thoughts. That's why he keeps talking about her as if she is alive. He knows Ashley hated and feared her tutor, and he is transferring those feelings to me."

"Thank you, Jim Parker," Joseph remarked. "I had hoped his paranormal mumbo jumbo would distract you."

"I don't understand, Kate," Adrian said. "What motive could Joseph have had?"

"Money. That's plenty of motive for you, isn't it, Joseph?" The anger that was surging through me finally enabled me to turn to him.

"I rather like it, yes."

"Who paid you to do it?" I asked.

Joseph didn't reply.

"Trent or Robyn," I guessed. "Robyn was horribly jealous of Ashley. And Trent had learned that she was my father's child."

Joseph smiled. "That's the delightful part about this family. They're the kind of people who provide plenty of cover for a murderer. Of course, nice people, like you and your mother, can provide cover, too, as Adrian has proven so well. It was he who hired me."

I turned and stared at Adrian with disbelief. "You," I said softly.

Adrian gazed back, his face mild, his blue eyes expressionless. He wasn't going to deny it.

"I told you he couldn't be trusted," Joseph said. "I told you, Katie, he'd burn everyone but a Westbrook—me, your mother"—his voice grew whiny—"but you didn't believe me."

"I can't—"

"Adrian couldn't endure the thought of his money going to a grandchild who wasn't his own blood," Joseph went on. "Corinne had made a fool of him, convincing him that Ashley was a Westbrook. Even so, he didn't want to cut off Corinne and Ashley, not publicly. Nor did Adrian want Trent to file for divorce. Either way, Adrian and Trent would have to admit they had been suckered by Corinne, and Adrian was much too proud for that.

"But if Trent did not admit it, if he took the blame for a failed marriage, he'd lose a large sum of money in the divorce settlement. That would never do. No, an *accidental* death was the only way to eliminate Ashley while saving face and money. Adrian wagered that Corinne, feeling nothing for Trent and having lost her darling brat on the estate, would leave, which she did."

"The two of you killed Ashley." I was still struggling to believe the horrifying idea.

"I baited her with the rabbit, yes. I watched her go under. Adrian likes others to do his dirty work. I told you, Katie," he said with the voice of a schoolteacher annoyed that a student hadn't listened, "he uses others, then discards them. He paid only half of what he promised me. Half! And he did nothing to get me admitted to the Conservatory."

"You never change, Joseph," Adrian said. "You're always blaming others for your own failures." He moved slowly toward the wall where there was a bench and sat down heavily. "I didn't pay the balance because you stupidly, lavishly spent the first payment within two days, calling attention to yourself and therefore to me, at the very time that Ashley died. You left me no choice. I had to stop the money and quickly take precautions against a police inquiry, hiring a private investigator, pointing him in the direction of Victoria, in case I needed a suspect."

I swallowed several times, but could not get the bitterness out of my throat. Adrian didn't care how many lives he destroyed as long as he kept the Westbrook money and reputation intact. I began to back away, not out of fear but repulsion.

Adrian eyed me and said to Joseph, "Now that you have set Kate straight, you have earned yourself another job. Kill her."

I froze at his words. It was a nightmare turned real: I had no voice to scream; my legs wouldn't move.

"Kill her, and you'll get your money. Please don't misunderstand, Kate," Adrian added. "I like you. I like you very much. It's a matter of priorities."

"Family first," Joseph remarked with a giggle.

"Exactly."

"But two for the price of one, Adrian, that's not fair. I want triple the money," Joseph said, laughing nervously, like a child who knew he was asking too much. "Ashley's fee, Katie's, and a fee to keep Patrick safe."

"You're ridiculous."

"Aren't I, though? Triple." Joseph continued to laugh in a high-pitched way that set my teeth on edge. My feet suddenly could feel again. I turned and ran.

"Get her!"

"Who, me?" Joseph asked.

"Stop her. She can sink us both."

"Toss me some money, Adrian. Make me a deal."

I dodged a handcart and kept running. I was halfway to the closest exit, the rear one, when I heard a door slam back against a wall and the barking of dogs. I glanced over my shoulder. Through a side entrance came a blur of motion, black and tan, two large shepherds. Joseph took off toward the front of the building. The dogs barked anxiously, eager to chase, waiting for their command.

"What are you doing?" Joseph shouted back at Adrian. "Put them away. I was bluffing."

Adrian laughed, then gave two commands. I glanced back again. The dogs separated. Joseph ran toward the balcony steps. I turned and raced down a row of chairs and chests.

A dog was quickly on my trail. I climbed over a sofa, landed hard on my ankle in the next aisle, and continued running. In a single leap the dog was there, in my aisle, getting closer with each second.

"Call it off, Adrian," I heard Joseph scream. He sounded higher up. "Call it off."

"Too late," Adrian replied.

Ahead of me was a line of bureaus, tall ones, side by side. I pulled out a lower drawer, used it as a step, and propelled myself over the furniture. The dog was confused for a moment, its bark changing tone. Then it found a desk farther down the line and slipped under, hot in pursuit again.

I couldn't look back, I'd lose too much time. Its baying grew closer. My heart pounded, my side cramped. Six meters to the door, half that between the dog and me. I wasn't going to make it. I couldn't.

The door opened.

"Sam!"

He charged toward me, grabbing a ceramic lamp, hurling it at the dog. The lamp shattered against the concrete floor and the dog shied away. It was distracted for a moment—barely a moment. I reached for a glass vase and threw it. A thousand pink shards exploded up from the floor.

But the dog would not be intimidated twice. It barely flinched. The position of its ears, the way it focused its eyes on me, I knew what was coming. Sam grabbed another lamp, a floor lamp with a long shaft. The dog lunged.

Sam brought the pole down hard, separating the dog and me. The animal's bark dropped in pitch to an ugly growl. Its upper lip pulled back; its teeth were wet with an excess of white saliva.

Joseph sounded as if he was on the balcony now. I could hear him screaming at Adrian and Adrian laughing, unconcerned with what was happening at our end of the building.

"Adrian!" I shouted, desperate to get his attention. "Adrian!"

Just then the dog rushed Sam. Sam swung the shaft of the lamp, slamming it down on the dog's shoulder, infuriating it.

"Run, Kate. Get out!"

The dog gripped the pole with its strong jaws, wrestling with it. Suddenly it let go and began to circle Sam. When Sam turned his head to see where I was, the dog stopped, its body quivering with tension.

"Don't take your eye off it, Sam."

The dog was positioned between us and the back door. But the door at the other end of the building was too far away. I'd be caught before I ran a quarter of the distance.

"Get up on a table," Sam said, keeping the lamp pole between himself and the dog. "Do you know how high these dogs can jump?"

"More than a meter—maybe four feet, five. A table won't do it."

"It will get you to that closet-thing."

I glanced back at a tall mahogany wardrobe.

"Shove the table against it. I'll knock it away once you're up."

"Once *you're* up," I corrected him.

"Just get there," he said between gritted teeth.

There wasn't time to argue. I shoved the table against the wardrobe, hoping the more massive piece of furniture was as sturdy as it looked. The dog's head followed the sound of the table's feet screeching against the concrete floor. Sam hissed to draw the animal's attention, and I scrambled onto the table.

"Are you up?" Sam asked, his back toward me, still keeping the dog at a distance with the shaft of the lamp.

"No."

The wood of the wardrobe was smooth and slippery. Each time I tried to pull myself onto the top, my hands slid over the edge. I licked them to make them sticky and jumped from the table to give myself a better angle. Getting partway on top, I pulled with all my strength. My arms ached. I scraped my ribs, slowly dragging the rest of my body onto the high, flat surface.

"Your turn," I called to Sam.

He backed toward the table, half step by half step, slowly, steadily. The dog moved with him. There was a heavy rope coiled on top of the wardrobe. I seized it like a weapon.

"Almost there," I told him.

His left hand reached back and felt the table, his right kept the pole between him and the dog. He slid onto the table, then carefully pulled up his feet. The dog's growl deepened.

"When you're ready, hand me the pole," I said.

"I can manage it."

"You'll have to turn your back to the dog. Give me the pole. I'll fend him off."

"You might fall," he argued.

"I'm not *that* clumsy."

"Kate, just stay still."

"Give . . . me . . . the . . . pole!"

But Sam, crouching on the table, rose to his feet and quickly spun around, letting the lamp shaft go, so he could hoist himself onto the wardrobe. The dog charged. Sam cursed.

"Kick! Kick!" I cried, then lashed out with the rope, using it like a whip on the dog. I brought the rope down hard again and again, trying to back off the furious animal. Hearing the rip of clothing, I pulled on Sam's arm.

He suddenly propelled himself to the top of the wardrobe, kicking over the table. Unprepared for the shift in weight and direction, I fell backward. Sam yanked me toward him, back onto the top of the wardrobe.

The dog leaped against the tall piece of furniture, charging it repeatedly, as if he had gone mad. Sam and I held on to each other and stared down at the animal.

A scream, a man's shout that pitched into terror, quickly drew our eyes upward. Joseph was in the loft, shouting to Adrian, "Call the dog off. Call it off!"

"You had your chance, several chances."

I could see Joseph backing toward the balcony railing. The dog matched him step for step, then began to close the gap.

"Call the dog off," Sam hollered. I shouted with him.

Joseph took a step up onto the flat metal railing. He climbed to the top, standing on a surface half the width of his foot. There was nothing for him to grab on to there—no pole, no wires—the ceiling high above him, the ground floor far below. The dog snapped at his feet. Joseph teetered.

I saw what followed as if played in slow motion. Joseph realized his fate, closed his eyes, began to fall. Sam jerked my head toward his shoulder, then buried his face with mine. We didn't see Joseph hit, just heard a sound like a pumpkin smashing against the concrete floor.

Twenty-three

"TONYA, MARCUS, COME!" Adrian commanded the dogs.

Sam and I held on to each other on top of the wardrobe. We couldn't see Joseph from our perch, but one of the dogs was nosing the area where he had fallen.

"Marcus, get out of there!" Adrian shouted at the dog. "I don't want to have to clean you up."

I sank against Sam, feeling sick to my stomach.

"I'm sure he's dead, Kate," Sam said quietly, "but as soon as the dogs are kenneled, I'll check him out."

"I can look for myself."

"Don't argue—not this one, okay? If it were someone I had thought was my friend, I would ask you to look for me."

I nodded mutely.

"Sam, Kate, we must talk," Adrian said, as if we, too, were obedient to him.

I ignored him. "How is your leg, Sam?"

"Marcus got a mouthful of pants."

"Did he? So, it's your pants that are bleeding like that."

"There is no need to stay up there," Adrian called to us.

Sam grunted under his breath, then said aloud, "When the dogs are inside, the door is closed, and you are farther from the door than we are, we'll come down."

"Of course, I understand," Adrian replied, sounding almost amused by our caution. "But don't leave. There are a few things we all need to understand."

As soon as he had secured the dogs behind the door, Sam jumped down from the wardrobe and rushed toward Joseph. He stopped suddenly. The way he gripped the back of a chair told me all I needed to know. Sam turned to me, his body bent slightly, his face distorted, sickened by what he had seen, then he buried his chin in his chest and walked swiftly back to me.

I slid off the wardrobe. "Let's get out of here."

"Not unless you have better lawyers than I do," Adrian called. He walked toward us, cell phone in hand, punching in numbers.

"Yes," he said into the phone, "this is Adrian Westbrook. I'm calling from Crossroads Auction House. I wish to report a break-in and what appears to be an unfortunate casualty resulting from it. . . . No, it's too late for medical assistance. The thief must not have realized we had guard dogs. He appears to have fallen. . . . Yes . . . Yes. . . . I'm not sure," he responded, eyeing me. "It is possible that more than one person was involved. . . . Thank you. I'll wait for you here."

Adrian closed his cell phone and gazed thoughtfully at Sam and me. "I called the sheriff, not the state police, to give us a little more time, though we don't have much. You need to make some choices quickly."

"The facts don't leave us any choices," Sam replied.

"Oh, everyone has choices," Adrian said. "Joseph here, chose to break in. His reason? One can only conjecture, but he cased the place last Monday with Kate—several people witnessed that. Perhaps, in the course of settling his mother's affairs, he became interested in the antique business. Perhaps he spotted a few valuable pieces he wanted but didn't wish to pay for. Too bad he forgot about the guard dogs.

"As for Kate, what choices does she have to make? Not only was she seen with Joseph on Monday, guests and employees at the hotel noticed her and Joseph together just before the break-in today. One has to wonder why a teenager would get involved in this kind of business—for a percentage of the profits? But wait, she was recently fired by the owner of the auction house."

He was framing me, blackmailing me.

"Don't look so grim, Kate," Adrian said, sitting down on

a Victorian settee, running his hand over the torn silk uphol-stery. "I was painting the worst scenario for you. In fact, you can choose to be quite well off for a seventeen-year-old. Your father must have left you a respectable sum. I would give you something rather more outrageous, with my guarantee that I will swear you had no part of this and with your guarantee that you will go along with my story to the police."

"But I won't."

I saw the perspiration on his brow, the first sign that he was less than sure things would work out his way.

"I don't think you understand the precarious nature of your situation," he said, "the little bits of information the police might be given that aren't very flattering to you, such as the poisoning of Patrick when he was in your care, the so-called accident at the pond, his distrust of you, not to mention the power of my testimony coupled with Sam's."

Sam turned to me. "Let's go, Kate."

"I would think twice before saying no to full tuition, Sam, tuition and board at an Ivy League college. I'd be delighted to give a decent education to a boy as bright as you. Did I mention I'm on Harvard's board of trustees? They have a fine hockey team."

"Over my father's dead body."

I heard a car engine. I wondered how two teens could con-vince a sheriff that they were innocent.

"I admire the honesty of both of you," Adrian said, his voice as reasonable as ever, though he was breathing fast, "but think it through. Ashley's murderer is dead. I have little time left—I'll be dead before a trial could begin. If death is the ultimate justice, justice will be attained. No one is in danger now from me—I'm not a common criminal. Most important, Patrick will be spared. Kate, you love the boy. Do you want him growing up knowing what his father has done?"

I didn't answer right away. I would have done anything to protect Patrick from more pain. I knew what it was like to grow up without a parent you loved deeply, to believe terrible things about that parent and try to hate her, hurting only yourself each time you did. If Sam and I covered for Adrian, we could give Patrick a few more precious months with his father and some happy memories. At seven years old, he had suffered enough.

"It's not what I want, but it's what is going to be," I replied. "I won't keep any more of your horrid secrets. In the end, secrets come back to haunt. I don't know how it will happen, or when, but someday Patrick will stumble on something that doesn't quite make sense. He'll start asking questions and realize that people lied to him in significant ways. Then he'll begin to doubt everything else he knows and experienced. He'll doubt even the good things that have happened to him. He'll mistrust people who try to get close, and become more and more alone."

Adrian rose to his feet, his face bathed in perspiration. At the same moment the front door of the auction house opened. The person who entered stopped just inside the door and gazed about. At first I didn't recognize Robyn. Her hair hung loose and untidy, as if she had yanked it out of its clip. Her shirttail, usually tucked in neatly, billowed out from beneath her short jacket. She strode toward us, her barn boots thumping against the concrete, then stopped midway down an aisle of furniture.

"This is a pretty mess," she said, turning her face away from the sight of Joseph lying on the floor.

From a distance, with her skin pale and her hair wild, her eyes glistening as if wet from riding in the wind, she looked younger, like a schoolgirl who had just ridden the newest horse in her daddy's stable. But as she grew closer, the shine in her eyes and the pallor of her skin looked unnatural. Her hands shook and her gait became unsteady.

"Hoppy was right about you being here," she said to her father. "There is nothing Hoppy doesn't hear or know."

"Robyn, you don't look well," Adrian observed.

"I feel wonderful," she replied. "I feel . . . liberated."

Adrian's brow creased, a look of apprehension spreading over his face. "Come, sit down for a moment." He patted the place next to him on the silk settee. "You see that Sam Koscinski and Kate are here."

He's warning her not to say too much in front of us, I thought.

"I see," she said, her voice flat. "I see that all my hard work has come to nothing."

Her words were uneven, as if she couldn't catch her breath.

"And why is that?" Adrian asked quietly, soothingly. He patted the seat next to him again, but she didn't sit down.

"Because I'm a fool! A total fool!" she cried angrily. "I have spent my life caring for you, pleasing you, protecting you when you were too cocksure to protect yourself. I knew she'd blow the whole thing apart," Robyn said, with a jerk of her head toward me. "Hoppy knew it too," she went on, "but you weren't going to be cowed by anyone." She shook her head. "All I've done for you, Daddy, all I've done for you. I tried to get rid of Kate, pushing her from the top of the stairs, getting Brook to break the window, as Ashley had, poisoning the cat, hoping to scare her into leaving.

"It didn't work. Hoppy had said it wouldn't. I was getting desperate, knowing it wouldn't be long before Kate figured out what I had guessed long ago about Ashley's death. So Hoppy laced the pie. When the plan went bad, I added the open bottle of cough syrup, and finally you fired Kate. Once again I had helped you. I thought it was all over."

"Then Patrick was abducted," I said.

She acted as if she didn't hear me.

"It was Trent who took him," Adrian told his daughter.

"I wish the devil himself had and he had carried Patrick all the way to hell! But you, you would have gone there to get him back. You would do anything for him, and yet you never notice what I do for you. You didn't notice with Ashley around, and you don't with Patrick, either."

She ran her hands through her hair, her fingers separating the strands, then bunching into fists, tangling them up. "All you could think about was your missing son. I saw that Emily was going to be as useless as ever, worrying about Patrick, not you, not even considering the effect of this on your health. So I phoned your doctor.

"That's right," she said, responding to the sudden lift of Adrian's head. "I spoke to your doctor about my fears for you." Robyn laughed out loud. "You know what she told me, don't you. You haven't been getting experimental treatment. Your cancer was cured."

I blinked.

"You've got the health of a man fifteen years younger—that's what your doctor said. You were manipulating us, Daddy! All of us, even your wife! You were dangling your money in front of us, seeing which dog you could make jump the highest!"

Robyn circled the settee, then sat next to him. "But once again I fixed things for you. I'm keeping you to the plan. There was poison in the cup of coffee I brought you today, the one you drank just before you left."

Adrian stared at her with disbelief.

"Surprised? Surprised as I was at what Daddy's girl could do?" She started to cry. "All my life, all I wanted was to please you."

Adrian bowed his head.

"But I didn't want you to die alone, Daddy. You know I wouldn't do something that horrible to you." She laid her head on his shoulder. "I drank it too."

"Robyn!" Adrian closed his eyes and rested his cheek against her head.

"Sam, we have to call a paramedic," I said.

"Too late," Robyn whispered. "Too late." She snuggled like a small child against her father.

"I need your phone," Sam said, reaching toward Adrian, but Adrian kept his arms around Robyn, slowly stroking her hair. Sam reached into Adrian's pocket to retrieve the phone, then flicked it open and punched in the numbers.

He was talking to the dispatcher when the sheriff arrived. I explained quickly as much as I could, then rushed outside to Patrick. I found him asleep in Sam's car, unaware of what was going on.

Robyn died in her father's arms before the paramedics arrived. Sam said that Adrian refused treatment and died shortly after.

Twenty-four

THE WEEK THAT followed the events at the auction house was, in many ways, more difficult than that which followed my father's death. When Dad died, I knew what I had lost. But while I felt depressed and saddened by the deaths of Adrian and Joseph, whom could I mourn—the people I thought they were? They were cold-blooded murderers. They had betrayed not only me, but people I loved, my parents and Patrick.

I could do nothing to ease Patrick's pain and confusion, not that week. In his mind, Ashley's fear of her tutor was still too vivid for him to trust me. But Sam knew better than anyone how it felt to be a little boy who had lost his father. He missed his hockey game Saturday night—didn't make it as far as the team bench—not because of the stitches in his leg, but because Patrick needed him.

If Dr. Parker was right, Patrick's sensitivity to Ashley would fade and finally disappear when Patrick's life became different from the kind she had known. The dynamics at Mason's Choice had already changed, and Emily was talking about leaving the estate, which I hoped would hasten the process. I knew I had to be patient.

Trent, Sam, and I spent much of that long week talking to the police, trying to patch together the recent events, though some things would never be verified. Trent told the authorities he had suspected that Ashley was murdered, but did not know who did it. While admitting he felt no affection for Patrick, he said that the prospect of another child's death was a painful reminder to him of the death of Ashley. He also realized that a child's death, occurring twice in a generation, would call unwanted attention to the family and create suspicion. After I was fired, he feared that Patrick was vulnerable, and removed him from the house till he could figure out who was threatening him. Looking back now, I should have realized that if Trent had wanted to hurt or kill Patrick, he wouldn't have brought him to a hotel in town and wouldn't have left behind such an obvious paper trail.

As for Mrs. Hopewell's and Brook's roles in all these events, we knew only what Robyn had claimed before she died. The housekeeper was gone by Sunday morning, leaving no forwarding address. Trent confided to me that she had a sister in Virginia, but he did not tell the police that, for I wasn't filing charges over the laced pie. I had no evidence to support what a court would consider the "hearsay" of a dead woman.

Brook left for Florida nearly as fast, after denying knowledge of any- and everything that had happened; one would have thought he was living in England for the last week and a half. While I will never know if he was the one who killed Patrick's hamster, my hunch is that he did it just for fun—his kind of fun, upsetting a child. In retrospect, I think Brook lacked his grandfather's steel, which had the curious advantage of making Brook nasty, heartless, and petty, but not actually evil. I think that when he realized more serious things were going on in the house, he pulled back from his own pranks.

Whatever the case, Brook will eventually be a very wealthy nineteen-year-old, for it turned out that Adrian did not change his will—had never planned to, according to his attorney. He provided for his wife and divided the rest evenly among his three children. Brook would inherit all of Robyn's portion.

During that week, Sam gave me his father's old notebook to read. It was Mr. Koscinski's jottings that had moved Sam to seek out Adrian the morning Patrick was missing. Putting together a log of the money spent by Joseph and bank reports on Olivia, whose cash had been tied up in her new shop, Sam suddenly realized that his father had been working on a new suspect—someone who had been present at the time of Ashley's death, someone with a surprising amount of money immediately after: Joseph. But who had paid him to kill Ashley? The most likely candidate was Adrian, Sam had thought, though Trent also had access to company funds.

Sam's plan had been to talk to Adrian and see what kind of visceral response he'd get when mentioning his belief that Joseph was dangerous. He never got that far. Robyn interrupted, bringing in her father's tainted coffee, then Joseph and I phoned from the hotel. Adrian asked Sam to follow him to the auction house so that he could drive Patrick home. I suppose Adrian wanted Patrick safely out of the picture while he talked to Joseph and me. He didn't realize how much Sam knew, and made a fatal mistake in assuming that Sam could be bought, as the young and ambitious Joseph had once been.

Sam, his mother, and I attended the private funeral of Robyn and Adrian. On a dreary afternoon they were buried in the family cemetery, a place that, for me, would always be full of ghosts. Three days later, Friday of that week, we went to a small memorial service for Joseph, given by his friends in Baltimore. It had rained all week; that day, it sleeted. I didn't think winter was ever going to let go.

Then Saturday morning dawned with a washed blue sky. The wind had a different feel, a lighter touch. Shy flowers called snowdrops raised their heads. In a sunny spot against a brick wall a crocus dared to open. I knew the temperature would drop again and that, for a while, winter would be mixed up with spring. My mother was coming in a week—she had sent me her flight number—I got hot and cold just thinking about it. Even so, it was time, time to find out if we could still be mother and daughter, time to find out if Sam and I could be anything more than friends.

I found him flat on his back, under his car.

"That's a clever way to protect the environment," I said, crouching down to peer under the old sedan. "Lie beneath your car and let it drop oil on *you.*"

Sam turned his head sideways. "So, you're feeling like yourself again."

"Yes and no," I replied honestly, sitting on the bristly grass next to the driveway.

He slid out from beneath the car and reached for a wad of paper towels to wipe his hands. "Actually, I'm involved in a complex operation. I'm trying to see if I can install a steering wheel on the right side of my car, so you can park it without threatening the lives of passing pedestrians."

I laughed, which made him raise an eyebrow.

"When I say something like that, you're supposed to act like a porcupine."

"Excuse me?"

"Get your quills up, Kate, do your cactus act. You're no fun anymore!"

I glanced away.

"Uh-oh. Sorry." He rested his hand on mine, as he had many times in the last week. His hand covered mine completely, and I wanted to turn my palm upward, to see what it felt like to slip my fingers between his.

I pulled my hand away. "There is something I have to tell you."

He waited, but not very patiently. "Spit it out."

"You have such a poetic way of putting things."

"*That's* what you wanted to tell me?"

"No!" Frustrated, I plucked at the grass on the edge of the driveway.

"Kate, you're starting to do that thing again—looking away, not meeting my eyes."

"I know." In the last week, I had needed his friendship and comfort so desperately, I hadn't thought about things like the shape of his hands and the luminous darkness of his eyes. But I was thinking about them now. Sometimes that was all I could think about.

"Want to tell me why you do that?"

I stared at a greasy wrench.

"Do you know why you look away?" he asked, his voice gentle.

I nodded.

"We've shared an awful lot, Kate. Can't you tell me?"

"I probably can if I don't look at you."

He threw back his head and laughed. "Sorry. That was funny. Okay"—despite an effort not to, he was still laughing—"what's the problem?"

"I'm in love with you."

His laughter stopped. When the silence became unbearable, I glanced up at him. "You look—you look stunned. I'll get over it," I added quickly. "You know when I put my mind to something, I do it. I *will* get over it, Sam."

"But I won't," he said.

"Sorry?"

"I won't . . . I can't. I've tried—it's impossible." He reached for my face and held it in his hands.

So that's *how it feels,* I thought.

"I love you, Kate."

I don't think I breathed.

"I have from the very beginning," he said. "Well, maybe not that moment when you nearly destroyed my car."

"Nearly destroyed! I didn't touch it."

He laughed and ran his thumb softly across my mouth.

How did he do that, make me feel his touch like heat beneath my skin—make me feel it everywhere even when he brushed only my lips.

"You can't have any idea how much I want to kiss you," he said.

"Maybe—maybe I do. Why don't you try and see?"

His mouth touched mine, lightly, carefully—too lightly and carefully—so I took over and kissed him.

"Maybe you do!" he agreed, when we had caught our breath again.

Turn the page to uncover more hidden secrets in

Dark Secrets 1

Legacy of Lies and Don't Tell

LAST NIGHT I visited the house again. It looked as it did ten years ago, when I dreamed about it often. I've never seen the house in real life, at least not that I can remember. It is tall, three stories of paned windows, all brick with a shingle roof. The part I remember most clearly is the covered porch. No wider than the front steps, it has facing benches that I like to sit on. I guess I was never shy, not even at six; in the dream I always opened the door, walked inside, and played with the toys.

Last night the door was locked. That's how I awoke, trying with all my strength to open it, desperate to get inside. Something was wrong, but now I can't say what. Was there something dangerous outside the house from which I was fleeing? Was there a person in the house who needed my help? It was as if the first part of my dream was missing. But one thing I knew for sure: Someone on the other side of the door was trying hard to keep me out.

"I'm not going," I had told my father back in June. "She's a mean old lady. She disowned Mom and won't speak to you. She has never had anything to do with Pete, Dave, or me. Why should I have anything to do with her?"

"For your mother's sake," he'd said.

Several months later I was on a flight from Arizona to Maryland, still resisting my grandmother's royal command to visit. I took out her invitation, the first message I'd received from her in my life, and reread it—two sentences, sounding as stiff as a textbook exercise.

Dear Megan,
This summer I will see you at Scarborough House.
I have enclosed a check to cover airfare.

Regards,
Helen Scarborough Barnes

Well, I hadn't expected "love and kisses" from a woman who cut off her only daughter when she had decided to marry someone of a different race. My mother, coming from a deep-rooted Eastern Shore family, has more English blood in her than Prince Charles. My father, also from an old Maryland family, is African-American. After trying to have children of their own, they adopted me, then my two brothers. It would be naive to expect warmth from a person who refused to consider adopted kids her grandchildren.

Now that I thought about it, the meaning of my dream the night before was pretty obvious, even the feeling that something was wrong. The door to my mother's family had always been closed to me; when a door kept locked for sixteen years suddenly, without explanation, opens, you can't help but wonder what you're walking into.

"Megan? You made it!" the woman said, crumpling up the sign with my name on it, then giving me a big hug. "I'm Ginny Lloyd, your mother's best old friend." She laughed. "I guess you figured that out."

When Ginny heard I was coming, she'd insisted on meeting me at the airport close to Baltimore. That October day we loaded my luggage into the back of her ancient green station wagon, pushing aside bags of old sweaters, skirts, shoes, and purses—items she had picked up to sell in her vintage clothes shop.

"I hope you don't mind the smell of mothballs," Ginny said.

"No problem," I replied.

"How about the smell of a car burning oil?"

"That's okay, too."

"We can open the windows," she told me. "Of course, the muffler's near gone."

I laughed. Blond and freckled, she had the same southernish accent as my mother. I felt comfortable with her right away.

When I was buckled in, Ginny handed me a map so I could follow our progress toward Wisteria, which is on the Eastern Shore of the Chesapeake Bay.

"It's about a two-hour drive," she said. "I told Mrs. Barnes I'd have you at Scarborough House well before dark."

"I'm getting curious," I told her. "When Mom left Maryland, she didn't bring any pictures with her. I've seen a few photos that my uncle Paul sent, showing him and Mom playing when they were little, but you can't see the house in them. What's it like?"

"What has your mother told you about it?" Ginny asked.

"Not much. There's a main house with a back wing. It's old."

"That's about it," Ginny said.

It was a short answer from a person who had spent a lot of time there as a child and teenager—nearly as short as my mother's answers about the place.

"Oh, and it's haunted," I added.

"People say that," Ginny replied.

I looked at her, surprised. I had been joking.

"Of course, every old house on the Shore has its ghost

stories," she added quickly. "Just keep the lights on if it feels spooky."

This trip might turn out to be more interesting than I thought.

Ginny turned on the radio, punching in a country station. I opened the map she had given me and studied it. The Sycamore River cut into the Eastern Shore at an angle. If you were traveling up the Chesapeake Bay, you'd enter the wide river mouth of the Sycamore and head in a northeasterly direction. On the right, close to the mouth, you'd see a large creek named Wist. The next creek up is Oyster. The town of Wisteria sits between them, nearly surrounded by water, the Sycamore River on one side and the creeks on the other two. As for my grandmother's property, it was the large point of land below the town, washed on one side by Wist Creek and on the other side by the Sycamore.

We crossed two sets of railroad tracks. I watched the scenery change from outlet stores to fields of corn and soy and low horizons of trees. The sky was half the world on the Eastern Shore. Ginny asked a lot of questions and seemed more interested in talking about life in Tucson than life in Wisteria.

"What's my grandmother like?" I asked at last.

For a full minute the only response was the roar of the car engine.

"She's, uh, different," Ginny said. "We're coming up on Oyster Creek. Wisteria's just on the other side."

"Different how?" I persisted.

"She has her own way of seeing things. She can be fierce at times."

"Do people like her?"

Ginny hesitated. "Have you spent much time in a small town?" she asked.

"No."

"Small-town folks are like a big family living in one house. They can be real friendly and helpful, but they can also say nasty things about each other and squabble a lot."

She hadn't answered my question about how others saw my grandmother, but I could figure it out. She wasn't the town favorite.

We rumbled over the metal grating of the drawbridge. I hung my head out the window for a moment. In Tucson, creeks were often just trickles. This one was the width of a river.

"We're on Scarborough Street now," Ginny said. "The streets off to our right lead down to the commercial docks, where the oyster and crab boats are. The streets to the left border the college. In a few blocks we'll be crossing over High Street, which is Main Street for us. Want to drive down it?"

"Sure."

We passed a school, went a block farther, then took a right onto High. The street had a mix of houses, churches, and small shops, all of the buildings made of brick or wood. Some of the houses edged right up to the sidewalk; a few had tiny plots of grass in front of them. Pots of bright chrysanthemums perched on windowsills and steps. The sidewalks on both sides of High Street were brick and ripply, especially around the roots of the sycamore trees that lined the street. But even where there weren't roots, the brick looked softened, as if the footprints of two and a half centuries had been worn into it.

"It's pretty," I said. "Are there a lot of wisteria vines around here?"

"People grow it," she said, "but actually, the parcel of land that became the town was won in a card game called whist. That was the town's original name. Some upright folks in the 1800s, who didn't approve of gambling, added to it. I guess we're lucky they weren't playing Crazy Eights."

I laughed.

"There's my shop, Yesterdaze." Ginny slowed down and pointed to a storefront with a large, paned window that bowed out over the sidewalk. "Next door is Tea Leaves. Jamie, the owner, makes pastries to die for.

"The town harbor is ahead of us," she went on. "Only

pleasure boats dock there now. I'm going to swing around to Bayview Avenue and show you where I live. You know you're welcome to stay with me if things get difficult."

"Difficult how?" I asked.

She shrugged. "I find it isolated out there on the other side of the Wist. And Scarborough House seems awfully big without a family to fill it up."

"Is that why my grandmother invited me? She can't get anybody else to come?"

"I doubt *that's* the reason. Mrs. Barnes has never liked company—whoa!" Ginny exclaimed, hitting her brakes hard, sending shoe boxes tumbling over the seat from the back of the station wagon.

A guy in an open-topped Jeep, impatient to get around a car making a turn, had suddenly cut in front of us. The backseat passengers of the red Jeep, two girls and a guy, held on to one another and hooted. The girl in the front seat turned briefly to look at us, laughing and tossing her long hair. The driver didn't acknowledge his near miss.

"Jerk," I said aloud.

Ginny looked amused. "That was your cousin."

"My cousin?" I twisted in my seat, to look down the side street where the Jeep had made another sudden turn.

"Matt Barnes," she replied.

"I thought he was in Chicago."

"Your uncle moved there, and Matt's mother is somewhere in the North, I believe."

"Boston," I told her. It had been an ugly divorce, I knew that much.

"Matt has spent nearly every summer in Wisteria. He transferred to the high school here last winter and is living full-time with your grandmother. You didn't know that?"

I shook my head.

"She bought him the Jeep this past summer. Rumor has it he's getting his own boat. Matt's usually carting around jocks or girls."

Spoiled and wild, I thought. But things were looking up. No matter what he was like, spending two weeks with a guy my own age was better than being alone with a fierce seventy-six-year-old. I'd just fasten my seat belt and go along for the ride.

"Does my grandmother drive?" I asked.

"Pretty much like Matt," Ginny replied, laughing.

When we got to Bayview, she pointed out her house, a soft yellow cottage with gray shutters, then returned to Scarborough Road.

We crossed the Wist, rumbling over an old bridge, drove about a quarter mile more, then turned right between two brick pillars. The private road that led to my grandmother's started out paved, but crumbled into gravel and dirt. Tall, conical cedar trees lined both sides. They did not bend gracefully over the drive, as trees do in pictures of southern mansions, but stood upright, like giant green game pieces. At the end of the double row of trees I saw sections of sloping gray roof and brick chimneys, four of them.

"We're coming up behind the house," Ginny said. "The driveway loops around to the front. You're seeing the back wing. That picket fence runs along the herb garden by the kitchen."

"The house is huge."

"Remember that you are welcome to stay with me," she said.

"Thanks, but I'll be fine."

Now that I was here, I was looking forward to the next two weeks. I mean, how much of a terror could one little old woman be? It'd be fun to explore the old house and its land, especially with a cousin my age. Four hundred acres of fields and woods and waterfront—it seemed unbelievable that I didn't have to share them with other hikers in a state park. A wave of excitement and confidence washed over me. Then Ginny circled the house and parked in front.

"Megan," she said, after a moment of silence, "Megan, are you all right?"

I nodded.

"I'll help you with your luggage."

"Thanks."

I climbed out of the car slowly, staring up at Grandmother's house. Three stories of paned windows, brick with a shingled roof, a small covered porch with facing benches—it was the house in my dreams.

I took my luggage from Ginny, feeling a little shaky. For the second time in twenty-four hours, I walked up the steps of the house. This time the door swung open.

About the Author

A former high school and college teacher with a Ph.D. in English Literature from the University of Rochester, Elizabeth Chandler enjoys visiting schools to talk about the process of creating books. She has written numerous picture books for children under her real name, Mary Claire Helldorfer, as well as romances for teens under her pen name, Elizabeth Chandler. Her romance novels include *Summer in the City*, *Love at First Click*, and the romance-mystery *Kissed by an Angel*, published by Simon Pulse.

When not writing, Mary Claire enjoys biking, gardening, and following the Orioles and Ravens. Mary Claire lives in Baltimore with her husband, Bob, and their cat, Puck.